Speak Softly, She Can Hear

Pam Lewis

Simon & Schuster
New York   London   Toronto   Sydney

SIMON & SCHUSTER
Rockefeller Center
1230 Avenue of the Americas
New York, NY 10020

SIMON & SCHUSTER and colophon are registered trademarks of Simon & Schuster, Inc.

For information regarding special discounts for bulk purchases, please contact Simon & Schuster Special Sales at 1-800-456-6798 or business@simonandschuster.com

Designed by Elliot Beard

Manufactured in the United States of America

10 9 8 7 6 5 4 3 2 1

Library of Congress Cataloging-in-Publication Data
Lewis, Pam, 1943–
Speak softly, she can hear / Pam Lewis.
p. cm.
1. Teenage girls—Fiction. 2. Female friendship—Fiction.
3. Children of the rich—Fiction. 4. Private schools—Fiction.
5. New York (N.Y.)—Fiction. 6. Betrayal—Fiction. 7. Secrecy—Fiction.
I. Title.
PS3612.E974S64 2005
813'.6—dc22   2004056563
ISBN 0-7432-5539-9

For my sons

The ghost's white fingers on thy shoulders laid . . .
—OSCAR WILDE

Part One

Chapter One

It was pitch-black. Black above and below. The only way to know up from down was by the pinprick stars. Ahead the sounds of Eddie Lindbaeck's boots fell heavily in the snow, his full weight coming down and then pushing off. Carole's footsteps were quieter because she'd worn her new Capezio flats to make her feet look pretty and to impress him. Capezio flats, black stretch pants with the loop under the arches to keep them from riding up, Naomi's gold mohair sweater, and her aunt Emily's brown parka with the cream vee. She couldn't help the jacket. It was all she could scrounge up in the warmth department. But now her feet were numb. She had to come down hard on her heels to get any traction at all, and it made her feel foolish.

She had the sinking feeling he'd forgotten she was even here. If anything, he was getting farther ahead. When he'd picked her up at the Double Hearth, he'd been aloof, not at all like he was on the train. A car passed them, whipping their shadows together. Afterward, it was even blacker than before.

"Is it much farther?" she called to him.

3

The sound of his boots stopped somewhere up ahead. "Is she tired?"

"No," she said. "She isn't. She's just cold." She wouldn't want him to send her back to the Double Hearth and ask for Naomi tonight instead. She'd won going first, and she was going through with this no matter what.

"It's not far," he said. "It's something out of *Cannery Row*. You girls didn't exactly go all out, did you?"

"You're the one who made the reservations."

Another car beamed from behind them, and she saw the sign up ahead. SNOWTOWN MOTEL. She knew exactly how far it was now because it was where the taxi had dropped him off after the train today. After the turn, the driveway snaked through a forest and then ended up at a clearing and the bunch of cabins, a big ring of them, with an office off to the left. Maybe it was crummy, but she wasn't going to take the blame for it. He was the one who'd supposedly been here before.

"You didn't give me much to work with." When she caught up, he put an arm around her shoulders and breathed into her ear. "No matter," he said.

The sound of his words triggered a spreading warmth, followed by a tight cluster of sensation, as though a string were being tugged deliciously somewhere deep within her. Naomi said the whole world is divided between those who have done it and those who haven't. *Men can tell.*

"I couldn't believe what you did this morning," she said.

Carole and her mother had arrived at Grand Central early and had had to wait near the information booth, where the floor was disgusting. Carole had Aunt Emily's skis and was wearing Aunt Emily's urine-colored stretch pants. In her suitcase she had Aunt Emily's long underwear and a hat she wasn't going to be caught dead in. She'd never carried skis before, and she kept hitting people with them by accident. When she set them down, they slithered every which way. Her mother kept trying to kick all the equipment into a tidy pile.

Carole had felt a little bad that her mother had gone to all the trouble of getting the skis from Emily when Carole didn't care about skiing. They'd had to get the car out of the garage and drive up to Tarrytown. Emily had taken the bindings to be oiled or something, and had the sides sharpened, and it was a very big production. She'd shown Carole and her mother those old pictures from a hundred years ago when she had been, in her words, *a big girl too.* Before she'd dieted herself into oblivion. Back then you had to walk up and ski down. Emily had said that a hundred times. Now they had chair lifts. Emily thought walking up made her superior. Emily was always saying things like that.

So Carole and her mother had been standing there waiting when they heard a voice bellowing out across the whole station. "You guys!" There Naomi was with Eddie right next to her on that giant marble landing that looked out over all of Grand Central. Carole had frozen on the spot. What did Naomi think she was doing? She had on all black and one of those serape things her father and Elayne were always bringing her back from South America. A sort of shawl in bright red. The odd couple, Carole thought. Eddie had looked preppie in his gray Shetland sweater and tweed jacket. He had blandly handsome features, a Scandinavian face—wide, high cheekbones, narrow dark blue eyes, and a full mouth. His lank hair was the color of sand. Naomi's eyes were thick with kohl, something she'd just started doing. Carole counted. *One one-thousand, two one-thousand, three one-thousand.* She knew exactly what was coming. On *four one-thousand* her mother leaned over. "Isn't it a shame what Naomi does to herself. She could be such a pretty girl."

Naomi and Eddie came barging through the crowd toward Carole and her mother, Naomi in the lead, Eddie following, carrying both their suitcases. Naomi pretended not to know his name. She called him "this nice man" and said he'd been kind enough to share his taxi, that if he hadn't, she'd have missed the train for sure. Eddie had grinned shyly as though embarrassed at all the fuss, as if, aw shucks, all he'd really done was what any decent person would do.

Carole had held her breath in desperate, paralyzing fear that any minute now her mother would catch on and Carole would be in the biggest trouble of her young life.

But her mother hadn't had a clue. She'd believed what Naomi had said and shaken Eddie's hand, her manner the same as when she met Carole's father's business associates—overly chatty and nervous. *What a nice thing it was of you to do . . . People in this city don't usually . . . Now where I'm from . . .* On and on, blushing and squirming in her coat like a complete idiot. She was forty, for God's sake, and Eddie was twenty-six. It killed Carole the way her mother could get, especially when *she* was the one going to bed with him later. It was so pathetic. She hadn't dared to look at Naomi, who she knew would be smirking dangerously.

"The nerve of you," she had said to Naomi when they finally ditched her mother and got on the train. "The absolute balls!"

They managed to get two pairs of seats facing each other and throw their stuff all over the other two. Then they'd had to fight people off who wanted to sit with them, saying the seats were taken. Naomi was best at that, coolly and calmly putting her hand on the vacant seat and saying, "I'm afraid these are already spoken for," ignoring people's dirty looks once the train got going and the seats stayed empty. If it had been up to Carole, she would have given them away. She was weak when it came to things like that.

Somewhere in Connecticut, Eddie made his way up the aisle and flopped down in the seat next to Carole. He leaned against her, and she let him, feeling his warmth. But that was nothing. The next thing she knew, Naomi, who was sitting opposite, slipped her stockinged foot between Eddie's big boots, inched it up the front of the seat between his knees, and rested it right between his thighs, wriggling her toes and laughing. Where had she learned to do that? He made a kissing motion at Naomi and then at Carole, and Carole dared to make the same noise back. After that, anything went. Whatever they felt like doing, they did. Whatever they felt like saying, they said. What a feeling it was. Think it, do it. For mile after mile of swaying tracks and stops and people getting on and off, staring at them, some of them making remarks. The girls switched places, took off their shoes and socks, touched his feet, each other's feet and ankles, until, some time in the afternoon, they all fell into a semi-sleep, tangled and barefooted.

"So I'll see one of you later," he said as the train was pulling into the Waterbury station.

"Me." Carole was drunk with him. Eddie had bedroom eyes, half shut all the time, with fat lids. And thick lips. His whole face reminded Carole of sleep, like you'd have to stick a pin in him to get his attention. So sexy, she thought.

"We had a race, and she won," Naomi said.

"You did?" Eddie said, waking up, a little confused. "A footrace?"

"Sort of," Carole said. Eddie's expression bothered her, and she didn't feel like giving him the details. It had been her idea and now it seemed sort of dumb and she was embarrassed. She and Naomi had chosen a course. Carole would start at 100th and Madison, while Naomi started at 20th and Madison. Whoever got to 60th and Madison first, the exact midpoint, won the right to go first with Eddie. Carole had won by six minutes.

"You must have cheated, eh?" Eddie pressed two fingers into Carole's belly and jiggled them. She knew what he was thinking. That she was too fat to outrun Naomi. But she'd only had to outwit Naomi. She'd zigzagged through the city, plunged into traffic mid-block, and raced through red lights. She counted on Naomi's getting distracted by stores and people, and she had.

"No," she said.

"Well, lucky me," Eddie said.

In the headlights of an oncoming car she saw him ahead now, getting ready to cross the road to the motel. He waited for the car to pass and then ran for it. She wished he'd wait for her, but maybe it was because he was an actor that he was this way. Maybe he was going over lines in his head or thinking about how to do a scene. She'd read in *Confidential Magazine* that Danny Kaye did that all the time. People would see him on airplanes and ask for his autograph, and he wouldn't even hear them because he was so preoccupied with a script.

He waited for her to cross the road. She couldn't see him very well and had to grope for him in the dark. Her hands hit the soft layers of his jacket. "Hold still," he said. His gloved hands came to rest on her arm, and she smiled secretly. He tucked her hand under his elbow and pressed it hard against his side. "Come on," he said. "It's fucking cold out here." The word thrilled her. She'd never heard it spoken like that, so casually, as if he said it all the time. He set off fast, but she couldn't keep up and soon her hand slipped from under his arm. He took a few steps without her and then stopped. Utter silence. She could be anywhere with anybody—it was that dark. She was too scared to take any more steps by herself.

"Eddie?" She groped the dark again. "Come on. This isn't funny."

He grabbed her from behind and she screamed. He clamped a leather glove that smelled like gasoline over her mouth. "Sshh," he said and kissed her, the warmth of his lips and tongue a sudden shock, more terrifying still. "Come on. Not much more." By now she could see a little bit of light through the trees ahead. She had her hand tucked in again between his elbow and his side and she was a little bit behind him. She liked it this way, the feeling of being taken somewhere. Against her will, but not really.

He led the way to the second cabin from the left. The ones to either side were dark, and the office was dark except for a neon sign with pieces of the letters missing. The cabin was dark wood, or painted brown, she couldn't tell. It had white shutters tilting off. She knew what he meant about it being crummy. "Ours is only a dorm," she said about the Double Hearth, where she and Naomi were staying. "At least you have some privacy."

He fumbled in his pocket for the key, opened the door, and switched on the light. "See what I mean?" It smelled of bats and mice inside, like a summerhouse that had been closed up. There were two twin beds with beige-and-brown-striped bedspreads, an armchair, and a bureau. His suitcase lay open on the floor. It was one of those fiberglass ones that you could drop from an airplane and it wouldn't break. His shaving stuff was spread out on a fake mantel. There was an electric heater. He switched on the heater, and they both watched the coils start to glow red. He went to one of the beds, jiggled the mattress, and grinned. He sat on the bed, took off his parka and sweater, and threw them into a corner. He started undoing the top button of his shirt and then stopped. "Don't just stand there," he said.

Her parka crackled with static electricity when she took it off. The yellow mohair sweater came way down over her hips, but even so she tugged it down and sat on the bed across from him, holding the parka in her lap. She had never thought about this part, the part right before. She had no idea how they were ever going to get from here into one of the beds. How she'd even get out of her clothes. How Eddie would. She studied the lamp on the table between the beds. It had a cowboy roping a steer on the shade. He probably wished Naomi was here instead of her.

Eddie unbuttoned the cuffs of his shirt, took it off, and threw it on top of the sweater and parka. She wondered if he would just keep on going and take off all his clothes. Then what? It was all happening too fast. But he stopped and sat staring at her in his undershirt and khaki slacks. Her father sometimes looked at her the same way. He'd once said she was never going to be cute. "No sirree," he had said. "You're going to be handsome. A handsome woman." She hadn't dared to tell that one to Naomi. She didn't want anybody to know. It was so awful. At the time, she didn't even dare ask what he meant—what women did he think were handsome? What if he said Golda Meir or Lillian Hellman? Well, no, she *knew* she didn't look like them. That much she could say. She didn't have a great big nose and little eyes, for one thing. Her nose was nice. And she had arresting eyes, everybody said, which was, in her opinion, too much like "handsome" to be much comfort. Her eyes were pale blue, like ice. In her wildest dreams she wondered about Sophia Loren. She hoped to God that Sophia was handsome. Generous features on Sophia, that was for sure. But dark. And Carole was so fair. Maybe, just maybe.

"Stop that thing with your foot, will you?" Eddie said. "It makes me nervous."

She took a breath and looked around.

"So?" he said.

"So?" she said.

He took a bottle of scotch from his suitcase, poured two little cone-shaped paper cups, and handed her one. The hot liquor ran down to her stomach like fire. He poured her another. "So you're eighteen?"

She remembered what Naomi had said. *Whatever you bloody do, don't bloody tell him you're only bloody sixteen. Bloody* was Naomi's word of the month. Naomi said he might not go through with it if he knew. He might think she was too young. "I got held back in the fourth grade. I couldn't get my multiplication tables." She added the last bit to make it authentic. Actually, she was young for her year and headed to Vassar in the fall. She had been accepted on early decision, the only girl in her class who had, and she would turn seventeen in her first month of college. She was a brain. She'd spent her whole life getting straight A's.

Eddie crumpled the cup in his hand and looked her up and down. There was something so bold in the way he stared at her breasts that it took her breath away, and when he slowly raised his eyes to meet hers, she felt so weak she could barely move.

"Give," he said. He reached for the parka she held, loosely now, in her lap. "Stand up and turn around. Let me get a look at you."

The old dread came back full force. She was fat, and her thighs rubbed when she walked.

"Just be natural. Trust me. Look at yourself in the mirror."

She stood and turned to the mirror over the dresser. Her face was flushed from the walk and the liquor. "Nice," he said. He stood behind her, examining her in the glass. He cupped her chin, pulled her hair back. It was blond and curly, almost frizzy. He lifted it from her back to the top of her head and kissed her neck, playing with the hem of her sweater at the same time. When she felt his hands along her bare midriff, she pulled in her stomach on reflex. "Don't do that," he said. "Just relax. You're fine."

"I don't know what to do."

"It isn't what you do. It's what *I* do. Lesson number one."

His hands lifted the sweater and she raised her arms automatically, like a child. When he pulled the sweater over her head, she was ashamed of the twisted and frayed straps of her bra. She covered the rolls of fat on her midriff with her arms as best she could, but again Eddie stopped her, smiling at her from behind in the glass. He undid the hooks of her bra and pulled it away. "Look," he said. She watched in shock as his fingers took her nipple and pinched it. It hurt just a little, but she didn't let him know that. She wanted to be brave. "They change." His smile held a trace of cruelty that only made her like him better. "Did you know that?"

Of course she did, but she shook her head. He'd said it was what *he* did, after all.

He unhooked her pants, ran the zipper down, and pulled them to the floor. She shut her eyes. She hated seeing herself all bigger than life. Without looking, she remembered the underpants she had on and blushed. They were gray and soft from so many washings. He pulled them to the floor and stood up behind her as his hands slid across her belly, down to the place between her legs, his fingers making small circles that suddenly felt good. Incredibly good. "You like that, don't you?" he said, and she opened her eyes and glanced at what he was doing, riveted now by the sight of his hand on her and the feel of his breath on her shoulder. She nodded. She could not speak.

Then he turned and went to the bed, where he lay down, leaving her stranded, with her panties and slacks around her feet. She wished he'd make this easier. But he didn't. He didn't tell her anything now, which wasn't fair. It was supposed to be about what *he* did.

He lay back on the pillows. "Beautiful," he said, and she was able to smile for the first time all night. "You're a diamond in the rough, you know that?" He beckoned her over and she went, kicking out of her pants. She lay down beside him easily. She felt as fluid as water while his hands traveled over her body, exploring, and she was carried along for what seemed like hours until he rolled away, stood beside the bed, dropped his pants, picked them up, and took something from the pocket. A rubber. He fumbled with himself, and she saw for the first time his thing in the dim light, bobbing and unruly. She couldn't take her eyes off it. The bulk of it, and that stocking thing dangling off the end. The fact of her looking at it that way did something to him, made him bigger. He lay down next to her. He touched her. "God, you're wet," he said.

"I'm sorry," she said.

It made him laugh so hard that he had to roll onto his back. He turned back to face her. "It's a *good* thing," he said. "I see we've got a lot of ground to cover."

She felt pleased with herself for making him laugh out loud, thrilled at his evident enjoyment of her although she didn't know exactly what had been so funny. Well, not funny. The way he laughed wasn't so much comic as appreciative. He liked her better for what she had just said. *It's a good thing.* She smiled, remembering the nice way he'd said that, as she felt his hands trace lightly over her abdomen and breasts and then make gentle, tantalizing circles, spreading slowly down, to her navel, below her navel. Her hand slid down his arm to his hand, wanting, needing whatever was next. She opened easily to him and felt again that sweet tugging and the sense that the place between her legs was the only part of her that existed, that everything else—body, thought, even consciousness—was gone, fully in the service of this sudden enlargement.

And then there was a moment of searing pain, and she realized that he was inside her. He started pumping rhythmically against her, aggravating the pain. She didn't want to cry out in case she was mistaken again and lay waiting for that flicker of pleasure to return, but it didn't. She shifted under him a little, and it did something odd. He hesitated as though he was listening for something, his body rigid and absolutely still. He seemed to get a second wind and boom boom boom. Then he slumped down on top of her with all his weight and stayed there until she could hardly breathe and had to squeeze out from under him.

Were they finished or was this still the middle? She waited for some other new thing to happen, but nothing did. She was getting her own second wind and wanted to go another round or whatever you'd call it. This couldn't possibly be all there was to it, not after what everybody said. "The central moment of the young wife's life," according to the book her mother had made her read. But he was snoring. She felt so wide awake. How could he be asleep so soon? She stared at the ceiling. It reminded her of summer camp with its plain pine boards. She used to lie on her bunk and stare at the knots until they looked like faces or animals, but she was too jumpy for that now. She considered racing out of here so she could tell Naomi. For once she'd have a leg up on Naomi. I did it *first.* But if she left, she might miss something. It wasn't even nine o'clock.

She looked around the room for something to do. There was no TV or radio. Not even a book as far as she could see. Just his stuff. She tiptoed to the suitcase on the floor and opened it up, but it was cold in the room and she went back and got his T-shirt from off the floor. The suitcase was olive green. Inside were a few pairs of those same khakis, all folded, and some shirts and underwear. She opened a drawer. Inside, there were a magazine, a box of rubbers, and some ten-dollar bills in a paper clip.

She opened the magazine. It was a dirty magazine on bad paper, with drawings of naked men and women in it and some fuzzy photographs. She pulled it out carefully and looked through it, glancing often at Eddie in case he woke up. She had a feeling he'd be mad if he knew she was in his stuff. She'd never seen pictures like this. Everything was the color of raw beef.

She opened the other top drawer and started to fill it with his underwear until it occurred to her that if he found all his things put away, he'd know she'd seen the magazine. That might not be okay. She didn't really know him that well. What if he thought she had taken some of the money? She undid everything, quietly slipping the clothes out of the drawer and back into his suitcase.

She went to the mantel, where his shaving things were all lined up. There was a little rectangular hairbrush and a tortoiseshell comb. She ran her hands over all his things as though they were her own. She picked up the hairbrush and ran it through her tangled curls. He had a leather toilet kit filled with half-used tubes and bottles. She went into the bathroom, emptied the kit out on top of the toilet tank, held it under hot water, and scrubbed. She flattened his toothpaste and rolled it tightly from the bottom. She wanted to take care of him now. Make everything easy and clean for him.

Her mother had explained about sex when Carole turned ten. It had been just awful. Her mother had been embarrassed, looking away most of the time and not meeting Carole's eyes. She had said that one day Carole would fall in love, get married, and then have intercourse. She'd blushed when she got to the part where the man's penis became rigid and was inserted into the woman's vagina. Even at ten, Carole had been pretty sure something was missing from the explanation, and now she knew. Her mother had left out the urgency of it all, how at a certain point there was no stopping. It had to be the whole reason anyone wanted to do it in the first place. Sex wasn't a chore at all but an unstoppable pleasure that could have gone on forever if only Eddie hadn't fallen asleep. When Carole had asked her mother about falling in love—what it meant, how it happened, how you knew—her mother had said, "You'll just know." Maybe it was happening right now.

"Where'd you go?" He was calling from the bedroom. She opened the door and looked out at him. "Don't go touching my stuff."

She sat on the side of the bed. "Do I look different? Now that . . . you know. They say girls look different after. That men can tell. I just hope Daddy can't tell. He'd kill me."

"You look fine. Don't worry."

"I feel different."

"You should."

"Can I see you back in New York?"

He lay back down and grinned at her. "So?" he said.

"So what?"

"Do you like me?"

"Yes," she said, flattered and a little taken aback to be asked. She wouldn't have dared ask him that question herself. What if he said no?

He pulled her down beside him. "Sure, you can see me back in New York."

"Can I go to one of your actor parties?" There was no question in her mind that he'd want her to. That really she was just making this easier for him. Saving him from having to ask. He'd said she was beautiful, after all.

"Maybe I can come to your place," he said.

The thought of Eddie in her bedroom electrified her.

"So tell me," he said. "You walk into your apartment, and what's there? Is it like a hall or what?"

She walked him through the apartment, starting with the dining room and the den off that, the corridor to her parents' room. He wanted every little detail—what was on the walls, what the furniture was like, what they could see out the window. She told him about the home for unwed mothers across the street and all the pregnant girls her age who played cards, watched TV, and waited for their babies. Her mother said it served them right.

"She's pathetic, isn't she?"

"Who?"

"Your mother."

She'd said her mother was pitiful a thousand times to Naomi. But she hated hearing him say it. "I don't know."

"I know, and I only met her for two minutes." He laughed. "Hot to trot."

"She has a hard life." What she meant was personally. Her mother

15

wasn't cut out for the life she was leading. She should have stayed in the Midwest, where the people didn't scare her. Her father's business friends made her mother so nervous that she sometimes drank too much.

"What if she knew?" Eddie said and laughed. "About this. Her little girl giving up her virginity to a cad." He rolled over and started kissing her neck, her breasts. "What if she knew I was doing this?" His hand slid down between her legs. "So answer me. What if they knew? Your parents."

"Well, they *won't.*"

"But just say, just *suppose* you were going to give me something in return for my keeping our little secret. What would it be?"

"That's not funny."

He sighed and rolled onto his back. "It's a *game,* for chrissake. Pick me out a present."

"Well, you don't have to shout," she said. Eddie sighed deeply. "Okay," she said. "There's a silver cigarette box lined in ivory, about yea big." She made the small shape with her hands. "There are always cigarettes in it left over from parties." It was her favorite thing. She loved the way it smelled of tobacco and the smooth, cool bone lining.

"You can do better than that. Something big," he said. "Something valuable."

She was a little hurt because she treasured that box. The only expensive items they owned, or at least the only ones she could think of, were the ancestor prints in the hall, but they were huge.

"Oh, forget it. Turn over," he said. She lay with her back to him so he could curl himself around her. "I like you," he said, running his hand back and forth along her thigh, then pushing up the T-shirt to help her remove it. "I like big women. That Naomi is skin and bone. A real Bony Maroni."

"She's going to be beautiful. Everybody says."

"Not if she doesn't put some meat on her."

Carole took a deep breath and relaxed. She'd never once expected him to like her better. It just never happened. "Naomi's mother went insane," she said and then stopped short. Maybe she shouldn't be telling him this.

"Oh, yeah?" Eddie said. She could hear the interest rise in his voice.

She nodded. Now she hoped he'd just let it go. She shouldn't have said anything.

"Insane how?" He tickled her side. "Come on, Carole. How?"

Well, when she thought about it now, she remembered how on her first day at Spence, Amanda Howe had pointed out Naomi and said, "That's the girl whose mother slit open her wrists with a fork and bled to death in a mental hospital." Her words exactly, so okay, maybe it wasn't really privileged information. It wasn't as though Naomi had ever sworn her to secrecy. Everybody knew.

"She died in an institution. She killed herself. Her stepmother, Elayne, she's Czech, she does Hazel Bishop commercials on *What's My Line?*" She paused to let him speak, but he didn't. "You know, Dorothy Kilgallen, Bennett Cerf, Arlene Francis, John Charles Daly. When they have a break, this red light goes on over on the left side of the set, which means she's on. Then her hands get all lit up. She's only twenty-four. She holds up a bottle of nail polish so you can see the lipstick and nails together."

Eddie ignored the story. "I bet that Naomi ends up in an institution too. Like mother, like daughter, don't you think?" It shocked her again, the way he was talking, but she liked it even though she shouldn't. "That one has a screw loose, no question about it." Eddie turned over, and in a few moments he began to snore again.

She'd been so afraid that she wouldn't know what to say and there she was saying too much. And it had all been so different from what she'd expected. Nothing like that idiotic book of her mother's, which mostly told how to use your elbows to keep a boy from touching your breasts. Oh, cripes. She had been afraid of Eddie seeing her naked, but he'd liked the way she looked. She'd been afraid he'd like Naomi better, and here he thought Naomi was skinny and crazy. She'd been afraid of everything, and now here she was, perfectly relaxed and not a virgin anymore. She pulled the covers to her chin and smiled. It must have been midnight, and he obviously expected her to stay overnight. She had never dared to think that might happen. Never in a million years.

She woke later because of a meowing sound at the door. It took a minute to remember where she was. The sound was human, though, somebody pretending to be a cat. Eddie sat up like a shot. "I'll get it," he said.

"They'll go away." Carole grabbed for his arm. "They'll go away if no one answers the door." She was afraid it was Naomi ruining her night.

"Let go." Eddie pulled away, wrapped the bedspread around his waist, and went to the window. He opened the curtain and strained to see out. Then he let the curtain fall. "Oh, for crying out loud," he said.

"Who is it?"

He turned the doorknob. Carole sat up, drawing the covers over herself.

Eddie opened the door slightly and pressed against the opening, whispering to whoever was out there. Carole strained to see, but Eddie was in the way. Then he said something she couldn't make out. She got up and stood behind him, her hand on his bare back. Startled, he turned from the door to face her. The woman outside used the opportunity to push herself past him and into the room. She shuddered, hugging herself and stomping her feet against the cold.

She had on a fur hat, pointed on top and tied under the chin, a navy-blue parka that came almost down to her knees, and big men's boots. She was carrying a large plastic pocketbook. Carole thought it was the motel owner's wife, here to kick her out. She'd heard you had to register as man and wife, and even then they made you prove it. You had to show them something with your married name on it. The owner must have figured out that Eddie had sneaked Carole in and wasn't going to have "it" going on in his establishment. She braced for the woman's anger, for a scolding. But instead the woman came in, took off her hat, and smiled. She had long reddish-brown hair, skin as pink as bubble gum from the cold, and a broad, plump face. She was a lot older than Carole.

"Let me take that," Eddie said to her, reaching for her parka.

"What's going on?" Carole said.

The woman turned her back to Eddie while he removed the parka. She shot Carole a look. Under the parka she had on a loose red sweater. She kicked off the boots and pulled off the sweater. Her olive-green dress had straps as thin as shoelaces that dug into her fleshy shoulders. She sat in the wooden chair beside the dresser, crossed her sausage legs, pulled a cigarette out, and held it up. "You got a light?" Her voice was higher than Carole would have expected, like a little girl's. He flicked the match with the thumbnail of one hand and dragged it across the tip of her cigarette.

"Eddie?" Carole said. If it wasn't the owner's wife, who was it? And who did she think she was, anyway? Sitting there like she owned the place. Carole went to the bed, the one they'd been in, and sat down. She'd been here first.

"It's okay," he said.

The woman smoked in a heavy, leisurely way, inhaling deeply and blowing out smoke from the corner of her mouth in a jet. She let the ash grow until it was almost as long as the cigarette. She held the pack of Kents out to Carole. "Want one?"

"I don't smoke."

Carole had the feeling that if she moved too quickly, something bad would happen. She watched the woman's hand raise the cigarette to her lips and only then realized that both of them, Eddie and that woman, were staring at her. She felt stricken, the way she felt when she had to stand up in front of the class and recite. "Eddie?" She wanted somebody to say something, to break the tension in the room.

The woman sighed, shrugged her shoulders, took another long, deep drag of her cigarette, and handed it to Eddie, who dropped it into a glass, the move all smooth and choreographed like they'd done this a million times. Eddie smiled, a disturbing kid's smile, and let the bedspread fall to the floor. "You dropped—" Carole began but stopped because the woman uncrossed her legs and let herself down to the floor, to her knees, right there in front of Eddie. She pulled her hair back with both hands, twisted it behind her neck, and then did something unbelievable. She took Eddie's thing in her mouth, and Eddie just let her do it. Instead of pulling away, instead of getting angry or upset, he stayed right where he was, looking down at the woman like he was in a trance. The whole thing made Carole want to gag. Wouldn't the woman get a disease? She should leave, get out of here. She looked for her clothing and saw Naomi's yellow sweater on the floor by the door. There was no way she could go over there so close to the two of them. And if Eddie wanted her to stay and she went, she'd never go to those parties in New York. She'd never see him again. He motioned for her to come over to where they were.

"Maybe I should go home," she said. What she really wanted was for the woman to go, and she wanted one of them to say that, but the woman laughed and pulled away from Eddie and got to her feet.

"Don't be silly." The woman looked at herself in the mirror, turning this way and that. "I'm Rita. Eddie isn't too good on the introductions." The easy familiarity with which she said Eddie's name made Carole's stomach heave.

Rita hesitated, then gave Eddie an uncertain smile. She came over to where Carole was sitting and sat down. "We met a couple of times. Get her a cigarette, will you, sweetheart?" Rita said to Eddie. "You should really smoke a cigarette, honey. It'll calm you right down." Rita's eyes were light brown, and for the first time, they seemed kind.

Carole shook her head. "No," she said. The truth was she'd made a deal with her parents not to smoke until she was twenty-one. They'd promised to give her a hundred dollars. Almost all the girls in her class smoked.

Eddie was looking from one of them to the other. "Nice," he said, grinning. "Say, Carole, why don't you help Rita with that zipper."

They were both watching her now. Eddie, erect, still standing where he was. Rita beside her, her face close and smiling. "What's your name again, honey?" Her voice was lower now, more like a regular person.

She shook her head. Her name was none of Rita's business.

"Carole," Eddie said.

"Aw," Rita said. "You and Jumbo here were having a nice time, right?"

Carole just stared at her.

"And in comes little old me," Rita said with a laugh.

"Right," Carole said.

Rita patted her hand. "I won't bite."

"Pull down the zipper," Eddie said, his voice stronger, almost demanding. He came over and sat beside her on the bed so that now she was flanked. "Come on." He kissed her neck. "You wanted an education."

Carole could have died. It wasn't like that. She stole a sidelong glance at Rita, who smiled back. "This might not work," Rita said to Eddie.

"Sure it will. Hand me that bottle there."

Eddie held the bottle of scotch up for Carole to sip. "A little lubrication is what you need," he breathed into her ear, nuzzling her hair back. "Trust me." She took the bottle and tilted her head back. The liquor came in a rush, filling her mouth. It seemed to explode inside her.

Rita burst out laughing. "Wow," she said.

"I told you," Eddie said.

Carole had to catch her breath. The liquor burned at her center and made her eyes water.

"She's good," Eddie said. So much was going on all of a sudden. The low light, the fetid but almost pleasant smell of the place, the sudden warmth she felt oozing out from the center of herself. She had to blink to see if it was real. "She's good," he said again. *Good.* It meant everything just then, like getting an A.

"Say, how old are you anyhow?" Rita's face was still pink, her brows bunched up.

"She's eighteen," Eddie said.

"She doesn't look any eighteen to me," Rita said.

"Well, she is," he said. "Right?"

Carole nodded. The scotch was making her feel soft and damp in her head.

"Let's get the show on the road." Eddie rocked from foot to foot. Rita turned and held up her hair so that Carole could take the little black zipper tab and pull it down.

"I don't know," Carole said. It was happening too fast. Everything was so confusing.

"Go on," Eddie said. "Just do it."

Carole pulled on the zipper and the dress opened, exposing more of Rita's fleshy back. Good. It was covered with ugly pimples.

Rita stood and wriggled out of the dress, leaving a dark green doughnut on the floor. She had on a red garter belt and black stockings. Nothing else. Rita winked at Carole, as though standing there nearly naked was cute or something. Carole had to look away because she felt embarrassed for Rita, whose breasts were long and walleyed, looking off in both directions. She was shaped like Sydney Saltonstall, a girl in her class who Carole had seen naked one time after gym and who had rolls of fat around her middle and no waist at all. Carole might be fat, but at least her body had a shape.

"Let's move these two beds together," Eddie said. "Up up up!"

They pulled away the little nightstand and shoved the beds together. "Rita's going to give you a back rub."

"It's okay," Rita said. "Lie down. Do like he said. A little back rub won't kill you." The sudden feeling of Rita's cold hand on her shoulder made her jump. "Hey, relax. I'm good at this." Rita's thumbs dug deep. They traveled up the back of her neck, massaging hard, and then into her hair. Rita purred things to her: "You're all tense. . . . That's

better. . . . Don't worry, honey. Nobody's going to hurt you. Honest."
Eddie draped a purple towel over the cowboy lamp, and the room went
all weird blue. His weight settled on the bed, then his hands on her, or
so she thought. She tried to picture the hands, but there seemed to be
so many. She felt herself losing her bearings. Through the fog of sensation, she knew this much: What was happening was freeing her. Rita
purred out the wrong name. "Garrett," she said. Or something like
that. Wrong guy, Carole was thinking dreamily. Eddie didn't say anything back. He liked her, Carole, and not Rita, she thought with faint
satisfaction. He wanted to see her in New York. He said she was good.
A diamond in the rough.

They surrounded her, wedging and shifting, their arms and legs
entangled, their skin growing moist and sticky. The sensation of
hands and lips on her body was strange but not frightening at all, not
now, and she felt carried along, lulled and excited, until everything
was happening by itself, until she was moving with them, on her
knees over them and then down, lying on her back, everything lus-
cious and thrilling. The beds slipped apart, and they crowded onto
the one close to the wall. Rita moaned, purred, whispered to Carole
what to do. She should touch Eddie here and then there. And she
was right because Eddie was like somebody new, kissing and touching her, Carole, and not Rita. She was the one he liked, she thought
dreamily. Better than he liked Naomi. Better than Rita. Maybe Rita
had set everything in motion, but now all of Eddie's attention was on
her, on Carole. All of it.

There came a sobering draft. Somebody had got up. She opened
her eyes and tried to make out who in the dim light. Eddie stood beside the bed, the bottle of scotch in his hand. He took a sip, then
passed the bottle to Rita, who passed it to Carole. She took a long
swallow and handed it back, but Eddie said to take another, and she
did. It was easy this time, the liquid rushing through in a pleasurable
way. She could see now why her mother liked to drink.

He shoved one of the beds aside. "Move over," he said to Carole,
his voice gruff. He climbed back onto the bed and straddled Rita.

He had something in his hands. Ropes or cords. "Watch this," he said.

He took one of Rita's hands, wound the rope around her wrist, and tied the other end to the bedpost. Then he did the same with her other hand. Maybe he was tying Rita up to get her out of the way. The thought made Carole giggle, the sound erupting in the silence of the room.

Eddie didn't even notice her laugh. He was different all of a sudden, serious, focused on what he was doing. Rita lay writhing, animal sounds coming out of her, egging him on—"Big boy, big daddy, come to Mama." Eddie's hand explored under Rita's chin the way Carole's speech teacher, Miss White, had instructed them so they could feel how the words vibrated in there. Eddie and Rita were taking up all the room on the bed, forcing Carole over to the side and off until she was kneeling beside the bed. The scotch made her feel outside herself, not knowing where she was, even though she knew she could remember if she would only try. And she did try now, slumped beside the bed, to shake off the unpleasant clumsy feeling gathering in her head. This was the motel they'd gotten. Snowtown. Stupid name. But that's where she was. With Eddie, who had only just tonight taken her virginity. Changed her forever.

She looked at Rita's upturned face, bland as cheese. Cheap, Carole thought. She wasn't even supposed to be here. Carole had even paid for half this room. He was hers, not Rita's. Carole rose, suddenly feeling bold, a little angry. She didn't care what anybody thought. She leaned in and tried to kiss Eddie, angling her face around, insinuating herself between him and Rita. But Eddie fell back on his haunches, and his hand slammed against the wall to keep from falling. "Jesus," he said.

"Eddie?" She'd only meant to keep it going like before. "Move over, okay?"

"You're too fucking big," he said. "Too much weight." He pushed at her shoulder. "Shit, you're big as a horse. Make yourself scarce."

Horse. The words hung in the stinking air, draining the life out of her. *Horse.* She felt so heavy with shame, as though she'd been struck in the stomach. She reached for the bottle of scotch and took a sip, then another, and it helped. Maybe she'd breathe again after all, maybe she'd live through this. And then another sip, longer this time, grateful for the way it dulled the humiliation.

"Hey," Rita said to her, lolling around, sort of out of it. She indicated with her chin the space at the head of the bed, between her head and the headboard in the tangles of rope. "Up here, honey. Just get the hell out of his way. He goes a little crazy sometimes." It was the only place Carole could be now, other than the chair, off by herself out in the cold, and she wasn't about to do that. No way.

She crawled over Rita's arm, into the cramped space between Rita's upturned face and the headboard. No space at all, not nearly enough for her, bracing herself, knees spread apart for balance. One hand on the wall, the other shielding her crotch from Rita's gaze. If she tried to leave, it was going to piss Eddie off again. The bed began to rock with his movements, and she was stranded. It was like being in the lavatory of a moving train—the way you can never get your balance, your legs useless and your body lurching all over the place. And the sounds of Eddie and Rita. Sickening sounds. The croon of their breathing below her and the steady pound of the headboard against the wall. She just wanted it to be over. She wanted to leave.

She shut her eyes, but the room spun and she felt nauseated. Eddie was breathing harder, grunting out every breath like an animal, and there were other sounds too, more tortured, the gravelly suck of air, which could be him or Rita. And then finally, finally, Rita relaxed, and Carole was so relieved she could have cheered. So there, she thought, Rita doesn't want to play anymore, and neither do I. But Eddie hammered on, and she was still on that train being thrown forward and then back, one side and then the other, bracing with whatever she could, her hands, her thighs, out of control until everything came screeching to a stop, with Eddie slumped beneath her, as motionless as if he'd been shot.

She didn't dare move until he raised himself and looked at her, his face inches away and grotesque in the dark purple light. "God, what a jolt," he said. "I bet you never saw anything like that before."

She waited for him to roll away before she crawled like an animal back over Rita's body, aware of her own immense size, her ungainliness and the awful picture she must make. She didn't know what she should say or do. She stood beside the bed. Eddie reached out, brushed her leg lightly, and grinned up at her. "First time for everything."

The room was very still, too quiet.

Something was the matter.

"Loosen up, will you?" he said. "Try to have some fun for once."

Rita's eyes were half open. "What's the matter with her?" Carole said.

"Nothing," he said. He whipped the towel off the lamp, throwing the room again into a stark cold light. "Believe me, she's better than she's ever been."

"Hey," Carole said quietly to Rita, but Rita still didn't move. She didn't even blink. "There's something the matter."

Eddie patted Rita's bare thigh. "Okay, sweetheart," he said. "Fun's over."

Rita still didn't move. Eddie stood, waiting, then scowled and knelt on the bed, leaning into Rita. He shoved her hard at the shoulder. "Hey, Rita. Hey, puss. Wake up."

He waited several beats, then placed his ear to her breast. He touched her neck with the tips of his fingers, just under the jaw. In that awful light, Rita looked bluish. He untied the cords and tried to raise her to a sitting position, but she was limp like a big doll, and he let her go like she was something dirty. Rita flopped to one side, her hand dangling close to the floor. They remained that way in silence, Eddie on his knees, Carole standing beside the bed.

"Oh, shit," Eddie said.

"What?" Carole wanted him to say something else, anything other than what she knew.

"She's dead."

Carole suddenly felt so sick to her stomach that she knew she was about to throw up. She bolted for the bathroom, barely making it to the toilet, where she dropped to her knees, thrust her arms around the toilet bowl, and vomited scotch and bile. When it was over, she stayed sitting on the floor, exhausted, hoping that when she went back out to the room, it wouldn't be true. She hadn't heard him right. Rita would be alive. Carole stood and looked at herself in the mirror. Her skin was gray, with dark circles under her eyes. She splashed water over her face and dried it with a towel. Then she went back into the room. Eddie was sitting on the bed. He looked up at her. "What the fuck did you do?" he said.

She felt she could throw up again. Her head was throbbing. "I didn't do anything. I only—"

"Only what?" He rubbed his face hard in his hands. "Only what? You only what?" Eddie leaned over Rita to look at her again. He touched Rita's neck. He nudged her head, ran his fingers along her neck. "You were all over her. Her neck's busted. You must have busted her neck."

"No." That wasn't possible. "No," she said again.

"Well, it wasn't me."

"There's a phone in the office," she said. "We can call somebody."

He took in a deep breath and shut his eyes for a long moment. "*Call* somebody?" He stayed that way with his eyes closed as though pained by her stupidity. "I don't think you understand." His voice was thick with contempt. "You stupid cow. You killed her."

"I don't see how—"

"You don't know your own strength, Fatcakes. I thought that the first time I saw you. She's a big girl, I said to myself." He looked her up and down. "A huge girl. A dangerous girl."

"But you said—" *Beautiful.* She was aware of her nakedness all of a sudden. Of her large body, the rolls of flesh across her stomach, the expanse of bare thighs. She crossed her hands over her breasts, then her abdomen.

27

"I told you to get off the goddamned bed, remember? But oh, no. You go crawling all over her. What's the matter with you?"

"She told me to," Carole said, looking down at her hands and then away, anywhere else.

"Don't bullshit me." He gathered a bedspread from the floor and threw it to her. "Cover her up." He went into the bathroom but came out again. "And don't fucking touch her. You got that?"

Not that she even could. Not that she could even look at Rita. She opened the bedspread and held it out, staring at her hands again, hands that seemed like they belonged to somebody else. And the room too looked like a place she'd never seen before, static and out of scale, like a room in a dollhouse. She threw the bedspread, which fluttered and landed in a tangle across the body.

When Eddie came back, he was calmer. He pulled a window curtain aside, holding his hand to his eyes, and looked out. Then he shut the curtain and sat on the edge of the bed, leaning forward, his elbows on his knees. "Here's what we do." She felt better hearing this, back on steady ground. They would do something. "Well, let me back up here. Before I get to that." He took in a breath, held it and then let it all out. "This is a big problem," he said. "A very big problem you have. Nobody can find out about this."

"But they will," she said. "When—"

"For somebody smart, you're not catching on. Maybe I'd better spell it out. Nobody is ever going to find out. Just you, just me. So here's what we do. We take her up there." Eddie indicated the window, the back of the motel.

"It's illegal."

She was afraid he'd hit her, the way his fists clenched. "What's illegal was you breaking her fucking neck." He pulled away the bedspread, raised Rita's head, and let it fall. Carole had to look away, or she'd throw up again at the sight of Rita's face, her eyes still partly open. "If you call the police, we have to tell them what you did."

"But I didn't mean to do anything." She was frantic, trying to think, trying to remember doing what Eddie said she did, but it was

28

as hopeless as remembering a dream. There, and then gone. All she could remember was the feel of it, the way she'd been thrown around in the dark. She had a memory of her hands on either side of Rita's head, and her thighs too, and hating the way Rita's hair stuck to her thighs and the hot fat feel of Rita's shoulder under the heel of her hand. All that she remembered. Maybe. Maybe accidentally.

He came over, so close she could smell him. Like metal or blood. "You were all over her." He spoke softly, nicely even. "You busted her neck." She was about to speak, but Eddie put a finger to his lips. "Don't," he said. "You were drunk. Shit, you're drunk now. Look at you."

"I never drank before."

"You were on her like a fucking gorilla," he said, still in the same soft voice.

There was a sound outside. Footsteps, right at the door. "Somebody's out there," she said.

Eddie switched off the light and they waited.

"I saw that." The voice was Naomi's. "Open up, you guys." She was right there, right on the other side of the door. She pushed it open. There was a rush of cold. "Pewey. It stinks in here."

Suddenly Naomi was standing before them in a raccoon coat, her mouth wide open, looking around. "You guys?" Her eyes traveled from one of them to the other. She burst out laughing and turned away. "Cover up, will you?" Carole snatched up a sheet and wrapped it around herself.

Eddie got up and put a hand on her shoulder, guiding her back toward the door. "Go on back," he said. "Get out of here."

"Wait." She was looking at the bed, at Rita. She took a step toward the bed. The bedspread had only partly covered Rita. Her hand dangled beneath it, her hair spilled down. A calf was exposed. "Who's that?"

"Shit," Eddie said and shut the door.

"Carole?" Naomi was still staring at Rita.

"You'd better tell her," Eddie said.

29

Carole shook her head.

"Tell her the truth."

"What truth?" Naomi said. "Somebody?" She looked from Carole to Eddie and back to Rita. "She looks—"

"Your friend's quite the pistol," Eddie said.

Naomi took a few steps toward the bed and stopped, staring for several seconds at Rita. "Everybody just shut up," Eddie said, even though nobody had said a word.

Naomi turned to Carole with a look of confusion, her mouth shaping the word *what*. Carole looked away.

"We have a problem," Eddie said.

"Not me," Naomi said. "Don't look at me."

"All of us," Eddie said. "But your friend in particular."

Naomi sat on the floor, her dark hair covering her face. "What did she do?"

"Let me lay it out for you," Eddie said to her. He put on a pair of underwear and a T-shirt, then he drew a chair over and sat facing Naomi, as though Carole wasn't even there. "Things got out of hand. Your friend here got carried away."

Naomi turned to look at Carole, her mouth wide in amazement, then back at Eddie.

"She got rough."

"I didn't mean—" Carole started.

"I don't have a lot of time for this." Eddie gestured toward Carole. "Fatcakes here leans on my friend while we're going at it. She's got the bitch's head in a knee lock." He demonstrated, spreading his bent knees, fists balled between them, like Rita's head. "And she lets fucking loose," he said, twisting his knees, fists flying out from the force. "And crack. End of story. I'm trying to help her. All I'm trying to do is get her out of this."

"Is she the . . . ?" Naomi indicated Rita with her thumb.

"The what?" Carole asked.

"Nobody," Eddie said. "She's nobody. You're here. Okay? You've seen. That makes three of us. Okay, okay." He flicked his hands as if they were wet. "Here's what we do." He opened the curtain again. It was still dark outside. "Who's got the time? Doesn't anybody wear a fucking watch?" He was getting so agitated. Fierce. He looked again.

"It's about four," Naomi said. "I waited up. That's why I came over here."

"Then we do this fast. Do it now. We take her up there, up over the field and the woods back there. We bury her in the snow. Nobody will know. Not ever. It's a fucking wilderness out there."

"We can't. The police. It's too fast," Carole said.

Eddie exploded. "Will you please ask your friend why she doesn't understand she fucking killed this girl, fucking broke her fucking neck, and I'm only trying to help her here?" He kicked the wall, slammed his hands against his temples. "Okay. You think it's too fast. Let me tell you about fast. Fast is when they get wind of this back at East Sixty-second Street. Fast is what happens to your dad's job at Ivey and Mason when this gets out. And all those boards of directors. What, Continental Pipe, the water company. Or your mom out there hobnobbing at Sign of the Dove. I know. I do my homework, Fatcakes. Fast is what happens when Mom and Dad find out where you are, who you're with, what you did. That's fast. Compared to that, this is molasses. Believe me. They'll turn on you so fast you won't know what hit you. And which college again? Vassar? Wellesley? It doesn't matter. You're not going anywhere when this gets out. Your dad will be shining shoes for a living."

How did he know all this? "But I didn't mean to do anything," Carole blurted out.

"So it was an accident. Big deal. Try explaining that. Rich spoiled fat girl from the city kills a little piece of ass from the sticks. Oh, it'll play all right. You won't have a chance."

He waited for a few seconds and then said, "The room is in your name." Her name? She couldn't take it in at first. "This. This room. Not that it matters. How's it going to look? Big-deal lawyer's daughter pays for a shitty motel room, pays to get herself fucked because nobody else will step up to the plate."

It was all coming at her too fast. The details about her parents and now the room. She couldn't keep up. Couldn't sort it all out, but it was bad. That was for sure.

Eddie sat on the bed. "Look, you two." His face glistened with sweat. "We're running out of time. We're going to take her out in back right now and bury her before it gets light."

"Not me," Naomi said. "I'm not going out there. It's freezing out there."

"It's not a choice."

"I didn't do anything."

"She's your friend. And you," he said to Carole. "Get yourself dressed."

Carole looked over the floor and tried to understand what he meant. Rita's dress lay at her feet, and her stockings and sweater were a few feet away. She wondered how she would ever find what she needed.

"Now!" Eddie bellowed, and she dropped to her knees and crawled about the room, gathering up what was hers, afraid to touch Rita's things. She couldn't figure out her own pants at first with those confusing straps under the feet, or the sweater. This was going to kill her parents. Their good girl. Their reliable daughter. She thought about the night at Giovanni's and her heart sank. Her parents had been a little drunk. It was the day she got her acceptance to Vassar. "You're going to make the grade," her father'd said. "It's just a matter of time."

Rita's purse was on the table next to the bed, and Carole watched Naomi pick it up and look inside.

"What's that?" Eddie said.

Naomi pulled out a red and blue plastic Minnie Mouse wallet. "God," she said. The way she held it up by one corner made Carole want to weep. She snatched the wallet from Naomi and thrust it into the pocket of her parka. "Nothing," she said.

It was hard to follow his orders. They were all mixed up, full of contradictions. He was telling her something about her shoes. Her

Capezios. The only boots were Rita's, and he made her put them on. They were short for her, and painful. He checked the window. "Hurry," he said.

Carole was in the middle, bearing the weight of Rita's wide hips, which were sickeningly hard, with Eddie at the front, facing her, walking backward, and Naomi at the feet. When he opened the door, there was a rush of cold air. Instinctively she gathered the spread over Rita to keep her covered from the cold. The body was heavy and warm. She had to pause and hoist again and again.

At first they moved well, quickly around the outside of the cabin to the edge of the field. But it was so cold and snowing hard, and the snow got in everywhere, at her neck, into her boots, her wrists, and she couldn't stop shivering. They dipped down and crossed a brook. In the field, the spread began to fall away from the body, bunching up at the hips so that Rita's breasts and face were exposed. Eddie and Naomi didn't seem to care. They wouldn't stop. They kept pushing forward through the snow. Carole had to adjust the cover the best she could, with one hand, or even with her teeth. They moved in starts, lost their balance. "Forget that," Eddie said when the bedspread fell away for the umpteenth time.

It was impossible to see where they were going in the thick snow, and Rita's body was slippery, harder and harder to hold onto. The spread was soaked through from dragging along the ground. Carole kept pulling it up and throwing it around Rita over and over.

"He said forget it." Naomi was hoarse from exhaustion. "Just let it go."

The field was uneven under the snow, with ditches and boulders, strands of barbed wire that wrapped around their legs. Twice they put the body down to untangle themselves. Carole could hardly move her hands. When they got to the woods, the going was even slower, a few steps at a time, ducking branches and stepping through thick brush, but at least the wind wasn't so fierce.

"Here." Eddie stopped and dropped his end. "We've got to dig a hole."

She fell to her knees and tried to wrap the bedspread around Rita, to cover her face and feet and tuck it in along the sides, but the ends kept coming loose.

"Help us!" Naomi screamed at her. They were scooping out snow with their hands. Eddie yanked her by the arm and pulled her down. "Dig, for Christ's sake." She scooped up the snow, her hands numb. Eddie got into the pit they were digging and worked in a kind of frenzy, like a dog. There was the sound of ice collapsing under him, and he sank slightly before her eyes. "Bingo." He stamped, breaking through underfoot. "This is good." He reached from the pit and started to pull the body toward him by the arm.

Carole tried to pull back on the body. "Don't just let her fall. Somebody get her feet."

But they shoved the body sideways toward the pit, and Eddie scrambled out of the way as the body fell heavily in. They stood quietly, all of them looking down. The pit, the snow, the color of Rita's skin were all the same gray except for the darkness of her eyes and lips, and the patch of her pubic hair. After some moments, Carole opened the spread to cover Rita.

Eddie snatched it away. "Are you crazy?"

"We need to cover her," Carole said. It was the least they could do.

"And have the cops trace it to the motel? And then to you?"

They pushed the snow back over Rita and smoothed it out. Eddie stamped on the filled grave, his boots making a soft, hollow sound. Carole fell to her knees, struck down by what they'd just done. Rita had been alive an hour ago, and now she was only a few feet beneath this perfectly smooth snow. It was impossible. It was a terrible dream, a horrendous dream. She blinked to wake herself, but it was real.

"Let's get out of here," Eddie said.

Carole smoothed the snow where Eddie's boots had left deep marks. "Rest in peace" was all she could think of to say. It was pitiful. It was not nearly enough. Nothing she did would ever be nearly enough.

When she stood, Eddie and Naomi were gone. It was lighter out, but still snowing and hard to see. She made her way back down through the brush and when she reached the edge of the field saw that the footsteps they made coming up here had already blown over. Only Naomi's and Eddie's new ones leading back down toward the cabin were visible. Soon the field would be swept clean.

She stopped to watch their two gray shadows ahead. She wished Naomi had waited. She needed her right now. She started walking again, but the sound of a car passing on a road nearby stopped her cold. What if it was someone looking for Rita? She held her breath and listened. The sound moved away and disappeared. But what if somebody else came? What if somebody was planning to pick her up and they went to the room? She had one terrifying thought after the other. Maybe lots of people knew where Rita had gone tonight and were coming to look for her at this very moment.

She sped up to keep from thinking and was relieved when she reached the ring of cabins, which sat quiet, motionless. She had to narrow her eyes against the murk and the falling snow to see, but she could just make out Eddie and Naomi. They were together in front of the cabin, drawing close to each other. Perhaps it was only one of them saying something to the other in a whisper. Or the fact that to be heard, Eddie would have had to lean down. But it looked like a kiss, and it lasted like a kiss. Longer even. She felt the last bit of life drain out of her. As she got closer, she got up her nerve to brush past them into the cabin. She found her Capezios and kicked off Rita's boots. Outside again, she passed Naomi and Eddie without a word, but he grabbed her by the sleeve.

"Hey," he said. "Wait a minute." He pulled her close. "You know, I know, Naomi knows. It would have been better if it were only you and me. Safer for you. But Naomi's your friend and she isn't going to say anything. We already talked about that. So there's only one way for you to have a problem and that's if one of us opens our mouth and it won't be me, got it?"

Carole nodded and turned to leave, but Eddie didn't open his grip. "You've got everything to lose here, Carole. Remember that. We're on your side. We're going to keep this quiet for your sake. Next couple of days we'll know if we're okay."

She pulled away and headed back toward the mountain road. It was light enough to see through the falling snow, to the towering jade evergreens, the road ahead of her. A few minutes later she heard the sound of someone running behind her.

"Wait up."

She stopped. When Naomi caught up, Carole turned to her. "Why did you put it in my name?"

"What?"

"The room, Nay. You're the one who made the reservations. You and Eddie. Why didn't you use your own name?"

"Somebody might recognize it. Elayne's famous, in case you didn't know."

"She's not famous."

"More famous than you," Naomi said.

Carole turned in a fury of tears and walked fast to get away from her. And then she remembered. She looked back. "What were you doing *kissing* him?" Her voice rang in the cold air.

"Shush," Naomi hissed at her. "You want to wake up the whole world?"

Carole turned away and broke into a run along the snow-covered drive, her lungs burning with a sharp smart pain, her feet stinging with cold. Where it turned to pavement she ran faster, harder, her feet crunching the pebbles of salt. She ran until a car rushed past going the other way, and stopped short. What if people saw? The car sped away, not even slowing. She breathed in relief. Maybe they hadn't noticed. Maybe they didn't care. A girl on the road before dawn like this. Maybe it happened all the time. Oh, please, God, if only.

Chapter Two

Carole Mason had entered Spence in the eleventh grade, and on her first day Amanda Howe was assigned to show her around and take her to morning classes. Amanda had broad shoulders and narrow little eyes that seemed to have sand in the corners all the time. She was the class president and always wore her Spence blazer. Her grandfather, she told Carole that day, had been a famous diplomat and her father was a doctor. Amanda passed her along to Shelly Taylor, who took her to lunch. They used the elevator to the sixth floor, a privilege, Shelly explained, that they were allowed because Carole was a new girl. Normally you could use the elevator only if you were injured or had to go more than three floors. Shelly led Carole down the elegant old corridor with its gleaming marble floors, past the drawing room and through the cafeteria, where white-uniformed women ladled out plates of roast beef, mashed potatoes, and green beans. In the dining room Shelly pointed out the dark gleaming mural of verdant battle scenes. It was actually one-of-a-kind wallpaper, very old, very valuable, and made especially for Spence in 1895. Shelly and Carole sat at a round table with Amanda, Deirdre Martin, and some other girls from her class. They were all talking about what they'd done during the summer, the boys they'd met at horse camp or in the Hamptons or France. Carole had spent the summer helping her parents pack up the house and move from Ridgewood.

Deirdre took over for the afternoon classes, including gym. Carole had been worried about changing in front of these perfect girls, but the locker room had little cubicles. There she put on her brand-new gym uniform—a stiff pleated navy-blue jumper with bloomers and a white middy blouse underneath. Deirdre came bursting out onto the basketball court, her uniform top densely covered in gold chevrons for all her years of varsity sports. There had been no volleyball at Ridgewood, and the Spence gym teacher kept blowing the whistle on Carole for violations, but she wouldn't stop to explain what she had done wrong. When it was over, Deirdre told Carole that everybody went to Havilands after school for cherry Cokes and she should come too. The three of them had been so polite, friendly, and full of information that Carole started to feel that Spence was going to be okay. Then, after school, Amanda, Shelly, and Deirdre ditched her and went off together. The next day they acted as though they barely knew who she was.

Maybe it had to do with her clothes. These girls wore stockings and flats to school. They had kilts and cashmere sweater sets when all Carole had were her old plaid dresses from tenth grade, saddle shoes, and the thick socks that had been quite the thing in Ridgewood, but totally dowdy here. And the glasses she'd thought were so great—cat's-eye glasses with glitter frames—were out to lunch. These girls wore tortoiseshell glasses. Real tortoiseshell.

Carole had cried herself to sleep that first week, wishing she were back in her old house, her old school, with her old friends. But the whole move had been because of her. Her father finally was making enough money to live in the city and send Carole to a good private school. There, according to him, she'd receive a real education and get into a real college, namely Vassar. Carole was supposed to carry the torch for the family. All their hopes rested on her. She knew her father wished she'd been a boy. Boys were better at torches than girls, but she was an only child and he'd had to settle for her. Buck up, he'd said sternly when she'd grown morose those first weeks. Stop feeling so sorry for yourself. She knew her mother hated New York as much as she did, but there was no help there. Her mother wouldn't ever stand up to her father.

One day in November, eight miserable weeks into the school year, Carole was sitting in homeroom, studying—at least she knew how to do that—when Naomi plopped herself down on the desk next to her. "Hey," she said. Carole had noticed Naomi. How could anybody not? Naomi was small and nervous and flashy. She dressed in bright colors and wore more makeup than she was allowed to wear. She was constantly being sent to the washroom to take it off. And she kept apart from the other girls too. Always at the end of the line for assembly. Always off to herself in gym. "Wanna go to Lamston's this aft?"

It was the first real invitation from anyone at Spence since her fateful first day, and she said yes, sure. She followed Naomi to the Eighty-ninth Street Lamston's, aware of what an odd-looking pair they were, Carole towering over Naomi, outweighing her by thirty pounds. Naomi had told her to do what she could to distract the salesladies, and Carole had wandered around asking the prices of things. Afterward they went to Naomi's apartment, where they streaked through a whole series of rooms to an enormous kitchen that had two industrial-sized refrigerators along one wall. Naomi dumped the contents of her purse on the kitchen table. Pens and lipsticks and key chains spilled out, along with things Carole didn't even recognize.

"You took it all?" she said. There had been times in her life when she'd been tempted, but she'd never had the nerve.

"Take what you want," Naomi said. She got up and checked one of the refrigerators. "We're in luck," she said. "Sometimes Elayne locks them." Naomi took out bottles of Coke, a platter of little cakes, and a jar of pickled string beans and set them on the kitchen table.

"I've been watching you from day one, you know," Naomi said. "And I can tell you a thing or two about Spence. First, and don't take this personally, but it's useless to try to make friends with anybody else because it's already way too late. New girls never get into a clique in less than two years, and fat girls don't stand a chance. No offense, of course. It's just the way things are." Naomi was so matter-of-fact that Carole didn't feel hurt.

Naomi said she'd been at Spence since kindergarten, moving each year from room to room and floor to floor. She knew everything about everybody, including the teachers. In particular, Naomi knew which ones were lesbians: the ones who wore tweed suits and would arrive together every morning and leave together at night. It's *very* common in these places, Naomi told her. "In fact," Naomi said, then stopped and looked appraisingly at her. "You're a virgin, right?"

Carole nodded.

"Me too, and we're almost the only ones." She went through the class girl by girl, telling who was a virgin and who wasn't. "Here's the thing," she said. "If we don't lose it before we graduate, we're going to wind up like one of those teachers. You most of all. Because you can bet that when those women were young they were just like you. Big and brainy and without a sense of fashion. Sex just passed them by and they had to settle for other women."

At first Carole thought it was just a joke, and she'd had fun talking about what they'd do and how they'd do it. Sometimes on the subway they'd pick out guys. Her mother had told her in that awful conversation about sex that her body was a temple, something that made Naomi scream, laughing. Naomi said that really, while she couldn't stand Elayne's guts, at least Elayne knew more than Carole's mother ever would when it came to sex. That was, after all, the reason Daddy had ever married her in the first place. It had to be, because there sure was nothing else to recommend her. Naomi did Elayne's Czech accent to perfection. *Ze first lover must be ze best to set ze expectations high for ze rest of ze life. Ze first iss ze standard!*

Naomi found Eddie Lindbaeck in January of their senior year at a huge party her father and Elayne had thrown at a restaurant. Eddie had crashed the party from the bar downstairs, which was good because it meant he didn't know her father or Elayne. That very night Naomi had asked him to do the honors, and he'd said of course. She came flying into school the next day to tell Carole the good news. Carole was going to have to meet him, of course. One morning in February Naomi sprang the meeting on her. All day, Carole could think only about how awful she looked. Her hair was more frizzed than usual and kept coming loose, and she was wearing her worst brown skirt and a plain white blouse that made her look even fatter than she was. She had on oxford shoes and falling-down bobby socks. She would have worn her best dress if she had known earlier, but Naomi said she just found out herself, which Carole didn't completely believe.

They'd met at Havilands, a big old dark coffee shop two blocks down Madison from school. Girls from school went there every day and stayed most of the afternoon, under a fog of cigarette smoke. A lot of girls were in there, not just from Spence, but girls in Nightingale Banford uniforms and Sacred Heart uniforms. Each group had a cluster of tables pushed together so they could huddle and gossip about one another. Carole was sure it was all mean. Everything they said. She skirted the edge of the place to a booth way in the back. She sat down and gently laid her books on the seat beside her. It didn't take Amanda Howe two seconds to come through the smoky haze toward her. "What are you doing here?" she asked with the emphasis on the *doing,* as though Carole had no right to be anywhere.

"Waiting for somebody."

"Who?"

"Just somebody."

"So why do you have to wait all by yourself? Be sociable, why don't you." It wasn't an invitation at all. She would be shredded if she sat with them. "It's not a *boy,* is it?"

Carole had her eye on the front door. Naomi had said Eddie was about five ten with sandy-colored hair and dark eyes. Drop-dead gorgeous. Carole didn't want him coming in with Amanda standing there.

Wouldn't want to have to make the introductions and wouldn't put it past Amanda to slide into the booth and ask Eddie a bunch of questions. God. If it ever got out what Carole and Naomi were doing, they'd be laughingstocks. Naomi had to have been insane to have her meet Eddie here in the lion's den with all these predatory bitches.

"None of your beeswax," she said. Amanda turned and went back to her table, where she obviously took pleasure in telling the others what Carole had said. They all shrieked, laughing at her. Nobody said beeswax anymore.

The waitress came over twice and finally said Carole couldn't sit there without ordering something, and it had to be more than coffee. If the other person didn't come soon Carole would have to go sit at the counter. She weighed the choices: order something and then be caught sitting with it, looking as if she couldn't wait to eat, or else go sit at one of those little spinning stools in full view of Amanda and her buddies when Eddie came in. She ordered a cup of coffee for herself and a hamburger, and when it came, in about two minutes, she slid it over to his side of the table.

The door swung open, and she knew it was him right away. He had silky light-brown hair that fell in his eyes, a black leather jacket over a dark blue Shetland sweater that made his dark blue eyes pop right out and, peeking out of the sweater, a pale blue button-down shirt. He had on penny loafers with no socks. When he got to her table, he winked at her, then let his eyes drop to her neck and her breasts, making her feel strange and weak. He slid into the booth across from her. He smelled of something. Some sort of strong aftershave. The other girls were staring. He was miles better-looking than their Trinity boys with their pimply faces.

"That's for you," she said about the hamburger. "They made me order."

He pushed it away, ordered a cup of coffee, and drank it in silence, looking up over the cup's rim at her with eyes like deep dark pools. "My mother used to tell me I had the map of Ireland on my face," he said. "What do you think?"

It sounded like something to do with his skin or veins or something. "You look fine to me."

He winked and grinned. "Naomi said you were funny."

But she hadn't meant to be funny. He reached out and touched her hair, swept it off her face and tucked it behind her ear.

"So tell me about you," he said.

"I moved here from Ridgewood, New Jersey, last year," she said.

He was looking around, preening. She felt a desperate need to speak faster, to hold his attention. "My dad used to commute. What about you? Where are you from?"

"New York." His eyes continued to sweep the room and returned to her as if she were only slightly more interesting than what was out there.

"You probably think it's the only place on earth, right?"

"You've got it."

She finally figured out what he'd meant when he first sat down. "But Lindbaeck isn't Irish, is it?"

"Norwegian," he said. "My father's the fish eater. My mother's the Mick."

"What school did you go to?"

He grinned at her. "I've been kicked out of all the best schools on the East Coast."

"Really? For what?"

"You name it." He leaned over the table. "Mostly sneaking out of the dorm at night to meet girls like you." He leaned back and smiled at her again. "I learn best in the theater of the real, if you will. Did Naomi tell you I'm an actor?"

She nodded. Naomi had told her all sorts of things. That Eddie was twenty-six, that he knew Doug McClure from *Checkmate* and George Maharis from *Route 66.* "What do you act in?"

He smoothed his hair with the palm of his hand and said he didn't act in anything she would have seen, like *Cactus Flower* or *Fiddler on the Roof.* Too sophisticated for that, was the impression he gave, although Carole wondered, guilty for being suspicious, if it was something else. He kept switching accents. It would be Brooklyn one minute, British the next. Sometimes southern. Maybe it was on purpose, but she didn't think so.

"So," he said, sitting up straight and looking her in the eye. "Let's talk about sex."

"Sshh," Carole said.

"Come on. What do you know?" he stage-whispered to her. "Tell me what you know."

She didn't know anything except for a guy in a furniture store who had exposed himself to her once, and she wasn't going to admit to that, and it wasn't exactly sex anyway. "Things," she said.

"Ever been kissed?"

"Of course."

"Deep kissed?"

She shrugged.

"Second base?" She didn't know what he meant. He glanced at her breasts, held up his hands, and wiggled his fingers.

"No," she said, feeling her face burn with embarrassment.

"Has anyone ever told you that a man undresses every single woman he sees with his eyes? I like what I see."

She felt herself blush crimson. She cast an eye around the place to the waitress, who was fiftyish and heavy. "Her?" Eddie looked and nodded, then shrugged and grinned.

"Not bad."

She started to giggle and pointed him in more directions. The two matrons at the window, a woman sitting at another table with her husband.

He leaned across the table. "You're going to be fun," he said. "I can tell."

It was the first time she knew it would happen. Really knew. Up until that moment it had only been something she and Naomi had talked about, giggling on the bus or whispering on the phone. Eddie knew a place in Stowe. He'd been there before, lots of times. And he knew the layout. "You're doing a very smart thing," he told her seriously. "And not for just a couple of hours in the afternoon at my place, the way Naomi and I had it cooked up at first, but a full week, so I can show you everything there is to know. Are you open to everything?" he asked her.

She said yes without hesitating, thinking she knew what everything was. Kissing and touching and then losing her virginity.

His hand crept under the table and rested on her knee. "More girls should have the courage to do what you're doing."

Chapter Three

The Double Hearth smelled of bacon and coffee, and there was a fire going in the bigger of the two fireplaces when Carole got back. A group of girls was waiting at the long tables for the kitchen to open up. They stared when she walked by them. She looked like hell, and there was no mistaking that she'd been out all night. After she passed, they laughed.

Upstairs, all she could think was that she had to get into a shower, to wash every molecule belonging to Eddie Lindbaeck off herself and get rid of the smell and the taste in her mouth. She had to wash her hair, scrub her ears, and brush her teeth. Then she'd know what to do.

The bunk room was crowded with girls running around in long underwear and rollers, wriggling into stretch pants. Carole's and Naomi's bunks were the ones at the end. Both were untouched, the blankets and sheets still pulled tight over them. She peeled off her black slacks, her yellow sweater, and her underwear and stuffed them between her bunk bed and the wall so she wouldn't have to see them again.

She rummaged around in her suitcase for her bathrobe, pulled it out. An envelope fluttered from the sleeve. Inside there was a ten-dollar bill and a note. "From Daddy and me," it said. "A little fun money for you. Love, Mom." Tears wet her face, and she crawled onto the lower bunk, her face to the wall, and sobbed, her whole body shaking. Somebody touched her shoulder, and she jumped.

"Sorry," a voice said. A girl's voice.

"Go away." She was so afraid people already knew her secret.

"You homesick or something?" the girl asked.

Carole didn't answer, and the girl left. She waited until the dorm quieted. It seemed like forever until everybody had gone downstairs to breakfast and she could sit up and look around. The place looked as if a bomb had hit it, stuff everywhere. She made her way down to the shower room, stepping over clothes, shoes, bedding. There were four shower stalls, each with a pink plastic curtain. A girl was toweling herself off. One of those slender girls she couldn't stand, with their sleek, shiny hair.

"Hi there," the girl said.

Carole glared.

"You feeling better?" It must have been the girl who saw her crying. Same voice. She was older than Carole, probably in college or something. "Look at this." The girl hoisted her foot up onto the sink and motioned Carole to look at something. "Boot burn. Worst I ever had." There was a chapped patch on the girl's shin, just above her ankle, scabbed over. Carole couldn't understand why it mattered about her shin. The girl put her foot down and stood there, hands on her hips. "You've been through the wringer, haven't you?"

"I'm fine," Carole said. Naomi would have done a job on this one. On the accent in particular, which was one of those top-drawer jobs that always sent them both right over the edge laughing. Her hair was auburn. "Please, just leave me alone," Carole said. The color reminded her of Rita's hair, the hardness of the skull beneath.

"Some of the guys up here can be real jerks," the girl said. "Especially the ones from Dartmouth."

"I'm sorry. I just—" Carole draped her robe and towel over the rod outside the shower stall, turned on the tap, and stepped in. It was a good strong shower with plenty of hot water and plenty of force.

The girl was still talking as though she could be heard over the running water. Finally there was silence. Carole washed between her legs, trying to get the soap up into herself, to flush out Eddie Lindbaeck. The night had left her with stinging sores. Her mother always said if the cure didn't hurt, it wasn't a cure. She scrubbed with a washcloth until her skin was red. She washed her face, inside her mouth, then lathered her hair. When she got out of the shower, the girl was gone. She dried herself off hard with a rough towel. There was someone in one of the other shower stalls. She wrapped a towel around her hair, put her bathrobe on, and waited. Maybe Naomi. Maybe she shouldn't have gotten so far ahead of her on the road. "Is that you, Nay?"

Naomi peered out of the shower stall, holding the curtain up. Her bony face was white and her eyes oddly small without makeup. "Boo."

"That's not funny."

Naomi shrugged.

"Oh, Nay. What if anybody saw?"

"We could hardly see each *other,* for Christ's sake." Naomi came out of the shower, toweling off. Carole was surprised by how angular and small her body was and looked away. She didn't want to think about bodies.

"What if they find her?"

"How can they? Eddie said she doesn't have any family. He knew her from before, from other times he's come up here. She lives by herself. He says there's no way anybody can connect you with her."

"Him either," Carole said. "Or you."

Naomi bent over to dry her hair. "I'm not exactly the one who got rough, Carole. Not that I won't stick up for you or anything, but come on."

"He invited that woman. He knew her."

"That's not *my* fault."

"No, but I thought we were only supposed to—"

"He *told* me what happened." Naomi righted herself with a whip of wet hair. "He said you probably didn't do it on purpose. It was just because you're, you know, big and all. You must not have realized—"

"Not you too," Carole moaned. "Please don't say that."

"He said you were all over her."

"Naomi, I mean, did you know about her? Oh, Nay, he got all scary and he knew all that stuff about my family. How could he know all that? Oh, God, Nay, you didn't tell him, did you?"

Naomi stuck out her lip and shook her head. "He said he kept trying to stop you, Carole. You were this crazy woman. You pushed her."

"No. It didn't happen that way."

"What do you remember, then? You've got to remember. Like exactly. Every minute."

"I only remember bits and pieces."

"He said you were jealous." Naomi made a face. "That when he wasn't paying attention to you every minute of the time, you got mad. You were pretty drunk. Is that true?"

"No! I just—"

"I want to believe you. Honest. But, you know, you don't remember," Naomi said. "And he does."

Carole moaned again. "Oh, Nay, if only I'd left when she came. If only I hadn't ever come up here in the first place. Oh, God, what were we even *thinking*?"

Naomi looked at Carole's reflection in the mirror. "If nobody talks, you don't have anything to worry about. And nobody will. Eddie won't. I won't, and you sure as hell won't. The end."

"I'm going to ask the guy at the desk when the next train goes. We can get a taxi."

Naomi turned. "We can't just *leave*."

"Just us. You and me. We'll make up some excuse. Pretend to be sick or something. All I know is I have to get out of here."

"Eddie said to act like everything is normal. Like nothing happened. We can't all go checking out. It'll look really weird."

"Eddie isn't the boss of us."

"He's a lot older than us," Naomi said. "He knows things. Anyway, even if I wanted to, I couldn't. Daddy and Elayne are away, and the little prick at the door is under orders not to let me in. They said."

"You could stay at my apartment." Carole noticed something in the way Naomi wouldn't meet her eyes. She remembered again the way Eddie's and Naomi's shadows had come together in front of the cabin. "Are you going to see him?"

"Maybe." Naomi looked back into the mirror.

Carole felt a spasm in her gut. It *had* been a kiss.

Until yesterday she would never have considered getting on that train and leaving Naomi behind. But yesterday was already a million miles away. Now she was alone.

On the train from Stowe back to New York, a man named Tom sat down next to her and started talking. He was divorced, he said, and he went to Stowe all the time. How about that skiing? He jabbed her in the side. Carole let him talk. She barely answered any of his questions, but it didn't seem to matter. He went on about his job. He worked on Park Avenue in the Fifties, something also about the window washers that he thought was funny or frightening. He wanted to know things about her too. What year in school she was. She said she was at Vassar. And what was she studying? She made it up as she went along. Medieval history. Maybe pre-med. She had another year to decide. She gave little fragments of answers here and there that kept him going on and on about himself. A week ago she would have given real answers to all those questions. She would have felt an obligation to explain things carefully. But everything was different. Now it seemed important not to let anyone know who she really was, and the only way to do that was to lie about everything.

The ride went by like that, a blur of fatigue, bad dreams, and Tom suggesting maybe they could get together sometime for a drink. Did she ever get away from school during the week? In New York? She said her name was Celia and gave him a phony telephone number. For the first time lying wasn't hard at all, and he believed every-thing she said.

As the train came in to Grand Central, she pulled her suitcase from under the seat and righted it, handle up, and ready to go. "I'd like to see you," Tom said.

"Okay." He'd never find her. She could say anything.

"Great." He put a hand on her knee and patted it.

"Don't touch me."

"I was just—"

"I said don't." Her voice was way too loud. People stopped what they were doing and turned to look. Calm down, she thought. No-body knows. Tom held up his hands in surrender. He was looking around at people on the train as if to say, "Beats me. I didn't do any-thing." The train lurched to a halt, and Carole bolted, pushing past Tom, through people in the aisle. Somebody lost his balance. Some-body swore at her.

She took the subway to Fifty-ninth Street and walked three blocks to her building, skis and poles clattering and shifting. She hadn't let her parents know she was coming home. She hadn't dared. She'd de-cided to wait until after she got to New York, thinking it would be easier then, but here she was, coming into the lobby, getting on the el-evator, where she experienced a brand-new horror. She'd only that moment remembered that she was going to need a reason for being home so early. She might have walked in the door, and they would have asked right away why and she wouldn't have been prepared. How could she not have thought of this until now? Until she was almost there. It was terrifying. There she'd been lying through her teeth to that guy on the train without a single thought as to what she was going to say when she walked in the door.

Naomi always said the deal with lying was to keep it simple. It was scary, though, because Carole had never lied to her parents. She'd fudged plenty, but that was different. Like broaching the sub-ject of going to Stowe, how she'd told about the ski lodge and how it catered to high school kids and ran a shuttle bus to the mountain every day. Her mother checked it out. She called the Double Hearth and found out that no liquor was allowed, that they locked the doors at night, and that there were dorms on separate floors. One for boys and one for girls. Her mother just assumed the rest—that Carole was going to be on that bus, asleep in the dorm at night, and learning to ski during the day. Just thinking about the Double Hearth made her all weak again. She stood in the vestibule. Diarrhea, she decided.

When she opened the door, there were voices. Many of them. She left her skis and suitcase in the hall. In the living room her parents were having cocktails with people. She knew the sounds by heart. They'd been the background noise of a lifetime, her parents' cocktail parties. Without even looking, she knew the women would all be sitting on the low living-room furniture, their legs elegantly crossed, the men standing and talking in little clusters. But she was glad. Her mother would be too busy, too distracted, to grill her about what had happened. She hesitated long enough to find her mother in the crowd. Her back, exposed almost to the waist in her black dress, was to Carole, and she was leaning in to some man with an intimacy that said she'd had a little too much to drink. Good, Carole thought as she slipped down the corridor to her room. They'd put fur coats on her bed. There was a pile of them, black and gleaming. She lay down, feeling the soft, perfumed fur against her face, breathing in the smoky scent. She listened to the distant sounds, the bursts of laughter. She knew who the people were. The partners in her father's law firm, their expensive wives. The Iveys, the Morrises, the Whites, all tuxedoed and slick, the women in their stiff coifs. Probably some of the clients too. It was the usual crowd of important people tonight, people her father needed to impress.

There was a metal tick of high heels on the marble floor. The door cracked open, and her mother was there. She was large and soft-looking, her plump cleavage showing in the black dress. She stood in the door staring, uncomprehending. "What on earth? What in the world? Carole!"

Carole buried her face in the fur.

"What on earth?" her mother said again. The bright inflection of her voice, like an actress's in a TV comedy, was more evidence that she was on her way to being drunk.

"I got diarrhea up there," Carole said. "Bad."

"Oh." Her squeamish mother was clearly taken aback by the suddenness of the word. "And you just came home? My lord, Carole." Her mother sat on the side of the bed, leaned over, and put a cool hand on Carole's forehead. "Do you have a temperature?" She paused a moment and withdrew her hand. She opened a blanket, shook it out, and stood to spread it over Carole, a gesture that must have happened hundreds of times before, her mother, smelling of liquor, covering her with a blanket, stroking her hair. It used to feel so safe.

"I might barf," Carole said.

Her mother made a sudden gesture to save the furs, reaching around and under Carole, gathering them up in her arms. She stood in the doorway, the furs spilling over. "I can tell them something's come up." She hoisted the furs to indicate the people out in the living room.

"I'll be fine," Carole said. Her mother's pretty face soured with indecision. "Really. If I need you, I can call the restaurant. Where are you going?"

"The Sign of the Dove." It was the restaurant Eddie had mentioned, and Carole shuddered at the memory of all he knew. "Oh, my. Chills?" her mother said.

"I'll be okay."

"Well, if you think . . . ." Her mother's voice trailed off.

"I think."

The sounds rose and fell as people put on their coats, used the powder room in the hall, and finally left. Carole took a shower in her parents' bathroom, with her mother's tough little nailbrush, which she used to scrub and scrape her skin almost raw. She let the hot water sluice over her. Her skin was chapped, the pain comforting. When she finished, she dried herself and didn't put lotion on. She wanted her skin and everything that might be on it to dry and flake. It was something she'd learned in biology in the tenth grade. That the body creates all new cells every seven years. At some point there wouldn't be a single cell in her that was there right now. Already there were new ones forming. Old ones dying and falling away. Already she was becoming someone else.

But how would she ever survive what was happening now in her mind? Now that she was home, there was nothing to keep the million nonstop memory fragments from eating her alive, the images and sounds from the night before, a constant screen of moving darkness shot through with atrocious pale scenes of snow, of night, of Rita's slick skin. She'd killed her. She'd broken her neck. The cold certainty shocked her time after time, and she wondered how she would ever quiet her thoughts enough to go forward. She would have to believe whatever she said, even if it was a lie. She understood that implicitly. If she didn't believe it herself, nobody would. Diarrhea. It was simple and familiar. It was a subject her mother would not press for details about. She clutched at her abdomen, willing herself to remember the train ride differently. *I sat in the row next to the toilet. The smell was awful, but I didn't dare get too far. The train rocked a lot. The door kept banging.*

She backed up, dispatching the night in Stowe in case they asked. *I had the lower bunk in the dorm, next to the wall. I hardly slept because I felt so bad.* The story was effective because she needed to generate nothing more. *The man at the morning desk helped me get a taxi to the train. Naomi wanted to stay and ski. And anyway, her daddy and Elayne are out of town.* It was amazing how easily you could fit lies into the truth, the truth into lies.

In the morning her mother came bustling in, sat on the bed, and put a cool hand to Carole's forehead. "You feel okay, but do you feel okay?" Her mother frowned and then laughed, her soft face lighting up with her own little joke.

Carole sat up. "Yes."

"I don't think we need to call doctor, do you? Just a little bit of rest should do it?"

"*The* doctor." It drove her crazy, the affectations her mother had picked up, as though they made her sound more cultured or something.

"So you'll be what, staying in bed today? Do you think?"

"I guess," Carole said. "Did the paper come?"

"Your father's reading it." Her mother's hands fidgeted in her lap. "I've made some plans for this week," she said. "I wouldn't have, if I'd known you would be here." She rolled her eyes. "Luncheons. Shopping." She sighed. "I'd give my eyeteeth to be staying home with you."

"It's fine, Mom." Carole was grateful that her mother had no spine. It was safer to be alone. There was less chance that she'd slip and say something.

Left alone in the apartment, she padded around barefoot, from her bedroom and into the wide dark foyer with the gloomy ancestor prints. Four bigger-than-life old men with wispy beards and faded ceremonial robes peered down at her without expression. Her mother was so proud of them. She had bought them at auction for a fraction of what they were worth, and if she ever decided to sell them again, she'd make a killing. They were always a conversation piece, and Carole was sure her mother had talked about them last night to whoever would listen. "So stately," her mother liked to say. "So inscrutable." Carole winced every time.

At the end of the foyer was the living room. It had dark Persian rugs laid out across the floor, left over from the people who had owned the place before. "Exquisite taste," Carole's mother liked to say of them. "Very cultured people." They'd also left some of their mahogany furniture and the heavy drapes along the wall of windows. Against this stuff, their own furniture stood out like a sore thumb. Naomi could tell the difference the first time she'd seen it. She'd picked out every piece that they'd had in Ridgewood. "Yours is the country stuff," she had said.

Carole glided around the room, touching things, trailing her fingers across the tabletops, and sitting in the chairs and couches. She almost never came in here. It was the formal room, used for parties, and she hadn't ever sat in some of the furniture. She liked the den better. Small and cozy, it had only the furniture from Ridgewood— the big leather chair her father liked and the couch covered brightly in red and yellow. The newspaper lay on the table beside his chair. She spread it out on the coffee table and went through it page by page, her hands trembling as she searched for items from Vermont. But there was nothing. Emboldened, she went through it again, this time studying the weather map, which showed cold and snow in Vermont, a drop in temperature. She refolded the paper and replaced it on the table.

She headed down the other corridor, to her parents' bedroom. It had the same dark paneling as the rest of the rooms, but it got more sun and the drapes were always pulled, so it seemed lighter. She lay down on her parents' bed. She'd been in this room the night she got her acceptance to Vassar. They all had. But she'd been sitting in the armchair, and her parents had sat side by side at the end of the bed, facing her.

It was after they'd come home from Giovanni's. Her parents were both sort of drunk, and her father had gotten all grandiose and said that when it came time for her to go to Vassar, he would have his secretary, Miss Palmer, establish an account. He would fund the account, and Miss Palmer would send the invoices directly to Carole at school, and she'd be responsible for paying her own bills.

None of the girls at Spence handled money. It was almost unseemly. But that was where her father broke with those other people, he explained. He wanted to teach her the value of a dollar, and this was the way he would do it. Carole remembered how he'd taken her mother's hand. "We have every faith in your ability to manage very well," he'd said. He'd brought out the family checkbook, a big ledger with three checks to the page, and showed her how they entered each check on the little stub at the side, how they made a notation about its purpose. He showed her bank statements, how they reconciled the statement against the stubs in the book. She'd been floored by the amount of money passing through the account. She'd had no idea.

The room was warm, and she fell asleep only to be startled awake by a dream. A large coyote dug in the snow exposing a dark mouth and eyes, a patch of hair, attracting other animals that circled and ripped at Rita's body, darkening the snow with blood, dragging a thigh here, part of the torso there.

She sat up, disoriented and sweating, to the distant sounds of her parents' voices from the kitchen. She tiptoed through the apartment to see if they were talking about her. From the dark dining room she could see into the kitchen through the pane of glass in the door. Her father sat with his drink and the evening paper, and her mother stood at the stove. Carole sat down at the dining room table, which was already set for dinner, and strained to hear. What if they knew everything and were just waiting for her to confess? But it was quiet except for the sounds of pots and pans. The door flew open, and her mother called "Dinner" before she saw Carole sitting in the dark. "What on earth?" she said.

"I was just coming," Carole said.

The dining room table had also been left by the previous owner. The son had done his homework on it or something and pressed down too hard with a ballpoint pen so it had marks on the surface, and the people hadn't wanted to take it with them. Her father sat at one end and her mother at the other, like people in a *New Yorker* cartoon, and she was in the middle. She was expected to pass the butter and salad by getting up and bringing it to one of them or the other instead of scooting it down or even handing it across like anybody normal would do. Her mother had made the corn and tomato casserole with hot dogs on top baked to explosion and then cheddar cheese dribbled over it. Usually Carole would eat three hot dogs, but tonight the first bite stuck in her throat.

I killed a woman.

Her father was talking about his day. He always talked about his day. Rattling off the names of people he'd seen and where he'd had lunch. She used to wish he'd talk about the trials. About the people he represented. She always wanted to know about that, even if it was just corporate law. But he said it was unethical to reveal certain details, so it was just better not to speak of it at all. That was the family philosophy on most things. They were bores. He told Carole and her mother about a house that Carl Morris had bought outside the city. Eighteen rooms on forty acres in Mamaroneck.

Her name was Rita.

Her mother envied people who had houses in the country. The only reason they didn't was because they needed the money for Carole's education. After Carole graduated from Vassar, they could spend their money how they wanted. Only four years from now. And anyway, those other people had family money, her father said. Inheritance. That's what kept all those other people afloat. Not hard work like Conrad Mason.

I slept with that guy from Grand Central and then I slept with him and her both.

The conversation swirled around her. Did they always compare themselves to other people this way?

I'm a very big girl. Three hot dogs a night. I broke her neck.

"Now you take the Macys," her father was saying. "They lived just the way we do until her father died and then they moved to that duplex."

They must not have found her. If they had, the police would break down your door and take me away. Your precious Macys and Morrises would find out. You'd be ruined.

"Carole?"

She must be frozen solid by now.

"Are you all right?"

From their seats miles to either side of her, both of them were looking at her. Pig in the middle trying so hard to act normal, but not remembering what normal was anymore. "Just a little bit weak," she said. "Think I'll excuse myself."

There would be no sleeping that night or any other, she would find out. Her mother came in to check on her, and she said she was fine, still a little wrung out, which seemed to satisfy her mother. After her mother left, Carole lay there. Rita's warm body would have melted the snow at first and then frozen, would be welded solid to the ice sheath around her ice body by now. It would stay like that until April or even May, frozen solid, so the animals would leave it alone and nobody would find it. And then the terror of these thoughts overtook her, and she broke into an icy sweat and had to get up.

She went to the window to watch the Home for Unwed Mothers. It was a Catholic place, and in the day she'd see nuns in billowing black wool habits strut about. Pregnant girls hung out in front of the building talking to one another and laughing and smoking all the time. The building was very old and low, only five stories and made of darkened brick. When they had moved into this apartment, the real estate agent had sworn up and down the home was going to be demolished because it was old and an eyesore, and when that happened their property value would go up. But it hadn't happened yet, and Carole wasn't sorry. She liked looking into the windows at night, seeing the girls in their rooms. She wondered who they were. Who their families were. Where they came from. She used to wonder about the boys who had gotten them pregnant. She used to be in awe. It was sad, of course, but impressive too.

Only one of the rooms over there was lit. The rest were dark. A girl in pink sponge rollers was leaning out the window, blowing smoke. Carole could see clearly into the room where another girl was sitting on a bed. The girl at the window dropped her cigarette and watched it fall to the street below, then shut the window. Carole went to the kitchen for a No-Cal, and when she came back, two rooms were lit. Good. The bedroom and the bathroom, which was all stark white. She'd seen girls go into the bathroom lots of times and hide things in the toilet tanks. Now the girl in the rollers did that while the other girl stood lookout at the door. Probably it was a liquor bottle.

They must have heard something because they both stopped to listen, made a dash for the door, and turned out the light. A few seconds later they were back in their room, doubled over laughing. The girl in the rollers threw open the window and leaned out of it again.

At the same moment the light went on in the bathroom and a nun in a white gown and long white hair was standing there, her hands on her hips. She flung open one stall door after the other until she came to the one where the girls had stashed the bottle.

"Hey," Carole yelled. The girl looked everywhere but up. "Up here," Carole stage-whispered. She pointed to the bathroom. "She found it," she called out. "That old nun!"

The girl ducked back into the room, and the lights went out. A few seconds later the light went on and the old nun was inside the room, flailing around, getting them out of bed. The girls knelt on the floor to pray, got up, put on their bathrobes, and left. As she walked out the door, the girl in the rollers waved behind her back, like Grace Kelly in *Rear Window.*

Carole stood watching after the lights went off, intrigued by what had just happened. She turned from the window and paced the darkened apartment. The corridor to the living room to the den and the foyer. Round and round she went, creeping silently through one room after another. She wondered what might be happening. Wondering how they punished pregnant girls.

All that week, she roamed the apartment at night and slept away the morning. She read the newspapers, searching for items about Vermont. Finding nothing encouraged her, and she would watch *Queen for a Day, The Price Is Right,* and *Search for Tomorrow.* When they were over, hours had gone by. Sometimes she would dial Naomi's apartment, in case she'd come back, but the telephone just rang and rang. She didn't dare call Stowe because the charge would appear on her parents' phone bill.

Her mother came and went each day. Before she ducked out, she told Carole where she'd be, what was in the refrigerator, and when she'd be back. Right after her mother told her these things, Carole couldn't remember what she had just said. When the telephone rang, Carole was never able to say when her mother would be home.

On the Friday before school was to start again, Carole heard voices and laughter in the foyer. She clicked off the TV and was trying to figure out who it was when her mother and Aunt Emily burst into the den. "Carole, darling." Emily gave her two little air kisses. "I was devastated to hear what happened. You poor dear."

Emily was their only relative. She lived in Tarrytown with Carole's uncle Jack. Carole wasn't supposed to know about Jack's money, but she did. He bought food that couldn't be sold in the United States and sold it to foreign countries. Substandard meat, corn with bugs in it. It was disgusting.

As usual, Emily was dressed to the nines. She had on a green hourglass suit and one of those little fox stoles where each fox had the tail of the one in front in its mouth. Emily and Carole's mother looked alike in a way. Both of them had very white skin and glittery dark eyes. But Carole's mother was the beauty—more shapely than Emily, with her hair in a soft bun at the back of her neck. Emily was reed thin, her black hair teased and sprayed into a helmet. She wore too much makeup too, fire-engine-red lips and rouged cheeks.

"I'm better now," Carole said.

"Emily just ducked in to pick up the ski clothes. Are they in your room?"

The panic ricocheted. She hadn't checked the clothes. The night she came home she'd taken them out of the suitcase and stuffed them away in the closet, where she wouldn't have to see them. There could be stains. "I was going to wash them. And send them to you."

"I rather thought you'd have already—" Emily said. "Oh, never mind."

"So where will we find them, dear?" her mother said. She was already heading for Carole's room.

Carole ran after them down the corridor, trying to think of a way to stop them, but her mother was already opening the closet and looking in. "Oh," she said. She picked up the suitcase. Under it, the parka and ski pants were all bunched up. Carole's mother lifted the pants and parka and shook them out, but it was obviously hopeless.

"Well, that's hardly the way to treat clothing that's been loaned to you," Emily said. "Or your own clothing, for that matter."

Carole watched the clothes pass from her mother's hands to Emily's. Emily laid them on the bed, smoothed them, and folded them into neat squares. Then she tucked them into a shopping bag.

"And you never even saw the mountain." Emily looked her up and down. "What a shame. It would have done you so much good."

That night Carole was still awake at four, drifting through each room, her steps creaking lightly. Across the street, all the lights were out in the Home for Unwed Mothers. Only the stairwell lights were burning.

If she could just talk to Naomi. She dialed Naomi's apartment, but still no answer. So she dressed and left the apartment by the back stairs. When she reached street level, she left the big gates in the alley open to the sidewalk so she'd be able to get back into the building without disturbing the elevator man. It was something she'd done since moving here because she couldn't bear to make him come all the way up to get her. It didn't seem right. She was only a girl, and he was an old man. That is *so* public school, Naomi had said when she told her. But she didn't care.

She'd never been outside on the street before dawn, so it was a surprise to her, another world. It was quiet and slow. The streetlights changed from red to yellow to green along Lexington even though no cars were there to stop and go. An occasional car passed, but there were no people on the streets, just dim burglar lights in the stores.

Grand Central was a tomb. The tunnel to the main concourse was dark and hushed. Bales of newspapers were stacked on the floor in front of gated doorways, but none of the stores was open. She prowled the corridors, her footsteps echoing loudly. A couple was asleep on one of the benches, lying head to head. A drunk watched her from another bench. Overhead, the Kodak sign showed a snow-covered mountain and a pair of skiers looking out over the valley below them. The woman was glamorous and thin, without a care in the world. Her mother had pointed to the picture when Eddie had asked where her daughter was going: "Just like that." Carole had been so embarrassed. She was about as far from that woman as anybody could be, and Eddie knew it. Maybe Naomi looked like that, but not Carole.

Naomi. She had to talk to her right now.

It was four-thirty, according to the big clock over the information booth. At the Double Hearth, the kitchen help would be getting ready for early breakfast, and if she said it was an emergency, she was sure somebody would get Naomi to the phone. She found a bank of pay phones and put in a lot of change, asked for information, then dialed the Double Hearth. A woman answered.

"I need to talk to one of the girls there, please."

"Nobody's up," the woman said. "Are you crazy?"

"There's been an accident," Carole said.

"You sure she's here?" The woman still sounded irritated.

"I can tell you the exact bunk," Carole said. "At the end of the dorm, the top one."

The woman let the phone dangle. It banged against the wall. In a little while footsteps approached and the phone was picked up.

"Who is this?" Naomi said.

"It's me."

"Jesus, Carole. What happened? What accident?"

"I only said that so she'd get you. I had to talk to you. What's going on?"

No answer.

"Is he still there? Have you seen him? Did anybody find anything?"

"It's four in the bloody morning."

"I can't sleep. I go to sleep and then I wake up two hours later and I can't get back to sleep. I keep dreaming about her. Oh, Christ, Nay, what are we going to do?"

"We?" The nearby sound of a steel shade rolling up the newsstand was as loud as a shot in the empty station. "Where the hell are you, anyway?" Naomi asked.

"Grand Central."

"Jesus, Carole."

"I need a newspaper."

"You stupid idiot," Naomi hissed at her. "Go home and go back to bed. And act normal, for Christ's sake, if it's even possible. Don't you think people will ask questions if you go running around New York at four in the morning? Use your head for once." There was a long pause. "By the way, we went back there, just to check. It's fine."

"Went back?"

"Go home."

"Is it okay?"

"It's so okay we couldn't even find it."

"We? You mean you went there with him?" She didn't dare say the name.

"Go home, Carole," Naomi said, and hung up.

She set the receiver back into its cradle and went to the newsstand, where she bought a *New York Herald Tribune* and a *Daily Mirror.* Then she walked across to the Lexington exit and headed back uptown.

It was a shade lighter, and the sky glowed with the approach of day. Traffic was heavier now, and fast. She felt disoriented in the dawn, like being late for school, at large when everyone else was where they were supposed to be. She ran toward home, hardly stopping to check the streets before crossing, half wanting to be hit.

At the apartment, someone had shut the iron gate tight. Probably it was one of the maids coming in early. She peered through to the steel door. That too was flush against the jamb. *Somebody knew.* She looked around to see if she was being watched. Lights were on in the apartments across the street, and traffic was thick. Her parents would be up any minute. She watched the street, where the traffic now was just a blur ripping uptown. She could step into the street and end everything. A minute from right now. An impact so hard it would knock the life out of her and not even hurt. The thought was a comfort. All her worry lifted, and she was clearheaded. She wouldn't do it. At least not now. But she would save it as a possibility. It would always be there, an option nobody else ever needed to know existed.

She walked around the corner to the canopied entrance, rapped on the glass, and waited. Heney came out of the mailroom at the back and squinted across, trying to figure out who she was. Once he recognized her, he hustled up and unlocked the front door.

"What would you be doing outside at this hour, miss?" he said with his heavy accent.

"Walking." She got into the elevator and watched while he drew the outside door across and then the brass gate.

"Didn't see you go out," he said. He kept his eyes on each floor marker as it went by. The elevator stopped at her floor, and Heney jockeyed it around so the elevator floor met the vestibule floor exactly. "The back door's not for you."

"I left it open," she said. "When I came back, it was locked."

"I know," Heney said, still not looking at her. "I locked it myself." He was waiting for her to get off the elevator.

"My parents would kill me," she said. She stepped off into the little vestibule outside her apartment door and turned to look at him.

He looked her in the eye. "They'd be right to," he said and pushed the brass gate across between them.

When she walked into the apartment, her father was in the dining room with papers spread out across the table, still in his pajamas and bathrobe. He looked up at her over the tops of black-rimmed half glasses. She hated those glasses because he looked so much more scolding in them. "Carole?" he said, rising and meeting her in the foyer. "You were outside?"

She had the newspapers in her arms. "I couldn't sleep," she said, showing him the papers. "I went out to get a paper." Stick to the true parts, Naomi once instructed her. And this part was true. She had gone out and she'd gotten a paper.

"We get the paper."

"But not these." She heard the indignation in her voice, as though it was perfectly normal to be outside getting newspapers at four in the morning, and who was he to challenge her. She'd never spoken to him that way, and he was really startled. He stood and took a step toward her. He smelled of bed, slightly stale and musty, his hair sticking up in back. "Just because I never went out for papers before doesn't make it wrong," she said, feeling reckless, challenging him in a way she never would have dared before.

He seemed about to speak and then changed his mind. "It's dangerous out there at this hour," he said.

"Well, I made it." She turned and went to her room, where she spread the newspapers out on her desk and went through them page by page and item by item. When she was done, she did it again to make sure. There were stories about murders in lots of places, but none about a murder in Vermont. It hadn't been discovered. It might never be discovered. If nobody had missed Rita yet, maybe they wouldn't ever.

She hiked up her sweatshirt and turned sideways to the mirror. She always looked a little slimmer that way. She slid her fingers into the waistband and found that it was looser. She smiled at this, but only her mouth moved. Her eyes wouldn't follow suit. The man on the train that day. Tom. He'd thought she was a girl named Celia, pre-med at Vassar. The memory of that lie pleased her unexpectedly now. She'd done it automatically, without agonizing at all because he was a total stranger and it didn't matter if he believed her or not. So it was possible to lie. Easy, even. And nobody was the wiser. She saw her lie to Tom as a sort of test run. Telling her father she'd gone out to get papers when she'd really been at Grand Central calling Naomi, and having him believe her—that was the proof.

Chapter Four

It snowed heavily on the first day of school, big flakes that clogged up the city like wet cake. The bus lumbered up Madison, packed full and smelling of damp wool and cigarette smoke. Carole got off at Ninety-first and jaywalked across Madison.

She was early. It was a good half hour before she usually got to school, and the place was dark except for the sconces in the main lobby that spilled a weak light over the heavy furniture and parquet floors. She took the stairs to the fifth floor, where she sat alone in homeroom with the lights out. It was so quiet, and it smelled of clothes and books and antiseptic. Over vacation, the desks had been organized into a tidy square in the middle of the room, five across and five deep. The walls had been stripped and the blackboards washed professionally so that they were exceptionally dark. Little by little the noises began on her floor. Teachers coming in after the weeklong break, chatting, commiserating about being back. They didn't know she was in there, of course. They were as bad as the kids, grumbling about how much they didn't want to be here. Someone flicked on the lights, which came up haphazardly across the ceiling. "Hey!" It was Amanda. She went to her desk and plopped down her books. "How come you're sitting in the dark?"

"I like it," Carole said.

"You would," Amanda said. "I went to Bermuda over break. See?" She held out her arm and shoved up the sleeve. It was brown as a nut.

"Bully for you."

The room filled up quickly. Girls everywhere. They'd covered the globe. Florida, the Caribbean, even Paris. But no Naomi. When the bell rang for assembly, Carole was swept along with the thundering rush down the stairs. In the gym they lined up with the lower grades first, kindergarten through six, then the middle school, and then the upper school, with the twelfth grade last. Carole stood alone at the end of the twelfth-grade line, watching the door for Naomi and unable to breathe in the noise and heat. She was desperate to talk to Naomi, to find out if anything had happened.

The music started up in the assembly room, Miss Polivka pounding away. A Sousa march. Miss P had a sense of humor, Carole always thought. The sound traveled across the mezzanine and into the gym, the signal to be quiet. That was when the stairwell door flew open and Naomi made a run for it across the polished floor, sliding into line. In that outfit Naomi drew attention to both of them, a shocking-pink sweater with thick embroidery all over it. Elayne and Daddy must have been in South America again.

Naomi, on tiptoes now, a big grin on her face, leaned up to whisper to Carole as they shuffled around the three walls of the gym behind the others. "God, what a week," she said. "I got blitzed every night. I had a ball." A ball? Was Naomi crazy?

Mrs. Danzig was posted at the door to assembly, mouth pursed in a tight, unhappy smile, welcoming everybody back and making sure they were not talking.

They filed into rows of folding chairs. Miss Steen, the headmistress, came to the podium. She was like a cartoon old lady in her long dress and oxford shoes, and Carole really liked her, liked the big smile on that homely old face. Miss Steen raised her hands, the signal they should sit. Naomi opened a hymnal and wrote in pencil on the inside back cover, "He wants to see you." She showed it to Carole, then erased the words. Carole shook her head. No way. Never again. Naomi opened the hymnal to another page. "Got to," she wrote. "Eddie said."

The piano pounded out a prelude, and they stood to sing "A Mighty Fortress Is Our God."

"No," Carole said, pulling the hymnal from Naomi's hands.

"You have to get your stories straight," Naomi hissed over the singing.

"What do you mean, stories?" Carole said. "He said nobody would find out."

Suddenly the room was quiet. A few girls in the row ahead turned to look. Others giggled. Mrs. Danzig motioned the other girls to sit, but Carole to remain standing. "Carole," she said. "Please tell us all what you and Naomi think is so important to discuss during the singing."

The whole school was staring at her. "Something that happened," Carole said.

"Well, of course, dear," Mrs. Danzig said. "But we'd all like to know what."

"Just something." Sometimes Danzig would make a girl stand there for three or four minutes until she told.

Miss Steen came to her rescue. "Well, it's our first day back, so we'll let it pass, but please let's not talk in assembly again, Carole. You may sit."

She didn't hear a word of what went on afterward, or all that morning. She went from class to class in a stupor. She'd never been singled out like that. And it made her doubly sure she wasn't going to see Eddie. No way. She'd already put a week between him and her. If she saw him, she'd have to start all over again keeping her mouth shut.

But at lunch Naomi slipped into the empty seat beside her. Across the table, Shelly, Amanda, and Deirdre had just been comparing tans and ignoring Carole. "This isn't funny, Carole," Naomi said. "You've *got* to go see him. I promised you would. After all he's done for you. God." Naomi's little face was all bunched up.

"If it wasn't for him—" Carole began in a fierce whisper. "Oh, forget it. I thought the whole point was to keep our mouths shut."

Naomi was quiet for a few moments, spooning up a dessert. "Look," she said in a whisper. "Eddie is a wreck. He's so worried about you, so worried about anybody finding out. He really cares about you. We went up there, up into the woods. The first time right after you left and then again during the week. It's okay. You can't see anything. And nobody asked at the motel or anything. But he said you had to go see him. Just once, just to make sure you have your stories straight."

Across the table, Deirdre raised her perfect eyebrows and tipped her head. "What stories?"

"Why don't you mind your own—"

"Beeswax?" Deirdre and Shelly gave each other looks and then doubled over laughing. When they lost interest in Carole and Naomi, Naomi continued. "He's doing the stuff you should have done yourself, you know," she said in a whisper. "He packed up all that woman's stuff. He couldn't risk throwing it away up there because somebody might have found them. Cheap crap. He brought it home in his luggage so he can throw it away here. You're really lucky, Carole. He's thorough. He's a genius."

"He got kicked out of all those schools," Carole said, but she felt guilty about the clothes. She'd never even considered things like that. What if there was more? What if there were things she should have done like that and didn't think to do?

"The point is, he got *into* those schools," Naomi said.

"Big deal." Carole remembered what he'd said. He got kicked out for being with girls like her.

"He absolutely forced himself to stay in Stowe all week." Naomi tossed her long hair over one shoulder. "I guess it didn't go so well with him and you." She glanced down at her manicure. First one hand and then the other. "He told me some of it." She paused. "Well, at least you're not a virgin anymore," she whispered, but Amanda must have heard.

"You're *not?*" Amanda said from across the table.

70

"Naomi didn't mean that." Carole picked up her tray and left the table, blushing crimson. Naomi came after her.

"Why did you have to say that?" Carole asked.

"All I said was you're not a virgin. Neither is she, for God's sake."

"You had no business."

"Okay, okay. But look. You've got to do this. He's staying in some-body's house. It's what he does. House-sits. I'll give you the address. Wait till you get a load of it."

There were only three hours until school let out, and one of those was gym. They chose sides, and she was the second to last chosen, just before Lucille Stoddard, who had one leg shorter than the other. Each team always got one of them. The fat one and the lame one. The game was dodgeball, and the other team split and lined up, one half on each side of the gym. Then they pelted Carole's team with the ball. They always went after her first, the easiest one to get out, but today they were especially bloodthirsty. They stepped over the lines, they fouled with every throw, and the gym teacher didn't stop them. Nobody blew the whistle. It made Carole so mad, she felt like fight-ing back. She got this idea, after she'd managed to stay in longer than usual, that the longer she could stay in without getting hit, the better her luck would become, the less the likelihood that anyone would ever find out what she'd done in Stowe.

Amanda and Shelly threw the ball with both hands overhead, hard. The big miracle was that everybody was getting hit but her. And the next big miracle was that the rest of her team, the ones who'd been struck out, were screaming for her, cheering her on. Finally, she was the only one in. This had never happened before. She felt light and strong because she wasn't eating. She darted and jumped. She thumbed her nose at the other team. And then out of nowhere came the image of Rita's shoulder, fat and pink with pimples on it. She stopped dead at the memory, and the ball hit her square in the breast.

The town house where Eddie was staying was on Sixty-sixth Street between Park and Madison, only four blocks from her apartment. It was the biggest one on the block, four stories high, made of a pale, pinkish stone with thick carvings around the door and windows. Scaffolding hung from the two upper floors, and workmen sandblasted around the windows, the sound deafening. Carole rang the bell and saw that her hand was shaking.

After about a minute an inner door opened, and Eddie stood in front of her, behind the barred glass. He just looked at her blankly, as if he didn't know who she was. He was dressed in a yellow sweater with a paisley scarf at his neck like that stupid Fred Astaire or something. Lord of the manor. He finally opened the door and pulled her into the foyer, his grip so tight on her arm that it hurt. One door and then the other slammed behind her, and suddenly it was silent. Eddie gave her arm another mean squeeze.

"Ouch," she said. "Let go of me."

"You little bitch," he said. "You leave me up there to pick up after you, and you skip home like the spoiled piece of shit you are." He spat when he talked. How had she ever thought he was cute? He made her skin crawl.

"Naomi said you wanted to talk to me, or I never would have come over here."

"Let's get one thing straight." He waited for her to meet his eyes. "You do what I say."

"Oh, sure," she said, trying to sound tough, to hide her fear.

He grabbed her arm again. "You're in the big leagues now."

She looked away, keeping her mouth shut. She hated him so much.

"Have you talked to anyone?"

"I talk to people all the time." She rubbed her arm, which still felt sore where he'd grabbed her.

"You know what I mean." He stepped closer.

"Of course not."

"I took care of everything. The room was clean. Not a trace of what's-her-name." He was scanning Carole's face. People did it all the time; her eyes were so pale they didn't give people a place to land. But this was different. It was intimate, like he was looking for something, some weakness or something. It gave her the creeps. "You know what I worry about? That you'll get religion or something. That you'll think it's better to confess when it's not. Look at me." He took her face in his hand, hard, so she had to look at him again. "You're naive. What you don't know is that shit happens all the time. People die. People get killed." He was nodding, as though he agreed with himself. "You didn't mean to do it. If it ever comes to that, I'll swear you never meant to do it. I'll tell them what happened. About your strength, you know? How I saw you there. Pushing on her. I tried to stop you."

"You did not."

He shook his head. "You just don't remember. You were putting away that scotch pretty good. You were like this split personality. Nurse Jekyll and Mrs. Hyde."

"Was not." But she had been. She knew that, and she knew that her memory of the night was not clear. She could never get a grip on the order of what had happened or how long anything had taken. She could not remember about Rita's neck at all, even though that was exactly the thing she had to remember.

"You blocked it out, Carole." His voice was suddenly, unexpectedly calm. "It happens. You got carried away. You were into it bigtime." His voice was almost loving now. He toyed with the edge of her jacket. "I can see it just like it was a movie. God, you were enjoying yourself. Don't pull away." He took a deep breath. "You know you did this. And it can be proved. There are ways, if it ever comes to that."

There were? That was such terrifying information she didn't dare to ask what those ways were.

"We need to be clear, you and me. You need to be clear. Because if you're not, I'm afraid for you. Don't mess it up. I want to hear you say it."

She nodded.

"Speak up," he said. "Say it."

"Say what?"

"I broke her neck."

"But I didn't mean to."

"Say it."

"I broke her neck," she whispered.

"That's right," he said. "You didn't mean to, but you did." He sighed and sat back on the couch, arms and legs splayed, breathing like somebody who'd just run a race, sweating at the edges of his perfect hair. He took off the silk cravat and wiped his forehead with it. He smiled at her. "Hey," he said.

"What?"

"You don't really hate me."

She looked away.

"You were a tiger that night," he said. "Now that we've got our little bit of business out of the way, I can tell you this. I can't stop thinking about our night. Come here." He patted the couch next to him.

"No," she said. The thought made her stomach turn.

"Oh, come on. You liked it. Admit it. I was your first guy. There's so much more to show you."

"When hell freezes over." She turned to leave, but he was right there again, grabbing her arm.

"You were going to get me that cigarette box, remember?" She thought he was talking about something in the motel room. Maybe something that could give her away. It was terrifying the way the panic could slide up her throat so suddenly. "You promised." He flashed a smile. "A souvenir."

Then she remembered. The one in her apartment. He made her describe it. "I can't," she said. "What if my mother notices?"

"Just give it to Naomi, and she can give it to me." His face was very close to hers. "I'll keep it closed up tight." He grinned meanly. "It'll remind me how we're all keeping our mouths shut."

That night she stole some of her parents' sleeping pills, eight in all. Four white (her father's) and four red (her mother's). She arranged them in piles of two. Six would be enough, she thought, but just to be sure, if she did it, she'd take all eight. No. Maybe she'd need more. She'd wait until the prescriptions were refilled and then steal more. It was a luxurious feeling to know there would be enough. She'd tried one of the red ones once to find out what it did. It had made her feel very strange, as if she were two people, one of them going about her business as usual, the other one floating alongside in a fog. Multiply that feeling by six and she was pretty sure it was plenty. Not that she wanted to kill herself. Far from it. It was just that if the police came to the door, or if anybody called the apartment to ask about Rita, she'd just march right in here and take them. No, wait. She'd go to the basement. Nobody ever went down there. It was dark and cold. She could take all the pills and die. It would be weeks before they found her. It was such unexpected comfort, like the traffic on Lex.

And it wasn't just the pills and the traffic. She imagined how it would be to fall from the highest point of the bridges in the city. At this time of year, the water in the East River was so cold that if the fall didn't kill her, the icy temperature would. She leaned out the window of her apartment and looked down at the street. Oh, man, there were so many ways it was a wonder anybody stayed alive. If one thing wasn't available, others would be. And what amazed her was that these thoughts weren't morbid. In fact, the thought of suicide cheered her. Whenever she thought about it, she felt relief.

The next morning at breakfast the telephone rang. Carole and her parents were at the dining room table, separated from one another, as always, by an acre of mahogany. Her mother disappeared into the kitchen, picked up the phone, and reappeared in the doorway, the cord stretching out behind her. "Emily," she mouthed to them. Her mother's conversations with Emily were always the same, long stretches of silence at this end while Emily talked. Usually Carole and her father made faces at each other, but she was too scared to do that now. "I don't know," her mother said at last. "I'll ask her."

She covered the receiver. "She wants to know who a Rita Boudreau is."

Carole had just picked up her spoon, but she was so shocked she dropped it and it clattered back onto the plate. Her mother's face was a pale moon hovering. They'd found out. "Who?" she said in case she hadn't heard right, in case there was any possibility.

"Who?" her mother repeated into the phone. She frowned at Carole while she listened, then covered the receiver again to speak. "She found a wallet belonging to this Rita person in the ski parka." Her mother watched Carole while she listened to what Emily was saying, then repeated it. "She's going to put it into an envelope and send it back to the address on the driver's license."

"No!" Carole blurted out. "I mean, *I'll* send it to her."

"I thought you didn't know her," her father said.

"Did you hear that, Em?" Her mother paused. "Carole says she'll send it herself."

"I remember now," Carole said. "I did meet her."

"The driver's license says she's twenty-eight." Her mother's face fell into a question. She put a hand over the receiver so Emily wouldn't hear. "They had grown women in the dorms?"

"She was on the staff," Carole said in a panic. "She worked there. She helped me when I got sick. I'll send it back to her with a note. I've been meaning to thank her."

"And you forgot *that*?" her father asked.

"Her name. I just forgot her name."

"But why would her wallet be in the parka?" her father asked.

Carole was unable to speak, unable to find any reasonable answer at all. Able only to say the truth of what she was thinking. That she didn't know how to lie her way out of this one, that she was caught. Finally. "I don't know," she said.

"You don't know," her father said, shaking his head and going back to his paper. She was stupefied at his reaction, or lack of reaction. She could hardly believe it.

"Be a dear," her mother said to Emily. "Send it to us here, and Carole will take care of it." She paused, listening. "She says it's no trouble," her mother said, "to send it there. Less in fact to send it here and then you send it. And when you think about it, she's got a—"

"No!" Carole said. She felt everything spinning out of control. "I said I'd do it."

"Well," her mother said into the phone. "You must have heard that. Would you mind awfully sending it here?" She listened a while more, then murmured a good-bye and disappeared back into the kitchen to hang up the phone. While she was out of the room, her father put down his paper. "What in creation was that all about?" he said.

"Since when is it a federal crime to forget somebody's name?"

"That's not what I'm talking about." Her father took a deep breath and sighed. The sound of her mother's heels on the kitchen floor clicked toward them. "You haven't been yourself."

"Then who have I been?"

"Don't talk back to me, young lady."

"You should call her right away and say you found it," her mother said, coming back into the room. "It's been almost a month."

The shocker was that she'd been caught unprepared and then been able to come up with something so plausible they still didn't have a clue. The bigger shock, though, was that she hadn't remembered the wallet, and if she could forget that, Eddie was right, she could forget anything. She could forget what she did in that room. She stole into the living room, slipped the silver cigarette box into the pocket of her sweater, and put her coat on over that so it wouldn't show. If Eddie found out about the wallet, who knew what he'd do. Better take him the cigarette box, like he said.

"Oh," her mother said. Carole stopped at the door to the elevator, her hand pressing against the silver box in her pocket. "You'll never guess who I ran into the other day." Her mother giggled and blushed. "That man from the train. You remember. The one who shared the taxi with Naomi when you girls went off to Stowe that day?" She looked so hopeful and girlish. "Well, he stopped me right out here on Lexington. At first I didn't remember, but then of course I did when he explained. He asked after you. Asked about your trip,

and I told him you'd gotten sick. He lives around here somewhere."
She sighed again. "Small world."

Instead of walking directly to Madison to catch the bus, Carole went up Lex to Sixty-sixth Street and rang Eddie's buzzer. He thought *she* was going to give them away, and there *he* went talking to her *mother!* When he answered the door, she knew what a bad idea it had been to come. The sight of him in his bathrobe, open down the front over nothing but his underpants, made her almost gag.

"What happened?" he said. "What's the matter?

"You stopped my mother on the street."

"Aw, for Christ's sake." He looked left and right, then pulled her inside. Paint-spattered canvas covered all the furniture. Two men were on stepladders painting the ceiling. Eddie glared at them. "I can't think straight anymore with all these people around."

Maybe he hadn't heard what she'd said. "My mother—" she began.

"I told Petey and Case I'd stay in the house if nobody started work before nine." He looked at his watch. "Shit." He pulled her through the living room and down a long hall to a small elevator. "I told you not to come here. I told you to work through Naomi." He swung open the elevator door. "We have to stick to the rules. It's the only way."

"I'm not going up in that. I can talk right here."

"Guineas'll listen to everything you say." He pushed her into the elevator. "Wop wop wop," he said.

On the second level he showed her into a room with a large unmade bed and clothing strewn across the floor and over the furniture. "This is exactly what you can't do," he said. "Panic and come here."

"You talked to my mother. Now she's going to talk about you. You have no idea. Now she's going to wonder stuff about you. Who you are, where you live, and what you do for a living."

"So what?"

"So everything."

"Your mother came at me gangbusters. Big sloppy grin on her face. She remembered me."

"That's not what she said."

"You think your mother's going to admit to chasing me halfway down the block?"

"That's a lie."

"She gives me this big yoo-hoo. I couldn't ignore her. I tried to get rid of her, but hey. That mother of yours—"

Carole had seen her mother do that other times. It was possible. "Move someplace else, then. You don't even live here. Those other people do. Pete or whatever. So why don't you even have a place of your own, anyway?"

He sat down on the bed and watched her. The nightstand was a mess—a full ashtray, crumpled packs of cigarettes, and a soiled scarf. "I'm in between apartments, that's why." He gestured around. "I deserve to live in places like this. I should have been brought up like this."

"I thought you were," she said. "I thought you—" She noticed a shocking pink sweater on the floor, the same one Naomi had worn the first day back at school. "Are you and Naomi—"

"She likes me. What can I say?" He lifted his filthy shoes onto a big soft silk comforter. "Let's make a little deal, okay? You keep your mouth shut, and I stay away from Mommy."

"I was already keeping my mouth shut. Why would you even—"

"I want insurance. It's for your own sake." He smiled cruelly. "I'd hate to have to let Mommy in on our little business."

She was stunned. "Why would you even think that? It's the whole point. It's them I'm keeping it from. God, Eddie, what's the matter with you?"

He was off the bed so fast she barely saw it happen, and then suddenly he was behind her, twisting her arm up, the pain searing her shoulders. "Nothing is the matter with me. Get it? It's you, cunt. Dropping in, disobeying. I asked you something, and now I want the answer. "Do. We. Have. A. Deal?"

"Yes," she whispered.

He relaxed his hand but stayed close to her, pushing himself against her. "What's this?" He fumbled with her coat, found the silver box, and held it to the light. He opened and closed it a couple of times. "Good girl. I almost forgot."

She loathed seeing it in his hands. Hated when he blew on it and rubbed the top with his sleeve. "I changed my mind." She reached to take it back, but he hid it behind his back. She wished he'd close the robe.

"Too late," he said. "No Indian giving."

"It's ours."

"Not anymore," he said.

She felt disoriented, dislocated. How long had she been here? He led the way, walking ahead of her. She watched his body move under the flimsy robe and remembered it from that night. In the elevator he said, "Hey. You have any money on you? I'm short of cash."

"No." He snatched her purse from off the pile of books she was carrying. "Give it back."

"You have ten," he said, fumbling in her wallet. "You big fat liar."

She tried to take the money back, but he held it from her and pointed to the living room, where the painters silently did their work. "Sshh."

Outside she was shocked by the noise of traffic, the bright sunlight. She hurried to Lexington, where there was a clock in the drugstore at the corner. It was nine-fifteen. Impossible. She ducked inside to ask if the clock was correct and was told that it was slow if anything. At school, assembly would already be over. First period would have begun, and she was twenty-five blocks from school. Half an hour away. How would she explain it? She hurried west on Sixty-sixth Street, crossed Park, ran the block to Madison, and checked south to see if there was a bus in view. There wasn't. She headed north. Already groups of women were shopping. Men in suits and overcoats were jumping out of taxis and disappearing into buildings. Maids were strolling along with children. The daytime world she'd never seen.

Carole bumped into people in her hurry, lunged through red lights between moving cars. He was a monster. She stopped and leaned against a building, suddenly weakened by the memory of his words. *Do we have a deal?* And Naomi's sweater on the floor. For the first time she understood how completely alone she was in this. She sucked in air until she could move again, but now, all around her, the street was thick with people. She tried to push her way through, but people pushed her back, accused her of cutting in. Cutting in? Cars were being directed by mounted police. She tried to cut around with the cars and back to Park, but a throng of people surged at her. There were sawhorses blocking the way, and people with signs milling around. Anti-Castro, anti-Communist, signs in Spanish that she couldn't read. What was happening? She snaked through, heading north as well as she could, and found herself at the front, pushing and shoving.

"I'm only trying to get through," she said to a man who elbowed her hard.

"So aren't we all," he said.

There was another ring of sawhorses blocking off the entrance to the Carlyle Hotel, a big clear semicircle of space. Something big must have happened inside the hotel. Maybe something terrible.

"What happened?" she asked a woman behind her.

"Nothing yet," the woman said.

The clock in the lobby said it was nine-forty, but that was impossible. It couldn't be. She asked a man the time, and he checked his watch. "Quarter to ten," he said. How could the time be going by so fast? It was after recess now. Second period. She'd never been late to school a day in her life.

From behind there came the sounds of car horns. Lots of them. A noise started in the crowd, shouting and chanting. Horns blared everywhere, and suddenly people were shouting from their apartment windows, dropping rolls of toilet paper and confetti. Across the way, police on horseback were separating the crowd, pushing them back to form an opening. The empty space filled with a line of gleaming black limousines, flags snapping over the headlights, making their way slowly up Madison. The sea of people parted. Men in dark suits ran ahead of the cars. A limousine pulled to the Carlyle's front door and stopped twenty feet from where Carole was standing. A man swung the door open. There was a long pause when nothing happened and the sound subsided, then a loud roar and thunderous applause all around as Bobby Kennedy stepped from the car. The wind lifted his hair in front, and he brushed it back. He was hunched, slightly untidy, and thinner than she would have thought, but energetic looking. He smiled. Somebody shouted something in Spanish, and he answered in Spanish. There was another roar, thunderous applause again. Grinning, he held out his hands to shush people. This happened three times before he could be heard. He thanked people for coming out to see him. He said something in Spanish and then he was gone, whisked into the hotel. The crowd stayed put, chanting and calling out things, but the police pushed them back and away. It was after ten. She felt sick to her stomach at what she'd done. She'd missed English and history. Her perfect attendance was shattered. They would have called her mother by now.

The police were pushing people away, telling the crowd to break it up. Any act of hers, any effort to move against the crowd, was futile. She'd read about panic, the need to quell it, to surrender and let herself be pulled and pushed until finally the crowd began to disperse. In only moments there were more police than people. She didn't dare look at the clock, but habit made her take a few steps back toward the hotel. It was ten after ten. She'd make it by ten-thirty. She'd explain about the crowd, about Bobby Kennedy. She'd say she got caught up in the crowd. That part was true. That Kennedy was there and she stopped to listen. She could even tell them she'd done it on purpose, a historic moment worthy of missing school for.

But then she spotted a familiar-looking girl with her black hair teased and sprayed in a huge bubble. The girl was rooted in place, staring at the door that Kennedy had just passed through. Who was she, though? The girl was certainly not a Spence student. Perhaps she was a clerk at Gristede's or Bloomingdale's? Or had Carole seen her on the bus? No. It was something else.

She moved closer, around. When she saw the girl full on and that she was pregnant, Carole remembered. The girl from the home, the bottle, the nun. Carole had thought often of the little flick of the hand behind her back that night, so intimate and friendly. She would just say hello and then she'd make a run for school. She approached and tapped the girl on the shoulder. "Hi," she said. "Remember me?" She had an urge to rub the streaks of teary mascara from the girl's wide, smooth cheeks. "From Sixty-second Street. That night."

"What night?"

"I saw you from my window? That old nun caught you hiding something in the john."

"God a-mighty." The girl's sudden smile took Carole by surprise. "Sure. Wow."

"Well," Carole said and didn't know what to say next. "I just thought I'd say hello."

The girl burst out laughing. "That's *all*? Jeez a-mighty. Who are you anyway? I'm Rachel Weaver." She flung her arms out to either side. Her coat flew open. "In all my glory."

"Carole Mason." Carole felt oddly dwarfed by Rachel.

"Shouldn't you be in school or something?" Rachel checked her watch. "It's half past ten."

"It can't be," Carole said. "That's impossible." She squinted into the lobby window to see the official time. In forty minutes lunch would start.

"Welcome to the trouble club." Rachel had a big loud laugh. "You skip for this too?" She indicated the Carlyle entry with her thumb. "I would have if I were in school. I mean real school, not that crap we get from the sisters."

"I didn't know he was—"

"I got goose bumps." Rachel had large, dark down-sloping eyes, like a puppy's. "I'm not sure which one I like better. Bobby or MLK.

83

It's a draw. I definitely like them both better than JFK, and I adored him. But, you know, you've got to move on. Who's yours?"

Carole shrugged. "We get taught to be objective all the time," she said. "Not to have favorites."

"So what?" Rachel said. "You can still have an opinion."

"Okay then, King." It felt thrilling to pitch that objectivity right out and go from the gut.

"Why's that?" Rachel said.

"He didn't get his job by being the president's brother."

Rachel let go a wallop of a laugh. "Right on," she said. Carole felt a surge of pleasure at how much she'd amused Rachel with the truth. It was exactly what she'd always thought about Bobby Kennedy. Sure he was great, but come on.

"I feel sorry for Ethel," Rachel was saying. "All those kids, I heard they don't even have enough beds in the house, and the kids have to sleep wherever." She patted her stomach. "I was due a week ago." She looked around. "If Sister ever catches me out here, she's going to kill me. They'll tie my legs together for punishment. They do that to some of the girls when they go into labor. To punish them. So they won't get pregnant again before they're married. They're barbarians. So?"

"So what?"

Rachel let out a rollicking laugh. "So are you going to school or are you going to skip? If it's skipping, come on. We can get some coffee." When Carole hesitated, Rachel went on. "Look, it's almost lunchtime. Take it from me, I've skipped a bunch. You're better off staying out the whole day than going in this late. You might as well. You're in trouble both ways. Enjoy the free time."

Almost lunchtime? It was like one of those nightmares where you can't do the thing you have to do no matter how hard you try. You keep doing something else instead, and it keeps getting later and later. Eddie kept telling her to act normal, and she was trying, but she just didn't seem able to do it. The school would be calling the apartment by now. They always called. Where was her mother today? She had to think. Maybe she was out. Oh, please let her be out and the phone ring and ring.

Rachel started walking. From behind you wouldn't even know she was pregnant. She stopped and turned, that big smile flashing. "Well?"

She'd go home. If her mother was out, there was still hope. She could answer the phone when it rang. But what if her mother was there? Oh, God. She caught up with Rachel, and they walked up Madison. Rachel careered into Eve's, a very expensive hat shop on the corner of Seventy-seventh and Madison. The windows were full of tiny pillbox hats with veils. Inside there were hats on little pegs on the walls, hats under glass, a counter where people could sit to try them on. Rachel plopped herself down and asked to see something that Lady Bird might wear. "How many times do I have to tell you you're not welcome here?" the saleslady said. Rachel grabbed Carole by the arm, and they ran out. Carole felt too numb to laugh as the time ticked away. What if Eddie had gone out and waited for her mother? He knew where they lived. What if he went to the apartment?

Rachel talked a mile a minute, pouring out her life to Carole, ducking around people and jaywalking. "You like to jaywalk? I *love* to jaywalk," she said. They tore across streets, ducking between cars. Rachel gave the finger to a cabbie who leaned on his horn at her. She said she was from Long Island, way down at the end, a place nobody's ever heard of. Her family was telling everybody she went to live with an aunt for her senior year of school. "Like anybody believes *that*," she said. "I don't even have an aunt, for crying out loud."

The boy was somebody she'd known all her life. He wasn't her regular boyfriend. Everybody thought it was, of course, but it wasn't, so let them think what they wanted. "What about you?"

"I never skipped school in my life."

"I know," Rachel said with a laugh. "You look like a deer caught in the headlights. What else?"

"Nothing." *I went to Eddie's house this morning before school because he shouted to my mother on the street and now I'm so scared he'll tell her what I did that I can't even get to school. I feel like I'm drowning.*

"Well, sure there is," Rachel said. "Everybody has things to tell. You don't need to be knocked up to have a story to tell. Like what's it like to live with all those rich people. They look snooty, but are they? Really? And that old guy at the door? He hates us over at the home, I just know it. He scowls at us."

"He hates everybody," Carole said. "Heney can't stand me. The more I go out of my way to be nice, the meaner he is."

Rachel charged through the door of a corner drugstore, slid into a booth, and ordered a Coke. The place reeked of disinfectant. She leaned over the table toward Carole. "That was Sister Crucifix that night," she said. She pronounced it *sistah.* "I would have been chucked out of there a million times by now if it wasn't for her. She hates me, sure, but she always picks me for waltzes. She has to pick the other girls for the fast dances, the polkas, and all, but I'm it for the slow stuff. I'm a great waltzer."

"You dance with them?"

Rachel roared with laughter. "Oh, the look on your face!"

"Well, it's weird."

"You're not Polish, are you? You've never been to a Polish wedding or an Irish wedding, for that matter."

Carole shrugged, a little embarrassed. "What will you do?" she asked. "After your baby."

Rachel ran her hands over her belly. "I'm not giving it up," she said. "I swear to God I won't." Her face soured, and her eyes filled. "Everybody wants me to. The nuns, my parents, Father Ryan. There's some couple that wants it, a couple that can't have babies of their own. They want me to meet them, but I won't."

"But it's your choice. It's your baby."

"They *steal* babies when they get born," Rachel whispered. "They tell you it died, but they really give it away."

"They can't," Carole said. The whole idea was impossible. "I mean, that would be illegal."

"Sweetie, they do whatever the hell they want," Rachel said.

"But you'd have to sign something, I think. They can't do it unless you sign."

"In your world, maybe." Rachel's face took on a new look, pleading and serious. Maybe Eddie was right when he said she didn't know anything. Maybe people died, people got killed, people stole babies, and nobody did anything. "Who's going to stop them? Not my parents. My parents would love it if somebody took this baby off their hands."

"I just thought—"

"Yeah, well, they're after me all the time, and I keep saying no, and then they tell me what a selfish girl I am. Not only nasty, but selfish too. They say there's nothing worse in the eyes of God than a selfish and nasty girl."

"You're not selfish." That was so plainly true. "It's your baby. Your possession. Your flesh and blood. What makes it selfish to want it for yourself?"

"Yeah?" Rachel said. "You mean that?"

"Sure," Carole said. "I just met you, and I can tell already."

"Are you a virgin?"

Carole looked down at her hands, and Rachel let out a big booming laugh. "You're not! You're just as nasty and selfish as I am, and you live in that fancy building. I wish those old nuns knew that. They're always holding up girls like you to us. 'Exemplary girls,' they call you."

"If they only knew," Carole said.

"This girl I know had a baby a couple of months ago and has relatives in Rochester. She said I can go there for a little while. After."

"My dad is a lawyer. He might know," Carole said. Rachel looked puzzled. "About whether they can just take the baby."

"Could you ask him?" Rachel grabbed her hand. "Oh, please?"

"I think so," Carole said. "I'll try. I know how it feels to be in trouble."

"You? How? What did you do?"

"What didn't I do?" She tried to make a joke of it so Rachel wouldn't ask more questions.

"Seriously, come on."

"I can't tell. I promised this guy I'd never tell. You just have to believe it."

Rachel pursed her lips and looked at something in the distance, then she leaned across the table. "Not to mess with you or anything, but that's what I used to think. I wasn't going to tell anybody. I was going to kill myself before I ever told."

Carole felt her face redden.

"Are you pregnant?"

Carole shook her head. "Worse."

"It probably isn't. I thought I'd let everybody in the world down. And then I told after all, and you know what? My folks went crazy, but it wasn't that bad. It's never as bad as you think it's going to be. After all, it's the truth, is all." She shrugged. "It just is."

When Carole got home, there were voices in the living room. Her mother and Emily. She shut the door silently and waited to see if they'd heard her come in. The chatter went on, and she listened. It was about the day. About something Emily bought. It sounded like she was holding it up to herself. The conversation was about the color. *Blue? More of a blue green. Teal.* So casual, so normal, that Carole was sure her mother couldn't have known she wasn't in school today. Her mother must have been out shopping when the school called.

But she wasn't out of the woods. Far from it. The school could call again at any minute. She slid into the kitchen, dialed the school number, and got the secretary. "Oh, Miss MacNamara," she said in the breathiest, sickest voice she could conjure. "My mother told me to call you. She forgot to call you this morning, and she's not home." It was a big chance. A huge chance. "I was sick today. I had a stomachache."

Miss MacNamara fumbled with papers for a few seconds. "I tried to call," Miss MacNamara said. "Let's see. Four times, and no one answered. Were you there?" Her voice dripped with suspicion.

"The phone's all the way on the other side of the apartment," Carole said. There were phones all over the place, but what did Mac-Namara know? "I must not have heard it. I thought my mother already called, but she forgot. She just called me to see if I was okay and said I should call you."

"Okay, dear. But let's try not to let it happen again. Let's talk to Mother about it, shall we? Let's remind Mother of the importance of that telephone call." Carole was so literal she thought MacNamara wanted to talk to her mother right then, before she remembered it was just the way she talked. *Let's not make so much noise. Let's not run in the halls. Let's clean our plates.*

"Of course," Carole said and hung up. They always believed her. She had a ton of currency built up because she was such a goody-goody. They called her that behind her back. She knew they did, Amanda and the others. Square too. Well, wouldn't they be surprised, she thought. It was almost too bad she couldn't go in and brag about taking a day off and lying to MacNamara and getting away with it.

She cruised into the living room, where her mother and Emily were sitting side by side on the couch. Her mother wore a brown dress that strained across her bust and she was smiling up at Carole the way she always did, a little nervous, a little shy around her sister, as though everything needed to go just so.

Emily had on a black suit with big fur cuffs, a red pillbox hat over that helmet of hair, and those creepy foxes chasing one another around her shoulders. Emily was like a Bedouin. She wore as much of her wealth as she could fit onto herself. She extended a bony hand for Carole to shake, her wrist thick with gold bracelets, fingers loaded with rings. She pulled Carole down to her level—she was surprisingly strong—and planted a waxy kiss on her cheek. Carole knew it would leave a dark red stain. While she was bent over, she saw the wallet on the coffee table. Blue plastic with a big red and white Minnie Mouse on it, and bent as though it had been folded in half. Carole snatched up the wallet. "You were supposed to send this to me."

Both her mother and Emily looked at her sharply in surprise.

"Really, dear." Emily's husband had probably poisoned half the Third World, but even so, Carole's mother was cowed by her sister, as though she'd never be as good. She started talking rapidly, explaining how Emily had made a special trip into the city to return the wallet.

"I think it was just fine to open it," Emily said, her eyes widening. "It feels very wrong to open a stranger's wallet, but under the circumstances . . ." In Carole's opinion, Emily would open anybody's wallet. "There's a ten-dollar bill and her driver's license," Emily noted. "I hope she hasn't had to go out and get a new one, retake her driver's test. I wouldn't wish that on my own worst enemy."

"Did she mention that when you talked to her?" Carole's mother indicated the chair opposite so Carole would sit down. "Carole called this woman and talked to her."

"You *found* her?" Emily said.

Carole nodded.

"Hmmm. I couldn't," Emily said. "I tried, but information had no listing."

"I got through." Carole hoped they wouldn't hear the tremor in her voice. She was so unprepared for all this.

"I tried twice. Are you sure?" Emily wasn't going to give up.

"Of course I'm sure. I called at the Double Hearth. Where she *was*. She's probably listed under her husband's name. Or her parents." It was so dangerous to create a Rita she knew didn't exist—a married woman, a woman with parents. But it was working.

"I'll see it gets mailed tomorrow," her mother said, holding out her hand for the wallet.

"No," Carole said. "I said I'd do it."

Emily gave her mother a sour look. "Common-looking thing. Open it and show your mother. That's her, right? That's the same woman?"

"Yes."

"You didn't even *look*," her mother said.

Carole looked quickly. In the space beside Rita's driver's license was a photograph of her sitting at a table in a kitchen. Her brown

90

hair, parted in the middle, hung down in curtains to either side of her expressionless face. She held a glass of something. Carole's hand trembled as she stared into that face with its sad accusing eyes.

"I still think it very strange that her wallet would be in your parka," Emily said. She could purse her whole face. "You didn't use it as a fake ID, I hope."

Carole slumped back into her chair. "Of course not," she said. So they thought she'd used this woman's driver's license to get served. She opened the wallet and held up the picture. "You think anybody in their right mind would think this is me?"

"They look fast," Emily said, quick in her own defense. "They want you to drink. All they want in those places is to say they looked at your ID."

"She *helped* me," Carole said, the implication clearly that Emily wouldn't understand anybody helping anybody else. It felt so good to use Rita against Emily, whom she'd never liked. She folded the wallet shut and stood up to leave. Her mother's face was slack with confusion. "I have homework."

In her room, Carole wrapped the wallet in a brown bag and put it in the top drawer of her dresser, under her underwear. That night, very late, she took the wallet from the drawer and studied the picture of Rita. It was the flat, bland face of a stranger half smiling into the camera, a person relaxed at a kitchen table. Rita must have liked this version of herself to keep it in her wallet that way. A flattering picture in ways. "This might not work," Rita had said. She must have known that Carole was in over her head. If only Carole had been able to hear the concern, the warning. Way over her head. *She doesn't look any eighteen to me.* It shamed her now, remembering what she'd thought of Rita at the time—that Rita was cheap, a rival wanting to steal Eddie away from her, when really, Rita had been trying to help her. She studied the information. *127 Baldwin Terrace. Morris Center, VT. Five foot five. 150 pounds. Eyes brown. Hair brown.*

Carole turned sideways to the mirror. She could suck in her stomach and make her skirt drop several inches to her hips. It was as though her body was morphing, disguising itself of its own free will, as though it had decided she'd be less dangerous if there was less of her. She went to the bathroom and got on the scale. One hundred and sixty-three. Thirteen more pounds than Rita. Back in her room, she wrote "163" down in tiny black numbers at the upper-left-hand side of a piece of graph paper. She got out another sheet for her measurements and did the same, writing the size of her hips, waist, and bust on the left side of the page. She tucked the papers away in the closet with the red change purse. Then she slipped out the service door to the back hallway, where the incinerator chute was. She pulled open the door. Down at the bottom she could hear the flames roaring, smell the fetid, garbagey draft. She was there for a long time with the grate open, her hair blowing, holding the wallet. Then she let it go.

Carole's father's secretary, Jackie Palmer, had a large smooth forehead and big eyes, but Carole could never recall the bottom of her face, which seemed to melt away into the rest of her. She always gushed to Carole. Her father said Jackie wasn't a very good secretary, and Carole figured she was trying to get points with him by being nice to her. She made a big deal of how much weight Carole had lost and how beautiful she'd become. *All grown up. A regular young lady.* Carole had to wait for her father on the settee outside his office for fifteen minutes listening to this. Finally he came out and ushered her in. He rubbed his hands together when he saw her. "Well, sweetie," he said. "To what do I owe this honor?"

"I have a question. It's sort of a business question."

He sat down behind his desk. "Shoot," he said. She could tell he thought this was cute.

"Do you have to sign a paper before somebody can take your baby away?" she said.

"What baby?" His face dropped.

"I mean, if you're not married. If you're under eighteen?"

He got up, closed the door, and came back to his desk. "What baby?"

"I told you. It's just a business question. A legal question."

"Is it about you?"

"Of course not."

"Naomi," he said, his anger gathering. "I told your mother it was something like this."

"It's not Naomi. Can't you just answer the question? Can't you just *say*?"

"You're not in any trouble, are you?"

She looked down at her shoes, which were scuffed and embarrassing. "One of the girls in that Home for Unwed Mothers across from us wanted to know. I said I'd ask. You don't need to make a federal case out of it, Daddy. It's just a question."

"How did you get to know one of them?" The way he said "them" made his dislike clear.

"What's the matter with *them*?" Carole asked.

"Well," her father said. "They're not our type of person, are they?" She'd never expected this from him. From Emily, but never from him. Not in a million years.

"And what type is that?" She raised her voice.

Miss Palmer cracked the door and looked in. "Anything you need?" she said. He waved her away.

"You're not to go giving my legal advice to one of them."

"I'm not asking you for advice. I'm only looking for information." She knew the difference. He'd told her often enough. There was advice and then there was information. Two completely different animals, although people mixed the two constantly.

"You're asking for advice, Carole. And you don't know it."

"I'll look it up in the library, then. I just thought you'd help out since you already know the answer."

He got up and came around the desk. "All this is getting entirely out of hand," he said.

"All what?"

"First you cut short your ski trip with no explanation."

"I had diarrhea," she said.

He ignored her. "Then you take up with one of those pregnant girls." All she could think was of skipping school, and if he didn't say anything about it, he didn't know. "You're going to Vassar," he said, crossing his arms tightly across his chest. "Vassar, for God's sake."

"What does that have to do with anything? Vassar is just a college," she said.

"It is not *just* a college," he said.

She rolled her eyes.

"It is one of the oldest, most respected institutions of higher learning for girls in this country, young lady, and don't you make that kind of a face at me. I won't have it."

She stared beyond him at the wall of photographs.

"I want an apology," he said.

Some of those photographs used to be in their living room in Ridgewood. She fixed on one in particular of her father and mother at Ruby Foo's restaurant in Montreal with two other men and their wives. The other men were friends of theirs from when they were all students at the University of Wisconsin, and the picture was old, taken before Carole was born. But one of the men was now the assistant secretary of the navy, and that, she realized, was why the picture was here and not at home. Here, important people would see it. In the picture below that one, her father was shaking hands with Vice President Richard Nixon. She didn't know where it had been taken. A reception someplace.

What if all those people on the wall found out? What if Miss Palmer and Heney and everybody at school and all the partners in the firm found out what she'd done with Eddie Lindbaeck in that room, and what if Nixon himself found out? And they could if she wasn't careful. They would bring all their hatred down on her, and on her parents too. It was like looking into the abyss just realizing what could happen and the power she had to bring their lives to ruin. Her father was still waiting for her to speak.

"Forget it," she said and turned to leave.

As she passed through reception, Miss Palmer looked over the tops of her glasses. Heard everything, she was sure. She hated Miss Palmer.

The Home for Unwed Mothers smelled like a doctor's office because of the disinfectant they used. There was a big lobby with glistening polished floors and no furniture except for a small desk and chair off to the side. A tiny nun sat smiling at her from behind the desk. "Can I help you, dear?" she said.

"I'd like to see Rachel Weaver," Carole said. "I'm her cousin." It amazed her what people just automatically believed. There was this whole layer of information you could give out and people wouldn't blink an eye. You could create a whole identity that way.

The little nun asked her to wait while she dialed the telephone. "Her cousin in the lobby to see her," the nun said into the phone, then hung up. "Somebody will be right down."

In a few minutes she heard footsteps on the stairs. The door below the exit sign opened, and a white-haired nun came through. Sister Crucifix. "Carole Weaver," Carole said. "My dad and Rachel's dad are brothers." People said the truth set you free, but that wasn't true at all. Lies were what set you free.

"As you no doubt know, Rachel is overdue and can't visit for long," Sister Crucifix said.

Carole followed the sister up two flights of stairs to a long corridor. They stopped in front of a door. "Your cousin is here to see you," she called.

"I don't have a cousin," Rachel yelled from inside.

Sister Crucifix smiled wearily at Carole.

"She can be such a pain, can't she?" Carole said. "Rachel, come on, quit kidding around. It's me, Carole."

The door opened a crack, and Rachel peered out.

"Oh," she said to the sister. "That cousin."

"I'll rap when time is up," Sister said.

"He wouldn't tell me," Carole said once she was inside the room and the door was shut. "He spazzed out over it. Thought I was the one who was pregnant."

Rachel shook her head. "It's okay. I finally got it out of them." She was grinning. "They can't take the baby unless I sign. You were right. Baby's all mine. I'm getting induced tomorrow. They're giving me a shot to start labor, so the baby will come like tomorrow or the next day. That stupid couple from New Jersey is coming in case I change my mind. If it's a girl, I'm naming her Carole. If it's a boy it's Pepper."

Carole grinned. "With an 'e,'" she said. "Carole with an 'e.'"

"I'm scared shitless," Rachel said with a big grin. She looked up at Carole and made a face. "It's going to hurt. They teach us girls a lesson, you betcha. They learned that from the Communists. We don't get pain medicine like regular women. We get nothing. I may not see you again. I'll be in the hospital for a couple of days, but I won't come back here after I have the baby. They don't want us telling the other girls what it's like. My parents said not to come home with any baby. It's okay, though. I don't want to go back there, little idiotic one-horse town. It's Rochester for me." She started to thump rhythmically against the back of the chair she was in. There was a sharp rap at the door, and it was time to go. Rachel caught Carole by the sleeve before she left. "Hey," she said. "Thanks. It's been real."

A few weeks later, a postcard arrived with an address in Rochester. "Pepper Weaver," it read. "Eight pounds even. Love, Rachel." Her mother left the postcard on the hall table for her. Neither her mother nor her father ever said a word about it.

Chapter Five

JUNE 1965

For graduation, all the girls had to wear white and carry a dozen long-stemmed red roses. Most of them had bought new dresses for the occasion in silk and taffeta and dotted Swiss. Carole had on a white linen dress of her mother's. It sagged off her shoulders and had to be belted tightly to give it some shape. Her mother had buzzed around her, trying to pleat the fabric that bunched under the belt. Once upon a time she'd wanted Carole to lose weight, but now she wasn't so sure. "Aren't you dieting a bit too much?" she'd asked.

"I'm not dieting," Carole had said. And it was true. She just wasn't hungry anymore. She weighed one hundred forty-five pounds, eighteen pounds less than when she'd started to keep her charts. But she was only half used to herself as that girl in the mirror with the flat stomach and thighs that didn't touch. In her mind she was still as big as ever. She might be on the bus or changing for gym, and she'd feel fat again. It was like the way people could still feel their limbs after they'd been severed. Phantom pain, it was called, and that was how it felt. No matter how she looked in front of the mirror, away from it she was still her cumbersome old self, still dragging all that phantom fat around.

They gathered in the gym before the ceremony, shortest in the front and tallest at the end this time. There was a hush when the music started and Miss P, accompanied today by some people from Juilliard, started to bang out "Pomp and Circumstance." It was music to make them cry, and they all did, even though they were glad to leave. Naomi was first in line in a white Chinese dress, tight as a drum. Carole was last, glad to be so thoroughly separated from her on the last walk into assembly. It seemed fitting. She marched across the mezzanine, step touch, step touch, the way they'd rehearsed, and sat through speeches and awards. Carole received the history and Latin prizes. After it was over she went out to lunch with her parents.

She'd had no intention of going to the graduation party. Once she was finished with Spence, that was it in her book. But her mother had been crushed when she heard that, and her father had taken action. It was important to stay out all night with *la crème de la crème,* he'd said. You didn't go to Spence and then miss the graduation party. No, sir. When Carole had pointed out that she had no date, her father had taken care of that too. A dental student named Jeremy Lyon, the son of somebody at the firm.

She'd agreed to go just to keep the peace, and that night she was looking at herself in the mirror. She had on a black matte sheath she'd bought for the occasion. Her mother had been disappointed in the choice. It made Carole look like a pillar, her mother said. Like a black column, which was a description that Carole actually liked. She turned sideways. Her breasts were no longer the wide, heavy things they'd been, bumping each other and in the way, but small and discrete, one from the other. Her old white bras puckered over these new breasts, bras meant for that other girl, that heavier girl, and definitely not right for a dress like this. In truth, she felt separate from her body. She liked becoming thin, feeling loose and disconnected inside her clothes, and it didn't matter what her mother thought.

Jeremy didn't pay attention to what she was wearing either. He was handsome in a soft-looking way, his features still boyish. He grinned at her when she opened the door and said to call him "Jer," but she preferred Jeremy, and he didn't seem to mind. He didn't mind anything.

There was a cocktail party at Amanda's apartment, with highballs served in fancy little glasses. Most of the girls were eighteen, or close to it, and most of them had been drinking for years already anyway. But this was the first time a parent had actually served, and it made them feel sophisticated. After the party, there was a dinner at a big private club on Fifth Avenue that had an enormous circular drive in front. Carole was glad about her black dress, the only black in the whole room, not counting the guys' tuxes. The other girls were in stiff pastel dresses or those op-art prints like Luci Baines Johnson wore.

It was a relief not to see Naomi. They'd hardly spoken for weeks. They were in different sections. Carole was an X, and Naomi was a Y, so they never had classes together. And lining up for assembly, Carole would wait until she knew where Naomi was before getting into line somewhere else. As far as Carole was concerned, the best way to keep quiet about something was not to talk about *anything*. You couldn't screw up that way.

Seeing Naomi made her feel shaky and exposed, as if Naomi herself were the danger. Over the weeks she'd watched Naomi reconnect with some of the other girls in the class. Deirdre and Amanda, the ones she'd been best friends with in third grade or fifth or whenever. They'd all known one another since kindergarten, and now that graduation was coming, they seemed to be closing ranks and getting nostalgic about the years they'd shared. Carole, being a latecomer, went back to being the class loner.

Naomi was still seeing Eddie too. One afternoon Carole was leaving the building, going through the front door out onto Ninety-first Street, and there he was, leaning against a car. He had his arms folded over his chest, his feet crossed so casually, like a model in an ad for expensive clothes. He raised a finger in greeting, but she walked the other way, toward Madison, not stopping until the corner, when she took the chance and looked back. He was still there, still watching.

The next day she sought out Naomi in the senior room. It was always filled with a smoke haze that started at shoulder level and went to the ceiling. To get out of the smoke, you had to lie down. Everybody did. But it was empty today because of midterms. Everybody else was in the library, studying. Carole could see Naomi's orange dress through the milky window in the door. There she was, lying on the floor, faceup, smoking a cigarette.

Carole opened the door, and Naomi looked up. Naomi's looks would serve her well now, Carole's mother had said. But later, when they were in their thirties, Carole would be the beauty. It had depressed Carole, one of those things her mother said to make her buck up that only made her feel worse.

Now she felt awkward and inarticulate. "I saw Eddie waiting for you yesterday," she said, looking down at Naomi. "I saw your sweater at his house."

"So?" Naomi took a long drag on her cigarette.

"I just wanted to know. Were you and Eddie doing it, even before Stowe?"

Naomi shut her eyes. "Oh, honestly, what difference does it make?"

"I want to know."

"Don't go getting all worked up. You make mountains out of molehills."

"So you were."

Naomi let out a big dramatic sigh. "It was like one week before Stowe, okay? Maybe two. That was all. I was talking to him all the time. I was the one who had to do all the work, if you recall."

Carole felt cold. "We were supposed to both—"

Naomi took another deep drag and let it out, like this was all too tedious.

"You let me win too, didn't you? It was all a setup." She hoped to God that wasn't true.

"It was your idea to play that stupid game, not mine."

Carole slumped down on the couch and watched Naomi crush the cigarette into a full ashtray. She knew the answer to the next question before she even asked it. "What about Rita? Did you know she was going to come?"

The two girls glared at each other for an eternity. "Maybe I did. Maybe I didn't," Naomi said.

"What's that supposed to mean?"

"It means, who cares? What's done is done."

Carole let out a whisper. "You knew all along. You and him. You pretended. And all that time on the train I thought— Oh, Nay, none of this would have happened. If I'd known I never would have—"

"Are you saying it's *my* fault? You turn this into my fault, when it was you who killed that woman?"

"Don't say that!"

"It's the truth."

"How can you even *stand* him?"

The door flew open, and Mrs. Danzig stuck her head in. Carole froze. Had she heard what Naomi had just said? She stared them down.

"What?" Carole said.

"You girls can be heard all over the floor."

Carole waited, but Mrs. Danzig said no more. "Keep your voices down." And she shut the door and left.

"Stand him?" Naomi hissed at her. "What would you know about anything? About love, about desire? You with your perfect little apple-pie family, your midwestern milkmaid mother, your dumb furniture. You're such a straight arrow, you know. Everything by the book. And you know something else? It's always me in trouble, but now it's your bloody turn, and you know what? I'm bloody glad. I like being the one not in trouble for once, if you must know. And I like it that you are!"

Carole could hardly believe her ears. Her life perfect? How many times had Naomi ridiculed her family? New Jersey hicks. "But Eddie Lindbaeck, Naomi. He's—" There were no words for what Eddie was.

"He's more fun than you'll ever be," Naomi said. "And anyway, I feel sorry for him. He's a lot like me. His family is a joke too. Just like Daddy and Elayne."

"It doesn't even bother you, does it? That woman died, and it's just business as usual."

"I'm not the one who killed her," Naomi said, glaring at her. "Anyway, that's the whole point, you moron. Business as usual. You're the one who doesn't get it."

Lester Lanin was playing his usual thumpety-thump music. "Come on," Carole said to Jeremy, grabbing his hand, but he said no and they watched from the sidelines, all those preppy boys with their elbows pumping.

When the table of parents dispersed, the real party started over at Shelly's apartment. Her parents were up at their country house. They'd left the refrigerator stocked with sandwiches and sodas and the freezer full of ice cream, as if they thought this was a children's party. But in no time the liquor closet was opened, the bedrooms were full, and drunken boys and girls with zippers open were staggering up and down the hallways. Jeremy took control of the stereo, playing "Satisfaction" at top level, "Wooly Bully" and "My Girl." When the downstairs neighbors complained, Jeremy led Carole into one of the darkened rooms, stumbling over bodies. They fell on a bed and lay there.

Around her were the sounds of people necking. A rustle of taffeta. An occasional zipper, something whispered. It was both private and public in the smoky overheated room. The so-called normal way people lost their virginity.

She lay in the hazy darkness, aware of Jeremy at her side, wondering if he was going to try to kiss her and what she'd do if that happened. She decided she'd slide away from him. She'd go get a glass of water. Something. But he wasn't making a move, so she relaxed. She wasn't exactly asleep but not really awake either. She was startled alert when someone said her name. There was a tiny figure in silhouette in the doorway. "Carole? You here?" Naomi came feeling her way along through the room in the dark.

A light went on. Ten or twelve people were splayed across the room. Kids waking up, their eyes puffy and blinking.

"There you are." Naomi weaved unsteadily and pointed at Carole. "I've been looking for you."

"Turn off the goddamned light," one of the boys said. "And shut up."

"Up yours," Naomi whined.

Kids sat up to see what was going on. "You found her, now hit the light," somebody said.

"What did *I* ever do?" Naomi whispered. "*I never did anything to deserve this. You're the one who did it.*"

"Shut up," the same voice said.

Carole rose to her knees carefully, as though a sudden move could cause Naomi to tell what she knew.

"Jesus," Naomi slurred. "I *helped* you. I carried that stupid woman in the goddamn snow, and you act like I'm the one who's poison?"

Eddie appeared from the hall, the tie to his tux undone, his shirttails out. "Excuse us." He put his jacket around Naomi's shoulders and peered into the room. "Lady's a little drunk."

"Am not!" Naomi twisted away from him.

Carole stood, terrified. Jeremy was fast asleep, snoring lightly, oblivious. If she left, Naomi would follow. She tiptoed down the dimly lit hall to the living room, where more bodies were spread over the floor. Eddie struggled to get Naomi into the jacket. She resisted, whining that she wanted to stay at the party. She wanted to find Carole. "I'm right here," Carole said. "Come on." They got her to the hall, down the elevator, and into one of those big cabs with the jump seats that you can unfold. They all piled in, and Naomi passed out between her and Eddie.

"She almost told," Carole said.

"She's just drunk."

"She almost told. She was about to." Why was he always after Carole to keep her mouth shut when Naomi was the real loose cannon?

"You're the risk, panicking like that."

"I didn't panic."

"Sure you did. You bolted in there." He pawed through Naomi's purse. "I need money."

"You mean for the taxi?"

"What do you have?"

"How can you not have money? Who *are* you, anyway?"

"Keep your voice down," Eddie said. "Or Jesus there is going to kick us out. Nothing a cabbie hates like a stiff."

"Stop, please," she shouted up to the driver. She'd walk the rest of the way. She put her hand on the door handle, ready to make a run for it when he stopped.

"Keep driving," Eddie said. "I'm telling you to keep going." He lunged for the jump seat in front of Carole, pulled it down, and was leaning into her, pushing her back against the seat. "You'll get out of this cab when I say you can."

She tried to slide across to the other door, but he grabbed her wrists. "Don't piss me off," he said. "When are you going to learn?"

"I want to get out and walk."

"You think you've seen me pissed off, don't you? Well, you haven't seen anything."

"Let me out," she said, hoping the driver would help her, but he was ignoring them. She slumped back against the seat and stared out the window.

"Look at me," Eddie said, but she wouldn't. She kept watching the traffic out on the street, the bright storefronts passing by. "You do what I say." She felt a searing pain in her breast, where Eddie socked her with his fist, a pain so intense it took the breath out of her. "When I say."

She ran first thing to the bathroom to see the mark he'd left on her breast in the mirror and touched the angry redness of it lightly. Then she went around turning off the lights her parents had left burning for her and slept away the sultry morning. When she finally got up, she felt groggy. She slipped out of her room. Everything was still and quiet. She found a note from her mother on the dining room table, saying she'd gone to meet Emily for lunch.

Barefoot and still in her nightie, Carole repeated the routine she had begun when she came back from Stowe, padding silently from one darkened room to another, convincing herself, crying, that last night was the last time ever. She no longer needed to go to school. She'd never see those girls again. Never see Eddie or Naomi. One giant step behind her.

She went to her parents' bathroom and opened their prescription bottles. Both were full, a sign that things would go her way. She took three pills from each bottle and put them into the change purse in her room. Then she paced until midafternoon and fell asleep in the afternoon light in the den.

She woke later from sounds in the hall. Her mother and Aunt Emily. "Carole," her mother called out sharply. She didn't respond. There was the shuffle of the women putting down their purses and shopping bags, maybe kicking off their shoes. A low discussion about something, one of them shushing the other. Then Carole's mother called her name again, louder this time. Carole pretended not to hear. Every time Emily came over, it was trouble. Maybe if Carole stayed quiet, Emily would leave. She tiptoed to the door of the den and peered out at them through the crack. They were at the door between the foyer and the living room, looking around and then at each other, waiting for her to answer. Emily shrugged, and the two of them disappeared down the hall that led to her room. Carole came out into the living room and followed. Her mother whispered her name at the door to her room. When there was no answer, they went in. Carole tiptoed farther down the hall behind them and listened from the hall.

Emily was in charge, commenting on the condition of the room, the unmade bed, the clothes strewn over the furniture. "You shouldn't allow this, Patsy," she said. "Mother would be appalled." There were other sounds, muffled. Then Emily told Carole's mother where to look. "Under the mattress. In the desk drawers. Try her pockets. The closet." She tried to remember with her sleepy mind what was in there that they might discover. The first thing that came to mind was the notebook where she wrote her measurements. Pages and pages of calculations. Her waist size, hips, chest, and thighs. Everything. She measured every day and calculated the loss as a percentage of the original. But so what? Her mother wouldn't even know what that was. Even if she did, it wouldn't matter. She'd been after her to lose weight her whole life, it seemed. But that little red change purse . . . She could hear drawers being opened and closed, the Venetian blinds pulled. She opened the door, and it was a few seconds before they noticed her.

Her very formal mother was down on all fours, looking under the bed. The woman who was so religiously careful about never invading her daughter's privacy, who wouldn't ever open one of Carole's letters or listen in on conversations the way other mothers did. It scared her to see her mother like that.

"What are you doing?" Carole asked.

Her mother blanched.

Carole came into the room and took the stack of papers that Emily was holding. They were just some old school papers. "Mom?" she said again. "What are you looking for?"

Her mother held a hand over her mouth as though she was about to be sick.

"Emily?" Carole said.

Emily threw up her hands. "Your mother is worried sick," she said. "It's not just this, is it, Patsy?" Carole's mother didn't speak. "She thinks something is the matter. You're not the girl you were," Emily said.

"People can change," Carole said. But what did they really know? What was this about?

"Your mother said you hardly ever talk to her anymore. Your manners are atrocious. Your grades are in the gutter."

"They are not in the gutter. I won the Latin prize yesterday, in case you hadn't heard. And the History prize." It was true she'd been quiet. She didn't dare talk anymore. She was always afraid of what might come out of her mouth.

"You didn't make the honor roll," Emily said. "You didn't even try."

"Of course I tried. And anyway, so what if my grades went down? It's not like I failed or anything. And what business is it of yours?"

"Your mother is my business."

Still sitting on the floor, her mother looked shell-shocked. She rose to her knees, then sat on the bed. She shook her head.

"Did you tell her all that?" Carole asked.

"You doubt me?" Emily picked Carole's black dress from last night off the back of a chair. "You treat your clothes so badly."

"And you live off other people's misery."

"I beg your pardon."

"Uncle Jack. He ships all that lousy food to people. It makes them sick. It must. It probably kills them."

"Jack's work is none of your affair, young lady."

"And my room is none of yours."

Emily reddened and trembled. "Are you going to ask her, or should I?" She waited a couple of beats for an answer. "Then I will." Emily looked Carole in the eye. "Are you pregnant?" Emily was triumphant.

"Oh, boy."

"It's not funny, young lady," Emily said. "Don't you smile at that."

"Stop it." Her mother was looking up at her for the first time. "Just stop it, both of you," she said.

"Good, Patsy. Finally!" Emily said. "Finally!"

"Leave us alone," she said.

"Not on your life," Emily said. "You can thank me for getting you this far. I'm not leaving now."

Her mother pursed her lips and shut her eyes. She got up and took Emily by the arm. "Leave us now," she said. She saw the surprised Emily to the door, shut it, and turned. She approached Carole. She was so close Carole could see tiny veins of lipstick over her lips. She concentrated on those veins. Her mother was saying something. "We had no business invading your privacy this way." She was shaking, and her voice was small.

Her mother sat down on the bed again, as though her legs wouldn't hold her if she stayed standing. She continued, but without looking at Carole. "I did tell her those things. I did say it started when you came back from that vacation. You didn't get sick." She glanced up at Carole and then away. "You fled, Carole. I know the difference."

Carole braced herself for the tidal wave that was about to break, the moment she'd been dreading.

"I'm not wrong, Carole. I'm your mother, and I know a thing or two. I know what I've seen. You used to come home in the afternoons and sit and talk to me. You used to tell me everything. What happened in school that day. You used to be so disciplined about everything. You used to laugh with us, with your father and me. About silly things." Carole remembered that. It was true. But she'd kept things from her mother then too. "Since you went to Stowe, you just stay in your room all the time. Like you're hiding something from us."

"I won't anymore," she said. "Now that school's out. Now that I don't have homework."

"It's not just that!" her mother said. "I'm not finished. We've never talked about this. You arrived home from Stowe without warning, claiming to have been sick, but in fact you were fine. There was no word all week from Naomi, which was peculiar given the way you two used to call each other daily. Not that your father or I mind, but that's beside the point. Your grades dropped. And things have been disappearing. That little silver cigarette box from the living room. And Miss Mac-Namara said something at the graduation about my forgetting to call one day when you were sick. But you never were. I was humiliated."

"It was—"

"I'm still not finished. You arrive out of the blue at your father's office with questions about pregnant girls." Her mother shook her head. "We don't know what to do. We don't know what's happening to you. To our family."

She had no idea her father'd told her mother. She'd thought it was over and done. Forgotten. "Nobody else has to tell their parents where they are all the time." It was weak, and she knew it.

"It's the *change,* dear. It's all those things together. And this." She opened her hand. There, squeezed small, was the red change purse. "Why?"

"Sometimes I can't sleep."

"You could have asked."

Carole had no answer for that.

"And so many," her mother said. "We couldn't figure out where they were going." She took several quick breaths, her bosom rising and falling, the sound of exhaling sharp in the quiet room. "You weren't planning—" She stopped, unable to say the words.

"Of course not," Carole said. "Oh, no, Mom. Really. I just thought it would be good to have some in case I needed to sleep and couldn't. You know, before exams or something. I didn't mean to—"

Her mother let out a long sigh, lifting her hands to her chest in a gesture of gratitude and relief. "I didn't think so," she said.

Her mother needed more, though, sitting there looking so fragile, so broken. She needed a lie. Carole sat down beside her on the bed. "The thing is, I've been worried about college," she said. She remembered something Deirdre had said rather melodramatically at lunch once, and she repeated it now. "It's such a big step. Spence is over, and I can never go back to these years of my life. Spence has been the best time of my life, and now it's over. And I'm afraid I'll miss home," she explained. "And what if my roommate's awful? I've never had to share a room with anybody. I don't know if I can do it."

Her mother, moist-eyed, looked at her, believing every word. Carole took a breath and kept going, verbatim from what she remembered of what Deirdre had said. And in fact there was some truth in it. There were so many things to worry about. "What if the work is harder? What if the other girls are smarter than me? What if I flunk out? What if I turn out to be the biggest disappointment of your life?"

Chapter Six

Jeremy turned out to be her summer salvation, already vetted by her parents because of where they'd found him. They saw only one side of him, though—how he came to pick her up wearing a coat and tie, sometimes with a little bouquet of flowers or a box of candy. Sometimes it was for Carole and sometimes it was for her mother.

Her father sat in the living room with a pipe in his mouth and the newspaper in his lap, looking like the dad in *Father of the Bride*. He waited for Jeremy to squeak down the hallway in his white bucks to say hello, to sit down opposite and talk about dentistry and the world at large. Her father had things to say about the Vietnam War and about Young People Today, how they no longer respected institutions, and what did Jeremy think about that? Jeremy said it was a shame. Some institutions needed to be questioned, no doubt about that. The Catholic Church, for one. But certainly not this wholesale questioning of the government and the whole military-industrial fabric of the country. Carole's father couldn't have said it better himself.

In fact, Jeremy didn't believe any of this. He was just saying what he knew Carole's father wanted to hear. His heart was really with the war protesters, the self-immolating Buddhists, and the underground. He told her that on their dates. He dug the counterculture, he said, and she'd been impressed. She liked that in him. It confirmed for her that the world was packed with liars and phonies after all. She had company.

Her parents were thrilled about Jeremy. In their minds the trouble they'd all had in the spring had blown over. That trouble with Carole had been only "nerves" over the end of the school year, over the prospect of going off to Vassar, all thanks to what she'd told her mother that day. It was a very quick coming-of-age. With some girls it took years. With Carole, it had happened in a couple of months, to hear them tell it. She'd lost her baby fat and gotten moody for a few weeks. Nobody mentioned the details. Nobody brought up the subject of the sleeping pills, the missed day of school, even the abrupt end to her friendship with Naomi. They were things of the past. Even Emily seemed to believe it.

The first night they went out, Jeremy took her to the Brasserie, where he apologized for falling asleep at the graduation party. He said he couldn't blame her for leaving him there, and he was glad she'd agreed to go out with him now. He told her that he was still asleep the morning after the party when Shelly's parents came home. By that time everyone else had left, and Shelly herself must have been asleep in her own bed. The bedroom he found himself in was the parents' bedroom, he explained with a laugh. They'd planned to come back early all along to check up on things, sneaky petes that they were, and there he was.

Jeremy had a broad nose with a galaxy of tiny pores and dark eyes under heavy brows. When he talked, he tipped his head down and looked up bashfully. He was always smiling, no matter what. "I got blamed for the whole thing," he said.

"What whole thing?"

"The place. It was pretty wrecked. Broken glass, spilled stuff on the carpets. The mother went berserk. I felt bad, sure. But I didn't do any of that, and I told them so. I said I came alone, that I was one of the extra guys, so I wouldn't get you in trouble. They reamed me out anyway. That woman swears like a sailor. They let the daughter sleep right through it all."

"Mrs. Taylor swears?"

"Oh, yeah," Jeremy said.

Carole used to think the world was orderly, everything was known by all, and that missteps were always noticed, especially her own. But life kept proving differently. Jeremy didn't know about Naomi screaming in the darkened room that night. He didn't know Carole had left not because of him but because she had been afraid of what he might find out. The Taylors hadn't known the kind of party Shelly planned to have, although everybody else had. When they found out, it didn't matter to them who had made the mess. They'd punished the sleeping boy in their bed when he'd had less to do with it than anyone. Apparently the truth went every which way. Apparently the truth was nothing special. She started to laugh about it all, and Jeremy joined in even without knowing what was so funny.

After dinner, he asked where she wanted to go. "Fort Tryon Park," she said.

Jeremy looked up at her with a smirk. "Really?"

"Sure. The Cloisters. I've never been."

"Now?" He dug in his pockets to see what change he had.

She'd meant sometime. But the challenge in his voice was too good to pass up. "Sure," she said. It made her feel a new kind of power to say yes and see if he'd really do it. "Now." The thought of heading off to someplace new so late in the evening made the night seem to stretch endlessly away, with nothing—no parents, no future—on the other side.

It was close to ten when they got off the express A train to 190th Street. Everything was closed, locked up tight, but they walked around the park in the dark. An unlit road took them through a parking lot and past a darkened cafeteria. They went farther along in the semidarkness, scrambling up the lawn toward the tower, walking beside the rampants and then back to the lookout at Fort Tryon. Down below were barges and tugs lit like little Christmas trees on the Hudson River. Jeremy was leaning on the wall, staring at New Jersey.

"You know what?"

"What?"

"Don't hate me."

"Why would I hate you?"

"Just don't." He was concentrating fiercely on the river below them.

"God, Jeremy. I don't hate you, I *like* you," she said.

"I like you too," he said, not taking his eyes from the scene below. In the movies, this was when he was supposed to kiss her. But he was so brooding and pulled into himself that she thought he might not. Even so, the very idea of kissing a boy, any boy, even Jeremy, whom she liked, made her sweat and worry. She pulled away protectively from him and began to walk back the way they'd come. She needed to be free of the feel of his body beside her, the way it reminded her of Eddie's and Rita's naked bodies on her skin, their sweaty hands, the feel of Rita's breast on her cheek and the crush of Eddie's weight.

Jeremy had always wanted to ride all 230 miles of the New York subway lines, and he couldn't believe his good fortune that Carole would do it with him. For her part, Carole didn't care that much about the subway, but it was fun to have a project, fun to be with someone who wrote down numbers and kept records the way she did with her weight, which was down to 142 and holding. There were parts of the city she could see with Jeremy that she'd been forbidden to see since she moved to New York. The whole city had been pretty much off-limits, since she was only allowed to travel between Ninety-first Street and Forty-second Street and only in daylight. Everything she needed to see and do was within those blocks and within those times, her father had said. But there was so much out there. There was Coney Island and Harlem. There was the Bowery and Greenwich Village, places she'd read about. Yankee Stadium and 125th Street.

They went everywhere. Dinner first and then the subways, although as time wore on, they skipped going out to dinner and went right down into the mouth of the Fifty-ninth Street station. She loved the hot summer dankness down there, the smell of grime and urine. They bought handfuls of stale peanuts and little miniature boxes of Chiclets from vending machines on the support pillars. They ate candy bars for dinner. They hardly talked to each other, which was okay too. Most of the time Carole just felt free. She would stand before the subway map, shut her eyes, and jab a finger somewhere. Jeremy would check his notes to see if they'd already done it, and if not, off they'd go. Whatever she wanted to do, he would do it too. By early July they'd done every mile of every line. "But we haven't been stopping," Carole said, not wanting it to end. "We've only ridden." He was more than willing to stop everywhere, and she had the sense that he too was a refugee from home, killing time until dental school started again in the fall.

They stayed out later and later, getting off at every stop. When she came in, at two or even three in the morning, her parents would be in bed and the lights would be out. But she sensed that they'd been waiting for her, that they'd turned out the lights and fled to their bedroom only moments before she came in, alerted by the sound of the elevator. Her parents the mice.

Nothing was ever said in the clear light of day about the lateness of her nights with Jeremy Lyon. They'd have been troubled if they'd known where she was going, so she took the offensive, offering freely the names of places they'd gone for dinner and what she'd had, lies her parents eagerly believed. And when it seemed that they didn't believe something, she tilted her head and looked at them in a way that said: You wouldn't understand. It was their vulnerability, and she knew it. Particularly her mother's, this sense that Carole had already journeyed beyond them. Carole tried not to use the tactic too often because afterward she felt bad. But if it helped to secure the brittle distance, then it was of value.

What she loved from her nights with Jeremy was the excitement of going up the subway stairs in a new place, the way her heart raced not knowing what they'd find. It might be a neighborhood of people and vendors and light or a wasteland of asphalt and tenement houses. Her father would have a fit if he knew.

Early one morning in late July they were sitting in a subway in Brooklyn. The car was empty except for the two of them. She'd been thinking a lot about the summer and about Jeremy and how easy it was to be his friend. How at first she'd gone with him to get away from home, and now it was just so natural. But something kept nagging at her about him. "Why did you think I'd hate you?" she asked him. "Remember? That night at the Cloisters you said, 'Don't hate me.'" She'd thought he was going to say that he thought everybody hated him or his parents did or maybe that he'd done something awful. That really was what she hoped it was.

"Because I'm not going to put the moves on you," he said, raising his voice over the noise.

"Oh." That was a surprise. Not that he wouldn't, but that he was saying it, that that was his big secret. "Okay," she said. "But I don't *hate* you." Anyway, by now she didn't even expect him to. She already knew he wouldn't. Somehow.

Jeremy faced her and said, "Because I'm not like other guys you've gone out with."

For a moment she thought he knew about Eddie, but one look told her no. It was something else. "Well, sure," she said. "You're already finished with college and going to be a dentist." She was deliberately missing the point, trying to steer him away from saying whatever it was because he was scaring her a little.

"Listen to me. I like guys." Now he was looking at her, his large dark eyes unblinking.

"You mean—"

"Of course I mean." He turned abruptly, staring out the train window into darkness, his misery plain even from behind.

She didn't know what to say.

Jeremy swung back. "See? You hate me."

"No!" From the furious look on his face, she would have thought he was the one who hated her. But she knew he didn't. He needed something from her. She didn't know what it was, but the moment was now. "No," she said again. "Please don't think that, Jeremy. I don't hate you."

He seemed to deflate. "I've never told anybody." He laughed, but his eyes were tearing up.

She strained to think of what she could say or do for him, something to hold out that would make him feel better. People needed that much. They needed comfort. She imagined if she had been the one to tell her secret to him and not the other way around. What would she need to hear? She reached up and stroked his cheek as gently as her fingers knew how. "You're not alone," she said, meaning herself. "You'll be okay."

He gave her a smile filled with disbelief. "Not alone?" Like it was the dumbest thing a person could say. "If my dad finds out, he'll kill me." His chin trembled, and not from the moving train, but because he might cry, this grown man beside her. "You don't understand," he said, his look full of need.

"I think I do," she said. "But there are worse things, Jeremy. Much worse." She was thinking that she could make his anguish disappear with her own. All she had to do was tell him about Rita and he'd be home free, his worry insignificant.

"Like what?" he said, smiling with new hope. "Name one."

She looked down into her lap, at her hands. "It's not like you *killed* somebody or anything," she said as steadily as she could, raising her voice to make sure he heard. And then she waited. When he didn't say anything, she looked up into his face, thinking now was her turn to face the music, but he was looking blankly, incredulously, at her.

"Well, of course not," he said, annoyance slipping into his voice at how far off the mark a person could be. "Jesus, Carole. I didn't push anybody over a cliff. It's not like that. You don't understand, and I shouldn't have told you." He sighed miserably. "But it's not your fault. I don't blame you for trying." She looked back at her hands, haunted by how close she'd just come, what she'd almost done. "Promise you won't tell anybody, please, Carole. Please." He took her hand and shook it as if to wake her up. "Don't tell your parents. You promise?" His words made her shrivel inside.

"No," she said. "Of course not. Of course I won't."

On a night in August so hot the heels of her shoes stuck to the pavement, she and Jeremy were on their way to Castle Clinton at the lower tip of Manhattan. They hadn't spoken again about what he had said. He'd called her again the next day. She hadn't been sure he would. And they'd gone train riding again, as if nothing had ever happened. That was how it was with certain secrets. So big you could only mention them once.

The subway doors opened, and a rush of skinny people came in, filling up the train with their tie-dye, batik, and minis. They were like clowns at the circus, the way they plopped themselves in among the other passengers and struck up conversations. Carole and Jeremy had seats smack in the middle of the train, and four people surrounded them right away—two women in expensive hip-hugger pants and hair to their waist, one of the men in a buckskin vest and leather fedora.

They were talking about a party—inviting everyone on the train to it. In the Village someplace. Great drugs, the woman cooed to Jeremy. Andy Warhol would be there.

They passed a bottle of vodka around and offered it to Carole, who shook her head. One of the men turned and started speaking fractured Spanish to two young women on the same bench. The women snapped angrily at him, and he backed away.

"We're going to Battery Park," Jeremy said, as though these people were owed an explanation. She imagined it was the way he must have felt with Shelly's parents. "But I guess we could—"

"Let's go," she said. "Let's just see." She asked the man, "Andy Warhol? Honest?"

"Maybe," the woman said. "Edie Sedgwick for sure."

"Who's that?" Jeremy whispered to her.

"Rich girl drug addict," Carole said. She had read it in the gossip columns.

"Oh," Jeremy said. "Of course."

"We'll just look," Carole said. "See what's happening. I've never been to one of these things."

They got out at Bleecker Street, and Jeremy noted it on his pad. A few other people from the subway came too—people like them, dressed in regular street clothes instead of weird getups. Now that they'd been recruited, nobody seemed to care if they came or not. They were more caught up in talking with one another and whacking one another on the behind and screaming. They came to a warehouse-looking place, somebody rang a buzzer, and the ground opened up. It was one of those dumbwaiter contraptions, with bells ringing to warn pedestrians about the sudden hole opening up in the sidewalk. A platform rose, and they all stepped on it and went down to the basement level, the hatch closing back over them. It smelled foul down there, the stench of something rotting. The light was low as they were rushed past a furnace and whole rooms full of metal garbage pails. Then a narrow staircase up four or maybe five flights of stairs. When the door finally opened, it was another world. Music so loud Carole could feel it in her teeth. Women were standing on platforms, naked except for G-strings, their bodies snapping like whips. The light was blue and white, streaking across the moving crowd. She held onto the back of Jeremy's shirt as they made their way through. "You okay with this?" he screamed at her.

"Sure," she screamed back. "You?"

He started to dance. They must not have danced at graduation, or she would have remembered this, the snaky way he moved his body, his eyes shut tight. He slid out of her view, hidden by the crowd, then reappeared, turned, and wrapped his arms around her, pulling her this way and that until they were at the edge of the crowd against a wall, where someone was screening pornographic movies. "Oh, man," Jeremy said, staring up. Carole watched for several moments. They were too close to see much, the images too big to comprehend. "I'm going to find a bathroom," she said. Jeremy nodded without taking his eyes from the screen.

There was a row of urinals hidden behind a wall of corrugated green fiberglass, and some toilets separated into stalls but without doors. At the far end, a small woman was standing with her back to Carole. She was barefoot, her nylons in shreds at her ankles, holding her shoes. Carole ducked into one of the stalls. When she came out, the woman was gone.

And so was Jeremy. The movies had stopped playing on the wall, and a mob of people had moved into the space where he had been. She looked out over the crowd of bobbing heads, cut by flashing lights. The room went black for several seconds, then the lights came up so bright she could hardly see. She started moving through the crowd. It was like being invisible. Nobody looked at her or moved out of her way. There had to be hundreds of people, and she wondered, with a flicker of fear, if she'd find Jeremy again.

"I thought that was you." The voice was loud, almost yelling, at her side. She looked down. "Naomi?" How was it possible? "What are you doing here?" Had she followed them? Was she being tricked? She recognized the clothes, the shoes she was carrying. Naomi had been the person in the bathroom. What was going on?

Naomi fluttered her hands and pointed somewhere and said something about Elayne. "But what are *you* doing here?"

"We got invited by people on the subway," Carole shouted, then wished she hadn't. It sounded pathetic.

"We?" Naomi was drunk, weaving slightly.

"Jeremy and me."

Naomi looked unsteadily out at the crowd. "I'm engaged," she said. She waved her hand in Carole's face, a giant diamond on her finger. "Baxter Oliver." She laughed.

Carole didn't even know the name. "Who?"

"Columbia Law. I met him on the bus." She had to shout over the music. "Love at first sight. For him anyway, and that's what's important." She sobered up. "Elayne practically wet her pants when I told her. She's been dreaming of the day I get lost ever since she married Daddy. She's doing everything in her power to make sure it goes through. That's why we're here. Elayne wants to impress Bax. She got us invited to this thing because Bax likes art. Some Warhol underling she knows from TV. She thinks these things are about art. Elayne's such a loser."

"Is he here?"

"Somewhere, yeah. Where's yours?"

Carole looked around the room for Jeremy, remembering the way he was dancing, not willing to have Naomi see that and make snide comments. She shrugged. "I was looking for him," she said. Naomi would make mincemeat of him.

"What about Eddie?" Carole had to ask.

"He had an audition for this new play. *Man of La Mancha.* Didn't get asked back. Happens all the time, poor guy." Naomi had to scream at her to be heard.

"I mean, do you see him anymore?"

Naomi wrinkled her nose. "Eddie doesn't see how my being married will be a problem." She looked around. "He might even be here," she said, losing her balance, spilling her drink. "He gets off on that. Being places where me and Bax are. Turns him on."

Carole quickly scanned the people around them, but the crowd was thick. Faces upon faces. Eddie could be anywhere. He could be watching at that moment. She had to find Jeremy and get out of this place. "I better go find my date," she screamed over the music.

She circled the outside of the room. Near the bathrooms, she caught a glimpse of Jeremy and drew closer. He was dancing with two men, gracefully, not touching, moving in that odd way, with his eyes shut and a smile on his face. He dipped and swooped like a child imitating birds, carried away. After a time he opened his eyes and saw her there. He gave her a private smile, and she pointed to her wrist. Mouthed the words, *Can we go?*

He snaked over to where she was. "Why the hurry?"

"There's somebody here I don't want to talk to," she said.

It took a while to find their way out of the building, and then Jeremy wanted to finish what they had started out to do—down to Castle Clinton and the Emma Lazarus Memorial and then to Essex and Delancey Streets and Herald Square. He didn't talk about the party or about dancing with the two men. He went back to writing the places they went to in his little book.

By the time she got home, it was almost light, the latest she'd ever stayed out. Jeremy waited with her until the night doorman let her in.

When she got upstairs, the apartment was dark and quiet. She paused inside the door and heard nothing. Tonight there wasn't even that ghost of her parents scurrying away. They must have gone to bed long ago, no longer interested in when she came in because in only a week she'd be gone. Still, she tiptoed down the hall, feeling her way along the walls. As she was about to turn left down the hall to her bedroom, she heard her father's voice from the living room. "Is that you?"

The living room was dark. She couldn't see him, but she knew where he was from the sound of his breathing, coarse and irregular now that he'd been wakened. "Where have you been all night?"

"Tavern on the Green," she said quickly, regretting it instantly because this was a restaurant he knew.

"No, you haven't."

"Yes, I was," she said.

"Not all this time. I had to call Jeremy's mother," he said. "Vulgar woman, his mother. I had no idea." She could barely see him, but, oh, the voice. "Do you know what it is to be humiliated? To have to ask the wife of an associate where my own daughter is?"

He turned on the light beside the chair. He was still dressed in his suit and tie, as if he'd just gotten home from the office. "The wife of an associate?" His hands shook in his lap. He got to his feet, looming over her. "Well?" he bellowed. "What do you have to say for yourself?"

"We went to a party."

"A party," he thundered. "At this hour? What party? Where?"

"Everybody goes. All the girls." It had worked before, this mystique about all the girls at the Spence School.

"I asked you where. I asked you what party. Whose party?" Her father was coming closer to her.

"Naomi's engaged to this guy. Baxter, that's his first name. I forget the last. It was down in the Village in this old warehouse." The lie had enough truth to sound convincing.

"I don't believe you."

"Well, it's true." If he wouldn't believe it, she would. "Andy Warhol was there. Edie Sedgwick."

"Who in the name of Christ are they?"

"Famous people."

Her father bellowed at her, "Do you know what she said?"

"What who said?"

"That boy's mother. 'Oh, Jesus, Conrad, I thought you knew.'" He did a shockingly cruel imitation of Jeremy's mother. "'It's a different world today. What with the pill and all.'" He got to his feet, looming over her. "Oh, Jesus?" he thundered at her. "What with the pill and all? Well?" he bellowed. "What do you have to say for yourself?"

Until right then she had thought Jeremy was telling his parents the same thing she was telling hers, making up vague stories about restaurants and nightclubs. But all along he'd been using her to reassure them that he was a regular guy. That Jeremy had told his parents they were sleeping together came as a big shock.

"I'm waiting for an answer." Her father wasn't as loud now. "Well?"

Everything cracked like glass inside her. She felt the tears well up and spill over. She began to sob for the first time since that night, but he wasn't moved. "Out until all hours with no explanation. We never know where you are. I had to learn from that woman that you and her son are—that you're taking the pill—"

"But I'm not—"

Before she had the chance to see it coming, the flat of his palm hit her so hard across her cheek, she sank to her knees on the carpet. He was standing over her, breathing loudly. She dared not move but stayed crouched where she fell, studying the dark pattern in the Oriental rug, a tufted blue line snaking through the burgundy.

She heard him get his breathing under control, the space between breaths lengthen. "I can explain," she said.

"There's nothing to explain. We'll have no more of this." He clicked off the light and left her alone in the now-dark room. She stayed where she was, his accusation ringing in her ears.

"The plum," he'd once said, "is the truth people tell at a point when they think they have no other alternative. It comes after skillful questioning by an attorney, a building, if you will, of questions or statements, one upon the other so that the person thinks you already know the truth and simply blurts it out in corroboration."

All spring, that was what hadn't ever made sense. He could so easily have done that. He could have gotten the truth out of her in minutes if he'd wanted to, the questions shooting out like bullets about what had happened in Stowe. *Think back. What did you eat? What was the first symptom? Did you vomit? What was in it?* He could have found out in a matter of seconds that it wasn't the food. Wasn't even diarrhea. *So then why DID you come home so soon?* And then the rest. *Why isn't Naomi home? What happened when you got up there? Where did you sleep? What did you do that night? Tell me about the other girls and boys.* He could have broken the night in Stowe into tiny fragments, found the flaws in her story, and put everything together in minutes. But he hadn't ever done that.

He hadn't wanted to know.

Chapter Seven

They drove to Poughkeepsie on a mild day. Carole sat in the back-seat, studying their heads. Her mother's hair was pulled into a shiny bun coiffed for the occasion with a royal-blue clip-on hat. There would be other parents there, people her mother needed to look her best for. Her father had a full head of hair at sixty. He had been forty-four when she was born, much older than most people's fathers, so he was sixty now. Or sixty-one. Her mother was only forty.

She liked the miles going by and wished she'd applied to another school instead of Vassar. Carleton College in Minnesota or even Stanford. It would have been good to have more miles separating her from her family and from that night in Stowe, which were, by now, sort of the same thing. The whole spring was behind her, though, and she thought of this trip as her escape from the fishbowl, as her real departure from all of it. She would never return to Spence. She would never again see Eddie or Naomi. Little by little, she would become free, like the coating on a grain of sand. That's what they did to make pearls. They dropped a grain of sand into an oyster. The irritation made the oyster secrete something that coated the grain so it wouldn't hurt so much. This went on for year after year until all those secretions

125

hardened into a pearl, and the original grain of sand was gone, never to be seen again. It was like amnesia. The thought of that pearl helped her to relax in the backseat and watch the scenery go by. Leaving home, more for good than any of them knew.

The day after the scene in the living room, her father had called her from work and told her not to see Jeremy anymore. That had been okay with her, though. Jeremy had told his mother she was on the pill, that they were doing it. Everybody lied to protect themselves, even people you liked. Sometimes they had to sacrifice somebody else, and she'd been it.

Her roommate's name was Josie. She was from Framingham, Massachusetts, and she reminded Carole of the girl from the Double Hearth that night, the girl with the chapped shins. She had the same neat pageboy, the same upper-crust accent. And she was immaculate in her madras Bermuda shorts, her sleeveless cotton blouse with the circle pin. Everything was neatly lined up on top of her dresser, the drawers full of folded Shetland sweaters, her closet an orderly row of plaid skirts. Josie had taken the best of everything by the time Carole and her mother got there, the larger dresser, the bed near the window, the larger closet. Carole had the sense that she was moving into bits of the room, here and there, fitting her belongings in around Josie's, and she stood there looking around. They'd said in the freshman letter to wait until your roommate got there so you could plan the room together, but Josie hadn't bothered.

Oblivious, her mother dove right in, asking where Josie was from and which school she had attended. "Farmington" came the answer and her mother gushed. Jackie Kennedy's school. Her mother remembered exactly which girls had abandoned Spence for Farmington, and she rattled all of them off, and of course Josie knew them all. Carole caught a glimpse of herself in Josie's full-length mirror. A wild girl with her frizzy blond hair, her beige cutoff jeans, and a black poor-boy sweater. Carole ran her hand over the tops of the two desks, then hoisted a suitcase onto the newer one, the one without the pen carvings on the top, and began opening the desk drawers.

"Oh, that one's my desk," Josie said. "Next to my bed."

Carole stared at her, deciding what to do.

Josie chattered on to Carole's mother about boarding school and how different this was for her, even though she'd been living away from home for years. It was as though she'd barely registered the impasse with Carole and everything was hunky-dory, but Carole could tell she knew exactly what she was doing.

"This is the desk I want," Carole said.

"Carole, *dear*," her mother said, nervously adjusting her hat, and then to Josie, "I'm sure she doesn't mean that."

Carole was struck by how timid her mother could be. How submissive in certain situations. Her mother was about to let Josie get away with this. She was about to let her commandeer the better half of the room just to keep the peace, even if it meant Carole, her own daughter, had to live with less. Carole understood her mother was just trying to get through the moment without conflict. But Josie was taking advantage. "Mother," Carole said. "She already has the better part of the room, the part with the windows and the sun. The least I can get is the desk without pen marks."

"Oh, but I'm sure she didn't mean—" her mother said. "We were a little late."

"I was only trying to be helpful," Josie said, looking as though her feelings were hurt. Fat chance, Carole thought. "To get organized so we wouldn't both be unpacking at once." Josie appealed to Carole's mother.

"I want that desk."

"Oh, for heaven's sake then." Josie opened the desk drawers and dumped out the contents on her bed.

They had an Indian summer that year, steamy and sultry long into September. Starting the first weekend, there were mixers with boys from Yale and Williams and Amherst. Carole was a fish out of water at them. She didn't know how to make small talk, how to run on at the mouth the way Josie did, flirting and giggling and saying almost nothing. Even so, boys sought Carole out. She found them smooth and confusing, so sure of themselves. And they drank a lot. There was almost always a bottle of liquor in the car or a flask in somebody's coat pocket. She didn't dare. She remembered what Eddie had said: *You were pretty gone on the scotch.* She'd vowed never to drink again. When one of the boys called her, she wouldn't take the call. Not yet. She wasn't ready for anything having to do with boys or liquor or anything else. Josie thought she was such a piece of work. *He's a Yalie! Are you crazy?*

She spent more and more time in the library reading newspapers. It had become a habit back in New York to scan the *New York Times* every morning and the *Herald Tribune* every afternoon, skipping the big stories up front and concentrating on the small items at the back, where there might be news of a body found, a murder investigation. But always there was nothing. Now she had so many more papers available, and she scanned them all—the ones from Burlington and Manchester and Boston.

She had almost nothing to do with Josie, who would spend hours lolling around the room with her friends, talking about boys and what the boys' fathers did for a living and where they lived and how rich they were or weren't and how you could tell. Josie said with great seriousness that she deserved to be married to somebody rich because she knew she'd be good at it, and Carole had said in disgust, "Everybody's good at being rich. It's poverty that's hard." Josie looked at the others and rolled her eyes. They hated Carole. At Spence they hadn't been friendly, but she was sure they hadn't hated her. Not like this.

They were almost never in the room at the same time. If Josie was studying at her desk, Carole went to the library. If Josie had her friends in the room, Carole headed outside. When Josie would be out, which was most weekend nights, Carole had the room to herself and lay on her bed, listening to the radio or reading. Going to Vassar was supposed to have been such a big deal, all those years with this as the endpoint. But how had she even known about Vassar? Had it ever been her idea? No. It was her mother's. Or maybe her father's. She couldn't even remember, but everything had pointed to Vassar, and now she was here and she couldn't see why. A few times she put in some effort. She memorized facts about the development of Western civilization and repeated them on the exam and got an A. But that didn't last. She'd lost her ability to concentrate. What's more, other parts of her life, when she thought back, were a lot better. She remembered Rachel in particular, who had been so straightforward, who always meant what she said. Carole smiled privately when she thought about the nuns and how it must have looked, all of them waltzing with those pregnant girls.

Sometimes she whiled away the afternoon at the Star Luncheonette in downtown Poughkeepsie, listening to people talking at the counter. Just ordinary conversations. A couple of pregnant women talking about how much weight they'd gained. A man trying to decide whether to put the snow tires on this week or wait until it snowed. Just normal life. Comfortable. She preferred that to school, and she was attracted by the order of the place, how it seemed all hit-or-miss the first time she went in, but then little by little she saw that everything, right down to the last fork, had a place and that there was a routine for everything. A few times, when the waitresses were shorthanded, she even helped out behind the counter in exchange for a cup of coffee. She loved it. She'd watched so much that she knew all the routines—how the waitresses filled the sugar, ketchup, and mustard containers when business slacked off. How they were always cutting up lemons and tomatoes and onions or filling the spare coffee urns so they'd be ready. How sixty percent of what they did was preparation, and only forty percent was serving the customers. It was a revelation. It took way more time to be ready than it did to do the actual work.

She skipped classes and didn't join any of the organizations at Vassar. But when her parents called, she had to say something, and it was Josie's life that Carole described to them. She told them she'd met a

129

boy from Princeton. She described the boy Josie had met at a mixer whose name was Neal, who was tall and redheaded, the son of a professor at Rutgers.

Her parents were thrilled, and over the months, Carole filled them in on all the details. She paraphrased letters that Neal had sent to Josie. She described the little gifts in Josie's top drawer—the little heart-shaped pin, the scarab bracelet.

One cold afternoon Josie piled into the room, still in her winter coat. A long camel-hair job with a belt slung low in back. "Guy downstairs for you," she said. "I told him I'd get you. He said you'd know."

"Know what?"

Josie put her hands on her hips. "I don't know what. Mrs. Beckley said there was a visitor for you and would I please give you the message. The guy was standing right there, and I couldn't say no. Very cute guy. And he just says 'She'll know who it is.'"

"Well, I don't."

"So go down and find out!"

"No," Carole said.

"What *is* your problem?" Josie went back down, slamming the door behind her, and came back to the room a few minutes later. "He says he met you in Stowe." Josie was standing, hands on her hips. "You're probably right. He's got the wrong girl. He's gorgeous."

Eddie sat cross-legged in a striped armchair in the receiving room. He watched her cross the room, looking her up and down as she approached. His hair was golden and he was tanned, like he'd been away. Seeing him, she felt that familiar loathing and fear again. Fear that something had happened, that the body had been found, that she'd been traced to the motel. Loathing for the man who looked up at her with those lizard eyes and said, "Long time no see."

"What do you want?"

"Let's go outside."

"What do you want?"

Josie came down with her friend Fiona, and the two of them fell giggling onto a sofa nearby.

"Okay," she said. It wasn't safe. "Let's go."

Eddie's car was parked on the drive. A blue station wagon that surely belonged to somebody else. He didn't own anything himself. Maybe not even the clothes. "Hotchkiss looks like this," he said, looking around.

"What do you want?" she said for the third time, sitting in the passenger side of the car, watching the windows start to fog.

"To see you," he said. "You're looking good. Really. I'm not just saying that."

"I don't care what you think."

He rested an arm on the back of the seat and slid a few inches closer while she, in response, pressed herself back against the door. In the late-afternoon light his face was only light and shadow. The neat eyebrows, the planes of his cheeks under high cheekbones, his pointed chin. "Naomi got married, the little bitch," he said. "She'll never be happy with him. Have you seen him? He looks like David Eisenhower. Like the class president everywhere I ever went to school. But he must be loaded. If Naomi married him, he's gotta be rich. She invited me to the wedding." He studied her face. "Were you invited?"

"You know I wasn't," she said.

"Everything she ever said about that father and stepmother was all true. You'd have thought it was that Elayne's wedding. She comes sashaying down the aisle. Mother of the bride in a red sequined dress. Couldn't take my eyes off her. And then Naomi in this little slinky number. Cute but no contest."

She didn't know where this was going. She would have to wait him out. And now Josie was going to start asking her questions about him. She had managed to contain her life in a neat package, and he showed up and poked a hole in it.

"Look, Eddie," she said. "I don't know why you're here, but the whole deal was for us to lay low. And stay away from each other. Why do you keep coming around? Just leave me alone, will you? I mean, why can't you? Naomi's married. I'm at school. And you're—I don't know, an actor."

131

"Not stay away from each other," he said. "I never said that. Keep our mouths shut. That's all." He leaned closer and touched her hair. "I like knowing what you're doing. Where you are. It's nice you're in college. I like that. Just a regular girl doing what girls do." She pulled away, out of his range. "You can't tell me you don't know what I mean." He let his hand fall to the seat. "You feel it too, I know you do, you have to. You and Naomi and me, but you and me most of all because she died right there with us, you know? We were all touching each other, and one of us dies. We're fucking, and she dies. Alive one second, dead the next. Jesus, Carole. Christ. It just blows me away every time."

"You make it sound—"

He leaned toward her and purred the words. "Yes, I do." Carole put out her hand to keep him from coming closer. "Nobody's asking any questions. Nobody even knows."

"Are you sure?" she said. She hadn't known how badly she wanted to hear that. "Nobody ever found her?"

"Nope," Eddie said. "Or if they did, they never put it together, what happened. They never connected us."

"I still don't know how it happened," she said. "I mean, I know it did happen. I've gone over it a zillion times in my mind, but I can't remember. I think I should remember. Shouldn't I?"

"You were smashed."

She remembered getting pushed off the bed, the slippery, awful way she kept sliding off the side to the floor, how cold she felt. "She said to get up on the bed, and I thought she meant up near the headboard, but now I don't know. Maybe she meant on her other side, but once I was there I didn't dare get off or do anything because you were so pissed, Eddie, so I stayed up there, but it was hard to keep my balance, and that's all I really remember." At least all she remembered in sequence—after that, it was all a blur. "I just wanted it to stop."

"I was pissed? I don't think so. You were the pissed-off one. You came at me. You lunged at her and me."

"No."

"She never invited you up on the bed. She would never."

This always happened. The way what she knew for a fact could slip right out through her fingers. "She was breathing funny, remember? Kind of rasping. Do you remember that?"

"Nah," he said. "She was fine."

"No. I remember that."

He thought for a few seconds. "Maybe that was after you did it," he said. "After you broke her neck."

She buried her face in her hands. "I think it was earlier."

"So you broke it later."

"I must have," she said.

"I saw you do it." Eddie smiled at her.

She pressed herself hard against the car door at his words. "Please shut up," she said.

"I didn't tell you that before, did I? How I saw what you did. It's how I know. Here you go over it a zillion times like you say, but you block out the main event. I saw what you did, Carole." Eddie whistled. "You must have been drunker than I thought."

She turned her face and looked out the car window across the drive to the lit doorway of her dorm, where a group of girls was pushing their way inside, all dressed in camel-hair coats and striped scarves. Girls without any problems. He must be right about what she'd done. She thought she remembered a pang of jealousy, anger that Rita had ruined their night. She remembered the feel of Rita's head, her hair, damp with sweat. She curled her hands in her lap. She didn't want him to say anything else. "Why did you come up here?" she said.

"I need a little bit of money."

"I don't have any money." She felt wary.

"Yes, you do," he said.

"I don't." She was thinking of her wallet upstairs. Maybe seven or eight dollars, that was all.

"You've got access to Daddy's money, right? Tuition money? You could spare a little bit."

"How did you know that?"

Eddie grinned. "How do you think?" He examined his finger-nails, then looked up at her again.

"Naomi told you that?" She must have. She'd told him everything else.

"So?" he said.

"No." It wasn't even her money. "Why don't you get a job, Eddie? Support yourself." She thought about all those schools. "What about *your* father? He must have money. If I give you money, I won't be able to pay for tuition, and they'll wonder where it all went."

"Make something up," he said.

"Your mother then. Get it from her. There must be somebody else besides me."

"You are so fucking ignorant," he said. She remembered how his mood had shifted exactly this way in the motel, how he could be talking pretty calmly and then turn ugly. "My mother," he said slowly. Carole could feel his breath on her face. Feel the cold of the glass against the back of her head. "Is nothing but a stupid cow."

She looked at the door to the dorm again. She wanted so badly to get out of the car, to go back inside, to feel safe. "You don't need to tell me about her," she said. "If you don't want to." She didn't want to know.

"Hell, no," he said. "You brought it up. You're entitled. My mother makes about five grand a year renting apartments. We're not talking Pease and Elliman here. We're talking crap. We're talking roaches. We're talking Brooklyn and Queens. Christ. She gives me nothing, not that that's the way it could have been if she'd just had the smarts to use the money Lindbaeck sent her for my education, but oh, no, she gets all up on her bandstand about how the money's for my education. Not for groceries, not rent, not clothes. Nothing but tu-ition and books." He laughed, throwing his head back. "He'd never have found out because he didn't give a flying fuck. He never even vis-ited. He moved back to Norway after I was born, and I never saw him again. And we're talking big-ticket schools, too. Collegiate, Hotchkiss, Kimball Union, a couple of colleges. For that we had to live in a walk-down in Germantown. I figured, Why not make the old man pay if that's what his game was? So I got myself expelled. They don't refund the money when you get kicked out, you know."

"You got expelled on purpose?" Up to now she'd assumed it had been recklessness and bad luck.

"Why not?"

She was silent. The information made him seem so much worse, so much more dangerous. All along, Carole had thought he was connected to something else, something big enough to absorb him. A family somewhere who'd gotten disgusted with him perhaps, but still a family. Still a connection he'd be afraid to blow. But there wasn't anybody. He was untethered, with no one to answer to. Except me, she thought.

"What if I don't give you money?" she asked him.

He paused. "But you will," he said. "You don't really have a choice."

She had to think fast. "There's hardly anything in the account right now. They'll fund it for second semester, though."

Eddie reached over to her, frightening her. "Hey," he said. "Relax."

"What are you doing?" she said as he reached again. "Don't touch me." She could hardly breathe.

"I just remembered something I wanted to ask you," he said. "You know what I heard?"

She opened her mouth to speak, but no sound came out.

He'd raised his hand to her shoulder and was running his thumb up and down her neck. It made her think of that night, when he'd checked for Rita's pulse. "Relax, will you? You're too uptight. I'm not going to hurt you. I just wondered—" His thumb stopped moving and pressed lightly just above her collarbone. "I heard this makes orgasm better. You ever hear that?"

"What?" She barked out the word. He was insane. "What?" she said again. "Of course not." She pushed his arm away, but slowly, not wanting to make a sudden move.

Eddie sat back and sighed. "Yeah," he said. "I didn't think it was true either. It's crazy. That's what I thought when I heard it. Shark fins, tiger balls. All just a lot of superstition. I just wondered if you'd ever heard that."

"I want to go now," she said, reaching for the door handle.

"Wait," he said. "Aren't we forgetting something?"

"I told you I can't."

"Write me a check. Postdate it or something."

"Okay," she said, pulling up on the handle.

"Do it now," he said. "Go on. Go up there and get the check."

She had another thought. "But Daddy will see it's made out to you, Eddie." She hoped Naomi hadn't told Eddie that she reconciled the checks, that her father never even saw them. "He'll ask me who you are."

She expected him to say "Make something up" the way he usually did, but this seemed to bother him. "Shit," he said.

She took advantage of the opening. "I'll get you cash during the break. It's the best way. Just tell me how to get it to you. Where to bring it."

"Don't you go finding me," he said. "I'll find you."

Chapter Eight

She skipped morning classes the next day and walked the six blocks to the Star, where she sat in the back sipping coffee. It was mostly men in the place at that hour—businessmen in suits and construction workers wolfing down big platters of eggs. And it was loud too, a lot of talk and laughter, much different from the women she was used to in the afternoons. She felt safer tucked away at the back, where nobody bothered her.

She hadn't slept after Eddie left. She had gone back to the room and found Josie and Fiona sitting side by side on Josie's bed waiting for her, grinning and sly.

"So," Josie had said. "You were holding out!"

"He's sooo cute," Fiona had chimed in. "You *parked* with him. We saw. The windows were steamed."

"Get lost," she had said to them and then gone straight to bed, not that it was possible to sleep with the two of them whispering about her—with her right there, the covers pulled over her head. They'd finally gotten bored and left the room, the lights still burning, so she'd had to get up and turn them all off, and by then she'd been completely buzzed, wide awake. She'd gone back to bed and counted the days until winter break. Nineteen. Less than three weeks before he came looking for her again, before he surprised her on the street or showed up at the apartment. Three weeks to come up with some money for him. He hadn't said how much, but he wasn't talking about twenty dollars, she knew that much.

But it wasn't just that. The whole idea of going home again at all, of being back in the apartment and back under a microscope, made her panic. Her parents were going to be watching her, asking a million questions, just the way they had at Thanksgiving when she'd gone home for three awful days of nonstop interrogation about her classes, about the other girls and what clubs she had joined, and of course Neal. Then Emily and her husband had come for dinner, which was even worse. Emily had sat at the dining room table talking about Carole as though she wasn't even there. "Awfully quiet, Patsy. Cat got her tongue, I suppose. And no word about the new beau either?" And then to her husband, "Carole has met a boy from Princeton."

Three whole weeks of that when she got home, plus always looking over her shoulder for Eddie, plus stealing money from her father, which it would be if she did it because the money wasn't hers, it was his, and she was entrusted with it. No mistake about that. And plus, she'd thought, feeling heavy as stone, there was going to be a vacation week in the spring and then the whole summer to get through with them. Over and over and over for four more years.

I saw you do it, Eddie had said. *I saw your hands.*

She watched Nancy, the counter waitress. She was so efficient, as though she'd been wound up and set loose. Not a minute to think, Nancy sometimes said of her job when things were slower. Carole watched her sweep tips into the pocket of her apron, then run a sponge over the counter, slap down a paper place mat and silver, fill a juice glass with water for the next customer, and reach for the coffeepot and start pouring refills up and down. Everything efficient and clean, the opposite of her own life. All that order was something to aspire to. Imagine being so busy with your work that you didn't have a minute to think.

At ten, she walked the six dreary blocks back to campus. She'd already cut two classes, and she knew she wasn't going to make the rest of them. She went into the room to find Josie and three of her friends sitting cross-legged on the floor, playing bridge. They had been talking when Carole opened the door but fell silent at once, which meant they'd been talking about her. Around them were ashtrays full to the brim with cigarette butts. There was a layer of smoke suspended in the air at eye level.

Carole opened the window and lay down on her bed. The silence continued.

"Your mother called," Josie said.

"When?" Carole said. Fiona giggled.

"A while ago. We had quite the chat," Josie said.

There was a whir as the cards were shuffled, then the slap, slap of their being dealt.

"She asked all about Neal," Josie said. The other girls, Caroline and Laurie, were staring at the floor.

"I said 'You mean *my* Neal?' To tell the truth, roomie, I didn't think you'd even noticed about Neal. I was actually flattered to think my life was of any interest to you."

Carole stared at the wall, her eyes prickling with shock.

"Guess what your mother said." Josie had stopped dealing.

"Come on, Josie," Laurie said. "Don't."

"No, no," Josie said. "I have every right." She stood and crossed the floor to Carole's bed. "She said 'No, *Carole's* Neal, dear. From *Princeton.*'" Josie had the inflection in her mother's voice in spades.

Carole could not move.

Josie continued. "I didn't know you had a boyfriend at Princeton named Neal too. What an *incredible* coincidence."

"Might we meet your Neal?" Fiona said with a mean smirk.

"Stop it," Carole said.

"But there's more," Josie said, her voice rising. "Didn't your Neal just give you the same little heart-shaped pin that my Neal gave me? Imagine that!"

"Please," Carole said.

"You're so jealous. I didn't know how jealous you were. You want my life so badly."

"I do not want your life," Carole said, furious, not caring for once. She looked at the four of them in their nearly matching outfits, their nearly matching hairdos. "Nobody in their right mind wants your life because you're spineless, Josie, such a loser, and you don't even know it. If it doesn't say Brooks Brothers, it must not be a shirt, right? If it doesn't go to Princeton, it must not be a guy. And you're vicious too. Stupid, unimaginative, and vicious is how I see you. No, I don't want your life, but my mother does. And I certainly don't want Neal."

"You couldn't have my life if you paid for it," Josie said.

Carole got up and made an imaginary line down the center of the room with her arm. "From now on," she said to Josie, "you keep your friends on your own side of the room."

"I want you to call your mother right now and tell her the truth. It's a violation, what you did," Josie said, looking at the others.

"Now," Carole said, shooing the other girls out of her territory.

"I'll call her myself, then," Josie said. "I'll tell her you're just so pathetic you made it all up. And anyway, Neal wouldn't look twice at you, just in case you were thinking—"

"*My* side of the room." Carole kicked the pile of cards across the imaginary line.

"You're in so much trouble," Josie said.

She didn't go to another class that day or the next. The house mother came to talk to her. Mrs. Minnehan, with her brittle red hair and crepe-paper skin, wanted to know what the trouble was. Josie had been talking. Then the nurse, Miss Saunders, knocked on the door and came in. She laid a cool hand on Carole's head to see if she was sick. When they left, Carole knew she couldn't stay. Pretty soon they'd make a federal case out of her. Her parents were going to hear about everything. And what about when Eddie came after her again, which he would over Christmas break, only weeks away?

That night, very late, she rose from bed and pulled open her drawers. She got her suitcase out of the hold at the end of the corridor and started piling in her clothes. Josie woke and turned on the light. "What's going on?" she asked.

"It's all yours." Carole opened her closet and pulled everything out at once, hangers and all, and stuffed it into the suitcase. When she was done, she sat on her suitcase and waited for dawn. Josie went back to sleep but woke later and watched Carole.

"You're so weird," Josie said.

Carole called for a taxi from the pay phone, then went back to the room. By now Josie had told other girls in the corridor. They were standing on Josie's side of the room, arms folded, watching. "You can't just go," Josie said. "You can't just leave without telling anyone."

"Sure I can," Carole said.

"Nobody ever just *leaves* Vassar," Josie said, almost pleading with her.

"Watch me."

When the taxi arrived, she asked to be taken to the station, where she waited over an hour for the train to Manhattan. She kept looking over her shoulder for Mrs. Minnehan or somebody else from Vassar. Nobody came.

That first night she stayed at the Hotel New Yorker, an enormous rambling structure on Thirty-fourth Street, way past its prime. The dim corridors upstairs went on forever, and her room was tiny, with barely enough space to walk around, but it felt safe, like the booth at the Star Luncheonette, tucked away, a place where no one could find her.

In the morning she went to the bank and emptied her bank account of what was left of her Vassar money. There was five hundred and eighty-seven dollars, sixty less than she thought she had. Her father would have given her a lecture about that. She was supposed to know to the penny. She folded the money, put it in her purse, and walked up Eighth Avenue, with the purse clamped tight against her stomach, starving. She hadn't eaten anything since breakfast yesterday, and she went into the first place she found, Bo's, a small diner, steamy and loud, squeezed between two buildings. Bo and his wife ran the place, shouting out a kind of shorthand Carole had never heard before about food. A blond with sand was coffee with cream and sugar. A raft was toast. The twins were salt and pepper.

She tucked herself into a booth at the back and scanned the newspapers people had left lying around, looking for an apartment. There were so many, and she had enough money, so how hard could it be?

The first place she saw was a single room on West Thirtieth with a bathtub next to the kitchen sink and windows that looked out on the building next door. The man who met her there watched her like a hawk and wanted to see ID. "Driver's license, birth certificate, whatever," he said. When Carole said she didn't drive and didn't have any ID with her, he asked where she'd lived before. Upstate, she told him. Where? He wanted to know. Poughkeepsie, she said. You bring a reference? he asked. The whole exchange lasted about a minute and a half.

"I have cash," she said, thinking that might be the problem. "I can pay." She brought out her roll of money, and the guy took a big step back away from her and waved his hands in front of his face as though she'd just pulled out a gun or something.

"Young lady, don't do that," he said. "Don't ever do that. Don't you go showing that around that way." He shook his head. "I'm sorry, but the law is the law. I can't rent to you unless you can show me some ID."

The same thing happened with the second place and the third, although she didn't show the money again. After each failure, she went back to Bo's and started all over again with other people's discarded papers.

"You lookin' for a place?" Mrs. Bo was a short, dark-haired woman who wore a small bow above her bangs that matched her outfit. She tipped the coffeepot and filled Carole's cup. Carole nodded. "How long?" Mrs. Bo wanted to know.

"Three days," Carole said.

"I mean how long you need it for? You looking for something permanent or temporary?"

"Just a while," Carole said.

"Then maybe I know somebody," she said. She narrowed her eyes at Carole. "What's the story on you anyway?"

Carole made it up as she went along, remembering Naomi's advice from way back to keep it simple and as close to the truth as possible. She was taking a semester off from college, she explained, to do some research on Henry James at the New York Public Library. "I have plenty of money," Carole said. "I can pay."

It turned out to be a sublet on East Thirty-first. The guy who was renting it had gone off for reasons that were never explained. But it was a nice enough place on the second floor. It had three deadbolts and a chain inside the door. The windows all had bars on them. Pretty bars, curved and filigreed, but still bars. The living room was long and narrow, with a high tin ceiling that had been painted so many times that the detail in it was blurred. The furniture was cheap—Scandinavian chairs with legs that tapered to little points and low plastic tables. The only windows were in the living room at the front and in the bedroom at the back. In between it was dark, and she needed to keep all the lamps burning, even in the daytime.

Mrs. Bo was the intermediary, collecting her money and telling her the rules. He only wanted fifty dollars a month, with four months paid up front, as long as she would take care of the place. "He's not allowed to sublet," she said of the apartment. "But he wants somebody in here to look after it. So if anybody asks, like somebody in the building, or if the super comes nosing around, you tell them you're the niece from upstate. That's all you say." She gave Carole an address in Iowa where she was supposed to send any mail that came in. She was supposed to keep the plants watered, she was not ever to answer the buzzer if it rang. And she was to let no one into the apartment. If she could promise all that, they had a deal.

Chapter Nine

She was sure they'd find her. Nobody like her ever just disappeared. It was just a matter of time before one of her parents showed up and all their lives fell apart. It was coming. It was inevitable. When she was outside, she was like a thief, watching constantly for her mother or father. Waiting for the bus, she kept her back against store windows, the better to scan the passersby.

But no one came. Weeks went by, and nothing happened. So maybe they didn't know where she was. Josie would surely have told them that Carole had left of her own free will, dropped out. And she'd probably told them the lie about Neal. Josie couldn't wait to tell everyone that story. Then there was Eddie. She hadn't known his name, but she would describe him, and Carole's mother would know. The man from the train, the one her mother had seen on the street. But Carole didn't want to think too much about that. It didn't help. For now she was beginning to feel safe. She was building another wall behind her. Every day that went by was another brick of safety.

The trouble was, she had only seventy dollars left, and she needed a job. She applied to be a saleslady at B. Altman, but when the personnel director asked for a Social Security number she excused herself and made a dash for the escalator. There was no way. Her parents would track her down in no time flat if her Social Security number got out.

She ducked into a little storefront restaurant around the corner named Earl's. She liked the name to begin with, written in plain letters across a heavy brown canopy over the front door. And the place was clean, with white tablecloths and heavy silver. She had tea, and Earl himself drew up a chair at her table. He was a big guy, bursting out of his starched whites and checked pants. He said he made it a practice to get to know his customers, but he wouldn't bother her if she preferred to be alone. Something told her this was okay, Earl was okay, and she said she'd like the company, sure, if he wanted to sit with her a few minutes and talk.

He wanted to know what she thought of the tea, what kind of food she liked, where else she liked to go in the city, and what she thought of all these kids you see today with their long hair and flowers. He personally found them refreshing. He'd grown up in Eugene, Oregon, in the land of backyard barbecues and ranch houses. "People didn't know how bored they were," he said. He'd been waiting a long time to see the world burst free and live. And the music! "So what about you?" he asked her, and then put up his hands quickly in a no-offense gesture. "If you don't mind my asking."

"I ran away from school," she said.

Earl nodded sagely. "It's a whole new world, isn't it?"

She said she liked seeing the people at Earl's, even though she didn't *know them* know them, if he knew what she meant. He did. He liked it too. He'd been around the block a few times too, and this was finally home for him.

One afternoon Earl was shorthanded, and Carole noticed that a man at a nearby table needed a refill on coffee. Without thinking, she got up out of her seat and brought over the pot. The man wanted dessert too. "What do you have?" *You,* as if she was the waitress. It felt so good to belong. "Crème brûlée, mousse au chocolat, sorbet, torte," she said. She'd heard the other waitresses run through that litany often enough. The man ordered, and she went to the kitchen to tell the chef. That was how it started. She went in four days a week to cover for one or another of the girls. Without even asking, Earl gave her cash from the register every week so she wouldn't be on the books, so she wouldn't owe taxes, so nobody could track her down.

And there was something else she liked about Earl's. The order of the place. Everything in the kitchen was arranged so it was easy to clean and easy to reach. Pots and utensils hung from racks overhead. At each station was something Earl called the *mise,* bowls of all sizes with chopped shallots, minced parsley, butter, salt. Some nights there were fifteen or twenty of these, depending on the menu, and something else he called a reach-in for the cold foods that he and the line chefs needed. When the restaurant was packed, she helped out by signing for deliveries that came in and checking over the orders to make sure everything was there, that the stuff was fresh and smelled right, that it was put where it belonged—in the freezer or the walk-in refrigerator. She had a knack for it, Earl told her. And she was tough too. When something wasn't right, she'd be on the phone to the purveyor, telling them to take it back or bring fresher or more, or whatever. Or else. The order of the place chased away her fear, time disappeared. She felt nothing but the urgency to get her work done.

She'd been at Earl's over a year and was serving lunch one day when three women came in. They were well dressed in their Courrèges outfits, like a bunch of geometry problems over opaque stockings and low-heeled shoes. As she stood at their table, her pencil poised over her notebook to take their order, she recognized Barbara Buchanan. A year ahead of her at Spence, Barbara used to terrify her playing volleyball in gym. She was in the glee club with her too. Carole's hand quivered as she wrote down their orders. *Chablis X3.* Barbara looked directly at her. "How is the salad prepared?" she asked.

Stranded, all Carole could do was stare at Barbara Buchanan and wait for the dreadful moment when she was recognized.

But it didn't happen. Barbara made a face, glanced at the others, and rolled her eyes as if to say, *What's with her?*

"However you like it," Carole finally said. "With or without the garlic. The choice is yours."

"Well, that's better," Barbara said. "I'll have it without." And with that she went back to her friends. Carole took a few steps backward from the women, who put their heads together and talked in low voices. When she got to the kitchen with the order, she could hear the blood pounding in her ears.

"You okay?" Earl asked.

She had to think a moment. "Yes," she said. She went to the little mirror at the back door. It was smeared and uneven, but it did the job. She looked at herself. Her springy blond hair was tamed into a thick braid down her back. Her face was bony now, the cheekbones and chin clearly defined, the nose larger. And something else. Her eyes were darker. She hadn't noticed the shift, but they were. They were a deeper blue, almost normal. A serious color instead of those child's pale eyes. She hadn't noticed because she rarely looked at her face in the mirror. Each morning she twisted her hair without watching herself. She checked herself at a distance to gauge her clothing, but she didn't want to look at her face. She leaned in to see better the deep blue specks that darkened them. She didn't remotely resemble the girl she had been.

One morning the following winter, she was painting her nails at the kitchen table in her apartment, making long syrupy strokes of red, one after the other. They didn't need her at Earl's, so she could do what she wanted.

She'd done six fingers perfectly. It was exacting work, requiring skill and patience. She had a rule that if she messed one up, she had to remove the polish from all the ones she'd already done and start over. This kept her focused on what she was doing, and it ate up the time. She had six colors to choose from in the bathroom, all lined up on the toilet tank, from the purple on the left to the red in the middle and the orange on the right. The color she was using now was her favorite, Candy-Apple Red.

She was about to start on another finger when there was a long buzz from downstairs. She'd sworn to ignore the buzzer. That had been part of the sublet deal, and her whole feeling of security depended on keeping that promise. All the promises. Anyway, nobody in New York knew where she lived, so it wasn't for her anyway.

But the buzzing went on for a long annoying time and then stopped. She stilled herself, the little nail polish brush poised, listening for the sound to start in one of the other units, and it did. Whoever it was tried all three units and then came back to hers again. It might be Mrs. Bo, although it was way too early for her. She came every four months to look around and collect the next four months' rent.

Fingers spread, Carole opened the door to the hall using the backs of both hands so she wouldn't smudge her polish. Then she went down the stairs to the landing.

Maybe whoever it was had left. She went down a few more stairs and bent over the banister to look. Suddenly the glass in the front door filled up with the shape of a man. He had on a fedora and an overcoat. He cupped his hands around his eyes, pressing his face to the glass, and peered in. She turned to run back up the stairs and stopped again at the landing to make sure. Oh, no. It was her father. And he'd seen her. She fled to her apartment.

She could hear him down there on the sidewalk now, shouting her name, banging on the glass so hard it could break. The buzzer sounded nonstop. How could he have found her? How was it possible? She watched him from behind the curtain. He flapped his arms in this terrible way, a way he would criticize in anybody else. He was so angry. That was what scared her. His anger. He'd hit her that time. Maybe he'd hit her again.

His hat fell off. It just dropped from his head to the street, bounced, and landed near the wheel of a parked car. She expected him to pick it up, but he didn't seem to know it had happened. That got her attention, the way he didn't notice the hat, a man who was always so careful. She slipped the window open a few inches. When he saw her, he crossed over to be just under the window, on the sidewalk.

"It's your mother," he said.

Oh, no, she thought. No.

"Let me in," he said. "Answer the door."

"What happened to her?"

"For God's sake, Carole. Open the door."

"Just tell me?" she said, more question than statement.

He flapped his arms in fury and looked around to see if anyone was listening. "Don't make me stand out here," he said. "You must open that door." He was looking up at her now.

She wished he'd pick up the hat. It killed her to see it there. It was going to get run over if he didn't do something. "I can't," she said, feeling desperate. "I'm not allowed."

He set his face in a way she'd forgotten, sucking in the skin around his lips so his mouth was a straight hard line across. He looked down at his feet, then looked up at her. "Not *allowed*?" he said. "What in the name of God is that supposed to mean? I'm your father." He looked so stricken, that was it. And baffled.

She just stared down at him, frozen, feeling the confusion roil up in her. Afraid of him, for him, afraid about what he'd said about her mother and of letting him in here to this place where nobody was allowed to be but her. Her chest tightened, and she couldn't take in a full breath. But she knew she would have to let him in, yes, in a minute she would, but right now she couldn't move. She could only stare down at him in shock. In a minute, she thought, I will. But then, as she watched, he threw up his hands in defeat, turned, and walked away, down the street.

"Your hat," she yelled. "Daddy. Your hat."

Either he didn't hear or he wouldn't hear. She watched the hat get crushed under a taxi. She slammed down the window. Her nails were a mess, of course, but she couldn't do anything about that now. What did it matter? Her hands were trembling so badly. She wanted to call somebody. But who? Who was there? Naomi? Out of the question. Jeremy? Maybe, but then Jeremy's father worked with her father. No. There was nobody left. Nobody at all. It was an astonishing moment, seeing herself this way. Up until now she'd felt surrounded. There was Earl and all the customers, the other waitresses, and the guys in the kitchen. But the truth was, nobody knew who she was.

She went to the window a few times and looked out, in case her father came back, but he didn't. Finally, when it was close to five, she called his office and talked to Miss Palmer, the same Miss Palmer who used to send the tuition bills to her at Vassar.

"I'm not supposed to talk to you," Miss Palmer said. "If you call, I'm supposed to put you right through to him, but he's not here." Then she added, "He's making the arrangements."

Arrangements. The word landed like a hammer.

"I'm not allowed to tell you anything else."

Her mother was dead. She must be.

"Jackie," she said. She'd never called Miss Palmer Jackie. Nobody did. Not even her father called her that. "Jackie, please?"

There was a long pause. She could imagine Miss Palmer looking left to right over her long nose. "Don't tell him I told you. You've got to swear." She paused, waiting for an answer.

"Yes, all right."

"I hate to tell you this, dear, but your mother passed away," Miss Palmer said.

"No."

"On Wednesday." Miss Palmer was unable to hide the agitation in her voice.

"No," Carole said again.

"A heart attack," Miss Palmer said. "On the street. They took her to Bellevue," she added, as though nothing could be worse than Bellevue, as though the cause of death itself was Bellevue.

"Bellevue," Carole repeated.

"Service is tomorrow," Miss Palmer said. "At the University Club," she added. "Everybody's coming." There was a long silence. "Oh, my God," she said. "I shouldn't have told you all this. He wanted to do it himself. Promise you won't tell him."

Carole felt cold and sweaty.

"Carole, please? Promise you won't? I wasn't supposed to tell."

Carole said nothing. This couldn't be happening.

"I can't say anymore. I shouldn't have said anything." Miss Palmer's voice was small and whispery. "I said way too much. He'd be so mad."

"Where is he?"

"At the funeral home, at Frank Campbell's, or the University Club. I don't know. He had a lot of stops to make this afternoon." The phone went dead.

Maybe it was a trick, she thought with a burst of hope. Maybe. Yes. It could be. Her spirits rose. They were saying it to make her come home. Her mother was too young. And who ever heard of a woman having a heart attack? Only men did, and old men at that. But something in Jackie's voice had been true, and she called Campbell's.

"Indeed," the hushed, calm voice on the phone said. "Mrs. Conrad Mason. Patricia." He said it *Patree-sha.* "Would you be a member of the family?"

She nodded, shocked that it was true.

"Miss?" he said. "Would you—"

"Her daughter," she said.

He talked on in a hushed voice. She had to ask him to repeat what he'd said, and he did, very patiently. Cremation had yet to take place. A final viewing if she wished to come right away.

Sitting numbly, watching the city pass by like some alien place, she took a taxi up Park and across on Eighty-first to Madison. The man at the funeral place gave his name, but she didn't retain it. He showed her into a small, well-lit room. "Shall I stay?" he asked, and she shook her head, then stood at the door after he'd left, shocked by what she saw. The room was empty except for a bed, or maybe it was a hospital gurney, on the other side of the room, miles and miles away, it seemed, and on the bed was a long white form lit like something sacred and covered in pressed white cloth.

She was still holding tightly to the doorknob, but she let it go and took several steps closer, her heart beating loudly in the still room.

She stopped again. She could see now the opening at one end of the form, the shroud, and her mother's face small and bare, the eyes closed.

Her throat swelled, her eyes seared with the tears that came. She went to her mother's side and stood looking down at her, supporting herself. "Oh, Mommy," she whispered, the name she'd called her as a child. Very lightly, she touched her mother's cheek and recoiled at the coolness of it. "Oh, Mom," she said, feeling more alone than ever. She rocked back and forth over her mother's lifeless body. "No, no, no, no," she said, the tears streaming down her face, sounds she barely knew she was capable of coming from her own lips, like the yowling sounds of animals at night. Her cries bounced off the bare walls, filling the room. The door opened, and the man asked if there was something he could do to help, and she said no, please, she wanted to be alone, and he shut the door again, his head bowed.

She was calmer after that, spent, remembering the last time she'd seen her mother, that Thanksgiving when she'd been at Vassar, and how tentative her mother had been, too timid to ask any questions. She'd mostly smiled nervously at Carole, wondering what was the matter. *Dear.* Her mother's favorite word for her, *dear.* So cloying once, but now she wanted only to hear it again. She leaned down to kiss her mother's forehead, shocked all over once more at its coolness, which brought home again and for good and for all that she was dead. Death was this. It was this clean white shroud, it was touching her mother's cold cheek. It was nudging her and getting nothing back. The stillness, the irrefutable stillness, of this thing on the table that was once her mother.

There was no fighting off the memory of Rita now, no avoiding the awful sloppy laxity of her body, the way it had slipped and slithered like a huge wet doll, how hard to hold onto. How different that had been from this prim form that had been her mother, virginal looking except for the dark stains of Carole's tears and the wanton smear of her lipstick. Both of them were dead because of Carole.

Drained dry now, despising herself. She knew it was true. She'd killed her own mother too.

She didn't know how long she'd been in there. The man opened the door a few times and then finally came to her, put a hand gently on her shoulder, and said perhaps it was enough, perhaps it was time to say good-bye. She leaned over her mother for the last time, kissed her cold cheek, touched her forehead, and said, "I love you. I'm sorry." And then she followed the man from the room and let the door close behind her.

In the lobby she asked to use the phone. She dialed the apartment, and a woman answered. "Mason residence."

"Is Mr. Mason there?" Carole asked.

The woman said he was out and asked who was calling. Carole hesitated and then gave her name. "It's Carole," she said. "Their daughter."

"Oh." The woman paused. "Is there a number where he can reach you?"

She gave the woman, a maid perhaps, the funeral home number and waited while she wrote it down and read it back. Half an hour later her father called. The old business veneer was back. "I don't know whether you know or not," he said.

"Yes," she said. "I do."

"On Wednesday your mother had a coronary and died. I'm sorry to have to break this to you, Carole. The service is tomorrow at the University Club. I've already arranged for cremation." That was it.

"What happened?" She wanted to hear it from him, not Miss Palmer.

"She was running for a bus." He waited. "When can you be here?"

"There?" she said. "The apartment?"

"Of course the apartment."

"Tomorrow," she said.

"What about now? My God, Carole. Enough of this. Your mother is dead."

She was a lot closer to his apartment than to hers, but she couldn't go. It was too soon. "What time tomorrow?"

"In the morning. The service is at one."

That night the old brownstone creaked in the wind and kept her awake. *Cremated.* The word hovered in the quiet hours of the morning. She had to get up and turn on lights to keep herself from thinking about the long chute, her mother, wrapped in white, sliding down it, arms crossed on her breast, and the roar of flame. She'd read somewhere that the body spits and crackles.

She spent the time until daybreak pacing. Running for the bus, her father had said. She imagined it over and over. She'd never been athletic. Her mother in a black suit, running erratically in her high heels, waving an arm. Yoohoo! Like that time with Eddie. And then falling, scraping her knees, bruising herself. She thought of her mother on the sidewalk, alone, strangers opening her purse to find out who she was, fumbling through her clothing, perhaps stealing from her. She was glad when daylight broke and outside the city began to move again. Glad for the noise, the distraction.

She dressed and undressed in everything she had, which wasn't much. Her old wool skirts from Vassar. Blouses ironed shiny over time. She finally put on one of her waitress dresses, the only black she had. It was too short, she knew, but she had no choice. She took the subway to Fifty-ninth Street and Lexington and came up the stairs to the street in broad daylight. Since coming back to New York, she'd come here a few times at night when she hadn't been able to sleep, when she'd needed to see her old home again, if only from the street. If only to know it was still there, that her parents were somewhere up there moving about those lit rooms, and that there was a chance that one day she could come home.

Now she saw that the Home for Unwed Mothers was a fenced-in construction site. A picture on the fence showed the high white apartment complex that would be there next.

The doorman was someone she didn't know. He made her wait while he called upstairs to announce her. "Go on, miss," he said. The man on the elevator was also new. He stood erect, with his uniformed back to her, watching the floors go by, then jockeyed the elevator several times to make sure the elevator floor met the vestibule floor exactly. She thought of asking about Heney but couldn't. What if he was dead too?

Her father was waiting at the elevator. Thinner and grayer. He raised his shoulders and dropped them as if to say, I give up. His eyes were red. Cautiously, because this was something she had never done before, she reached out to hug him. The feel and smell of him, the way he so stiffly kept his distance, made her pull away again.

"You came," he said, fighting back tears.

"I don't—" She wanted to say that she hadn't meant for this to happen. It was all her fault somehow. Her father looked anxious, his head swiveling from her to the apartment. The guests. He was as nervous as she was. "Do people—?" She wanted to ask if they knew she'd dropped out of sight.

"People from the firm," he said, meaning who was there, inside. "Your aunt Emily, of course." He was pulling her into the vestibule as he spoke.

She got passed from one person to the next. They all told her how sorry they were. The women kissed her. The men embraced her lightly. She felt carried along by the waves of their concern. At any moment, she thought, her mother would walk into the room. It seemed impossible that all this was because she was dead.

One of the junior partners took Carole aside. In a soft, wet voice he asked her, "Will your mother be there? At the University Club?" She couldn't understand the question. She looked around, feeling almost panicky. Then she realized he was asking about the coffin, or about the ashes. Where were they? "I don't know," she said. She turned away from him, down the corridor and to her old room. She stopped in the door and leaned against the jamb for support. It was all happening so fast.

The chair from the den was in the middle of her room, and beside it was a table with a book of crossword puzzles and a tray of pens and pencils. Her mother's eyeglasses. She opened and closed the stems, held them to her nose, and breathed in. The faint, familiar odor made her weak and slightly ill. She sat on the edge of her mother's chair and opened the small drawer at the front of the table. There were photo-graphs of her as an infant and the proofs of her Spence yearbook photo, taken the autumn before graduation. In them she had the calm, intelligent look of a girl you couldn't surprise. A girl who knew exactly where she was going. One of the photographs and half of another had been ripped from the sheet as if in anger.

Under the photos were her report cards from Spence. Each was a single sheet on which her grades, all A's, were recorded in blue ink with notes from the headmistress at the bottom. "Will do well what-ever her field of endeavor," the last one said. Even getting away with murder, she thought ruefully. She pushed them to the back of the drawer, where her fingers felt something else. She drew out a small stack of mail, bound with an elastic band. There were four letters, all addressed to her and all unopened. She knew the writing because her mother had forwarded a letter to her at Vassar. Rachel must have kept writing to her here, she thought, feeling a flutter of pleasure at the idea of somebody who liked her.

Footsteps sounded in the hall, and she slipped the letters into her purse. "She practically lived in here," her father said. He was stand-ing in the doorway. "She thought if she was in here for long enough, she'd know why you left."

"It wasn't anything she did."

"She didn't know that."

She felt vulnerable and ashamed in the chair, guilty for having the letters, which she was sure he hadn't seen. If he'd known about them, he would have opened them all. He walked to the window. "Why did it have to take this to get you back?" He didn't face her, but the question was real. He wanted to know.

"I thought I had more time." It had never occurred to her that one of them might die.

He wheeled to face her, visibly angry. "Well, you learn the hard way, don't you?"

She was about to speak, about to lash out, but he put a finger to his lips and squeezed his eyes shut. "I promised not to do this, not to be angry. I promised that if you came, I would say 'no questions asked.' I want it to be like that, and not like this. So I'll say it now. Please come home, Carole. Or at least talk to me. Let me know what's happening now. Not then but now." He forced a weary smile. "No questions asked. Your mother said it was the only way. I wish she were here to see you." He stopped himself from crying the same way he had done on the street, by sucking in his mouth.

The tenderness was far worse than anger could have been. She stepped to the window with her back to him and looked down on the hole where the Home for Unwed Mothers had been. "I'll bet she hated to see that," she said. "They'll build something higher than us."

"Think about it," her father said and then left.

She stayed there alone for some time. It had always been her mother's face she thought about when she thought about home, never her father's. She'd been so sure that after enough time had passed she would hug her mother again, and now that would never happen. Please come home, her father had said. Could she? Looking around her room, she felt an ache of regret. If he really meant that, *no questions asked,* then for his sake, maybe yes. For her father's sake and for her own. He had nobody now.

"Well, look who decided to show her face."

Emily was there, tiny in a dark outfit. "Everyone else has gone ahead. I told Conrad I'd collect you, and we'll meet him downstairs."

Emily's face had softened since Carole had last seen her, fleshed out a little so she resembled Carole's mother more. "Oh." Carole checked her watch. "I didn't know."

"Of course you didn't." Emily's words were charged. She didn't move from the door.

"Excuse me," Carole said.

"Your mother suffered." Emily blocked the door.

"They'll be wondering—"

"They'll wait for the sister and the daughter." Emily's voice was stone. "The blood relatives. The only blood relatives, and they'll wait for us, by God. You're not leaving here until I say my piece."

"You don't understand, Emily."

Emily snorted. "Understand? How dare you speak of understanding! You broke your mother's heart. You might just as well have shot her, taken a knife and plunged it into her. Day after day. It ate her up. She used to sit in this room. Your room. She was waiting for you to call, to come home. 'What did I do?' she would ask me. And I tried to tell her she'd done nothing. She'd been an exemplary mother. It was you. Ungrateful, spoiled child. You had every advantage. And you have the audacity to breeze in as though nothing has happened." Emily glared at her.

"Everything has happened."

"A week ago. If only you'd come a week ago." Emily broke down, holding her white gloves to her face, smearing them with lipstick.

"Daddy's waiting."

"Don't want to upset our daddy, do we?"

"What's that supposed to mean?"

"You're just like him."

Carole edged past Emily and into the hallway to the main corridor. She wasn't like him. She couldn't be.

"Their marriage was falling apart." Emily caught up to her, her little face fierce, the eyebrows like a pair of chevrons, her features bunched in fury. "Ever since you left, and don't go acting surprised. Your father with his stiff upper lip, telling her to get a hold of herself."

The door to the vestibule was open. Carole ran for it and pressed the buzzer.

"You could say you're sorry." Emily was right there, slamming the door to the apartment behind her.

"Of course I'm sorry," Carole said and felt her heart fracture, felt the rush of tears again.

The elevator door rattled open. They rode in silence until Emily tapped the operator on the shoulder. "Broke her mother's heart, right, Maurice?" He turned partway, nodded politely, and then faced front again. "You saw it. You had to see it. Everybody did."

"Leave him alone," Carole said.

158

Downstairs, her father was waiting in front of the building beside a shiny black limousine. He checked his watch in annoyance, then hopped into the front next to the chauffeur. Carole took her place in the backseat and sat staring at the back of her father's head. At the hair over the collar of his shirt. Her mother was dead. The thought was stunning all over again. It couldn't be true. But it was, and she was going to the funeral.

They were ushered into a red brocade room at the back of the University Club. A minister read from the Bible and then began to speak of her mother, calling her Patsy so often that Carole wondered if her mother had been going to church. He mentioned the loss of a devoted wife to Conrad. "And a loving mother to her daughter, to Carole. There is nothing so deep as the bond of mother and daughter," he said. Her father apparently hadn't told the minister anything about the family after all. The minister was talking about other people, some mythical family.

After the service, the room swarmed with men and women in dark wool suits and dresses, gold jewelry and perfume. They sought her out, one by one, introducing themselves, telling her how they admired her mother and, again, how sorry they were and asking if there was anything they could do. She'd seen the sympathy cards at home, all the people who couldn't be here today. It was the great wide web that her parents inhabited. The vast network she'd once known, if only peripherally.

Waiters appeared with trays of food and glasses of wine. She watched her father glide through the crowd. The women kissed him, the men shook his hand. Carole came up beside him and touched his elbow. He turned and smiled at her, his eyes brimming at the sight of her. They moved together from cluster to cluster, accepting sympathy. Three people gave her their business cards and urged her to call them. They understood she was at Vassar. Perhaps she would be looking for work when she graduated. They could help.

So nobody knew except Emily. To everybody else, the family was intact, perfect except for the death of the mother.

At the far end of the room, someone caught her attention. She looked again, but the crowd had shifted. Her father passed her to a woman with tears in her faded old eyes, who kissed her and then wiped lipstick from her cheek. He introduced her to someone else. He had his arm around her waist, holding on to her for dear life. "Client of the firm," he said about the man now shaking her hand. "Client and friend," her father added, but he was already in another embrace. This time a woman had him by the ears and was saying something close to his face. Her father's arm loosened at her waist. He let her go. He was moving away from her, being swallowed up by another group.

A waiter handed her a glass of sherry, and she set it down untouched. Without her father shepherding her around the room, people left her alone. She edged toward the door, away from the thickest part of the crowd, where she could watch her father's progress through the swarm, catch a glimpse of his gray head bobbing, hidden and then emerging.

She felt a hand grip her elbow firmly and thought, for a moment, it was her father, but she caught a glimpse of him in the distance, so it couldn't be. There was a flash of longish dishwater hair and dark mutton-chop sideburns. A waiter, she thought at first, but why was he gripping her so tightly?

She turned to take him in, face him full-on. It couldn't be. She blinked and looked again. "Eddie," she said. The horror of it, that he would be here, in this place with these people, the invader making what was already dark so much worse.

"How did you know?" She scanned the crowd, frantic to find her father, see if anyone had noticed, as if her drumming heart was so loud people would have fallen silent, watching her. But they weren't. Nothing had changed out there. "How?" she asked him again, more forcefully.

"Announcement in the *Times*," he said, smirking. He was so calm. "I just happened to notice—I don't usually read obituaries, so depressing, don't you think?" He took her wrist in his hand and held it tight. "I'm really sorry about your mother. Honest."

"Don't you dare even speak about her," she said.

"She was a lovely woman."

"I said, leave her *out* of this."

"But I *knew* her." Something in the way he said it made her turn to see his face. He smiled at her, cocked his head. "In the biblical sense, if you know what I mean."

He couldn't mean what she thought he meant. It wasn't possible. That he and her mother had— No. She shut her mind to it. "I had to leave Vassar. I flunked out," she said.

"No, no, you didn't," Eddie said. "I went up there. Your little friend Josie told me all sorts of things about you. You left. No flunking out."

She searched the crowd again for her father and found him at the center of a cluster across the room, safely at a distance. She had to get Eddie out of here before her father noticed.

"She flagged me down one day," Eddie said. She thought he meant Josie. It was so hard to get her bearings. The room felt unbearably hot. She was sweating. "You remember. You were pissed. You thought I'd accosted her, remember? But it was the other way around. Honest, *she* was the aggressor that time, and then again last spring on Lex." He meant her mother. "I was house-sitting nearby. Same neighborhood as before but a much better gig. Those people were civilized. They didn't care if I drank the liquor, and there weren't all those workmen. The noise. Remember?"

"Stop it," she said.

Eddie winked. " 'My daughter? The one you met at the train? You wouldn't happen to know?' " Her mother's voice leaked sickeningly from him, the way it had from Josie. "Seems you'd vanished into thin air from college, and she never knew where you were. Ran away from Vassar. Did you get kicked out? Join the underground? Are you one of those college girls running around with drug addicts and ex-cons? Well, your mother was distraught. Your father wanted to hire detectives. Where, oh, where could she be?" He paused and looked around the room. "Well, I couldn't let it go. I had to know too. Have to know. Present tense. If there were to be detectives, perhaps there would be police, even though the police wouldn't touch it, since you'd obviously left of your own free will and you were of age. Well, by now you are. By the way, you lied about your age that night. But if there had been police—well, there was no alternative."

"Alternative to what?"

"To *comforting* that poor woman." He had a predator's grin, all teeth. "So lovely. So mistreated and misunderstood. And so responsive. Much more than you. Is that him?" Eddie pointed to her father, who had moved closer and was speaking to a group of people.

She tried to focus on something in the room, her eyes darting from one spot to another, one face to another, but what she saw was her mother's white plump body beneath Eddie in that room Carole had been in, the one strewn all over with his clothes. Her mother on that bed, her eyes shut, her head thrown back. He would have told her mother she was beautiful, she was special, and then he would have asked, *So where do you think Carole might be?* She could hardly breathe all of a sudden. It felt as though her throat had closed.

"Easy," Eddie said. "You'll cause a scene."

"What did you tell her?"

"Interesting you should ask that, because that was always *my* question. What did *you* tell her? What did she know? It took several times to find out. I had to proceed so gingerly. She was not in a frame of mind to talk. I had to come rather close to our little secret to find out."

"No, oh, please, no."

"I said close. That business in Grand Central. I told her we'd met up again in Stowe, and she wasn't really that surprised. She never did like Naomi." He paused and straightened up, looked around. "Tell me, where did it happen? I understand it was a heart attack. Did she go quickly?"

She froze. Her father was watching them, a quizzical look on his face.

"So that *is* him. I thought so. That's what I thought he'd look like. Patrician and cool. Did you know that he had an affair not so long ago? Gloria something. She might even be here." He sighed. "Your mother was quite the tiger. She'd lost her own virginity at an even younger age than you did, and not to your father, although he never knew that. She was under the impression that you'd come to find me at some point. She thought you'd have a soft spot in your heart for the man who'd deflowered you. And when you did, I was to let her know pronto. I was her connection to you in her mind. Poor thing. She never breathed a word of this to Conrad, though. She was quite afraid of him, but you must know that."

"There you are." Her father was approaching them, striding over, a drink in his hand. "And you are?" He thrust out his free hand to Eddie.

"Ed," he said.

Her father studied Eddie for a moment, squinting at him, waiting for more, and when no more was forthcoming, said, "Conrad Mason."

"I'm so sorry about your wife," Eddie said, then excused himself, saying he'd be right back.

"Ed?" her father said. "Can't place him."

She shrugged as if to say she didn't know either.

"I've been trying to get your attention. People I want you to meet." Her father stared into her face. "What's the matter?"

She didn't trust herself to speak. She felt the beginning of tears.

"Oh, sweetie," he said. He gave her a quick hug. "I know, I know."

"Just give me a minute," she said. "You go ahead. I'll find you." She didn't want Eddie to come back, didn't want him anywhere near her father.

"Don't let me down," he said.

She committed his expression to memory. His high forehead and thin lips. His caved-in expression of concern for her at that moment. She watched him cross the room away from her and get lost among other people. She was sweating, overly warm in the room, and she had to lean against the wall, which was cool. Eddie was returning, carrying two glasses of sherry. "There's one more thing." He offered her a glass, which she waved away. "Not to worry about the money you promised that night. There will be more. Quite a bit, in fact, and all yours."

"I will never give you one red cent," she said.

"Oh, yes, you will." Eddie took a pen from his pocket and held it next to his glass, as if ready to tap the glass and bring the room to a hush. She didn't dare call his bluff right then.

"Okay," she said.

"Good girl," he said. "Let's see how much you get."

"Get me a drink," she said. "A real drink."

"That's more like it." And he was off again.

She slipped from the room to the great, drab cavernous lobby of the club. There was a door to the right, and she went through it down a hall lined with bookcases. She turned to see if Eddie was following, but he wasn't. She took the emergency exit to the street, praying as she opened the door that it wouldn't set off an alarm. She found herself in a narrow alley. She'd left her coat, but that didn't matter now. She slipped down the alley to Fifty-fourth and ran crosstown until her lungs burned. Miss Palmer, she thought. Miss Palmer must have told him, must have fallen for some story he told, that and his smooth voice. Or worse. He could be sleeping with Miss Palmer too, prying secrets from her.

There was no question what she'd do. Pack her things. Disappear. If nobody knew where she was, she would be safe. Eddie would not try to get money from her father. She was sure of that. Women were Eddie Lindbaeck's domain, people smaller and weaker than he was.

The apartment was still strewn with her clothing from this morning, and she moved from room to room, picking the few things she wanted. She kept checking the window in case he had followed her. She stuffed her toothbrush and comb into her purse and felt the letters again from Rachel. She sat down on the bed and ripped them open. They told of the baby Pepper, how he had rolled over and cut new teeth. Of living in Rochester and the cold. There were pleas for Carole to write back and questions about what she was doing. Carole ripped through them, looking for an address. The last of them was postmarked San Francisco: "You should come out here. Haight-Ashbury is where it's at. It's wild. It's fantastic. We're the last house on Stanyan before Seventeenth Street."

Part Two

Chapter Ten

There was a lull now, the bulk of customers having left for the evening. Only a few tables were left, finishing up their desserts or having a last beer or cup of coffee. It was a good moment, Carole thought, the planets in alignment and all that. She'd learned to recognize these times. They didn't come all that often. When she felt one, she stopped what she was doing and let herself enjoy it.

She had been putting a fresh cloth on one of the tables. She'd snapped it the way one does a bedsheet so it landed smartly over the table, leaving one dark table corner exposed. She left it there, half done, and slipped to the back of the restaurant, her own restaurant, Chacha's. Someone had put on "Midnight at the Oasis." Maria Muldaur's throaty, slightly whiny voice filled the room, low and pleasant.

Her job was mostly done for the evening. Soon the customers would go home and just she, Will, and the Weaver-Lears would be left to plan out the year's nighttime cross-country ski trip. They'd done the trip in each of the past four years. Every year it was the same, and

167

every year they met here to plan it. She liked knowing what to expect after all those years of moving around.

She caught sight of herself in a nearby mirror and stared. She had changed in the past ten years. She had grown into herself, you could say, become set; she had a slightly wary look, as though she were endlessly expecting something to happen. Her eyes were hollow looking, her mouth neutral, but beautiful too, Will told her. He said she had a certain elegance of bearing in her tall, thin way, a kind of grace and purpose. "And that hair," he would say, burying his fingers in the kinky ashy-blond nimbus around her face, "your great shimmering halo."

She'd met him on a dare not long after she'd opened Chacha's. Back in the days when her life had exactly one dimension, when she was still scared silly about whether she was doing it right, doing all the work herself, putting up deli platters à la Bo and dinners à la Earl, furnishing the place with tag-sale tables and chairs. She was buying the food and cooking it and serving it and washing up afterward. Every night she counted her money down to the last penny, left it in the night drop at the bank, and went home to sleep, only to start the same thing all over again the next day. And the customers were starting to come. Mostly they were kids from the colleges and hippies from the surrounding towns and people Rachel called the voluntary poor, who seemed to do nothing but always paid their bills. They'd come in and sit around playing checkers and nursing a beer and sometimes staying for dinner. Carole didn't have many rules for the place. She didn't want them. And she certainly never told anyone where to sit, not after growing up with her father, who always asked for a different table. Every single time, even when the first table was a good one.

On this night, though, the place was deserted because of a storm that had dumped over two feet of snow and shut down the whole town. Rachel was there, stranded and waiting to go home with Carole. And the only other person in the place was a man sitting at the bar, watching the news on TV and sipping coffee. He was a big guy, probably six feet three or four, and wide through the shoulders. He had on a leather jacket and Levi's. And he was black, which you noticed because it was unusual for Montpelier.

"I dare you to go over and strike up a conversation with him," Rachel said to her. Carole had come over to see what it was doing outside. She was looking down Main Street, which was bone white, silent, with snow coming down thickly. "He looks cool," Rachel added.

"Dare?" Carole said, turning to Rachel. "What is this, third grade?"

"Okay, double dare," Rachel said. She was tucked into the corner of the sofa, her feet drawn up, wrapped in a gray shawl she'd knitted herself, and she was knitting something else, something big and brown for Morgan. A sweater maybe.

"Well, I've already talked to him, so I guess I win," Carole said.

"Not patron to customer." Rachel widened her eyes as if to say *duh*. "Woman to man."

"This is a restaurant, Rach," Carole said, glancing over at the guy and hoping he wasn't listening. "Not a singles club." But the truth was that she had already noticed him, and not as a customer either, but as a guy, and when he'd spoken to her, asked for coffee and a bagel, she'd felt the slightest fluster and had shaken back her hair and then felt exposed and a little foolish.

"I'm not suggesting you take him home with you. I just think you could use a little practice, and don't get me wrong or anything, but you need to branch out a bit."

"I've got a lot to do," Carole said. "I can't go striking up conversations with the customers just for the practice."

"Oh, come on," Rachel said. "You've got nothing to do. Nobody else is coming in here tonight in this weather, and you know it. You could close up right now and not lose a dime. Hell, you'd even save on electricity if you closed now."

Carole looked over at the man, all by himself, and she felt a little bit sorry for him. Will later told her that he'd heard every word, that he was trying to keep a straight face and look a little lonely.

"Maybe you don't have the nerve," Rachel said.

Carole walked right over, sat down on the stool beside him, swiveled to face Rachel, and gave her a *so there* look. The man—well, Will, but she didn't know his name yet—just kept staring at the TV screen overhead as though he hadn't noticed her sitting down.

Carole cleared her throat to get his attention, but he didn't blink. Rachel made a sign with her fingers: *Say something!* But what was there to say? She had no experience in this. If she was on the other side of the bar, she'd know exactly what to do, but here? Next to him like just another customer? She scowled at Rachel again, but the trouble was, she couldn't exactly get up and admit defeat. Her only option was to pretend she just happened to have sat down on this particular stool, when all the rest of them were available. She tipped her head up and watched the TV too, feeling so bloody foolish and ticked off at Rachel for getting her into this, and she was going to get even, oh, yes. Look out.

It seemed a woman had died in the snowstorm the night before. Her car had veered off the road and gotten stuck in a snowbank. She had left it and set out on foot. Speculation was, she was headed for a house she must have remembered passing. She was found dead in a snowbank less than a quarter of a mile from her car. "Dumbest thing she could have done," the man said to the TV. "She should have stayed put."

That did it. He'd blown it now. "In the *car?*" Carole said. The words practically exploded from her lips. "You think she should have stayed in the car?" What kind of a guy would blame that poor woman for her own death?

He took a calm sip of coffee and spoke, still staring at the overhead TV. "That's what I said. She should have stayed put. She could have run the car now and then for a little heat. It's a shame."

"Oh, please," Carole said. "The car was disabled. They just said that on the news. She needed shelter." Over on the sofa, Rachel must have heard everything and was shaking her head.

Now, finally, he did turn to look at Carole, but slowly. He had the kind of face where you could see the structure right underneath, as though it had been assembled out of clay and covered with skin the color of cider. He was very good looking, and she suspected he knew that. He took the time to look over her whole face feature by feature, as if searching for something in particular. Her eyes, her nose. When he looked at her lips, something totally unexpected happened to her. It was a kind of collapse deep within her, a delicious pooling warmth that caused her to sit up straighter and again, as she'd done earlier, push her hair from her face over her shoulder. He grinned at her. "She already *had* shelter," he said.

"A car isn't shelter." Carole knew instantly that she was wrong. Of course a car was shelter, but she charged ahead. "A house is shelter," she said as levelly as possible. "Her body told her to get out of the car and go to that house, where she would be warm and safe." She felt the exposure of talking about a woman's body and what it was saying when her own body was doing plenty of talking on its own. She'd been in a deep freeze for such a long time and now she was thawing out so fast she ached.

He smiled at her and shook his head. "Her body told her to stay put, believe me. But she didn't listen to it."

Carole turned to see if Rachel was watching, and she was.

"You think I'm being a jerk," he said.

"Maybe a little," she said. "Well, no, not a jerk. You're just—" Her right hand reached up and fiddled with her hair again. "Opinionated," she said. "I see you have opinions about this."

"Will Burbank." He extended his hand. "I should," he said. "It's my field. I teach this stuff at the community college."

"You mean you teach—" She didn't know what to call it. She was thinking about what they taught at Vassar—the history of western civilization, the poets of the Victorian period. She'd never heard of a college course in why not to get out of your car in a snowstorm, and she was confused by the feel of his hand in hers.

"Survival," he said.

"But what's there to know? No offense, but is it a whole subject?"

"You're not from here, are you?"

She shook her head and shrugged as if to say, *Got me.*

"So, Chacha," he said, using the name of the place since she clearly wasn't going to tell him her real name. "Try this one. Who's the most important person in a rescue? The victim or the rescuer?"

"The victim," she said immediately, even though it was probably a trick question.

He looked almost apologetic. "It's the rescuer."

"But if it's the victim who needs help—" She laughed. "How does anybody ever get saved?" She pictured a scene in which somebody was drowning, calling for help, but the person on the beach was just standing there saying "No way. Too dangerous."

"Sometimes a victim shouldn't be saved. The rescuer needs to assess the danger to himself. He knows what he's doing." His hand was still on her wrist, heavy and warm. "Do you want to hear?"

She did, actually.

"If the rescuer dies, so does the victim. Do you see? It's automatic. The rescuer has to keep himself alive to do any good, and that means putting himself first."

"Or herself."

"Or herself. She has to be number one, or they both die." She liked the way he shifted genders for her without missing a beat.

"What else?" she said, ever the student. "Try me on something else."

He did, but she flunked every test. She'd swim for it if she fell out of a boat far from shore. Wrong—she should do something called the survival float to retain heat. "I can teach you that," he said, causing her heart to pick up speed for a couple of seconds at the very thought that there might be more, later, some other day, with him.

She also got the falling-through-the-ice rescue wrong. You don't walk to the victim. You don't even crawl on hands and knees. You get down on your stomach, spread your body weight over as large an area as possible, and slither.

"You know my best credential in this area?" he said. "It's being from Queens and not from up here. I tell my class that on the first night. Every time. Brings home to them that survival is learned behavior. It's not instinctive. For most of us, our instincts will kill us."

They moved over to the armchairs, where it was more comfortable, pushing them close together so they could talk in low voices and not wake Rachel, fast asleep on the couch. Carole told Will that she'd dropped out of college and supported herself for a year working in a restaurant in New York, then hitchhiked to California on the day of her mother's memorial service. There had been nothing left to keep her in New York. It was the most she'd told anyone except Rachel about herself.

"What about your father?" he asked her.

"Dead," she said, and felt miserable about the lie, except that Will's reaction saved her by being so cerebral and absent of pity. Not a shred of *oh, poor you*. "So you're alone," he said. "Any other family?"

She pointed to Rachel and told him how, when she'd hitched across the country, all she had was a scrap of paper from Rachel. "'We're the last house on Stanyan before Seventeenth Street,'" it said. When I think back on it, I was lucky. I hardly even knew her." She paused, uncomfortable about brushing up against the truth of her past. "Now it's your turn," she said.

He'd grown up in Queens and he'd gone to NYU and moved up to Vermont along with every other hippie, to get back to the land, and here he laughed. To the land anyway, not exactly *back* in his case, since he'd never been from the land in the first place. He'd moved in with some purists in Adamant who voted to become vegetarians midway through raising a pig, some chickens, and a steer. All the animals were set free and died of starvation over the winter. "It got me to thinking about survival and how none of us knows enough about it, and worse, a lot of people are so sure they have it knocked. They don't know how little they know. Like you, right?" he said. "You thought you knew. It's not a criticism. It's a fact."

He'd received training from the Red Cross and taken courses at the University of Vermont, so he knew what he was talking about. Right now he was doing what he could to teach it to others—in schools, to groups, at the community college.

She knew she was twisting her hair in her fingers too much and lowered her hands to her lap, only to find them sliding around again, to her throat, her ear, her hair again. Like she was pointing out parts of herself to him. *Look here, look there. My lips? My hair?* She wriggled and squirmed, all the while trying not to. The thing was, she felt like kissing him. Not any big passionate kiss. It was just a sort of friendship kiss. And she asked him, interrupting, "Do you mind if I kiss you?" He'd laughed out loud, loud enough to cause Rachel to stir, so when Rachel woke, there was Carole kissing Will Burbank—just lightly, demurely, on the lips, but still kissing him.

Carole took a quick detour into the kitchen, with its stainless-steel counter and fluorescent lights, to check on the state of things. The wash-up crew—two kids from Goddard—was at it. Steel racks of washed glasses and plates were steaming, and the counters were clear. Sandy, her best waitress, was putting some desserts together.

"These are the last," Sandy said of the desserts. "And I'm out of here."

She pushed back out through the swinging doors and went over to join the others. "Squeeze in," Rachel said, hoisting the baby, Dylan, to her other side. Rachel had gained weight with the pregnancy and wasn't planning to lose it. She was happy, she said, to give in to the whole earth-mother thing once and for all. She hoisted herself around, setting off the muffled sound of the bells she'd sewn into all her clothing.

"Squeeze indeed," Morgan said, shifting his long scissors legs aside for her.

They watched Will and Pepper play checkers for a while, listening for the sounds in the kitchen to end. Pretty soon, Sandy and the kids came through the swinging doors, laughing and shrugging on their parkas and saying good night. Then Carole brought out the plates of food she'd made for tonight. Stuffed mushrooms, spinach salad, and hot bread. She drew beers for Morgan and Will, glasses of seltzer water for Rachel and Pepper, and another cup of tea for herself.

Will slid the topo map out of its plastic sleeve, unfolded it, and spread it across the table. A black dot on the map indicated where she and Will lived; another indicated Morgan and Rachel's place. Between the two, razor-thin brown lines grew dense, far apart, and dense again, indicating steep hills and deep valleys.

"February twenty-eighth?" Will looked at each of them in turn, then touched the dot indicating his and Carole's house. "We start here. Five o'clock." He went over it all, showing where the trail ascended, where it forked, where it crossed a ridge, where they'd stop. She looked around at the others, their faces serious in the light of the hurricane lantern. But her attention was drawn to Pepper, to the shiny scar that ran down his forehead and came into sharp relief in the light. The ugly red thing shocked her all over again with its size and depth, the way it severed and puckered his eyebrow. In ordinary daylight the scar was hardly noticeable, and she could go for weeks or months without thinking of it, the way she could go for long periods without noticing a person's accent or some other small habit that set them apart. But then something would happen, like right now with the light the way it was, to make her aware again. Pepper must have felt her gaze, because he put his hand to his forehead, a self-conscious gesture she'd come to recognize, and she looked away, ashamed to have been caught staring.

After that night at Chacha's, Will had driven Carole and Rachel home over snow-covered streets to the Capitol apartments. Already she felt safe with him. He drove carefully, stopping at lights and signs even though theirs was the only car on the road. Rachel had asked him if he wanted to come in, wanted even to crash there, given the weather. "It's a bitch out, right, Carole?" she'd said. Will had smiled and shaken his head. Thanks, but that was okay, he'd be fine. He'd reached across the front seat to open the car door, and the feel of him so close, of his hand brushing past her, had been electrifying. He'd waited in the car, looking up through the windshield until Carole turned on the light in the apartment and came to the window to wave that she and Rachel were safely inside.

He called her the next morning while she was still padding around her apartment in her robe. "Will Burbank from last night," he said.

"Oh," she said, sinking into the couch with a giddy pleasure at the sound of his voice. She'd stayed awake long into the night thinking about him, reliving every inch of their conversation, awed at what she'd done, asking for that kiss, but not regretting it either. Not at all.

"So how are you," he'd said to her, and something in the downward cant of his voice with its emphasis on the word *you* told her that he'd already made up his mind about her. Now all she had to do was make up hers about him.

He came back into Chacha's that afternoon and settled in at the bar with a cup of coffee and the afternoon newspaper. She felt his eyes on her as she hustled beers and sandwiches, as she bumped through the swinging doors to the kitchen, hip first, and then out again. She found herself preening under his gaze, tossing her hair, rolling her sleeves, tapping her pencil against her lower lip while she took orders, and glancing sidelong at him whenever she could. She went to ask him if there was anything she could get for him, but instead of asking from behind the bar, she came around beside him and leaned in to point out items on the menu so that her hair pressed against his face and she could breathe in the slightly smoky smell of him.

"What time can you get off?" he said.

"Anytime," she said. Business was light again today, and Rachel would cover for her.

"I'll cook you some dinner."

He took her up to his house, the same house where they now lived, which was four miles out of town on a dirt road. It had a steep driveway, the snow so deep on either side she could barely see over it. The house itself was nestled into a clearing with a view of the White Mountains on a good clear day. It had a big woodstove in the living room and a cathedral ceiling he'd made himself by knocking through the upstairs room. He'd put in skylights and a big fan to keep the warm air from collecting up there. There were two big couches in faded plaid in the living room, a coffee table made from a pocked telephone wire spool, and a million books on all the walls. Beyond was the dining room and then the kitchen, which was all business at one end and all indulgence at the other, where he'd installed a Franklin stove and a big armchair with a good light. She sat in the armchair and watched him make their supper of rice and beans and leftover pork, a salad and fresh oranges for dessert. He told her his whole story over dinner, as if getting it over with, as if he already knew it had in it the things she would want to know. He said he'd had a two-year marriage that had ended eight years earlier, and that his only long-term girlfriend had moved back to New York a year ago. And then the floor was open to her, and she'd felt shy. "I've never been married," she said. "I've never really even dated."

"You're kidding, right?" he said, letting go his booming signature laugh. "A good-looking woman like you?"

"I've been busy," she said. "I've got my work."

He apologized right away, as if he'd insulted her. He said he hadn't meant to pry. And then he cocked his head and said, "But it's true. You are a good-looking woman, Carole." She smiled and stared down at her hands and then looked into his eyes for a dangerously long time.

He pushed his chair out from the table, took her by the hand, led her to the stairs, and she followed oh so willingly, oh so eagerly. She wanted, or at least her body wanted, what was in store, even as her mind objected all the way up the stairs and into his bedroom. *Look out. Be careful. Remember the last time.* And when she reveled in the feeling as he unbuttoned her shirt, kissed her neck, and pulled her gently to the bed, her mind ratcheted up its objection and conjured images of Eddie and Rita in that motel room, him demanding, like a spoiled child stamping its foot, that she *obey*. But her body won out, her melting body and the delicious comforting feel of his kisses and whispered assurance that he knew this was too soon to say it, but he loved her.

She had moved in three months later, when her lease was up. That was where they lived, and that was where they went after making plans at Chacha's with the Weaver-Lears, driving the four unlit miles in their usual companionable silence. Often on nights like this they had to leave the truck at the base of the driveway and walk up, but tonight they sailed over the snow-dusted drive and pulled to a stop in the dooryard. Will turned on the porch light, and they went inside, took off their boots at the door, padded into the dark living room in stocking feet, and warmed themselves at the woodstove.

Besides the glow from the stove, the only light in the room came from the red blinker on the answering machine. There were more messages than usual, and the sheer number made her curious. On her way to the kitchen, she hit the start button and listened as she got the coffeepot ready for the morning and checked the refrigerator to see what they had for breakfast. The first call was just a bleep, followed by a long silence. Whoever it was breathed into the receiver a few times and then hung up. The one after that was a woman's voice. "Blast from the past!" The voice laughed, and Carole stopped, frozen in place, staring at the machine. "It feels so bloody far out to hear your voice on that machine after all this time. I was so freaked out just now that I hung up. That was me, the last call, by the way. Or maybe it was the answering machine that freaked me out. I never would have expected you to have one. You of all people. I don't even have one. Hardly anybody does."

Carole hit the stop button hard and stood staring at the machine. It can't be, she thought. It just can't be. Not Naomi after all these years. How could she have found her? How had she gotten the number? What did she want? She looked around to see if Will had heard, but he must not have. He was nowhere in sight. Heart pounding, she brought the answering machine closer to herself and huddled over it, turned down the volume, and then hit the start button again. "Carole, baby." Oh, the voice, the familiarity of it, as though no time had passed. "Okay, here it is. You'll never believe what I've done. Call me as soon as you get in, okay?" Naomi screamed out the word *soon*. "This is just so bloody groovy I can't believe—"

Carole stopped it again because Will's footsteps were approaching. He went through the dining room to the kitchen, where he turned on the faucet and let it run a few moments, drank a glass of water, then passed through the dining room to the woodstove, which he banked every night before they went to bed.

Once he was busy with that, she hit the start button again and listened with the volume lower still. "Where the hell are you? I can't keep waiting. Don't ask. Same old thing here." Laughter. Carole felt ill at the sound of it, at the way Naomi could be so carefree, as if this was all some great big joke when it wasn't. And the big question begging an answer: *How had she found her?*

"Look, I'm going to be away for a few days, but meet me at the class reunion on Friday, okay? You *are* going, right?" The phone clicked off. And then the last message came on. "Oh, shit. Of course you're not going. You never go to reunions. Well, you've got to come to this one." Laughter. "I have news. 'Noose,' as they say in Brooklyn. We're going to be neighbors. I'm moving up there. I've already found a house and everything, and it's not even that far away. It's over in the Shady Rill section. Oh, God, Mason, there's so much to catch up on. Tons of water under this bridge. I can't possibly go into it all now over the phone. Ten years' worth of stuff, can you believe it? But I haven't forgotten you for a minute, you know. My shrink said I should do zero-base thinking, so I did. Start from nothing, no expectations, no baggage, nothing. Who's the person you admire the most? he wanted to know. Not now but in your whole life, and I said you right away. Didn't even miss a beat. It came as a surprise to me, but the minute I said your name out loud, I knew it was true. I know we sort of lost touch, but hey. Oh, God, we had such a great time in high school, re- member? All the stuff we did, how close we were? Seriously, though. See you Friday." There was a long pause. "Be there, Mason, please." Another long pause. Carole stared at the telephone while the tape re- wound, clicked, and buzzed. She'd never once thought it would be Naomi who would find her. She'd thought Naomi was gone, off and married to that guy. Bax, that was his name, living some jet-set life somewhere. She never, ever expected this. Eddie maybe, but never this, never Naomi.

"Who's that?" Will said, making her jump. She hadn't heard him come in.

"Nobody." She might have shouted it. "Somebody I used to know." She felt numb all over, like nothing in her—mind or body— would work. She was caught in a collision of her two lives.

"I got that much," he said. "And she's moving up here—"

"She doesn't mean it," she said.

"Sounds like she meant it to me. Who is she?"

"You don't want to know," she said, and oh, God, what a lie it was. Her skin was beginning to hurt. Something throbbed behind her eyes. The thing about dread was how it gripped you like an all- over vise, how it obliterated everything but itself.

"I don't?" He was grinning at her, expecting her to open up the way she always did.

She had to say something to stay in the here and now with him. "I think she's an alcoholic. I could hear it in her voice, couldn't you? And crazy, if you want to know the truth. Unpredictable. I don't know what she's thinking. A real city girl. Born and bred."

Will just stared.

"Well, it's *true*," she said, slapping the table with the palm of her hand. "No matter what you might think."

He put up his hands, his old *I give* gesture. "Whatever you say."

"Well, it's not just whatever I say, Will. It's the truth."

"Christ," he said. "Okay." She looked away, her signal that there was nothing else to say.

After he went upstairs, she listened again to the tape, this time like a thief, turning the volume way down. Then she dialed the operator and asked for Naomi by her maiden name. But there was no listing. Of course. Baxter, that was the husband's name. But Baxter was his first name. And for all Carole really knew, no matter what she'd said to Will, Naomi might not even live in New York, might have called from some other place.

She went back to the machine and listened again. *We're going to be neighbors. . . . I've already found a house and everything.* This was crazy. She couldn't possibly mean— Carole dialed the operator. There must be a way to find her, to call and stop her. "I got a call," she said. "They didn't leave the number. Is there any way to trace it? To find out the number she called from?"

"I'm sorry," the operator said. "We're not authorized—"

"But it's an emergency," Carole whisper-shouted.

"What sort of emergency?" the operator said.

Carole slammed down the receiver. She played the message again: *. . . already found a house.* Found! So there! Not bought, only found. That was so much different. There was still time. Carole could hear the liquor for sure in Naomi's voice this time. She had seen enough drunks to know they flew high on an idea and forgot it in the morning. She became aware of Will again, standing at the door to the dining room, watching her hunched over the telephone like something wounded. "What?" she said. "Why do you keep sneaking up on me like that?"

"Is everything okay?" he said.

"Of course it is," she said. "What makes you think—"

He raised his shoulders slightly and let them drop. *Isn't it obvious?*

"I might go," she said.

"Where?"

"To that reunion."

"You're kidding," he said, frowning. "You've never—"

"I know that," she said. "This is different."

"Different," he said. "Okay. I'll buy that. When is it? Where do you have to go?"

She was glad for the solid ground of the when and where questions. "Friday. New York. I'll call the school to double-check."

He was watching her, waiting for more. He gave her a long time, the space she needed to tell him what was really going on. When she said nothing, he came over to kiss her good night.

Stay calm, she told herself. It was only a telephone call. Don't take the leap from those phone calls straight into some full-blown catastrophe. And it was a drunken telephone call. She'd seen plenty of those at Chacha's, usually women at the pay phone late at night dialing one number after another. Not a snowball's chance Naomi would really come here to live. It had been nuts of Carole to even consider the truth in that. This was one of Naomi's crank calls.

She went directly to the nearest mirror to look at just exactly what Naomi would see. Not the chubby full-faced sixteen-year-old. No. She looked long and hard at her image. Her hair was pulled back from her angular, very serious face. She looked worn for twenty-six. The other women at the reunion would be much better preserved. Naomi most of all. They would already be thinking about saving their faces, and it would show. Carole had fine lines at the outer edges of her eyes, between her brows, and around her mouth, but she liked the age that showed in her face. She liked the speed with which she was getting through life.

She was stronger than Naomi. Maybe she always had been. She would go to the reunion, and she would tell Naomi not ever to set foot in Montpelier. She had to. They had a secret to protect, and the only way to do it was to turn away from each other, although sometimes, God, it seemed she was the only one of the three of them who understood that.

Chapter Eleven

SAN FRANCISCO
1968

The San Francisco house Carole had come to after leaving New York was a great dowager of a place at the edge of Haight-Ashbury. It had a sagging roofline and a weedy, overgrown yard. It wasn't one of the good communes—one of the political or famous communes they wrote up in the *Examiner* or *Time.* It was just a big old house that was falling apart. People came and went. You never knew who would be there from one day to the next.

When Carole arrived, she came through the open front door and saw Rachel sitting cross-legged on the floor in a circle of seven or eight lackluster people. Rachel's hair covered her shoulders almost to the elbows like a great dark shawl, and she looked up and stared at Carole for several seconds over the tops of her little wire-rimmed glasses, then jumped to her feet and shouted and danced like they were long-lost sisters. "Of course there's room," Rachel had screamed. Hadn't she said so in all those letters? Later, in the kitchen eating spaghetti, Carole brought out the packet of letters she'd taken from the drawer in her parents' apartment, all opened by now. "But there were more," Rachel had said.

In a long, breathless monologue, Rachel explained how the nuns had made her pack everything in the middle of the night when her water broke. They'd taken her by taxi to a hospital outside the city, where she'd had the baby. The couple from New Jersey came to the hospital for the birth and expected to take Pepper away with them, but Rachel refused to sign the papers, even though she was tripping on the anesthesia. The nuns had been furious. They wouldn't bring the baby to her until he was screaming with hunger. "Next baby I home-deliver," she said.

She'd stayed with that girl she'd met at the home who'd been taken in by her aunt and uncle in Rochester. She lived with them for two years. The uncle was cool, she said. He helped with the babies, took care of them while Rachel worked at a temp agency and her friend waitressed. But it was so boring. She wanted more action. In the spring of 1967 she got a ride with some university students she met at a gas station. They were heading west. One of them was Morgan. She pointed to a very tall, spindly-legged, black-haired man standing against the counter, who smiled broadly, just like Rachel, and gave Carole the peace sign in greeting. He was from Hardwick, Rachel explained, a little town in Vermont near the Canadian border, and someday they were going to go back there and build a geodesic dome in the woods. They'd plant a garden and have six kids. "Morgan is brilliant," Rachel said. "Everything he touches is a work of art, and I can't wait to have children with him. They'll be spectacular children," she said.

Carole stole a look at Pepper, who didn't seem to have heard.

"And what about you?" Rachel said. In a million years she hadn't thought Carole would come. She'd never written back, for one thing.

"My mother died," Carole said, which was all she needed to say to Rachel to make her face collapse in sympathy. Rachel brought her to a room on the second floor with a sliver view of the city if you stood way to one side of the window and a single mattress on the floor. Carole sat there on that first day, her suitcase beside her, and thought,

What now? She'd had her hopes pinned on this all the way across the country and now here she was.

Although Carole didn't know it at the time, she had arrived in Haight-Ashbury just months after its heyday, on the cusp of its steep and rapid decline. Hard drugs and crime were beginning to roll through the district, filling the vacuum left by the flower children who were already vacating for Sebastopol and Santa Cruz and Oregon. On some days Haight Street was just a sea of chrome, hundreds of motorcycles glistening in the sun and Hell's Angels taking over the sidewalks and bullying passersby. On other days it was a wasteland.

Her memories of the year in San Francisco all held a nightmare edge. Her family was gone. Her mother was dead, and her father must have hated her. On top of that, the weather was always gloomy, and nobody ever bought lightbulbs. They were too much of a luxury, so instead of getting new bulbs, they moved the ones they had from lamp to lamp until only a few good ones were left, and all of them in the bedrooms. The common areas were always dark, and people got used to feeling their way around the place.

"So if you're not doing drugs and you're not into sex, what in hell are you doing here anyway?" a fifteen-year-old girl named Jaya asked Carole once. Jaya was typical of the kids who passed through the house—lost waifs who were very sure of themselves in matters of sex and drugs, but children in the important ways. They got sick a lot, ate poorly, and didn't see the point in picking up after themselves. That day Jaya slipped Carole some speed, saying it was an aspirin, then followed her around and watched the speed take hold. Carole hadn't known at first that she'd taken anything, only that she felt suddenly punched up with energy, that she had this stunning new optimism and could live smack in the present. No future, no past, just pure moment. Pure now. She walked all the way to the marina that day and back. When she got home, she cleaned the kitchen until early the next morning. She asked Jaya for more.

She was on speed again the night she got a job waitressing and busing at Magnolia Thunderpussy. She was willing and energetic, and she knew a thing or two about restaurants. Magnolia hired her on the spot and taught her how to make outrageous ice-cream sundaes like Marty's Montana Banana and Pineapple Pussy. Her life fell into a rhythm of late nights on speed, getting up midmorning, and going first thing to find Pepper, Rachel's precocious, bright little boy who called his mother by her first name. Rachel would yell out to whoever was around that she had to go to Golden Gate Park for a demonstration or down to Market Street to throw blood on people. It was always something like that. And whoever heard her was expected to keep Pepper out of trouble, but God, look at who they were! Carole was the only one who ever really did it. She was the one who sought him out, gave him baths, combed his hair, and took him to the library and the playground down the street. Then Rachel would take a sudden interest in him and sweep him off to the combat zone to make sure he understood that life was not the peaches-and-cream existence of the commune. Or she'd march him up to see the mansions on Nob Hill so he could see the Wasteful Way Those People Lived. Rachel said he was acquiring street smarts. "Remember knowing how powerful you really were but your parents thinking you couldn't do anything?" Carole didn't remember any such thing.

"They arm kids in the Congo at six, did you know that? They make fighters of them. And gypsies. Those kids are on their own, even younger than Pepper. We pamper kids in this culture, and then they don't stand a chance in the real world. I won't do that with Pepper."

"Those kids in Africa get shot," Carole said.

"That's the beauty," Rachel said. "This isn't the Congo. All the advantages. None of the disadvantages."

One night in March, after she'd been there a year and was used to the sounds in the house, Carole woke very late; she heard an unfamiliar noise on the stairs. She sat up on her mattress and listened, and sure enough, it was the sound of someone barefoot on the stairs. But the sounds were too light and playful to be one of the adults. She got up and opened her bedroom door in time to hear the front door open and close, so she followed, pulling on her bathrobe as she went. Outside, the night air was cool, and there was a slight wind coming from the Bay and up the street. She stood on the porch and peered out into the night.

Pepper stood, barefooted and wearing only his pajamas under the light at the corner of Stanyan and Seventeenth. He turned and ran down the sidewalk, right past the house, a spindly little thing with arms spiraling, making noises like an airplane. He didn't see her as he ran past, and she didn't want to startle him by calling out, so she went down the steps to the sidewalk and followed him. At midblock he turned and came her way, stopping short when he saw her there.

"Pep," she said.

He grinned.

"What are you doing out like this?"

"Playing," he said.

"Let's go back," she said, and he came with her willingly, still making airplane noises as if there was nothing at all unusual about his being outside.

Just before they reached the house, she saw a soldier on the other side of the street. He was clean-cut with a shaved head and a khaki uniform that even from a distance looked crisp. Lots of soldiers came through San Francisco on their way to or from Vietnam, but usually the only way you could tell was the haircut. People swore at them or worse if they showed up in uniform like this guy. The soldier watched her and Pepper walk up the street and onto the stone steps to the house. Once she was inside, she checked from the living room window, but he was gone, and she was glad. The sight of him and the way he'd been watching her made her feel queasy. It was dangerous for those guys to come around the Haight. People hated them.

When she woke the next day, she could tell by a thin ray of cloudy light coming in slantwise from her window that it was late in the day. She lay in bed and listened for sounds in the house but heard nothing. She went down the hall to the bathroom, peering into empty rooms as she passed. She listened for sounds from the turret, but that too was quiet. "Pepper?" she called, and received no answer.

Being alone gave her a luxurious and rare feeling of peace. She took a long, blistering shower and shampooed. If there was enough sun, she would dry her hair in the little yard out back. If not, she would dry it on the radiator in the kitchen. She looked at herself in the bathroom mirror, peering in close for the details of her face. The speed wrecked her appetite, and she'd lost more weight. Her cheeks were slightly hollowed, her eyes deeper set. Her body was thin but well muscled, her legs strong from the walks up Stanyan Street to the house. You're letting that body go to waste, Rachel sometimes said. Carole's abstinence was famous in the house, like she was some kind of saint or pariah, one or the other. But her body was only a body. A vessel—she'd heard that term as a kid, and it fit so well. A vessel that held her, not a thing in and of itself. Not like Rachel, who was all sexual urgency with Morgan, so the house reeked of their lovemaking most of the time. She looked again. This was how she looked to other people, but she didn't feel at all like it.

She put on a cotton robe and belted it tightly, then she took a hit of speed and sat down on the toilet seat to wait for the very slight sweating, the feel of her heart quickening, the sense of excitement. She checked outside for sun, but there was none. It was a gray drizzly day, with dark clouds settled low over everything. Just as well, because soon her pupils would start to dilate and the murk of the house would feel better than bright sun.

In the kitchen, she boiled water on the stove and made some instant coffee, then pulled a chair over to the radiator and sat with her back to it, fanning her hair over the hot metal bars, fluffing it to hasten the drying, restlessly turning this way and that to expose the hair underneath to the heat. She heard footsteps in the hall at one point and stopped to listen. People went barefoot or they wore sandals. These footsteps were hard, made by real shoes. Real heels and soles. "Who's there?" she said, standing and crossing the kitchen.

The hall was dark, lit from behind by the open front door. She saw the silhouette of a man, a soldier. "Hey," he said.

But not any soldier. He came toward her, his arms out as though he expected to embrace her, and she took a step back. "Carole," he said, and hearing the voice, she knew. She felt cold and sick, with the hopeless feeling that again and again he would find her and keep on finding her for time everlasting. He was blocking her access to the front door. The back door was open, but beyond it there were trash barrels and junk. If she tried to run, she'd get caught up in all the debris. *How had he found her?* She backed away, trying to imagine an escape route. No one knew she was here but Rachel. Only Rachel. And why? Why now?

Afraid, she backed into the kitchen and flipped the switch, but the bulb was dead. The only light came from a bluish strip of fluorescence on the stove, and she could barely see his face. She went behind the table to keep it between herself and him. "What?" she asked. All she could think was that something had happened. He knew something. Something about Rita. It was over.

"At ease," he said. He had on one of those caps with a point that sat low on his forehead. He could be anybody. If she passed him on the street, she might not know him. But he wasn't anybody. He was Eddie. "I came by to say hello. Shit. I've been in 'Nam. I've got exactly twelve hours in San Francisco, and this is the reception I get?"

He was slightly out of focus because she was at that point in the cycle of speed, just past the peak. "You never just come by to say hello," she said.

He picked up one of the kitchen chairs. Dropped it in place, and she jumped. "Sure I do," he said. His head jerked to the side, like he had developed a tic. She couldn't be sure.

"How did you find me?" She tried for the calmest voice she could. No point in upsetting him. Not if he was wrecked, which he might be.

He undid the button of his shirt, took out some pieces of paper, and handed them to her. In the bad light and with her eyes dilated the way they were, she couldn't read them, but she didn't need to. She knew that one was a letter from Rachel that had been in her mother's drawer. The other was a graduation picture of her that had been ripped from the proof sheet.

"Your letters were never opened. Quite a woman, your mother. She had a thing about privacy, but I guess you know that." He opened the refrigerator. "What do you have to eat around here?" He pulled out the jug of Thunderbird wine and swung it to the table.

"I don't have money, if that's what you want."

"Who said anything about money?"

"I just—" she began. "The last time."

"Well, this isn't the last time. This is a guy dropping in on an old friend. A little hospitality wouldn't kill you, a little 'Nice to see you again, Eddie. What have you been doing with yourself lately?' 'Oh, thank you for asking. I've been in fucking Vietnam getting fucking shot at while you've been sitting here in your hippie house doing drugs and balling like a jackrabbit.' That's what I want. A little fucking respect, because you have no idea what it's like over there."

"Okay," she said. "Okay, that's cool. Sure."

"Good," he said and took a long drink from the jug of wine. "You look good. Yeah. You do."

"Thanks," she said.

"You lost weight, but you've got some size on you. I like that. Not like those gook broads. Another species. Like fucking an otter."

Carole drew away from him.

"So?"

"So what?" she said.

"So how do I look? Huh? Now it's your turn to tell me I'm looking pretty good myself."

"Sure, yes," she said. "You look fine."

"You can do better than that," he said. "Say it like you mean it."

"You do," she said. "You look good. The service and all. It agreed with you."

"The service did *not* fucking agree with me." He smacked the table with his open hand.

"Okay," she said. "All right. Sorry."

There were sounds at the front door, and Eddie visibly jumped. People were coming into the house, coming down the hall toward the kitchen. Pepper burst into the kitchen at a run, saw Eddie, and stood staring at him with frightened eyes. He was used to strangers, so it wasn't that. It was the uniform. Even at four he knew this wasn't right. Then Rachel was standing in the doorway behind Pepper, squinting through the dark at the stranger. "He's just leaving," Carole said, blurting out what she hoped was true, as if she had any way to make that happen, anything to head Rachel off. The second that Rachel recognized the uniform, and she had already, Carole could see it in her posture, the gathering rage of finding somebody who'd actually gone over there, who'd killed women and babies and napalmed a zillion acres of jungle and all the rest of it right here in the kitchen. Her kitchen.

"Like hell," Eddie said. She noticed his hands twitching and that tic again with his head. "We were just getting it going."

"Who let you in here?" Rachel said. "I mean, who the hell do you think you are?"

"Who let *you* in?" Eddie said, mocking her.

"You're in *my* house."

"Door was wide open," Eddie said, smirking.

She looked at Carole. "He's not a friend of yours, is he?"

"No," Carole said.

"What was that you said?" He'd been tipped back in his chair and now he brought it forward with a bang. "Let me tell you—"

Rachel walked over to where he was sitting, stood over him, and spat in his face.

"Oh, Rach," Carole said. "No."

Eddie drew his hand slowly across his face to wipe away the spit. He looked at it, then reached over to Pepper, who was standing at the stove, and wiped it on Pepper's shirt. He looked at Rachel. "You bitch," he said softly. But she wasn't scared. She drew herself up and spat again. Eddie was on his feet in a flash, his fist out, and Rachel dropped like a stone. It all went so fast then. Pepper was screaming screaming screaming. Carole rushed over to Rachel. She thought she was dead, the way she lay there, but she sat up on her own, holding her face in both hands. Eddie was standing over them both. "You see what she did?"

"What *she* did?" As if that justified hitting her, knocking her to the ground. "You come in here where you're not wanted and hit a woman half your size and then you say it's *her* fault?"

"Make that kid shut up," he said, holding his head in both hands, his voice neutral, as if she was going to do what he said, the way she always did. That was what got to her.

That was when Pepper kicked Eddie in the shins. It couldn't have hurt much. Pepper was too little, and he was barefoot, but you would have thought Eddie had been shot by the look on his face. "You little shit," he said. Pepper went at him again. Eddie reached out and grabbed him by the upper arm and must have swung him. Carole didn't see it happen, but she heard the sound, a loud crack as Pepper's head slammed into the edge of the kitchen counter, where the tiles were chipped and sharp. Blood streamed down Pepper's face as Eddie stamped out the back door. Carole could hear the trash barrels toppling and rolling as he fled. "Don't think this is over," he shouted, and then it was silent.

Pepper started screaming again. Thank God, because it meant he was alive. Rachel was pulling herself up. Carole ran from the room to get bandages, a little tin box she kept in her suitcase. She went by feel, because her pupils had to be as big as pies by then, found the box smelling of rust, went back downstairs, and pressed a wet towel to Pepper's head, but there was so much blood, way too much. She remembered from her mother that you doused a cut with warm water over and over to clean it and then patted it dry with something sterile, not that there was anything clean around. She used the lapel of her bathrobe, cleaner than anything in the kitchen. She pressed it against his face while she drew out a Band-Aid, pulled the little tabs apart to expose the square of gauze, pressed it to the wound on his cheek just underneath his eye and peeled the tabs back, pressing down to make them stick.

"There," she said, but Pepper rubbed at it furiously.

"You put it in the wrong place," he said, and tried to press it higher on his forehead, but it wouldn't stick, of course. It was so wet. The dark spot had formed on his forehead and was running all down his eye. She reached for it, to correct her mistake, but he pushed her hand away. "You're so wasted," he said.

She got the keys and made both of them—Rachel and Pepper— get into the van and then drove them down Stanyan, left on Judah, and up the hill to the medical center, around to the emergency room, where she let them off and parked the van. She was still barefoot and wearing only her bathrobe, which by this time had blood on the front and the sleeves, and in the stark fierce light of the emergency room people stared at her. The linoleum felt bitter cold underfoot. They took Rachel and Pepper into different rooms, and Carole went from one to the other, answering questions about what had happened. Rachel was released, her face painted with red disinfectant, and the two of them sat side by side in the bleak waiting room. Carole felt exhausted and shaken. Her mouth was dry.

"Who was he?" Rachel asked her.

She was so weary, so tired of keeping secrets, and now another lie was called for and she had none. "The devil," she said, looking away, feeling sick and ashamed.

" 'The devil' doesn't exactly cut it, Carole. He almost killed Pepper. He could have. So who was he?"

Eddie, Eddie, Eddie, Eddie. The name hammered at her, daring to be spoken aloud. *Lindbaeck,* that hateful, ugly name, more hateful because she was so afraid of it. That was the disgrace of this moment. That was her shame. All she could manage was, "He would have left."

"Not what I asked," Rachel said, and Carole felt cornered, her defenses at the ready. Every situation has more than one truth, she thought with growing self-justification. None of this would have happened if Rachel weren't so hot-tempered about soldiers and uniforms and the war. "You're the one who spat on him."

"You're on his side now?"

"Of course not." Anger felt a lot better than fear. "But you should have let me handle it. I was getting him out of there."

"I don't think so," Rachel said. "You should have seen yourself. You looked scared to death in there. Cornered, is how you looked. He wasn't about to go anywhere. It's why I stepped in. You have any more surprises? Anybody else coming to beat us up?"

"Nobody knows where I am."

"Well, he sure as hell did."

She didn't want to think about that. Not even for a second. "Look, I'm sorry, okay? What more can I do?"

"Maybe we can turn him in," Rachel said. "Call his unit or whatever. Military police. Oh, forget it. You really don't think he'll be back?"

"He said he had twelve hours."

"I hope he gets killed in the war," Rachel said. "Serve him right."

Two nurses came out and asked to speak to them, but separately. Carole was taken to a small office. The nurse had forms to be filled out, but Carole couldn't see them because of her dilated pupils, which angered the nurse. She had to ask each question aloud and write down Carole's answer. The questions were about where they lived and what had occurred. All Carole said was that an intruder, a man, came in off the street and started a fight. It was clear the nurse didn't believe her. Then she was sent to another room, where a man in regular clothes interviewed her. What were the conditions of the home? Had the child been hurt before? Where was the child's father? Which one of them was the mother, and what, exactly, was their relationship? Carole realized they were looking for signs of abuse. "You don't understand," Carole told the man, but the way he looked at her let her know he did understand.

They kept Pepper overnight for observation. Rachel slept on his bed, and Carole slept on the floor. Morgan came up late and paced up and down the hall most of the night. When the nurse released Pepper grudgingly the next day, she said she would schedule follow-up visits in the home and that someone would contact them.

Back in the van, Rachel took the wheel, and Carole sat in the passenger seat, with Pepper between them. "Look at that," Rachel said, touching the line of tiny black stitches that ran from Pepper's hairline down his forehead to his eyebrow. "They're butchers. Look how it puckers."

"We can go back," Carole said. "They can do it over."

"They cannot," Rachel said, as if this were the stupidest thing she'd ever heard.

"There's a way they do," Carole said. "They can reopen it. I'm pretty sure." A girl she knew at Spence had had a scar removed once. "Really, I think we should at least ask," she said. "It's right on his face."

Before all this had happened, Rachel would have listened. You think? she would have said, eager to learn, hear Carole's advice. But not now. Now Rachel was the only mom. She pulled the van over. "I said no. Listen to me, Carole. You're not putting him through anything else. You've already put him through enough."

Back at the house, Jaya was in the kitchen, and when they came in, she started in on them right away about how freaked out she was. She'd come all this way from Lakewood, she said, only to have violence in the house of love and peace. It wasn't fair. Carole set about cleaning up. Nobody had even wiped up Pepper's blood or put the wine back in the refrigerator. Once she was finished, she went to her room and slept away the day. It was about eight at night when she awoke. She heard voices in the kitchen and went downstairs.

Morgan and Rachel were sitting at the kitchen table, Rachel all tense, with her knees drawn up, swathed in some big India-print garment, and Morgan overly relaxed as usual, his long skinny legs stretching across the top of the table. "You brought harm into our lives," Rachel said. She'd obviously been practicing with Morgan what she would say. "If it was just me, that would be one thing." Her hand lifted to the painted bruise under her eye. "But it was Pepper. You brought Pepper into this. We need a meeting."

A part of Carole rose up in objection again. If Rachel hadn't spat on Eddie, it wouldn't have happened. That's what had started it. Well, Carole may have started it by knowing him in the first place, letting him into their lives. But the spark for the fight, that had been all Rachel. You didn't mess with Eddie that way. Not with all the macho bullying swagger of his, the unpredictability. But she wasn't about to say that again. She'd said it once, and she felt ashamed of herself, given Rachel's bruises and Pepper's cut. She was answerable, no question. When it came to Eddie, she was at fault.

The three of them went upstairs to the room where Rachel's consciousness-raising group met. Tinfoil covered the windows, candles and pillows dotted the floor. Rachel lit the candles and invited Carole and Morgan to sit. "We need a cleansing," Rachel said. "We need to get our feelings into the open." She sat quietly for a few seconds. "I'm very freaked out about what happened. Also"—she glanced at Carole—"I'm disappointed in Carole. I feel that our home was violated and she allowed it to happen by allowing that soldier to enter our space in spite of knowing how I feel on that subject and without any discussion. Even though she knew him, it was a violation. I trusted her with my baby, with Pepper. That's all. That's all I have to say. I feel violated."

Morgan spoke up. "I wasn't even in the house. So I'm not going to place blame here. All I can say is, Rachel is unhappy, so I'm unhappy. And my kid has a scar for the rest of his life. I wish it hadn't happened. But it makes me sure of one thing. We need to get out of here. The whole district is going to hell. Street people moving in. And bad drugs, man. That's not what we're about here."

"I would prefer to stay on the subject," Rachel said.

"Hey, Rach, it *is* the subject," Morgan said.

"Carole?" Rachel said.

Carole took a deep breath. "I'm sorry for what happened," she said. "I didn't mean for it to happen. You have to know that about me, Rachel. You have to. You too, Morgan. And as to letting him in, I didn't do that. He just walked in through the door. People do it all the time, so it's not exactly fair to say that part was my fault." She paused. She didn't want to go splitting hairs about who was at fault for what. And anyway, Rachel would never admit that spitting at him had started the whole thing. "But I'm with Morgan about leaving," she said, trying to play down her excitement over what he had said. The possibility of getting out of that house where Eddie had found her, moving to where he couldn't possibly track her down—now that was the real solution. If that happened, then yes, they really were safe. She could promise that.

"I see," Rachel said, and Carole could tell Rachel felt as if she'd been betrayed all over again. Here was her group, her room, her idea, and Morgan and Carole were changing the subject and running away with it.

"It's a solution," Carole said. "We had a problem, and this is the solution. He won't find me if we move."

"But who was he?" Rachel was solemn. "That's what I want to know."

Carole took a deep breath. She owed Rachel that much. "Remember that day after we saw Bobby Kennedy, we went to the drugstore, and I told you I knew trouble, and you didn't believe me?"

Rachel nodded.

"That was him, okay? He got the address off one of the letters you sent me. Don't ask me how. It's how he found me. And if we move, he'll never find me again."

"You promise?"

"Cross my heart," Carole said.

"Things will just get worse here, Rach," Morgan said to Rachel. "More dangerous guys coming through that door, unless we keep it locked, I guarantee it. And what about the social worker? Eh? I don't want to scare you, but those people are dangerous. They come in and if they don't like what they see, good-bye Pepper, hello California State judicial system."

Rachel reached out for Carole's hand as if she were grasping it for life, and Carole took it and held it in both of hers. Then Morgan slid over and took Rachel's other hand, and the three of them sat in the flickering candlelight, heads bowed in silence.

They were all packed up and on the road two Mondays later. They were headed to Vermont, to a place way up north where they would homestead, Morgan called it, by which he meant, they would build their own house and grow their own food and keep chickens for meat, maybe a cow for milk and cheese down the road. She'd told Morgan that the only place she'd ever been in Vermont was Stowe, and even that felt risky to say out loud, but she had no choice. She had to find out before she got into that van how far it was from Stowe. Morgan made a face like she'd said something about the sewer. He said Stowe wasn't even Vermont. Stowe was another world. Nothing but tourists and high prices and trendy places, he said. It's like a suburb of New York. Where they were going was something else altogether. They'd be in the real wilderness. If she was thinking Stowe, she'd better think again. Which was almost all the reassurance she needed.

The land Morgan took them to was a landlocked acre up in Worcester that his uncle had given him. His uncle owned bits of land all over the state that he'd been buying for years. He'd paid peanuts for each piece in the belief that one day the owners of the surrounding land would pay a king's ransom to own the whole piece. He'd turned out to be wrong, and he'd given the piece in Worcester to Morgan to avoid having to pay taxes on it.

The piece was in the center of a tract owned by someone living in Florida. It came with a contentious right-of-way, a narrow path from the road that snaked through a bog and uphill through a stand of spruce. They'd had to clear the acre first, cutting trees and pulling out brush, then carry the building supplies in themselves. The Florida people wouldn't let them widen the path even temporarily for a truck to go through. But the three of them had done enough that summer, and by fall the completed dome resembled a large sleeping animal, the color of peanut butter and the texture of leather. It had odd-shaped Plexiglas windows here and there. Inside was a single large room heated by a woodstove at the center, its pipe heading directly out the top.

Carole stayed with them through the summer and fall. They learned the hard way about everything—chimney fires, insulation, and leaks in the roof. They didn't have running water or electricity that first year. They'd had to bring water in from the stream each day, then boil it on the stove and decant it into jars. They'd had to cut and split wood for the stove. There'd been days when Rachel and Carole would fall over laughing at what had become of them—two girls from New York homesteading on this little piece of land. But underneath it all, Carole had felt so safe tucked away there. No one knew where she was.

Come winter, though, everything took much longer to do. Darkness fell by four-thirty, and with only candlelight available, they'd be in bed by seven or eight. Rachel and Morgan's "room" was a double mattress separated from the rest of the space by a blanket strung across. Carole's and Pepper's mattresses were side by side on the other side of the dome. Often on those nights, Carole would have to cover her ears with her pillow to keep from hearing the muted sound of Rachel and Morgan making love. She would lie rigid, her heart beating, frightened and waiting for the sounds to stop. They filled her with dread. They brought shame.

Most mornings, she woke at five-thirty. She would cook a breakfast of oatmeal and eggs and suggest to Pepper that he might want to go to school that day. If he said yes, and he usually did to her, she would make his lunch and dress him as well as she could against the cold.

She went about it this way because Rachel believed that school was entirely Pepper's decision. She said it was up to the school to keep his interest, and if he didn't feel like going, she was not going to force him.

Carole and Pepper would walk the long path to the main road, where the yellow school bus stopped. When Pepper got on the bus, there was no doubt that the other children found him curious. She could see all their little faces pressed against the windows to see whether or not he would be there. She knew how strange he would seem to the other kids—a little boy who was absent so much of the time, who didn't seem to come from a house but from the woods. They must think Carole was his mother.

By spring the half-mile path from the dome to the road was well worn and deep. It ran with snow melt for several weeks before turning to deep mud. She and Pepper forged detours around the boggy parts and bridged the worst of it with logs they dragged from the forest. It was the first time she'd ever heard the term *unlocking* for what went on each spring in Vermont. The ground just let go. You could almost feel it happen. You could smell it. It was as though all of life had begun anew.

One morning in early May, she woke and knew from the soft warmth of the air that winter was over for good. She lay on her mat on the floor, looking up through the window at the apex of the dome to a sky that was, no question about it, a gentler shade of blue. It was still way too early to get up. She felt the optimism that always comes with spring, and then, little by little, she recognized again the sounds coming from the other side of the dome. Rachel and Morgan were taking care to be quiet, but even so, the sounds were unmistakable.

That morning, however, instead of pulling the pillow over her ears, she lay still and listened without anxiety to the sound of the bedclothes, the sharp intake of breath and whispered moans. She felt calm and even a little bit curious. She wondered what it would be like to have the warmth and comfort of another person's body always available, the way Rachel and Morgan had with each other.

After those sounds subsided, others took their place as Rachel and Morgan spoke in low whispers. She assumed they were talking about the day and what they would do, and with this realization came a new understanding. She knew absolutely what was in store for her if she didn't leave this place and begin a life of her own. She would become one of the children. Already there were times when it felt as though Morgan and Rachel were the parents and she and Pepper were the children. Just the other day Rachel had said, "Carole, why don't you and Pepper go out and hunt up some wood for the stove," as if she were the older sister instead of an adult. This was Rachel and Morgan's house—their design and their dream. This place was their future, not hers.

That same day she pulled her hair into a ponytail, dressed in the last of her Vassar clothes, and borrowed the van. She drove into Montpelier and applied at the Howard Johnson's for a waitressing job. It was the only work she knew how to do. She didn't give her address to the manager. If he found out where she lived, she might never get the job. She made up a post office box number, said she'd just moved, didn't have a telephone, and that she would come the next day for his decision. Lying about who she was and where she was from came so easily. It was just another disappearance. The manager hired her on the spot.

Chapter Twelve

NOVEMBER 1975

Carole stood on Ninety-first across from the school. It was a handsome stone building, nine stories high, with heavy carvings over the windows and doors. A private walled garden belonging to somebody else—Carnegies or Mellons, she thought—went from the school all the way to Fifth Avenue. She watched as women poured through the red door. Some of them were tiny with age, their little silver heads bobbing in the November sun. The young ones were sleek in dark minicoats and long smooth hair. A few got dropped off by limousines or taxis, but most came on foot in groups of two or three. They all seemed confident as they pulled open that door.

She had on her new parka. She'd just bought it at Gray's in September, and it was quite stylish in Montpelier. But here? All these years later, and she would still miss the boat when it came to clothes. She had on a long black skirt and a black sweater. When she was getting ready this morning, Will had suggested her silver earrings and a bright scarf. "For color," he'd said. "You need a spot of color." And when she was dressed, he'd stood back from her and said she looked great.

They'd had an awkward few days after the telephone call. He'd wanted to know more about the woman who called, why it was such a big deal if she moved up here. If Carole didn't like her, she could just ignore her, couldn't she? He didn't get why Carole was so undone by the whole thing. It wasn't like her.

Carole had said he didn't understand, and he'd said, laughing the way he did when she was so obviously missing the point about something, as if she were missing the point on purpose, "So *explain!*" She'd snapped his head off and then felt sorry about it, but she hadn't opened the discussion again. This time had to be the last time, it just had to. Her whole life, it seemed, was about hiding and running and close calls. Why couldn't they just leave her alone? Naomi and Eddie both. They kept taunting her with what had happened, with Rita, with her own guilt, like a couple of wolves working the herd and singling out the weakest prey. They would hunt her down until she fell. But if she could just make sure that Naomi wasn't coming, that she was staying put where she was, then she'd know what to tell Will. It all depended on that. She checked her watch: 11:27. At Chacha's they'd be setting up for lunch right now. A few early birds would already be there. Will was taking the day off and filling in for her.

A woman who looked familiar passed her. One of the other grades, not hers. Maybe one of those girls she used to look up to. Okay, it was 11:30 exactly, time to take the plunge.

She checked up the street for traffic, headed across, and got swept into the lobby with a noisy group of women who all arrived at once. All around her women were hugging and talking. She tried to remember faces, voices, but it was all confusing, so bright and fast. There were signs on the walls telling them what to do, a guestbook to sign, and forms to complete about tours of the new wing, requests for money. In her whole life, she'd never gone back to any place of significance and she was unprepared for what happened to her in the blink of an eye. She was that girl again—the girl she once was, feeling the tremor of intimidation among all these women who were so polished and sure of themselves. She went to the stuffed cloakroom, took off her parka, hung it on a hanger, and found a mirror. Her face looked small in all that bushy wild-woman hair, but she had an intensity. Her don't-mess-with-me look, Will called it. Maybe it was born of fear this time, but so what. No one could tell. She stood up straight, throwing back her shoulders, and then went back to the lobby determined not to look around pitifully for somebody she might know. The only person she wanted to see was Naomi, and Naomi would have to come to her.

While she waited for the elevator, a calm settled over her. She went over what she planned to say again. She'd take Naomi aside. She would tell her in no uncertain terms that she was not to move to Montpelier, and if she'd already bought a house, which was so unlikely as to be ludicrous, well, tough. She'd have to sell it. She knew drunks well enough to know their remorse and guilt after a bender. More than likely, Naomi would be ashamed of herself for making the call and would acquiesce easily.

And anyway, she would add, they weren't friends. Once Naomi had succumbed, Carole would tell her what a good decision she'd made not to come. She'd be solicitous even, telling Naomi everything would be okay. She'd appeal to the snob in Naomi. You wouldn't have liked it anyway, she would say. Montpelier is just old brick buildings and aluminum-sided houses. It has two bars and a few restaurants, most of them just burger-and-fries joints. At four o'clock when the state and the insurance company let out, the streets are a gridlock of bumper-to-bumper. People do their shopping from the Sears catalog and get their merchandise delivered to the post office. Really, she might say, if you want Vermont, there are better places to look.

On the sixth floor, the brass grate rattled aside, the outer doors parted, and she stepped into a wide corridor packed with women, glints of gold at their ears and wrists, a rush of smoke, the scent of Joy, and excited conversation. Uniformed maids circulated, carrying silver trays of canapés and sherry. Carole drew in a quick breath as a grinning blonde in pink, the current headmistress, grabbed her hand and pumped it vigorously. She had too many teeth and a raspy voice.

"Class?" she asked.

"Sixty-five," Carole said. The headmistress pressed one hand firmly into the small of her back, pointed to the far end of the corridor with the other, and gave her a little push. "Down there. Do you see them?"

The turnout was dismal, only four out of a class of twenty-eight. Carole narrowed her eyes to see who they were. Louisa, Joan, Deirdre, and Amanda were huddled in a tight circle. No Naomi. They'd been a miserable year, fractured by cliques and rivalries, one of those classes that never really jelled. She had no idea how their lives had turned out. She took a few steps forward. All four were talking furiously, hands flying. She knew their type so well. The last she'd seen of them was in the master bedroom of Shelly's parents' apartment that time, sprawled out with Jeremy Lyon among tangled sheets with another couple. She forgot who. There had been other bodies spread across the floor. The room had been dark and smoky. She remembered looking around at her classmates and their drunken boyfriends. How Naomi had staggered through the room toward her. She had thought that she would never see any of them again after that night.

She made her way over to the little group of four. Deirdre barely glanced at her as she went on talking to the others. It was Louisa who finally recognized her. "My God, it's Carole? Is it really? Is it you?" There was a chorus of excited little shrieks as they took her into their small circle with hugs and handshakes, telling her how fabulous she looked. She'd lost weight, right? Without waiting for an answer, they were filling her in on their lives. What they did, which wasn't much, mostly volunteering at the Met and taking courses when they had time away from their children.

"And what about you?" Louisa asked.

"I run a bar," Carole said. She felt pleased to say that. She'd made a life for herself, while they hadn't done much. They nodded and blinked, not knowing what to say. A bar? Carole? "It's called Chacha's." She shrugged.

"Are you married?"

"Sort of," she said.

"What's that supposed to mean?" Amanda said.

"It's a long story," she said.

"Who else is coming?" Louisa said. "Who has the list?"

Amanda pulled one from her purse and cruised the names, rattling off bits of gossip. "Naomi." She looked at Carole over the tops of half-glasses.

"She's coming," Carole said.

"Whatever happened with you guys?" Amanda asked. "You were like this." She twisted her first two fingers together. "And then boom, all of a sudden—" She splayed her hand open. "We could never figure it out."

"Everybody thought it was that guy she brought to the graduation party."

"No," Carole said, thinking yes. That guy. It scared her a little that they would remember Eddie.

Up and down the hall, the sherry was making the women loud. There was more laughter and faster talk. Word spread that it was time to go in to lunch. The huge double doors were drawn open, and the women moved in groups into the dining room with its famous Revolutionary War wallpaper. The smell brought it all back. If she shut her eyes, she was fifteen again, and not a mirror in sight.

The whole event quickened after that. Everybody was looped. Photographs were passed around, and Carole stared at husbands in seersucker suits, blond children at the seashore. There was a volley of questions for each photo. *Who was that? Where was it taken? What were the names?* And *Oh, isn't she adorable, isn't he handsome.*

She rummaged through her purse for a photograph of Will. She'd just come back from getting a roll developed, and she passed one of the snaps along to Louisa on her left. It showed the two of them sitting on barstools at Chacha's, Will's arm around her, his face pressed against hers. Louisa had to put on her reading glasses. She stared at the picture but said nothing, her silence speaking volumes.

"His name's Will," Carole said. "Will Burbank."

"Oh." Louisa passed the photo around, and Carole watched it pass from hand to hand.

"That's us at my bar," she said, since no one was saying anything. The silence that accompanied the passing of the picture told it all. He was black. They didn't know what to say about that, so they said nothing. She suspected they would be feeling sorry for her. A cliché. Fucking her way into the black experience, she'd once heard someone say, and it had hurt her. She'd told Will, and he'd thought for a second and then roared laughing. "Nobody would want to do that," he'd said. "That's crazy."

She kept an eye on the door, waiting for Naomi to show up. Her salad got taken away and then her lunch. While the dessert was being served, they were gaveled into silence. A very elderly woman rose from a table near the dais and walked stiffly to the microphone. "I don't know what I'm doing up here," she said in a wobbly voice. "Since the real speaker in the family is my husband, not me." She looked out over the crowded room and smiled fondly. "Most of you remember my husband." At a nearby table, the senior class for that year, all bouncing girls in short uniform skirts and lug-soled oxfords, rolled their eyes at one another and stifled laughter at that dotty old broad. How could anybody remember her husband? She had to be ninety.

The woman pointed a bejeweled hand toward the window behind her, in the direction of Central Park. "We had chaperones in my day. They came along when we went for tennis lessons in the park." She paused. "And this made it very difficult to smoke." The room burst into relieved laughter. "Smoking was the height of wickedness, so it was, of course, what everyone wanted to do." More laughter. She went on, describing places in the building where the girls of her day went to sneak a cigarette—the cast room behind the stage, the room that opened onto an alley that led out to Ninety-first Street. They were places Carole remembered too, where she and Naomi used to go.

The table of senior girls whispered among themselves, shook out their hair, rewound it, let it go, twirled spoons around in their melting desserts. By now, it was clear that Naomi would not be coming. Carole stopped glancing at the door. Some students were gathered on the dais, preparing to sing. Someone sounded a pitch pipe, there was a tune-up hum, and they opened with the same lovely obscure pieces that Carole had been taught as a girl, "Who Is Sylvia" and "Hodie." These were followed by a medley of songs from the sixties—"Leader of the Pack," "It's My Party," "He's So Fine," sung with the same careful attention to each note as the chants. There was no hard edge to the music, though. The notes were right, the words clear, but they held none of the tough energy that had made that music so great.

As they filed out of the dining room, dismissed by the headmistress after a plea to contribute to the building fund, Carole ducked into the drawing room and swung the enormous doors shut behind her. It was lovely and quiet, exactly as she remembered it, with high ceilings, pale brocade-covered furniture. A painting of Miss Spence hung over the fireplace. Two satiny sofas faced each other across a polished coffee table. As underclassmen, they'd been permitted in that room only once a year to have their class pictures taken.

Yearbooks were fanned across the coffee table, and she found her year, the white one. She flipped through the senior pictures, one page per person, all by Bachrach, all with the same Mona Lisa smile. It wasn't until you reached the back of the book—the candids—that you saw the differences.

Here were pictures taken out of school, around the city, and during vacations, dances, and dates—the pictures that told the real story, that showed bodies in action and faces in anger, concentration, and wonder. On the last page was a picture Carole remembered well. The two of them—Carole and Naomi—stood side by side in the Senior Room. The Inseparables, they had been called, and not kindly. It had been taken just before spring break, before the trip to Stowe. Carole was the tall, heavy-set, grinning blonde on the left, dwarfing Naomi, dark and petite. In the photograph Carole is pressing a snapshot into her breast. Only the edges were visible. It was their best secret. At the moment the photograph was taken, they'd said his name in unison. "Eddie." It was why they were smiling that way, with open, surprised-looking mouths, as though they were singing.

"Excuse me?"

Carole looked up to see the headmistress standing in the door to the drawing room. "I'm going to have to ask you—" She gestured to the empty hall behind her. "We're having to lock up."

"Oh," Carole said. "I guess I got carried away in here."

"I understand," the headmistress said. "These things happen."

"Tell me," Carole said as they walked together, the headmistress's hand again at the small of her back, guiding her firmly toward the elevator. "I was expecting to see someone today, but she never showed up. Is there a way to get an alum's address?"

The headmistress frowned, and Carole knew she was trying to decide whether it would be quicker to say yes or no. "Come along," she said. "And we'll see."

They took the stairs up one flight to her office—the same sunny, carpeted room with the mahogany desk that the headmistress had had when Carole was a student. Carole remembered sitting there, dragged in after Naomi had taken her shoplifting that time. The storekeepers had recognized Naomi's school blazer. Naomi was the one to get into trouble; Carole was quickly off the hook. She could do no wrong in those days.

"Let's see," the headmistress said, flipping through a file box that held reply cards for the reunion. "Sometimes they tell us. Leonard, Leonard, Leonard. Here we go." She pulled out a card. "'Naomi Leonard. Mrs. Baxter Oliver,'" she read. "Let's see if she filled—yes, here it is. One thirty-one East Seventy-fifth." She drew her lips over her enormous teeth and smiled. "I think you might have had just as good luck with the telephone book, but let me write it down for you anyway." She pressed the piece of paper into Carole's hand and steered her back through the door, to the elevator.

Outside, the late afternoon was raw and fiercely bright. She walked down Madison to Seventy-fifth Street and then east across Park to Naomi's building, which was one of those high, grand old things with doctors' offices on the ground floor and a dark green canopy over the entrance.

"Does Naomi Oliver live here?" she asked the doorman.

He looked her up and down. "Whom should I say is calling?"

"Then she lives here, yes?"

"Your name again?" he said.

"Just tell her it's Carole," she said.

He disappeared into a little room off the lobby. A minute later he reappeared with a slip of paper. "Carole Mason?" he asked.

She nodded.

"Mrs. Oliver has stepped out," he said. "But she's left word you're to wait for her."

"Stepped out? When?"

"I don't know," he said.

"Well, I mean, was it just now or an hour ago?"

"I can't say." He pointed to an upholstered chair in the lobby that was chained to the wall. "You can wait there."

It frosted her that Naomi wasn't here, and worse, she obviously expected Carole to come looking for her. She'd fallen into that same trap all over again: thinking she was playing a game she'd already lost.

That summer after senior year, a few days after she'd seen Naomi at that strange party where Andy Warhol was supposed to show up, she'd gotten a frantic call from Naomi. They just *had* to get together, and it *had* to be that day. In retrospect Carole must have leapt to the conclusion that Naomi had information from Eddie; she'd gone to the restaurant immediately, an expensive little French bistro in the West Fifties that Carole could never afford with her own money. Naomi had told her to get a table. She'd pay. Bax, the new fiancé, was loaded. Naomi wasn't there yet, and there was no alternative but to be seated at the reserved table and accept the cup of coffee and a plate of rolls, which she ate while she waited. And waited and waited. Until she had to pretend she was going to the ladies' room and then sneak out a door at the back and run. No Naomi. No explanation. You could know a thing and still be powerless to change your own behavior in the face of it. That was the awful truth, she thought as she waited yet again. She'd give her another five minutes, and if Naomi didn't show, she'd leave. She took out her checkbook so she could get it up to date and was subtracting the checks she'd entered when the door clicked open and a gust of arctic air blew in, swirling a few leaves and bits of paper across the marble floor. A small woman, swathed in a huge black coat that brushed the floor, was standing in the doorway. Her face, squinting into the lobby, was perched on top like a toy. It took Carole a minute to recognize her.

"You came!" Naomi shrieked. "I knew you would." She minced across the lobby in high-heeled boots, arms wide open, still the old Naomi in that huge coat and heavy makeup. Her hair was across her face from the wind, stuck on her pink lipstick. "You look fabulous," Naomi said, going up on her tiptoes to give Carole a kiss on the cheek. "Come on upstairs."

Carole ran her hand across her cheek, where Naomi had just kissed her. "You drag me all the way down to that awful reunion and then you don't have the courtesy to show up."

"Oh, God, I'm sorry." Naomi glanced up, making a pitiful face. "Forgive?"

"No, Naomi." Carole used to forgive Naomi almost everything. It used to enrage her mother the way, as she put it, "Naomi can lead you around by the nose."

"We'll talk upstairs." Naomi put an arm through Carole's. She filled up the elevator with her voice, the smell of her perfume, the constant wriggling. "I couldn't deal with those bitches at the reunion, not with all that's happening. And maybe they've heard. So tell me everything. Louisa and Amanda were there, right? Who else?" She rummaged through the pockets of her coat and pulled out a tortoiseshell barrette with the tags still on it. "I was at Saks. I picked this up for you." She grinned. She touched Carole's hair. "It'll look fabulous on you. Love your hair like that. I had my eye on a better one, but I didn't dare. Not after what happened. Come on, take it."

Carole took the barrette and looked it over.

"It's just faux," Naomi said.

"Forty dollars for a hair clip?" Carole held out the tag. "I can't take this."

"You have no idea the risk I took for you."

"You stole it?"

"Oh, get with the program," Naomi said.

It stung the way it always had. Naomi could make thieving or anything else sound perfectly fine, cool even, as though everybody worth their salt was doing it. Only Carole was too square to have any fun. She had to remind herself, as she stood staring at the elevator gate, that she was a grown woman. She had a house and a business. She had responsibilities. And it was wrong to steal.

"I'm going to stop. My shrink is working on it." Naomi took a deep breath. "You see, I got detained at Cartier. That's what they call it these days. 'Detained.' It was just this plain ring, not even that pretty, but they stopped me at the door and I had to go talk to the manager in the office. Said I must have forgotten, but of course they don't buy that. The thing is, one of the partners in Bax's firm—Bax is my husband, *was* my husband—is on the board there, and of course they all got wind of it. The shit hit the fan, and they had to fire Bax. They said it was going to be a big PR problem if they didn't let him go, much as they loved him, yadda, yadda. So you know what he did instead? He got a divorce. He said it was all my fault. But it's okay, really. I'm hip with that. We hadn't been in sync, if you know what I mean." She made a circle with her thumb and forefinger and ran her other forefinger through it a couple of times. "The thing about a divorce is. By the way, you divorced?"

"No."

"Well, after all the pain, divorce is actually good for you. It makes you take stock. I mean, really look at your whole life and start fresh. Because you lose all the friends you ever had. The parties stop cold.

Nobody calls for lunch anymore, except for losers. You just have to think back to what worked in your past."

"We've got to talk," Carole said.

"What do you think I'm doing?" Naomi said as they got off the elevator. In the vestibule, putting the key into the lock, she turned. "Ignore the mess." It was dark in the apartment, and they had to grope their way down what seemed to be a hallway to a room that was lit by daylight. Carole felt things underfoot. "I think this one works," Naomi said. She clicked on the light, and Carole looked around. It was appalling. They were in the living room. The windows all had heavy drapes. Around the edges, you could see that the glass was filthy and scarcely let in any light. The furniture was covered with files and books. There was clothing on the floor. Old shopping bags, new clothes with the tags still attached.

"Everything happened at once," Naomi said. "My father dies, and then Bax and I get a divorce, and now I have all this *shit* to deal with. Look." She pushed through one room after another, turning on the lights as she went, shoving things out of the way with her feet. There were two dining room tables, chairs stacked against the walls. "That's why I decided to sell it all. Start over, you know? Remember that?" She was pointing to a lacquered Chinese cabinet. "That used to be Daddy's. I hate it. Always have. You look healthy as hell, by the way."

"Will you please calm down," Carole said.

"First, a drink." Naomi led the way through the dining room to the kitchen, and Carole had no choice but to follow. "One more reason to stay away from that reunion, if you ask me. All they serve is those itty-bitty glasses of sherry."

She poured out two tumblers of vodka. "Hope you don't mind the glasses. Bax wanted the crystal, and I didn't." Carole put the glass down. "Sit anywhere." Naomi picked up an open box of Cheerios and offered it. "Want some?"

Carole moved a stack of paper bags from the chair and sat down. "You can't move to Montpelier."

Naomi fed herself a few Cheerios, put down the box, and

shrugged off her coat without unbuttoning it. It fell in a heap at her feet, and she stepped out of it. She had on a black turtleneck and blue jeans. She plunged her whole forearm into the box of Cheerios and rooted around for something. "There's supposed to be one of those press-on tattoos in here." She pulled out a little cellophane package and ripped it open with her teeth. "Look," she said. She wet the tattoo with her tongue and applied it to the back of her hand. "Ta-da!" she said. "Smiley face. Have a nice day."

"Did you hear me?" Carole said.

Naomi's little face bunched up in a pout. "I heard." She hopped up on the counter next to the sink and took a long sip. "I hate this stuff, but it's all I've got."

"We were friends, sure. But ten years have gone by. Everything has changed. You're different, I'm different." She scanned Naomi's face for a reaction, but Naomi was difficult to read. She plowed ahead anyway, her script in shambles. "You'd hate it up there. There's no place to shop. People talk about how much wood they burn each winter. They talk about wax for their cross-country skis, for God's sake."

Naomi swung her feet a couple of times, and they banged against the cupboards. She shut her eyes. "My shrink disagrees. He thinks it's healthy, me moving to Montpelier because I *know* people there. I know you. We go back. I don't know anybody here anymore. He said the sick thing to do would be to stay where I'm not wanted. I.e., New York City. I'll come down to see him twice a month, and I'll get on the horn twice a week. We've already figured all that out."

"Stop lying to your shrink, Nay. We don't know each other. Not anymore."

Naomi sighed like a perplexed teacher explaining something to a child. "You have to look at the whole scope of things." She spread her arms out wide. "Your whole life, not just now, but the past. I *never* had a friend like you."

"That was so long ago. We're not friends now."

"I went around with this real estate agent up there, and she said to

me, 'People like you will want to live in South Burlington or Shel-
burne.' And then she tells me who's who out there and she even drives
by their houses and tells me what they cost and which ones she's been
inside and how they're done up and who has taste and who doesn't.
But no way in hell am I living there. So I ask her to take me to Montpelier because I went to school with someone who lives there and I
want to see it, and I find a house! She tells me they've got hippies and
communes around Montpelier. Except for the insurance company
and the state, it's a backwater town, not for me at all. Said the hippie
kids are always getting head lice and roundworm. Is that true, by the
way?"

"Yes. That's what I'm trying to tell you."

"You know the road that goes out past the swimming pool, the
one shaped like a dish." She paused. "You take it to Shady Rill, then
hook a left. It's a dirt road off that, maybe two miles in. It's old. An
old farmhouse. It used to be owned by a bunch of sisters. The last
one died about a year ago."

"The Rowling house?"

"Yup. That's the one."

"But you can't." Carole'd read the last of the Rowlings had died.
The house was in the vicinity. Her vicinity.

"Well, I did."

"Did what?"

"Bought it." Naomi turned her head so that Carole could see only
her profile, her small upturned nose peeking out from behind a curtain of hair. "You might just be a little nicer," she said.

Carole took a desperate breath and said very loudly, because
Naomi didn't seem to hear anything, "Nay. You. Cannot. Do. This! I
see this all the time in women who come into Chacha's. They get a divorce, and they go through a crazy period. Divorce lawyers really
ought to warn you. Either they get really depressed or they're all
charged up with liberating rage. They reconnect with old boyfriends
or old friends as though they can go back to some earlier time. But

they can't. You can't. They get over it, and so will you. Believe me. You'd just get yourself up there, and six months down the road you're going to think, oh, my God, what have I done?"

"It's my life, and I'll do as I damn well please. Anyway, what the hell is Chacha's?"

"My bar."

"Oh, right."

"You can't come!" Carole shouted. "And you know why too. That other business." The situation was slipping out of her control. She was just grabbing at straws as she fell.

"What?"

"Stowe, Eddie. Don't pretend you don't know exactly what I'm talking about either. We have to live our separate lives. It's safer."

"That was a long time ago, and nobody ever found out." Naomi waved her hand dismissively. "You can't just let that govern you."

"We still—"

"I never even told Bax. That was the whole point, in case you forgot, which I hope you didn't, for your sake."

Carole took the barrette from her pocket and handed it to Naomi. "I don't want this stuff. I don't want you in my life. Can't you get that through your head?"

"Hand me that if you're not going to drink it." Carole handed over the glass of vodka. "You've obviously lost your sense of humor," Naomi said. "Anyway, I won't embarrass you up there, if that's what you're worried about. I only took the barrette for old times' sake. I've got it under control. Daddy was between wives when he died, so I got everything. I mean everything. It's taken forever just to figure it all out."

"Are you listening at *all*?" Carole asked.

"I'll be good, I promise." Naomi gave her a bright childish smile. "And what you said? You know, talking about wood or wax or whatever? It sounds good. It's what I've needed all these years. Back to the land. Really, Carole. You'll hardly even notice me."

Carole hesitated. She needed to say something that would break any friendship right smack in half. "You were never my friend, Naomi. You were like this default position, if you must know. I needed you to get through Spence."

There were sounds in the hall of the front door opening and slamming shut. "Hello?" a man's voice said.

"In the kitchen." Naomi didn't seem to have heard a word. She winked at Carole. "Boyfriend *du jour,*" she said. "Wait till you get a load of him."

A man suddenly filled the doorway to the kitchen. He was dark, slight, and smoothly groomed. Longish brown hair and a dark coat with a patterned scarf. He leaned down to kiss Naomi, a kiss that went on for a long time. After they finished, Naomi smiled at Carole, her eyebrows raised in victory.

"Hi," the man said to Carole.

"Can we continue this alone?" Carole said to Naomi.

The boyfriend left the room. Carole could hear him stumbling through the dining room in the dark, tripping over things. "Sorry I didn't introduce you," Naomi whispered, "but I'm always afraid I'll get the name wrong. You know how that is."

"No, I don't know how that is," Carole said. "Look, Nay. Maybe I didn't mean that about a default position, but how many times do I have to say it? Don't come. That's the only reason I came down here. To tell you not to come. Not to start the friendship, not to talk about the past. One reason only. You've got to stay here. Or someplace, just not Montpelier."

Naomi flicked the hair from her eyes and took the last swallow of her drink. "Oh, what the hell," she said.

"Did you close on the house yet?"

Naomi shook her head.

"So don't, Nay."

Naomi hopped off the counter, toppled slightly, then recovered. "Whatever," she said.

The boyfriend wasn't getting very far out there in the wreckage of Naomi's apartment, and Carole thought he'd be coming back in any minute. She had to know one more thing. "Did you ever see Eddie again?"

Naomi grinned and put a finger to her lips. "Sshh," she said.

"Well, did you?"

Naomi narrowed her eyes at Carole. "Lay off already," she said. "Sheesh!" She went to the kitchen door and called into the dark apartment. Carole could hear the boyfriend finding his way back to the kitchen. "Arthur," Naomi said. "His name is Arthur."

"Yes or no?" Carole said as Arthur blundered back in, and Naomi just smirked as if to say, What's a girl to do? Carole had no choice but to leave.

The day outside was colder and grayer than when she'd walked to Naomi's building. A wind had picked up and was swirling papers and old leaves along the sidewalk. Carole walked to Lexington Avenue. She'd lost all her resolution. She felt disoriented, depleted, and out of place. She hadn't set foot in New York since her mother died, and it wasn't that she had an interest in seeing her father, it was more the familiarity of where she was that made it natural to keep walking toward Sixty-second Street just for a glimpse of her old building. The man at the door, portly and red-faced, stood aside for her.

"Conrad Mason?" she said.

"I'm sorry, miss," he said. "Nobody by that name."

"Did he move out?"

"No idea," the man said. "Never heard the name."

Not that she'd have talked to him. But all this time she'd imagined him living in the apartment, working in the Chrysler Building, everything going forward the same as it had before, just without her and her mother. All this time she had assumed that if she ever wanted to find him, she would at least know where to go.

Chapter Thirteen

Her truck was a snow-covered lump alone in the train-station parking lot. The snow dragged at the hem of her skirt and spilled into the tops of her boots as she walked, cold trickling down her insteps. She yanked at the door, but it wouldn't budge. She went around to the passenger side and yanked again. Nothing. She took off her mitten and felt for her keys in the dark, rummaging around the bottom of her bag.

Never lock the car door in winter, somebody had told her once. "Oh, shut up!" she said to whoever it was. Not Will. Not his style. So she'd locked it. So she forgot. How was she supposed to know everything? Way too much. Every day something new. Some new hazard to avoid. It was on the news at night. It came from people talking in Chacha's. *Don't burn green wood. Don't burn soft wood. Don't flush the toilet if the electricity's out.* Endless. And Will, more subtle, and with much better timing, but still—it was all exhausting information. *The keyhole ices over, and you won't get the key in.* She found the key and stuck it into the keyhole, turned it, but not too hard. *You can snap a key in half.* She peered inside. Her flashlight was in the trunk, along with the battery cables and God knew what else. If Naomi had just left her alone, she wouldn't be here now, locked out of her lousy truck and stranded in the cold with no way to get help. The day flooded back, the sights and sounds of New York, her father's apartment—or not his apartment now. And Naomi and Spence. The smell of everything.

She gripped the handle and pulled with everything she had, so the door burst open and flung her back. She threw her purse onto the passenger seat and started up the ignition, feeling a blast of cold air from the heat vents, watching lights cast a beam over the white sea ahead. She inched forward, concentrating now on what she knew how to do, to drive ever so slowly across the parking lot at the steadiest possible speed, making the turn so gradually in the untouched snow that there was little chance for a wheel to slip and spin, and then out to the main road, where the plow had come through, where her tires had purchase once again, where she could afford to go a little faster, where everything was normal. She knew what she had to do. She knew the time had come for it.

She took the left in Montpelier and then the four slow miles up East Hill Road. Halfway there, she turned off the headlights and drove by the light of the moon. When she rounded the corner at the base of the next hill, she could see the faint glow of the porch light from the house on the hill above. Will must have left it on. She pulled to a stop in the little parking area at the base of the hill. There was a buried electrical line from the house for nights like this. She plugged it into the socket under the hood to keep the engine from freezing, then headed up the hill in the pitch dark, hardly making a sound.

In the mudroom, she dropped her purse, stepped out of her boots, and hung her coat on a hook. The heavy double doors to the living room were ajar, and she brought in an armload of wood, which she dropped into the bin beside the stove. She chucked them into the stove one at a time and pushed them to the back to catch later, then latched the stove gate and went upstairs, pausing before she entered the bedroom to look at Will, massive under several down quilts. He'd leave her if he knew. Everybody would.

In the morning, she was aware of Will rising and getting dressed. The world had changed. She heard the roar of the Gravely when he started it up in the dooryard and then its fading sound as he moved slowly up the rise and down the driveway to the road, blowing snow. She shut her eyes, focusing on those last few minutes. *Whatever,* Naomi had said, but what had she meant? *Whatever you want.* That was the explanation Carole wanted. She stared at the ceiling. Whatever, as a way to avoid addressing Carole's plea? That was the other possibility. But think of the apartment, the mess, the clutter, all that furniture. Not the apartment of a woman getting ready to move. Not at all. It was the apartment of a woman who felt like making trouble, who couldn't control herself. And she'd made her position clear to Naomi. But really, the bottom line was that Naomi wasn't up to a move. Naomi was a wreck. Naomi couldn't move across the hall, let alone up here.

Will came back in, his black hair dusted white, and she listened as he showered, dressed, and slid the change from the dresser top into his pockets. He brought her coffee and sat heavily on the bed beside her. "I dug you out down there and turned the motor over. You shouldn't have any trouble."

She nodded. "Thanks, toots."

"Trip go okay?"

"Mmmm," she said, sitting up.

"You going to tell me what it was about?" Except for laughter, which from Will was frequent and so wide open it could swallow her up, he was hard to read. His face could look completely neutral, as it did right now, but he wasn't being neutral, she knew. He was being careful. He was bursting with curiosity.

"A reunion," she said. "We sang the school song and they asked us for money. None of the people in my class have changed that much. I don't know. We had little glasses of sherry, and the senior girls sang pop tunes."

221

"Sherry," he said. "You're kidding."

"I told you, it was a hoity-toity school."

"See any old boyfriends?"

"It's a girls' school."

"Oh, right," he said. "Girls' school. So what was the big attraction? Are you going to tell me about the old friend?"

She loved his face. She could never get enough of that great big face, the wide lips, the high forehead and kind eyes with those chiseled-looking little eyebrows. "There's not much more to tell, actually. That girl on the phone that morning, I talked to her, and I don't think she's moving up here. She's kind of a mess."

"A mess how?" The details of people's lives fascinated him.

"She drinks too much, she steals, she has roaches—the insect kind—she can't remember her boyfriend's name. Shall I go on?"

"Sounds pathetic," he said. Pathetic was the worst thing he could call somebody. Will's ultimate dismissal. Once somebody had hit pathetic, he was no longer interested. "Hector keeps calling," he said. "You never called him back the other day, and he's hyperventilating. He wants you to come in before lunch today."

Once Will left, she got out of bed, showered, and shampooed her hair because it smelled of the city. Then she dressed and beat it down the hill to her truck. Years ago, Earl had told her how fast things slide when the owner isn't around, no matter how great the staff and how much you trust them. It's human nature to slack off.

But the place was fine. Carole poured herself a cup of coffee in the kitchen, sat down at her desk in the alcove, the only private place there was, and went through some receipts.

"There you are!" It was Hector, dressed to the nines in a white suit and green bow tie. He gave her a swift kiss on each cheek. "So, what do you say, Carole. Was I right or was I right?"

"About what?" she said.

"The picture, you ninny!" He pulled the week's menu from his jacket. "Don't tell me you forgot!" He showed her the menu. It was on bright orange paper and folded in half. Inside was the menu, on the back were the puzzles, and spread across the front was a picture of a grade-school class, all lined up in front of a school building. Under the picture it said "Identify the people, the date, and the event. Win two free lunches."

"The color is dreadful," Hector said. "But the picture came out splendidly, if I do say so myself. They're having a ball out there," he said, pointing to the dining room. "It's the fourth grade at Union Elementary, 1934. Lots of them out there are in the picture. Significantly changed, of course."

She peeked out the door. Thursday lunches had started attracting leathery old farmers and their soft, plump wives since Hector had taken over the menu design in return for a few free dinners. He'd make up a crossword puzzle or a word jumble or connect-the-dots. You had to have lived in Montpelier as long as these people had to get any of the answers. Word had spread, and the Thursday crowd was always the biggest. It was the day the new menus came in. Carole was embarrassed about forgetting the photo. He'd spent some time as a school photographer, he'd said, all excited. Why not put those pictures on the menu and see who can get all the faces?

Carole looked around the restaurant. There must have been forty or fifty people. She did a quick mental inventory of the food they had on hand, what had come in on Tuesday, what was left for today. Cases of potatoes and lettuce. A forequarter of lamb, forty pounds of beef. Thirty pounds of fish. Enough.

"Come with me." Hector pulled her to the bar, where he had laid out some photographs. There were the usual classes of kids lined up in front of schools, groups of Rotarians and Elks at tables, as well as miscellaneous shots—outdoor scenes with people standing around. "I want you to see the range. The caliber of the work."

"They're nice," she said.

"You're not even looking, Carole."

She bent over them and took a better look. The Elks Club pictures were wonderful. They looked as though they were taken in the 1940s. The men had wide lapels and fedoras.

"I want to expand," Hector said. "As I mentioned to Will, we can do so much more with the menus."

"The puzzles and things were getting a little tired."

Hector looked stung. "I don't believe I said tired. I believe I said a change would serve us well."

"Sorry, maybe I'm the one who's tired."

"That's what you get for gallivanting to New York like that." He sifted through the pile and drew out a photograph of a nude woman lying facedown in a clearing, arms outstretched and toes pointed in.

A chill shot up the nape of Carol's neck. "Hector. Who is that?"

"Isn't she a beauty? That's the lieutenant governor's wife. Nineteen hundred and forty-five."

"She's dead. How . . ."

"No, she's not," Hector said. "Quite alive. Still is, I believe."

Carole studied the picture more closely. The woman looked like an alabaster statue. *Like Rita.* She had the same heft, the same smooth fullness of body, but her hair was jet black, and she was facedown, not faceup. Carole had a flash of precise memory of Rita in her grave. How disarranged she'd looked, with her limbs askew, knees up, her head forced down into her shoulder because the space was too small. This woman's photograph had been taken in summer, in the heat. By now there had been many summers in Stowe. By now the heat had reduced Rita to nothing but bone.

"Lucky shot," Hector was saying. "I just happened to be doing some work next door, and she just happened to be . . . well, one wouldn't call that sunbathing, exactly. An odd woman, she was. Is. But a beauty too."

She caught a glimpse of Rachel and Pepper. She hadn't expected them, and the sight of them annoyed her unaccountably. Here it was a Thursday, and Pepper was again out of school, and not only that, but Rachel rewarded him for not going to school by bringing him in here, as if not going to school was some sign of great intelligence on his part and not just a misguided effort to please his mother. Rachel flopped back on the couch and began to nurse the baby again. He must have made a peep. Just the littlest thing, and Rachel would undo her blouse, which also angered Carole. That couldn't possibly be good for kids. All that feeding when the baby might not even be hungry, when he might want something else, like love and attention, was going to make the baby crave food just as Carole had when she was younger. Not that she could say anything, since she had no kids herself, as Rachel would be quick to point out. Carole knew this anger was because of Naomi, at least the root of it. It wasn't as though Rachel was doing anything new, nothing she hadn't done a hundred times before. But Carole didn't want to even talk to her today. In fact, she didn't want to talk to anybody. Not the staff, not Hector, not the customers. She hung back where Rachel wouldn't notice her, wouldn't yell out for her to come on over and join them. She didn't feel like it one bit right now. Didn't feel like being with children and babies. Not ever. She herself had been fitted for an IUD because she didn't think people should have children unless everything was exactly right, which it wasn't with her and would probably never be because, she thought, feeling like she would cry, what was she going to tell any child of hers about her life if she couldn't even tell her own friends? What if her child wanted to know about school and growing up? What could she say? Kids had a right to know your whole past, or else what was the point of bringing them into the world? While Will had a full, lively history that went way back, hers just stopped. Any child she brought into the world would be a partial child. He would be the child of amnesia, and hadn't she told Will that a hundred times?

She turned away before Rachel saw her, before Hector would need anything else. She took her parka from the peg and, coffee in hand, went down the back stairs. She might as well be taking speed again for the way she felt today, all jitters and good for nothing and needing—needing suddenly—some answers, to find out what had happened up there in Stowe after she'd left.

She had always known this day would come. It had loomed for

years. Stowe, that shadowland to the west of Montpelier. Every morning on the radio she would hear the report from Stowe. Somebody skied down the mountain and told the conditions. Restaurants in Stowe advertised in the *Times Argus* and on the radio. There was the constant belief of the chamber of commerce that people going to Stowe would want to stay in Montpelier. But that was a dream. Stowe was another world. A rich world. It wasn't a town at all. It was only an idea.

That she would go back to look had been ordained the day Rita Boudreau died, a given fact of her life. She sipped coffee as she drove, feeling, she thought, like someone going to the execution chamber, taking a last look at the world around her, full of dread but with a sliver of hope, too. Illogical, crazy hope as if something good was going to come out of this. It pulled her along. If she could just see the place again, she'd know. Know what, though? There the question went cold. Maybe she wanted to feel worse. Had she ever thought of that?

She had the radio going loud. There was only one station, and it played sappy music, but it took her mind off things. "My Eyes Adored You." "Thank God I'm a Country Boy." How did people write that frivolous garbage? And then there it was. Stowe, straight out of a stage set. People walking around in Day-Glo ski clothes. The cars were shinier and bigger, with ski racks mounted on their roofs. She gunned the truck when the light turned green to keep her nerve from failing. She felt out of context, her mission unholy in this sparkling-clean place.

She had no idea how far it would be. Snaking around those turns as though at any moment somebody would jump out at her, she hoped the Double Hearth had burned down. The Snowtown too. It was exactly the way she hoped for different endings in movies she saw more than once. Every time she saw *Bonnie and Clyde,* she hoped this time they wouldn't be deceived. They'd see the ambush and escape.

But no, the Double Hearth suddenly loomed ahead on the right, a big barn of a place with a silo. The sign read: DORMS. PRIVATE

ROOMS. WEEKLY RATES. BREAKFAST. She pulled into the parking lot and snapped off the ignition to kill the radio, which was much too loud. The moment she opened the car door, she smelled the faint and slightly rancid combination of bacon and toast that had filled the Double Hearth the morning she'd come back here. She leaned against the warm truck, tasting bile.

"Can I help you?" a man inside asked her. He was sitting on a couch next to one of the hearths, glancing up at her over the tops of his glasses. She knew how she looked to him. One of those hippie chicks. People were used to her in Montpelier. Up here was another story. *Steal the pictures right off the wall.*

"I was here once before. Years ago. Just thought I'd—"

That did it. He gave her a big smile. "Oh, sure. We get people coming back all the time. Take your time." He went back to his newspaper.

To the left was the doorway that had a thick blanket across it. She pulled the blanket aside and went up to the landing and through the door to the girls' dorm. It was again the smell of the place that kept getting to her. Of cosmetics and deodorant and bedding. It was the same smell as when she and Naomi had been here. The rows of empty beds were in disarray, with blow dryers and clothing all over the place. She walked slowly down the aisle to the last pair of bunks against the wall. The lower was unmade, a pink flannel nightgown on the pillow, an open suitcase at the foot. She sat down on the bed and waited to remember, sure she was alone.

She lay back slowly on the bunk, then reached up and touched the coils of the one overhead that had been Naomi's. She raised her feet and pushed slowly up, bowing the mattress above. A suitcase slid from the bed and banged to the floor, the contents spilling.

"Jesus," somebody said, making her bolt upright. Other voices sounded up and down the room, and when she looked down the row of bunks, she saw faces here and there, groggy girls and boys looking for where the noise had come from. "Fuck you," somebody said. "We're trying to sleep."

She bolted from where she was to the bathroom, remembering the girl with the chapped shins. She must have been about twenty to Carole's sixteen. Twenty seemed young now. Twenty was nothing. There was a girl ironing her hair next to the sink, and the room reeked of singed hair. A boy came out of one of the toilets, paused to watch the girl at the sink, and then left. "You want the iron after me?" the girl said, looking at Carole's hair.

"No, thanks," she said. Back in her truck the radio came roaring to life.

Tried to hide
Break on through to the other side

The sign to the Snowtown was bright blue with gold letters, a joke for such a dump. She took the turn and drove slowly down to the ring of cabins, all newly repaired, shored up and painted pale blue with white shutters, like dollhouses with porches and wreaths on the doors. In front of each one was a blue and gold sign. Someone had named each of the cabins. The one second to the left was the Putney. She stopped in front of it. The music changed, screaming at her.

Eyes that sparkle and shine.
You're sixteen, you're beautiful and you're mine.

She cut the engine to kill the radio, feeling conspicuous, aware of how the old truck stuck out here in fairyland. But the place was deserted. She looked back up the road. She should leave. What in the name of God was she doing?

But there was no way not to look. She felt a compulsion unlike anything before. She had to see. *Then* she would leave. She was out of the truck and up the steps quickly, pressing her face to the glass to see through the shadows. She tried the door and it opened. Heart pounding, she entered the room. The two beds were unmade. The bureau opposite and the fake mantel held someone's belongings. She willed herself to be caught at this. She willed someone to walk in on her as she opened the door to the bathroom and went inside. To punish her for this intrusion. Breaking and entering. B and E, she'd heard Will call what she was doing.

It was all painted a pale blue now. The room was so small, but that night it had taken a lifetime to crawl across on her hands and knees away from Rita's lifeless body and gather up her clothes. In her memory it was enormous. A sound somewhere made her jump. Then another. The sound of a door slamming.

Get out, she told herself. Get out of here *now*. But as if in a dream in which her limbs won't obey, she stopped to see what she looked like in the mirror that would have held her reflection then too. Only then would she believe that she was here, and yes, the panic in her eyes, no matter how hard she tried to scare it away, there it was like somebody screaming. A woman in a black sweater, her hair wild in her face, eyes hollow.

She was down the stairs, but not into the truck as she knew she should, but off, around the side of the cabin, looking up the field in back. The sun was hot on her back, burning into her black sweater, the sky a brilliant, sharp blue. The ground was oddly smooth underfoot, a perfect white carpet, her boots pulling up perfect sole-shapes of snow, baring ovals of bright unnatural green. A rich kelly green, and the grass cut short like a crewcut. She stopped to look over the weird unwrinkled field.

It took several moments to realize she was on a golf course that ended at a parking lot far in the distance, glistening hotly with cars. She had a sense of total disorientation, as if she'd come to a place entirely different from where she'd intended or had leaped from some other reality into this, whatever it was.

The woods and the field of her memory were gone, stripped bare. They'd brought in bulldozers and backhoes and whatever else it must have taken to rip through the forest. Now the scene she remembered was gone forever. It was sealed over, taped shut inside herself. Somewhere beneath the glittering razzle-dazzle of what was before her lay Rita's white bones and teeth. Her hair.

The tears began slowly. They rose up painfully behind her eyes and spilled down her cheeks, soaking her fingers as she tried to wipe them away, but they kept washing down. She could not move from where she stood. She had wanted to feel again what she had felt that night, she knew that now. She had wanted to be cracked open and relive the whole event, as if then she would know what to do. But there was only a sadness so overwhelming it pulled her to her knees and kept her there, even as the cold seeped through her skirt, and then down again until she was lying on her side, her cheek pressed into snow-covered grass.

Someone was calling her. A woman's voice coming nearer. She must not be caught here, she thought, alarmed, but still too heavy to move until the woman was almost upon her and Carole sat up in the brilliant sun, blinking. The woman had been running so fast her blond ponytail swung from side to side. "Are you okay?" she kept saying. "Did something happen?"

Carole scrambled to her feet, dusting snow from her skirt, wiping her eyes.

The woman stopped, hands on her hips, her head cocked as suspicion replaced concern. "That's private property up there," she said. "Are you with one of our guests?"

"I just wanted to see," Carole said, the fugitive once again, circling around the woman who was now in her way, between herself and the truck. "I didn't realize—"

"Is that your truck in front of the Putney?" The woman's voice was accusing now. Carole passed her, smiling weakly, her mind gone blank because there was no explanation for what she was doing other than the truth. *I came back to the place where I killed a woman.* There was just flight.

"I'm leaving," she said.

The woman ran after her, calling out, "What were you doing up there? Who *are* you?"

At the truck the woman caught up. "You stay away," she said. "I don't want to see you around here. You had no business."

Running from the scene. In her truck, hightailing it down the driveway, going left instead of right. She'd been the moth touching flame, flirting with exposure. And then the sickening possibility occurred to her, that she might not be anonymous. She might be known here in Stowe. It was possible, and not as the girl from ten years ago but as the business owner from Montpelier. She felt sometimes that she had a million fragmented identities, as though she was only a filament of reality. *What you see is what you get.* But not in her case. In fact, she thought as she drove north on a wet narrow road hugged by steep granite walls, she was nothing like she seemed.

"Paint what you see and not what you know," an art teacher had once instructed her, a difficult exercise because it meant looking fully at an object and not thinking *flower* or *shoe,* or whatever it was but concentrating only on line, shadow, and color. The teacher would stand behind her and say, "Where do you see that?" And of course it wasn't there. She was certain now that Will loved what he knew and not what he saw, and why shouldn't he? She wouldn't allow him to see her.

She drove until she came to a sign. "Entering Morris Center." She pulled to the shoulder and let the van idle. *127 Baldwin Terrace, Morris Center, VT. Rita Marie Boudreau,* the license had said. *Five foot five. 150 pounds. Eyes brown. Hair brown.* Twenty-eight years old.

One-twenty-seven Baldwin was a drugstore, the old kind with a soda counter and a little bell that jingled when she went in. There was a man behind the soda fountain dressed in stained whites, like the soda jerks of her youth. The name HOWIE was embroidered on his breast pocket. He looked her up and down. "What can I do you for?"

Careful, she told herself. Take it easy. Don't do anything rash. She had to remember where she was, in the dead silence of this place.

She browsed the shelves, which had only scant merchandise on them, rows of dusty Band-Aid boxes, some toothbrushes. End of the line, she thought with some relief. Her memory of the address must have been wrong. "I thought this was a residence." She looked around. The store was clearly old. "I must have the wrong address."

"Who you looking for?"

"I thought it would be a home. I'm wrong."

"We got an apartment upstairs, if that's what you mean." He pointed to a door in the back. "Hasn't been rented in a while." He had two different-colored eyes. One brown and one blue. She thought one of them might be blind and looked from one to the other, wondering which of them could see her. "Take a look if you want," he said. He took a large ring of keys from his belt and picked out one of them. "It's just through there." He showed her to the door in back, opened it, and ushered her through to a dark staircase. She could feel him close behind her and turned. "Were you working here in 1965?" she said.

"I was twelve in 1965," he said with a laugh. "My dad owned it." He followed her up the stairs and opened the door. "Give a shout if you have any questions." She went inside, but Howie waited at the door and watched her.

"If you don't mind," she said.

But he still didn't move. "Is it just you?"

She put a hand on the knob. "Just me." She pulled the door gently toward herself until she heard him turn and go back down the stairs. Then she shut the door tight.

She was in a musty room with a single window that let in the afternoon light. It was bare, and you could see where the floor had been shellacked around the edges but left raw in the middle, to be hidden by a carpet. She walked across to the kitchen, the floorboards squeaking underfoot. The kitchen was large, with peeling wallpaper—a yellow background with clumps of brick-colored cherries. There was a small rusted stove against one wall and a refrigerator and a sink against the other. The window looked out on a house and an overgrown yard behind the drugstore. The bedroom was off the kitchen through another door. It still had a narrow metal bed in it as well as a small bureau and one of those freestanding full-length mirrors. The pale green curtains at the window were torn.

Carole went over to the bed and sat down, her hands folded in her lap. It may have been Rita's bed back then. And after Rita, dozens of people would have slept on it, but still it counted for something. She shut her eyes for a few moments and then looked up. Rita might have come from this very room that night. She would have looked at herself in the mirror before she went out. She would have adjusted the straps on that olive-green dress, then turned to see how she looked from behind. Maybe she teased her hair. Carole stood up. She raised her hair over her head and back-combed it with her fingers. It was what they did back then. And then Rita would have sprayed it. She turned in the mirror, again as Rita must have once, to see if the seams in her nylons were straight. It was as though they were sisters and she was watching Rita get ready for a big date.

She opened and closed each drawer in the dresser. She opened the closet, which was shallow and small. A few wire hangers hung on a wooden rod. She touched one of them, thinking it might have held Rita's parka, her dress. She wondered what they would have done with the other clothes when Rita never came back. The door opened behind her. Howie again. "So?" he said.

She'd fallen apart at the motel, come within a hairsbreadth from getting into real trouble. She wasn't going to do that here.

"I need a little more time to consider," she said, desperate to hold on to the moment with Rita—so unexpected, so satisfying, to be Rita for just a few moments more.

"Look, for you I'd cut a deal." He came to the bed and sat down. She felt like he'd stolen from her. If he'd only left her alone for a few more minutes, she'd have—She didn't know exactly what. But something. It was like being pulled from a dream and then trying to recapture it. "It would help if you'd—" she said.

But Howie lay down on the bed. "Two hundred, heat included."

She took a last look in the mirror. She could see him on the bed behind her, but so what? She swiveled, fluffed out her hair.

Howie's expression said he thought this was all for him. "You're something else," he said.

"Right," she said, a sense of alarm creeping into her. "But I guess it's not exactly right. The apartment, I mean." She was closer to the door than he was, and as she crossed back through the living room, she heard the bed creak behind her as he rose and followed her out, but at a distance. It was okay. He was fine. She had another thought, feeling bolder again. "Can I use your phone?"

"Maybe, maybe not," he said, behind her now.

"I'll pay," she said. "I wasn't asking to use it for nothing."

They were back in the drugstore, and she felt safer. "Who you looking for? I know just about everybody in Morris Center."

She smiled at him. "Just somebody I used to know," she said. "I'm curious."

"Who?"

She cocked her head and shrugged a little, giving him a look that said, Sorry, but this isn't really any of your business.

"Whatever," he said. That word again. He indicated the wall phone behind the cash register and handed her a thin phone book. "It's a dime for local calls." He was suddenly cool to her, rebuffed, but so what? She shielded the phone book from him while she looked up the number. "I'll bet a dollar I know your party," he said.

She forced a smile at him as if she hadn't really heard.

There were two Boudreaus. A Paul and a Lionel. She dialed the Paul number. Howie moved closer and was tidying the shelves behind her. The number rang twice before she hung up. What was she doing?

"Busy?" Howie said.

She nodded. She used the dime to dial again, this time letting it ring through. It clicked and buzzed, and then she got a recording that the number was no longer in service. She went over to the counter and sat down.

Howie slipped behind the counter, poured a glass of water, and slid it down the counter to her. "No answer?"

Carole didn't dare raise the glass to her lips. She hunched over the counter and tipped it with both hands to keep it from spilling, but even so it sloshed over the counter. She took a deep breath. She tried to fish another dime out of her purse to pay for the next call, but her change spilled, spinning this way and that. Howie helped her collect it. She held open her purse so he could drop the money in.

"You could use a calmer-downer." He indicated the whole drugstore with a sweep of his hand, and when she smiled, added, "We got everything here. Just name your poison."

"I have to make another call," she said.

He frowned and shook his head. "Suit yourself."

She called the second number. It rang once before a man picked up. "Hello?"

"I'm calling to ask," Carole said, her voice low. She waited until Howie moved away.

"Speak up," the man on the phone said.

"I'm looking for the family of Rita Boudreau." Was she crazy? She should have found a pay phone someplace else. What if Howie could hear? She looked over, but he was sponging down the counter.

"Who is this?" the man said.

"Are you related to her?"

The man said something to someone else in the room. The sound was muffled, as though he was holding his hand over the receiver. Then he came back on the line. "You tell me who you are first, young lady."

"I went to school with her. I was just wondering."

"Well, I'm sorry to tell you I don't know who you mean." The man hung up.

Howie had drifted back toward her and was standing nearby, pretending to study one of the shelves. "You never went to any school with her," he said without looking at her.

Trembling, Carole gathered up her purse.

"You weren't looking for an apartment either, were you?"

"I need to go now," she said. "Thanks for—"

"They found her in Stowe. Dead. Shit, you think I'd forget that?" He headed her off as she went for the door. "Hey! You listening?"

Her truck was several cars down on the left. She pulled open the drugstore door, and the bells sounded. Howie was right behind her. "Hey, wait," he said. "They told my old man to let them know if anybody came looking for her, you know. What's your name? Hey."

She ran from the store and down the street. She had to get out of there before he could see her license plate. Howie was on the sidewalk outside the store when she sped by. He gave her the finger as she passed.

What was she doing? She'd panicked. Why had she ever thought she needed to go to Stowe again? The idea of it had lain out there all these years like some kind of mission she had to fulfill. Something she would do, something she needed to do. *Returning to the scene of the crime.* She cursed herself for doing it so impulsively. Hadn't that been the trouble in the first place? She'd spent all these years taming her impulses, only to give in to them and then take those awful risks. That woman at the Snowtown and then Howie. Now two people had seen her and would remember the bizarre way she had behaved. It was as though she wanted to bring on the danger. Would Howie call the police? Would he describe her truck to them? She stepped on the accelerator, then slammed on the brake. Don't draw attention. *Try to act normal,* Naomi had said that night on the telephone at Grand Central. *If that's even possible.* Naomi should talk. It was her call that had set off this backward slide, that had sent Carole trespassing and calling attention to herself. It made her wonder now if all three of them—she, Naomi, and Eddie—were drawn to one another and to these places like ants to sugar, as if a certain amount of time passed and then each of them needed to take another look. What had Eddie said that time in San Francisco? *Don't think this is over.*

Chapter Fourteen

Carole and Will drove the frosted back roads to Rachel and Morgan's for the Saturnalia dinner, a ritual event they held each year in mid-January to cover Christmas and Thanksgiving at once. Eight weeks had passed since she'd gone to New York for the reunion and then to Stowe, and there had been nothing from Naomi and nothing from Howie or anybody else. Not a phone call, not a letter, not a visit from the police. The dread had gone from a constant hour-to-hour, sick-to-her-stomach vigil to something less sharp. But it was still there, a sort of dull wariness, until she began to wonder about that house Naomi had mentioned and why she hadn't even thought to check it out. The Rowling sisters' house. She wasn't sure where it was, but Rachel would know. Rachel knew everything about the area. It was on a back road somewhere out in Middlesex, Carole knew that much. There had been four unmarried sisters, and the last of them had died a year or so ago at the age of about ninety. Carole had read about it in the paper. If she could see the house, she'd been thinking, yes, if she could see it abandoned, falling into disrepair the way it had been described in the paper, then she would be sure. That would seal the danger, she was almost sure. All this would be over, a thing of the past.

It was still early in the day, and sun sparkled through iced trees. In the backseat she had platters of corn bread and antipasti, a pan of vegetarian lasagna and Will's turkey drumstick, still warm in its aluminum foil on the seat. When they pulled off the road, Carole got out and checked the garage, a big homemade corrugated metal box, to make sure Morgan and Rachel really were home. It was padlocked, which meant the truck was inside and the Weaver-Lears were there. They'd set the date weeks ago, but since her friends didn't have a telephone, it was always iffy.

Carole and Will struck out along the icy, ridged snowmobile tracks. It was lovely in the woods, with gentle sounds as lumps of snow fell from branches and plopped onto the snow. Just before the long final curve, Will stopped and held up a hand for her to stop so they could listen one last time to the stillness of the forest. "Will?" she said, so safe that she was willing to be reckless. "Remember that girl from Spence who called that night?"

"Sure I do. The mess. The one who drinks too much and steals."

She nodded. "Here's what I was thinking. I never heard from her again."

"Well, good," he said. "I guess it's good. You didn't want to, right?"

"Maybe tonight, after, we could drive by that house she was talking about. The Rowling place. I'm just curious."

His parka hood was pulled in tight so only the center of his face showed. "Sure," he said. She thought he was smiling in there. She hoped he was.

They rounded the bend and stood looking at the dome hunkered down among the trees. Morgan and Rachel had improved it over the years. They'd put in running water and electricity, added on a mudroom, and built a chicken coop. It still felt like home to Carole, like the place where she was from.

She could see Rachel framed in the door, waiting. When they got close, Rachel threw her arms around them and drew them inside. She had on a muslin India-print dress, red and brown, and she twirled in it to show it off, the long, droopy sleeves flying out like streamers.

The house was hot and steamy and smelled wonderfully of roasting squash. Light streamed in through murky Plexiglas panels overhead, giving the room a warm yellowish glow. A large couch was in the center of the room with shawls and blankets on it. The stove, a square black Defiant from down in Randolph, stood free in the center of the room with its long silvery chimney going straight up. The only other furniture was a low table, pillows thrown here and there where people could sit, and a long dining table that separated the living space from the kitchen. The floor was covered with books and magazines. The kids' and Rachel and Morgan's bedrooms were still separated by blankets strung across.

Pepper was sprawled on the couch, sipping water from a jar. "Hey, Pep," she said. Pepper raised two fingers in a victory sign and grinned at her.

There was a banging noise somewhere, and Carole looked around the room. Dylan, naked except for a diaper, was slapping the crib rail with his fists. Pepper got up, dragged him over the crib rail, and then fell to the floor under his brother's weight. Then he hauled the baby onto the couch and removed the diaper. He worked quickly, holding the pins in his mouth while he wrapped a clean diaper around the baby. "Watch him, will you?" he said to Rachel. She picked up the baby and held him while Pepper disappeared behind one of the blankets and came back with clothes and shoes for Dylan. "There," he said when the baby was dressed. He started picking up the place after that, straightening out magazines and stacking pillows. "Place isn't safe," he said to Carole and Will. "I keep telling them."

"*You* survived it," Rachel said.

"You know what I want to be when I grow up?" Pepper said.

"A cop!" Rachel said to Carole and Will. "Where did I go wrong?"

"Maybe highway patrol," Pepper said. "Maybe the marines."

"Oh, please," Rachel said.

"It's good to know what you want," Carole said. At ten she'd been completely under her parents' thumb. At ten, they'd already made Vassar a fact of her future. It amazed her that Pepper could be so independent so soon. "What made you suddenly decide?"

Pepper shrugged and looked around. "Stuff," he said.

Rachel smiled wanly. She handed Carole some armloads of bittersweet for the table decoration, prickly, difficult stuff to work with. Carole set about untangling the vines.

"You always said it was up to me." Pepper never knew when they were kidding and when they were serious, which was probably why he wanted so much structure.

"And it is, kid," Rachel said. "You make your own way in this world."

There was a noise outside, and Morgan stomped in, shaking off snow. "God damn," he said. "I almost bought the farm out there." He unzipped his snowmobile suit and hung it up. Underneath he was wearing a plaid Nehru jacket. He'd put pomade or something on his hair to slick it down. It made him look like Keith Richards, with those spindly legs and his dark smile.

"What happened?" Will asked.

"Fell," Morgan said. "I'm up in back, about halfway between here and the tower. Place I don't recognize. Looks like it had been planted for Christmas trees or something, although I don't know how anybody'd be able to harvest way up there."

"You fell through?" Will said.

"It was so deep I couldn't get up. I got all tangled in the branches under the snow."

"You got lucky," Will said. "Could have been a real bitch."

"It *was* a real bitch," Morgan said. "I should have been wearing snowshoes. The snow got so deep all of a sudden."

"Good thing you weren't," Will said. "They can get stuck in the branches. Probably a spruce trap. So how'd you get out?"

"I swam," Morgan said, doing a breaststroke for them. "Swam right out until I could stand up again."

Carole looked at all the books on the couch. *Soul on Ice,* Isadora Duncan's autobiography, and *Peyton Place.* "You reading these?" she said to Pepper. He nodded.

"The classics," Rachel said.

"Let me show you what I've done," Morgan said to Will, and the two men left on the annual tour of the place, with Morgan showing Will where he'd caulked windows or plugged up holes or put in something new with those odd-looking antique tools he had. Built to last, Morgan liked to say, although the house looked inconsistent. The kitchen cabinets were beautiful, handcrafted of cherry wood, but the appliances were scattered here and there, and there were no counters. There was a magnificent staircase to the mud-floored cellar, but the walls were flimsy and leaky and the doorways had no doors on them. Morgan called in that he was taking Will out to see the barn. They'd be back in a few.

After they'd gone, Rachel poured wine for herself and seltzer for Carole, took a tin box of cheese crackers from the shelf, and sniffed them. "Not too bad," she said. She'd taken to wearing her hair parted down the middle, braided, and then the braids coiled into thick rounds at the ears.

"You look like those Von Trapp chicks," Carole said of the women who sometimes walked around Montpelier in their dirndles and braids.

"I can leave it like this for days." Rachel peered inside a big mason jar of flour. "Damn," she said. She took the jar to the compost tray in the corner and upended it. The flour spilled out and puffed into a white cloud, and miller moths flew out.

Carole bit her lip. At the restaurant, she kept everything squeaky clean. She had to. People could get so sick. The fallacy, of course, was that Carole had been eating Rachel's food for years and never got sick. It made her smile. You thought a thing was true, but maybe it wasn't.

"What do you know about the Rowling house?" Carole asked, sitting down at the table.

"That one up on Molly Supple? What about it?"

"Do you know if it's been sold?"

"Why?"

"Somebody I used to know. From New York. Said she came up here and looked at it, maybe to buy."

"Get out." Rachel sat down at the table opposite Carole. "Who? Like high school?"

"Yes."

"You keep *up* with those people? I thought you cut all that off."

"She just got in touch out of the blue. Said she was moving up. I told her to stay in New York."

Rachel sipped her wine carefully. "How did she know where you are? I mean, really. I always thought nobody knew."

"No idea." And Carole was afraid to know exactly. Could Naomi have tracked down her Social Security number? She'd been using it for the restaurant. The danger was that if Naomi could find her then so could Eddie. He hadn't yet bothered to do it, so just maybe he never would.

Rachel pushed the tray of cheese things toward Carole. "You're all bottled up again, you know that? God, just look at your fingernails, bitten down to the quick." Carole made fists of her hands. She wished Rachel would just answer the question. "There's a new CR group at the Episcopal church. You should go, you know. It's never too late."

"I don't think so," Carole said. Rachel had gotten her into the consciousness-raising group in San Francisco once. It was all women who took turns talking, and the rule was that you had to let each person talk. No cross-talk was allowed, which meant that there were lots of long, awful silences.

Carole had hated it. It had embarrassed her the way one after another of the women talked so openly about their private lives. One woman said she had bought a dozen doughnuts and eaten them all in the car. Another was trying not to live in her head, as she put it, but in her body. Carole had found the discussion annoying. Finally a woman named Jo said in this little voice that she needed to speak because she'd cheated on her husband. Carole had perked up. She expected a chorus of questions. *With who? When? Does Dave know?* She'd forgotten the rule about no interruptions, and the women had waited in silence as Jo labored through some disjointed, off-the-wall story about being on a ladder and some guy holding onto her hand too long and Dave getting in his moods and something that she'd seen in a magazine. Jo was all over the map with her story, and it made no sense at all to Carole at first, but then the parts of it began to fall into place. It was a complete story told in fits and starts and out of sequence, with Jo weeping sometimes and laughing other times, adding up to a very clear whole picture of what had happened and when.

Jo stopped talking, and there was another long silence. Carole by this time had been fully sucked in by the story. She wondered what the other women were going to do. They couldn't leave it alone. They would need to do something. And then, as though at some signal, the women crept forward toward Jo. There were seven or eight of them altogether, and they surrounded her murmuring things like *It's okay. You're only human. These things happen.* The soft sound of all those voices was unexpected. They stroked Jo's hair and took her hands in theirs. Carole's eyes welled with tears. All that forgiveness. All that comfort.

"Suit yourself," Rachel said. "But if you ask me—"

"I did ask you Rach," Carole said. "I asked you about that house. The Rowling place. If you know anything."

Rachel frowned. "No," she said. "It's probably a dump."

"Okay, then."

"I'm trying to put myself in your shoes," Rachel said. "I'm thinking that if somebody from my old school showed up. I mean, they *all* must have known what happened, me leaving school so suddenly and then never coming back. But if they found me, I'd want them to see me, see that everything's cool now. How I've done all right for myself. How I live. How I kept Pepper and how great he is. I'd want to see what they looked like too, how they changed. If they had at all. God, I'd be riddled with curiosity." She poked Carole in the arm to make her look up. "Aren't you?"

"I've already seen her. I went down to New York a few weeks ago to head her off. I told her not to come."

"To New York City? What's the story?"

"There's no story. I just told you the story."

"You did not, Carole. Try to remember who you're talking to here."

"She has an agenda."

"Which is?"

"It doesn't matter. She won't be coming. I was firm."

"Firm?" Rachel grinned. "You? What did you say?"

"I told her she wasn't welcome, that I'm not her friend and never will be."

Rachel stared. "You're kidding."

"Will and I might take a ride by the Rowlings' on the way home," Carole said. "See if anybody's there."

"It's not exactly on the way home," Rachel said.

Morgan and Will came stomping in just then, chuffing from the cold, and it was time to fill their plates to overflowing with squash and lasagna and cheese and vegetables canned last summer from the garden. They held hands around the table. On one side, Carole had Dylan, on the other, Will. One big heavy hand and one tiny one. In that circle she felt a current travel among them, connecting them. She was thinking about how good it felt to be here with her friends, so comforting and safe.

They ate quietly, passing the food up and down the table. After several minutes, they started to talk about holidays when they were kids. Rachel's childhood had big family dinners after mass. Morgan's sounded pretty bleak. There never seemed to have been much food. And Will told the story of his mother's turkey. . . . Carole was silent, as she always was when the talk turned to the times before they'd known one another. But she was remembering something so vivid

244

she couldn't get it out of her head. That incredible Christmas tree and the presents at Naomi's house their senior year.

Naomi had insisted on Carole's going over there. Carole just *had* to see this. They had a real tree this time. And, she'd said with excitement, Daddy and Elayne were not waiting until the last minute or blowing the tree thing off altogether like they usually did. No way. This year she'd begged and begged because it was her senior year and who knew where she'd be next Christmas? And not only had they done it, but Carole had to see the thing. It was so incredibly beautiful, it made up for all the other years.

Carole had gone over, and sure enough, it was the most gorgeous tree she'd ever seen. It sat in front of the windows in the living room with a million small white lights, covered in big pink and silver bows and shiny ornaments. It had been sprayed with something pearly so it looked like it had been snowed on. But the really amazing part had been the presents, heaped in piles underneath. There had to be fifty, from huge to tiny, and there were only the three people in Naomi's household. The presents were all wrapped to match the tree. Pink and silver and gold. Naomi had been out of her mind about it. It was as though they'd finally *noticed* her, she kept saying. They had finally done something that was important to her, and not just grudgingly but in this really big way.

Carole and Naomi had sat on the couch and admired the tree for a long time. They were giddy with speculation about what might be in the boxes, and it was inevitable that they'd slip off the couch, kneel on the floor, and start shaking one or two, knowing full well they weren't going to stop there. They were going to open a couple and rewrap them so nobody would ever know.

Naomi had picked one of the presents. She shook it and made a face. No sound. She'd taken another and done the same thing. So Carole had started rooting around. She picked a big package, the kind of box that a coat might come in. She was expecting the weight of something like that, but the box was so light it slipped from her hands.

Naomi ripped the paper off the package, and it was empty. She opened more, and they were all empty. She'd just sat there staring at all those empty boxes. Carole knew right then that things like this probably happened to Naomi a lot, but she never talked about them. What made this so much worse was having Carole there to witness her humiliation. Then Elayne had come barging in just like a madwoman. She'd been taking a nap, and when she saw the tree, she'd started screaming. *Stupid girls, what do you think you're doing?* She needed the tree to be perfect for a party they were having. When Carole left, Elayne was on the phone to Naomi's father barking orders for him to call that window-dressing company and do it pronto. Naomi didn't call Carole for days after that, and when she finally did, she never mentioned the tree.

"And speaking of old times," Rachel said, pulling Carole from her memories, "this one has a high school friend who maybe bought the Rowling house and maybe didn't or won't— Oh, you tell them."

Carole felt loose and out of control. It was one thing to tell Will and then to tell Rachel, one to one, to be in charge of what she said. It was another to hear the information spoken aloud, suddenly everybody else's property, up for grabs. She wanted to gather it all back in, to vacuum it up. "Just somebody I used to know," she said. "I didn't mean to make a mountain out of a molehill."

"Call information," Morgan said. "When you get home, just call and see if there's a new listing."

"They're driving by," Rachel said. "After."

Carole felt her life spilling out again, becoming public.

"I want to go, too," Pepper said.

"I know right where that house is," Morgan said. "You go—" His long fingers began to gesture. "It's hard to explain, but I could show you. I could take you. Hell, we could all go."

"Oh," Carole said.

"We do need to get out," Rachel said. "We've been here for four days straight." She glanced at Carole. "You cool with that?"

To say no would make it all flat-out bizarre. It would put up a red flag in all their minds. "Sure," she said.

They cleared the table and put out the pies. Apple, mince, and pumpkin. Then, together, they washed the dishes, which was an ordeal in that house unless, as Morgan said, you really got into the moment Zen-like, enjoying the bubbles, enjoying the great tubs of scalding water that were heated on the stove and brought over for the dishes. By the time they headed out, Carole was feeling confident that the house would be dark and all this worry would be over. But just in case, she wanted to make sure the others understood absolutely. "We'll only drive by. We won't stop."

Rachel crossed herself. "Scout's honor," she said.

Morgan, Pepper, and Dylan left on the snowmobile, and by the time Carole, Will, and Rachel got to the road, Morgan had the truck idling. Carole and Rachel climbed into the back and sat on a pile of lumber. Carole zipped her parka to the neck and held tight to the side of the truck as they started down the road. Rachel yodeled a few times. She hauled Carole to her knees and made her do it too. Scream at the top of her lungs. She did it until Morgan threw on the brakes for a turn, and they were slammed against the back of the cab. She had a vague idea of where the old Rowling sisters lived. Somewhere out in the hills. Molly Supple was a familiar road name, but she'd never been on it. There were so many little dirt roads crisscrossing out there.

The truck slowed almost to a stop, then took a sharp right. Overhead branches snapped and whipped at them, and they had to crouch even lower down. "This looks like a damn driveway," Carole said. "We shouldn't be going up any driveway." She got to her knees and banged on the cab roof to get Morgan to stop. He banged back.

By now the truck was fishtailing and lurching. Its wheels spun and caught. A dog barked up ahead. Carole held on to the rails of the truck bed. She peered around the edge of the cab. "Turn off the headlights," she yelled at Morgan, and he did. But they were already in somebody's yard. Before them was a house in full view, every window blazing with light. A Jaguar and a new Toyota Land Cruiser sat in the driveway. Rachel let out a low whistle that set the dog off again. "Shush," Carole said to the dog.

Carole could see right through the picture windows to new Sheetrock, all hospital white. In all that light she couldn't make out where the dog was. But then it moved. It was tied up at the back door, a white dog as big as a calf, with a huge head, working the air with its nose.

A sound from the house set the dog off even worse. The back door opened, and Naomi stepped onto the porch, looking out into the night. She had a glass in one hand and took a sip. "Shut the fuck up," she said. The dog snapped at her.

"Let's get out of here," Carole said. But the next thing she knew, Naomi was coming across the front walk toward them, a tiny, thin shadow skittering along in high heels, the dog straining for her on its tether, barking and snarling. She stopped a few feet from the truck, cupped her eyes with one hand, and peered at the truck bed. "Carole bloody Mason?" she said, "Is that you?"

"You'll pay for this," Carole said to Rachel.

"Sorry," Rachel whispered. "Really."

"I'll be damned," Naomi said.

The light was so bright behind Naomi that it was hard to see her face. "We were just going by," Carole said. "We're leaving."

"Who do you have with you?" Naomi peered into the cab. "Oh," she said. "Kids." Then she noticed Morgan, still at the wheel. "Hello there," she said.

"We can't stay," Carole said.

"Of course you can." Naomi opened the door to the cab. "There's nobody here but me."

"No," Carole said, but Pepper was already out of the truck and headed up to see the dog.

"Hey, you," Naomi said sharply. "Leave the dog alone."

As they got out of the truck and stood in the glaring artificial light, Naomi looked each one of them up and down. Carole knew exactly what would be going through Naomi's mind, the way she would take in every detail. The safety pins in their clothing, the way their boots were mended with duct tape. Rachel's bells, the tattered baby carrier for Dylan. Everybody would reek of failure in Naomi's eyes. As they followed her to the house, Rachel whispered again to Carole that she was sorry, but she was looking at the house in amazement, at the light pouring out, the brilliance of white inside. "You *still* know people like this?" she asked.

"Five minutes," Carole said. "And we're out of here." She walked with the others toward the house, walking into hell in a way, in shock that this was actually happening, this house, the voices around her, and her own peculiar willingness to keep on going, as if her body had to imitate the others because she couldn't think at all.

In the kitchen Naomi pulled items out of her cupboards. Jars of nuts. Six-packs of soda, a tube of anchovy paste. She had a bottle of scotch in one hand, clutching it so tightly her knuckles were white. "This calls for a celebration," she said. "Put your jackets anywhere. The closets aren't done yet." She was watching them closely, looking at the jackets, mittens, and scarves they dropped on chairs in the living room. There was a pair of men's shoes next to the back door. Carole wondered if the boyfriend was in the house somewhere. Arthur. That was his name.

Naomi noticed her looking at the shoes and dropped one of the parkas on them. "So who are these people?"

"These are my friends," Carole said, aware as she said it of her emphasis on "these," as if to say, *and you're not.* "Will Burbank. Rachel, Morgan, Pepper, and Dylan Weaver-Lear."

But it was lost on Naomi. She'd obviously been drinking before they arrived. She went from one to the next, extending her small glamorous hand tipped with its little red nails to each, even to the baby. Then she went back to Morgan. She stood close, looking up at him. "You do the honors, okay?" She held out the bottle of scotch to him.

Morgan took the bottle from her. "Sure," he said. "Glad to."

"Cheers," Naomi said, handing them each a glass. "You're the first real people I've seen. Other than workmen." She gestured around the house.

"Workmen are people," Carole said, knowing it sounded petulant.

"You know what I mean."

"Morgan's a workman."

"Oh?" Naomi said. "As in?"

"Carpenter," Morgan said. He was uncomfortable, rearranging himself over and over.

"But I'm *looking* for a good carpenter," Naomi said.

"You wouldn't like me." Morgan cleared his throat. "What I mean to say is, my work is different. It wouldn't fit in here." He was being diplomatic.

"Well, *sure* it would." Naomi must have thought Morgan was being shy and all she needed to do was coax him out.

"Morgan's work is museum quality," Carole said. "Fine and painstaking. You'd get impatient."

Will grinned at her.

"Whatever." Naomi took another sip of her drink and tossed her hair. Something in the gesture caused Carole to look from Naomi to Rachel. Somewhere along the line Rachel had undone that funny hairdo, and now her black hair, shot with early gray, covered her shoulders. It surprised Carole to see the two of them side by side. Rachel was taller and larger than Naomi, her features rounded and soft, and yet Naomi was the one who took up space. She was all tight nerves, always in motion. When they'd been girls, Naomi had discovered that she could stay thin by eating what she wanted and then sticking a finger down her throat. Carole wouldn't be surprised if she still did that.

Naomi latched on to Will's elbow, digging her nails into the fabric of his jacket. "Let me show you around."

"Carole wants to get going," he said.

"She said five minutes," Naomi said. "I heard." She checked her watch. "We've still got time." She turned her back and started running on to Will about how she wanted lots of light, *needed* lots of light, but look around up here and all you see is houses with little windows. "Like pissholes in the snow, if you ask me."

"You're losing a ton of heat through that glass," Carole said. "It's getting sucked out, and it's going to cost you a fortune in oil. Light too. You might consider some thermal window coverings. Vermonters know this stuff."

"Money isn't exactly something I worry about," Naomi said. "But I'll keep your advice in mind." She winked at Will, then turned and headed for the stairs. "I want the whole thing in white." She spoke almost intimately to Will as she guided him, leaning on his arm. "Glossy. Walls, woodwork, everything. I like it bright, you know? What I really want," she told him, leaning over closer, confidentially, "is for it to look like a loft in SoHo. That way, if I never look outside I can pretend I live in New York. Maybe get a tape of street sounds. Hey, there's an idea." She walked over to the telephone, picked it up, and dialed a number. A minute later, she was talking to someone named Zoë. "Just lean out the window with your recorder and send me the tape." She winked at Carole. "Say hello to Will." She handed the receiver over. "Her name is Zoë. She's a trip."

Will handed it back.

"He's got a case of the quiets," Naomi said into the phone. "I've gotta run. I've got a houseful, and they're all staring at me like I've flipped." She made a yakkety-yak sign with her hand to indicate that Zoë was still talking. When she hung up, she said, "What a brainstorm that was. Taxis honking. People swearing. You know. Life."

"Why did you move here if you like New York so much?" Rachel had a wide-eyed smile plastered on.

Naomi pointed at Carole. "Yours truly," she said. "My bosom buddy in high school. We were absolutely wild in those days. Little Miss Good Citizen and I used to shoplift."

"Naomi!"

"Really?" Pepper was staring up at her.

"Lamston's five-and-ten," Naomi said.

"We've got to go," Carole said.

Naomi checked her watch. "Two more minutes." She spun around and headed to the second floor. After a moment, Morgan went up behind her. He turned at the stairs to shrug at Carole. "I've got to see this," he half-whispered. "She's making a mess of it." The others followed, even Carole, encouraged now that she knew the spirit in which they were all going along with this. Naomi had had the whole upstairs gutted so it was just a huge open space, all newly Sheetrocked, with shiny hardwood floors. The bunch of them stood in awe, looking around. Even the bathroom was exposed. The tub, the toilet, the sink in one corner, but raised on a platform. There was a razor and a can of shaving cream on the sink. Where had the boyfriend gone?

"Not much privacy there," Morgan said. In the center was a large round unmade bed, and on the ceiling was a mirror.

"It's like a bowling alley," Pepper said.

Carole put the baby down, and he ran across the floor in delight, his loud happy cries echoing in the large room. "And a bitch to heat," she said.

"We've already *had* that conversation." Naomi looked from Will to Morgan as though sure she had their agreement.

"Cha's right," Will said. "These old houses had registers in all the rooms. You could direct the heat to places where you needed it most and not heat everything."

So there, Carole thought.

"What did you call her?"

Will smiled. "Cha," he said. "Sometimes I just like to call her Cha."

"Like an alias?" Naomi cocked her head coyly. "Are you in *hiding* or something?"

"You found her, didn't you?" Rachel said.

"But that place of yours. Chacha's. It's so, I don't know, *Spanish*."

"How *did* you find her?" Rachel asked.

"Easy," Naomi said. She backed away and gestured around. "So this is it. This is my house. You like?" She spun around but toppled slightly and was caught by Morgan. "Oops. Damn shoes." She took them off and threw them, and they clattered across the polished floor. No one answered the question.

Naomi went slowly down the stairs, her glittering nails cutting the air, the gold bracelets tinkling as she talked on and on about the house and more plans she had for it. A new room off the kitchen. A garage. She complained about the road to her house, what a mess it was to drive, how they never even came up there with the snowplow. Morgan said it wasn't a town road, but Naomi cut him off. "Of course it's a town road. It's a road, and it's in the town, isn't it?" And Morgan gave up with a laugh, as if her ignorance was more charming than maddening.

As a girl, Carole had been the pathetic one—tall, gauche, and brainy in a way that soured people on her. She'd envied Naomi back then. Naomi had always been so sure of herself, for one thing, and she had flirted her way through everything. "I sat out the sixties," she was saying to Will, and then laughed, an oddly husky laugh for her little frame. "Well, the political part, not the sexual revolution. I was right in there with that, oh, yes." She didn't understand that it would cut no ice with Will, who had done just the opposite, ridden out the hedonistic part but not the political part. And then she guided the conversation back to all the money she had, oh me oh my, how she just kept on inheriting from one distant relative after another. "And it'll keep on going," she said, eyes wide, as if it were an affliction. "There are still some aunts to go and an eccentric old cousin who thinks I walk on water."

Time to get the ball rolling. Time for everybody to clear out, but Naomi segued into talking of a party she wanted to have. "I've wanted to entertain of course, in here. That's the point of all this space. And all of you people, well, you're invited. Hell, you'd be the guests of honor, being Carole's friends and all. How about in three weeks? Yes! That's enough time to order the stuff and get out some invites." She ran on about it, and nobody said anything until she was all done, until she said, "And of course the kids."

All along, Pepper had been standing beside her, looking up, taking in every detail of her. "I'll bet she'd like the night ski," he said to the others, and Naomi laughed a shrill, tinkly laugh.

"Oh, no," Carole said. "She wouldn't like it."

"Why I'd *love* it, sweetheart," Naomi said. "Whatever it is."

Will cleared his throat. He explained that she probably wouldn't want to come. It was long and cold. Really cold. They often skied all night except for building a campfire if the weather permitted and later having something to eat at the cabin. You had to be really fit. Anybody else would have understood that the invitation was being withdrawn.

"If Carole can do it, I can do it."

"She's experienced," Will said.

"And I'm a quick study," Naomi said. "I've got all the stuff. I got it down at the sports store. The skis, the boots, the poles, even snow-shoes. Just tell me when."

"Really, Nay. Listen to Will." This whole discussion mustn't go any further.

"February 28," Pepper said. "Right?" He looked at Morgan, who shrugged.

"No," Carole said.

"Well, that's settled. Now how about something to eat?" Naomi said. "I'll bet I've got something." Naomi lurched into the kitchen and started to rummage around. She held up the things she'd taken out earlier. "Oh, God, look. I never offered you this stuff. Well, have some now."

"We're leaving," Carole said.

"We already ate," Rachel said by way of explanation, or maybe apology.

"Thanks anyway," Will said.

Carole was putting on her parka, and Naomi was suddenly at her side, close, whispering. "It's that thing about that woman, isn't it? Back in Stowe?" Naomi's head quivered more than shook. She was so wired.

"Keep your voice down," Carole said, looking to see if anyone had heard, but they hadn't. Will, Pepper, and Morgan must have already gone outside. Rachel was still fussing with Dylan's jacket by the door and out of earshot.

"My lips are sealed, Carole. They always have been. Don't be such a worrywart."

"I wish you'd just stay away," Carole said. "Just leave me alone."

"May I remind you," Naomi said, pulling herself up to her full height, "that you're the one who came to me. You're the one who dropped in on me, and not vice versa. You and all those friends of yours."

The trouble was, it was true. "We were just going to drive by, that's all. I was hoping you wouldn't be here."

Naomi looked up, her eyes narrowed in defiance. "Well, here I am," she said.

Chapter Fifteen

Naomi greeted them at the door wearing a white caftan and a gold turban wrapped around her head. She had long multicolored earrings that brushed her shoulders and tinkled lightly. Her shoulders were dusted with sequins, like the ones that had fallen out of the invitation when Carole opened it. Leave it to Naomi to make you have to run the vacuum cleaner after opening the mail. She'd fumed as she cleaned up. Will had watched her from the couch and said for the hundredth time that they didn't have to go to the party. It wasn't a command performance or anything, and why didn't Carole just call her up, say no, and be done with it? For somebody who never wanted to see this woman again, going to her party was a peculiar thing.

But by this time, Naomi had become a magnet, and Carole didn't dare stay away. It was better to go than to sit at home and wonder who was there and what Naomi was saying about her, because she had no doubt Naomi would talk up the fact that they'd known each other a hundred years ago and no doubt lace their story with lies or, worse, the truth. Better to go and see for herself and at least cut Naomi off at the pass if she started blabbing when she got drunk, which she would. And besides, Rachel had come in to Chacha's and hinted around pretty broadly that they all wanted to go because of the food and because, as she put it, "God, Carole, it's just so bizarre. *She's* so bizarre."

As usual Naomi had way too many clothes on her small form. She threw her arms around Will, gave him a kiss on the mouth, then pulled Carole toward herself, grabbed both their hands, and guided them into the room, hanging on for dear life as she pushed through the crowd. The room had that cocktail-party sound, a rumble of voices so loud that Carole could barely hear when Naomi introduced her and Will to people they already knew.

Since that last time, Naomi had done things to the living room, smothered it in fabric. Whatever happened to "I want everything in white"? Carole wondered. The living room ceiling had a big blue button in the middle with pleated fabric spiraling out to the four walls, like being inside a big cushion. It resembled the apartment Naomi had lived in as a girl, which had seemed at the time like a pastel fairyland. And she remembered New Year's Day of her junior year, a nasty wet day just like this one, when Naomi had called her. "You've got to see this," Naomi had rasped into the phone. "Get over here, only don't ring the bell."

Carole had left a note so her parents would know where she was. She'd walked up Lex to Eighty-fourth and then over to Park. When she got off the elevator, Naomi had hustled her into the apartment. She was wearing some outrageous costume that made her look like a Guatemalan doll—a peasant blouse, too big for her, pulled down at the shoulders, and a flouncy turquoise skirt. Naomi always swam in her clothes, even then. The sleeves were always too long, the shoulder seams drooped. She had her hair all piled up on her head and wore thick makeup. "I got bored," she'd said about the makeup, pulling Carole into the apartment and shoving her down the hall like a trained bear. And then the first shock, the huge wet liquor stains all over those lily-white walls, the very walls Elayne had had painted umpteen times to get exactly the right shade of white, idiotic as that had seemed at the time. And in so many colors. Brown, maroon, yellow. Naomi giggled and danced in her spike-heeled shoes as she went from one stain to the next. She picked up a half-full glass from the side table and flung it at the wall. "Cointreau."

"What have you done?" Carole asked.

"Not me, stupid," Naomi said. "Them!" She indicated the hall where her father and Elayne's bedroom was.

The place reeked. It stank to high heaven. But that was nothing compared to the living room. That beautiful pastel room was now a shambles, the furniture overturned, all the powder-blue taffeta cut to ribbons. Naomi's eyes glistened. She was wired, proud of being able to show off the ravages of her family life.

Naomi picked up a scissors that one of them must have thrown on the floor and began snapping it open and shut. Carole could recall its steely sound in the quiet apartment. Naomi looked around and then punched the scissors into the couch.

"Don't," Carole said.

Naomi snipped out a circle of the blue taffeta and stuck it in her hair like a flower. She pointed to a fireplace poker in a corner. "You can use that."

Carole picked it up and watched as Naomi cut into a chair that her father and Elayne had missed. "Don't just stand there!" she said. "Wreck something."

Carole rested the tip of the poker on the plump pink fabric of a chair, staring at the ugly charred metal and the dent it made. With very little force, she nudged the poker so it split the fabric. White batting pushed through the hole. She did it again a few inches away. "Way to go," Naomi said. She handed Carole a tumbler and filled it with some green liquor and told her to throw it. Carole remembered how she'd stood there with the glass in her hand, not wanting to and then doing it anyway. She remembered the green hitting the wall and dripping down, how Naomi laughed.

"They'll never know it was us." Naomi tugged at one of the curtains. The bracket pulled out a patch of plaster, then the whole rod fell, burying Naomi in fabric. She fought her way out of it, laughing and swearing. "They'll think it was *them*. We could torch the place, and they wouldn't care." With that Naomi smashed something else made of glass against the wall. She was still wrecking the apartment when Carole let herself out a few minutes later. The next day in school, Naomi said her father and Elayne had gotten up at dinnertime and gone out. Not a word about the mess. While they were gone, Naomi had done some damage to their bedroom. She figured it would be cleaned up by the time she got home that afternoon, and Elayne would be out buying more furniture.

Here at Naomi's party it was a peculiar crowd. There were women with little diamond tennis bracelets on, admiring the renovations, turning over the china and looking at the marques. And their husbands in navy blazers and gray slacks, rocking on their heels. The women lit up at seeing Carole and finding out she was somehow related to this sudden, colorful new presence in town. The Weaver-Lears were all there, hanging around the edges of the room and watching, chatting to one another. Morgan had on his plaid Nehru jacket from the Saturnalia dinner, and Rachel was in her usual dark layers and bells. Nobody else was talking to them. Pepper stood by the window, watching Naomi.

Carole should have predicted that Naomi would be more interested in upscale people. The ladies who lunch. The wives of the insurance executives, the doctors, the lawyers in town, and those other shadowy figures—people with summerhouses and ski chalets up here. Not many, but they were out there. She'd have no interest in the patrons of Chacha's, who were poor and who, excepting the Weaver-Lears, were conspicuously absent.

Naomi pushed Carole and Will into a nest of people like a couple of prize show-dogs. "We went to school together! Imagine! We were like this!" Naomi held up a hand with two fingers wrapped together. "And then Carole just dropped out of sight, and bingo! Here she surfaces in Montpelier, Vermont, of all places. I could hardly believe it! I would never in a million years have expected it. I mean, if you knew her when, well, you'd never have believed it. She was actually chunky!"

One of the wives stepped right up. "Chacha's is just fabulous," she told the others. "Really funky." She gave Carole a warm glance as though she had fond memories of the place, when Carole knew she'd never set foot in it.

Naomi dug her nails into Carole's arm and dragged her off to meet a little gaggle of doctors from the Barre hospital. The energy in the room had a frantic quality to it. Everybody was talking at once, their voices rising to be heard so they were almost shouting at one another. When Naomi raced off to talk to somebody else, Carole looked around. Will had somehow managed to escape and was over talking to Morgan and Rachel.

She snaked her way through the crowd. When someone tried to engage her in conversation, she just pointed to the corner of the room where she was headed, apologetically, as if someone was waiting there and she had to go. She landed among them finally. They had staked out a spot between the kitchen and the dining area. They were all sharing a plate heaped with hors d'oeuvres. Carole pushed into their midst.

"Try this," Rachel said, offering her the plate. Carole shook her head. "They get it from someplace in New York. That woman over there." Carole turned to see who she meant. A stout woman stood at the kitchen counters. In front of her were dozens of white containers in all sizes that she was emptying onto plates. She was dressed in yellow silk pajamas, and her hair was cut in a long shag. She looked up just as they were all looking at her. Her face broke into a smile, and she waved. A few seconds later she pushed through the crowd toward them. "Zoë," she said with a long, dramatic sigh. "I'm Naomi's friend from New York. I'm just exhausted. Slave labor. Think I'll take a break." She looked around at them. "I'll bet you're Carole."

Carole nodded.

Zoë clapped her hands. "Naomi has done nothing but talk about you for months. I just knew it had to be you. God, you two must have had a ball as kids."

She leaned into the group conspiratorially. "If you ask me, this is a mistake. Not that you *have* asked me, but Naomi in this godforsaken place? She's absolutely undone by the divorce, of course. That bastard. Baxter the bastard. The great *white* bastard, I call him." She glanced at Will. "Oh, sorry," she said. "But he's a prick to just walk that way. Naomi fell apart. Completely went to pieces. Which is the only way I can even begin to make sense of this move up here. Now Stowe or Sugarbush, I could understand for a few months of the year, but this? But, you know, she kept talking about you, about how close you two were as girls. And she had this thing about coming up here. You've been *immensely* helpful. She talks about you all the time. Introducing her around and all."

"I haven't done a thing," Carole said. "I discouraged her from coming."

Zoë burst out laughing. "Well, I know that, but I mean once Naomi makes a decision . . ." She looked around the room. "And just look at all the friends she's made so far. I mean, she hasn't even been here a month. Well, maybe that. But hardly at all, and just look. She fits right in, doesn't she? She's the kind of person who can fit in anywhere. I'm so jealous."

"You've known her a long time?" Will asked

Zoë nodded. "Oh, yes. Last year. We met at my exercise club. I was going through exactly the same thing. Dumped, if you can believe it, after almost ten years. We're like sisters," she said. "We're soul mates." She gave Carole a light swat on the knee. "Which is why I'm just so excited to meet *you*. We can all be soul mates together, right?"

"Me too?" Rachel winked at Carole.

"Of course, yes," Zoë said.

Rachel pointed to one of the bits of food on the plate. "You know what's in these?"

"Not a clue," Zoë said. "She ordered it all from Panky's, this place on Third. I brought it up with me. Picked it up frozen yesterday. Well, my traveling companion picked it up, and I picked him up. Everybody in the city has them cater their parties. It's, like, you don't miss the party if Panky's is doing the food."

Naomi pushed herself into their circle. "Did I hear Panky's? You having fun? I see you've met Zoë. My compadre. We've been in the trenches together, haven't we, Zoë baby?"

"Where did you find all these people?" Rachel said. "Such a mishmash."

Naomi flashed a bright smile. "You've got to be social in a new place," she said. "When I meet people I like, I just hand them an invitation. It's as simple as that. Of course, now that they're here, now that I've had a chance to talk to them all"—she raised her eyebrows and pursed her lips—"I see I've made some mistakes."

It made them all look out onto the room, wondering who she might mean.

"See that guy over there in those awful pants?" Naomi pointed to Jim Sawyer, a great tree trunk of a man with bristly hair. He had on red slacks and a plaid jacket. Everyone knew his son had died of leukemia just months ago. He gave them a little shy wave when they all turned to look. "Total bore," Naomi said. "He's off the list next time."

"They want to know what's in these things." Zoë popped a round doughy-looking thing into her mouth. She chewed reflectively. "I'd say fish or something like that. All I know is, it's good."

"I never ask," Naomi said. "I just said to send their best, and they did. Not like that dreadful little market in town. The Sanford Market. Those guys don't know shit from shinola, and they're all so bloody old. Ick."

Zoë passed the plate to Morgan, who helped himself to a handful of the canapés. "I bet you can eat whatever you want and never get fat," she said with a sigh, popping another into her mouth.

"Oops, someone new has just arrived." Naomi withdrew and was gone in an instant.

"She's *such* a good hostess, isn't she?" Zoë said. "Always presiding. Like Leona Helmsley in those ads, you know? *Where the queen stands guard.*"

"Oh, please," Carole said.

"But she's fabulous. Talk about a woman on her own. Now that woman really puts the *b* in *bitch.* In a good way."

Carole wasn't sure if Zoë was talking about Naomi or Leona Helmsley. She would have asked perversely, but a deep laugh from behind interrupted their conversation.

She turned to look, and there he was. Oh, God. Eddie, beefy in a brown velvet suit with wide lapels, smiling at her with perfect white teeth, leaning in to kiss her cheek, reeking of cologne. She pulled away, but he slid his hand up her back and gripped her shoulder. He extended his other hand first to Morgan and then to Rachel. "Ed Lindbaeck," he said, leaning closer against her. "I knew Carole in New York."

The room rolled and pitched like a ship, and she felt that tumbling sense of seasickness. She would have rushed for the bathroom, but she was fixed in place as she watched Rachel lean in and shake Eddie's hand, her attention fully on his face with a peculiar curiosity that was way too big, that had to be recognition. Carole had a vision of that night in the van and Rachel in the dark, with Pepper on her lap saying, *I hope he gets killed.*

Now Rachel's face twisted in pain, her mouth opened wide, and she let out a shrill sound that turned heads. Her hand flew up, but not at Eddie. She was bent over, grasping at her hair and her ears, and only then did Carole see that Dylan, who was in his Gerry pack on Rachel's back, must have pulled Rachel's hair or her earrings. Rachel swung away from them, with Morgan following to help.

Eddie turned to Will. "We go back, Carole and me," he said. *Further than you,* was the implication. "She's surprised to see me."

Carole couldn't catch her breath. He was digging his fingers one by one into her back in some sort of secret code. She shifted to her other foot and tried to step away, but his hand tightened and he drew her closer. He slid his thumb between her arm and her side, pressing the side of her breast. His whispered breath was hot in her ear. "Haven't we fucked before?"

"Hey, man." Will took a step toward Eddie. He couldn't have heard, but he had eyes.

"He's just—" Carole said to Will, trying to laugh it off. Don't make a scene, she thought. *Not here, not now.* Eddie could say anything. In the kitchen, Naomi was watching, her eyes glassy and dangerous. She made her way toward them.

For Carole, everything was happening in slow motion now. She was trying to figure it out. Him and Naomi. It had to be. Nothing had ever come between them, not even Bax. Eddie's hand slid down her side and rested on her hip. She took a deep breath to steady herself just as Naomi pushed her way in between them. Her smile was huge and her eyes bright and wet. "You guys." She clapped her hands. "I can't begin to tell you what a treat this is." And then to the others who were watching, to Will in particular, "We all knew each other in school."

"Let's have a toast." Eddie filled Naomi's glass. "Anyone else?" Nobody did. Carole sought out Rachel and found her sitting down with the baby on her lap, doing up her hair. So she hadn't recognized Eddie. She didn't know. Eddie held his own glass up and smiled at Naomi, then touched the glass to his lips but didn't drink, while Naomi took a long swallow. He caught Carole's eye briefly and winked. The implication was that he was helpless to stop Naomi. Carole turned to make her way across the room for the door. She felt a hand grab her elbow, turned, and saw Naomi looking up at her, the gold turban tipped and catching the light. Naomi dug her fingers deep into Carole's flesh. "Be happy for me."

"I don't believe this, Naomi. How could you bring him up here? It's bad enough with just you, but him!"

"Don't be pissed, Carole. Please don't be!" She gave Carole a big smile and shimmied her head stupidly.

"You're so drunk, Naomi. You're disgusting." Carole tried to pull away but was startled when Naomi held on tight. "Let go of me."

"No," Naomi said, so loudly that people near them turned to

look. "I'm not drunk. If you think this is drunk, you should stick around. Let's sit down."

She pulled Carole to a pair of chairs in the corner. Carole looked back at the party to see Eddie and Will still in the circle with Zoë and the Weaver-Lears. "Say you're not mad, Carole." Naomi seemed dead sober all of a sudden. "You were my only friend, you know. The only real friend I ever had. With everybody else it was always just take take take." She smiled a little. "Even Eddie, but I forgive him for that. It's not like he's trying to hide it or anything. But never you. You've never asked for a thing from me."

"Sure I have. I asked you not to come up here."

Naomi shrugged as if that didn't count. She went on. It was as though she'd rehearsed this. "You were such a brain at school. You could have hung out with the preppie crowd. With Amanda and them. They'd have taken you in like that." She tried to snap her fingers but fumbled it. "It was because of me you didn't. You were a real friend." Carole didn't think that was true at all. Naomi kept talking. "Even Elayne and Daddy. I was just an annoyance to them. Elayne actually said that once. And you know what else? Bax made a deal with them. A deal! There I was thinking it was love at first sight on the Madison Avenue bus one day, but no way. Elayne set it up. She told him where I was going to be. And sure enough he comes up to me and starts talking. It was this deal for money. Like a lot of it. He never loved me. Didn't even like me. That whole Cartier thing I told you was true, but it wasn't the reason we got the divorce. No, sir. We got divorced because Bax never meant to hang around in the first place."

She bit her lip. "I came up here to find you. Eddie was against it, if you must know. He only came because I came."

"He should have stayed away."

Naomi pulled herself up and tossed her hair. "I hate to say it and all, but, well, Carole, you owe me. I kept my mouth shut about what happened, and I'm always going to keep it shut. Anyway, here I am. How bad can I be? And anyway I don't know what you have against him anyway. All he ever did was try to help you."

Eddie suddenly appeared. "What are you girls talking about?" He leaned down to kiss Naomi, smiling at Carole. She remembered the two of them that night, their gray shadows coming together outside the motel. It must have been going on for years with them. He whispered into Carole's hair. "You be careful." She remembered with a shiver of disgust how he'd pushed himself inside her. She stood, and immediately Will was there too, an arm around her waist.

"Let's go," Will said.

She let him pull her through the room by the hand, and as they went, faces blurred together. By the door, she dug through the pile of coats for her parka and finally found it. She and Will were heading for the car when she heard Naomi clatter down the icy path behind them in her high heels. "Hey," she cried, lurching and reeling toward them, the white sleeves of her caftan billowing like a ghost. "We're on for that thing, right?" she called out. "That ski thing?"

Will revved the motor and maneuvered his way through the ragged line of cars parked down the driveway to the road. He drove for several minutes, then pulled over. It was bitter outside, and their breath soon frosted the windows. "What's going on? That guy was all over you."

"Who?"

"You know who. That guy from New York. What is he, an old boyfriend or something?"

"Naomi's," she said. "You don't think—"

"He had his hand on your ass."

"My arm."

"His hand was on your ass, Cha. You let him keep it there. I've seen guys at the bar get clocked if they got too close. Just tell me what's going on, okay?"

She remembered the oily weight of Eddie's arm on her shoulder. The way he let his arm slip down her back. Her paralysis as he did it. Sometimes in Chacha's men would come on to her. Usually they just said things to her, waiting to see if she'd ratchet it up, and when she didn't, they let it go. But once in a while a guy might try something

266

physical, and she'd let him have it right away. An elbow, a hip. With Eddie she'd been afraid even to move away. If she'd shrugged off his arm, he'd have raised his voice, attracted the attention of everyone there. Bad enough that he told Will he'd known her and Naomi years ago.

"I need you to believe this, Will. It's nothing. Nothing like that. I knew him briefly in New York. He was Naomi's boyfriend then, before she married Bax. I let him keep his hand on my shoulder for Naomi's sake. She likes him. She said she loves him. I didn't want to make a scene. I'm telling the truth."

Chapter Sixteen

At four o'clock Carole stood on the deck to check the weather. She had on a purple bathrobe over sweats, a stocking cap, and Will's slippers over two pairs of thick socks. She shifted her weight, and the snow crunched underfoot. Ten to fifteen degrees, she figured from the sound. It was a promising kind of night. There was no wind, and the sky was an opaque blue, draining to turquoise. It would be a brilliant, starry night, the visibility perfect. In the weeks since the party, Naomi had called four times. Will had taken the calls, and Naomi's questions had been about what to bring. She already had the best skis, bindings, and poles, but she wanted his advice on the kind of pack, how to layer, whether to bring a compass. She was buying everything brand new, no doubt. The calls eased things between Will and Carole. The more he talked to Naomi, the more he thought Naomi was a dipstick. Not somebody he would have picked out as Carole's friend, even from a long time ago. But their unresolved discussion about Eddie still hung in the air between them. Once Carole had asked Will whether Naomi had mentioned anything about Eddie. She'd tried to sound nonchalant, but her voice gave something away. Will had suggested that if she was so damned interested, she should call Naomi herself, and she'd said, as lightly as she was able, "Oh, come on, Will, please," as if it was all in his imagination. She'd felt an awful mix of guilt and relief when he'd said he was sorry. The truth was, she was stuck. Nothing was safe anymore. She had no idea about Eddie—where he was or what he was doing.

A pair of headlights came over the hill in the distance. The car disappeared for a few moments, then reappeared, more slowly than before. She could see the car turn in the drive. She wasn't ready yet. She went back into the house.

Inside, Will was standing over their two open packs and ticking off the items he'd packed. "Flashlights, batteries, matches, camera, binocs, Jell-O. Okay. Two pairs of socks, scarf, hat, spare gloves. Okay."

"People coming," she said.

"Already?" He checked his watch. Will would never show up even one minute before he was expected, which was funny because he was so laid-back about so many other things. "I'm not done yet." He pointed to the couch in front of the fire. "I put out your clothes to warm. Go ahead and get dressed. They'll just have to wait." She knew he'd take his time, making sure the packs were exactly right for tonight.

She grabbed the hot clothes from the back of the couch and took the stairs two at a time. Upstairs, she stripped off the bathrobe and climbed into the warm long johns. The heat was delicious.

Outside, the truck was just now coming over the culvert, the muffler loud and ready to drop off, no doubt. She looked in the mirror, swept her hair into a twist in back, and secured it with hairpins, listening to the sounds accumulate downstairs and outside. She ducked into the spare bedroom and looked down to see what the noise was. The Weaver-Lears' truck was parked down there, and Morgan, Rachel, and Pepper were milling about, taking skis off the roof, pulling gear from inside. There was no sign of Will, and she knew he still was inside double-checking the compartments of their packs.

She went back to the bathroom to finish. Downstairs a man

laughed loudly, a jarring sound. It wasn't Will, and she'd never heard Morgan laugh like that. She adjusted the mirror to check her hair from the back. When the man laughed again, it caused her hand to slip. *Eddie. Damn it. No.*

She went again to the window to look down. Naomi's little Jaguar sat behind the Weaver-Lears' truck, with skis strapped to the top in neat lines. Four of them. Two pairs, one pair a lot longer than the other. Carole cupped her hands to her eyes against the inside light, in case she was mistaken. But there was no doubt. Four skis, and both doors to the Jaguar left wide open. And then the loud laughter from downstairs again. A noise behind her caught her attention.

Will stood in the doorway. "We have a problem," he said.

She nodded. "I know."

"You know?"

"I saw the skis. Just now, from the window."

"Right," he said, a shade of disbelief in his voice.

"You certainly don't think I had anything to do with it."

"I don't know anything," Will said. "The more I think I know, the less I know."

"They can't possibly be up to this. It's not like Central Park on a Saturday afternoon."

"She said she's done some around here, getting ready. I don't know about him. I just know I don't like the guy."

"Well, neither do I." She followed him downstairs.

Eddie and Naomi stood in the living room, all done up in some sleek space-age outfits, black, shiny, and wet-looking. She had a black patent-leather backpack covered with zippers and little compartments.

"Look," Will said to Eddie. "We're going to have to give you a rain check on this. I don't like to have people on my runs if I don't know how they'll do."

Naomi's red mouth formed a surprised little O. "Come on," she said, using her little girl's voice—both demanding and seductive.

"He's an ace." She giggled. "And we have food, look." She dropped her pack on the coffee table, opened one of the compartments, and removed some, crushed sandwiches wrapped in foil. She laid one on her thigh and pressed it with her hand. "Well, it's food anyway," she said. "I packed it myself."

Rachel, Morgan, and Pepper came in just then, bundled in layers of flannels and old sweaters and patched parkas.

"Will says Eddie can't go," Naomi whined to them.

"Why can't he go?" Rachel said to Carole.

"We had it figured for six of us," Carole said. "Not seven."

"Whatever." Morgan handed his pack to Will. "You want to check this for me, man?" he said.

"So you agree?" Naomi asked Morgan, as though suddenly Morgan was the enemy.

"Will's in charge on these things." Morgan unzipped the big compartment and started unloading items. "Whatever he says."

Rachel pulled Carole aside. "There's something about that guy," she said. "About Eddie. He looks familiar."

"You met him at Naomi's," Carole said quickly.

"Well, I know that," Rachel said. "Duh."

"God," Naomi said to Will. "You let these people bring a *baby*, and you won't let Eddie come when he's such a good skier."

"Baby?" Will said.

"Hey," Morgan said. "It's cool."

Only then did they notice Dylan strapped to Rachel's back.

"It's colder than hell out there," Will said.

"We've done it before," Rachel practically barked at Will. She'd been expecting this. "We do it all the time at home."

"No," Will said. "I won't take him. It's too dangerous. He won't be moving the way we will."

Eddie beckoned to Carole. At first she tried to ignore him, but he started toward her, leaving her no choice. "What?" she said, her voice flat.

He slung an arm over her shoulders. She tried to shrug it off, to move away, but he wouldn't let her. "For myself I don't give a shit. But my little princess has her heart set on it. And if we don't go, she'll be pissed. And when she's pissed, she's no fun."

"That's your problem."

"Not exactly." He looked pained. "These people think you walk on water." He pulled her closer and pointed to Rachel with the hand that was resting on her shoulder. "I wonder if *she* ever killed anyone."

"Why are you doing this? Why don't you just go away?"

"We have the kind of secret that—how can I put this? It's *useful*. You're so scared all the time. And to tell you the truth, it's fun." He paused. "Look. My baby has her heart set on tonight. Who cares why? She gets on these kicks, but I don't need to tell you that. You're it for now. She's a little in the bag too, not that I hold that against her. She's easier to get along with that way. So talk that big jungle bunny of yours into letting us come along."

Carole's eyes bored into his. She turned away, back to the others, where the discussion over Dylan was still going strong. Rachel and Morgan were showing Will the way they'd lined the Gerry backpack in down. He'd be fine. They did it all the time. Will was beginning to give in. She could tell by the way he was examining the pack, taking out the down quilting and feeling the loft.

"We can all go," Carole said. "Naomi and Eddie too. There's enough food."

Will glowered at her. "What the hell is going on with you?"

She didn't respond.

He threw up his hands. "I'm not responsible. Everybody hear that? You're each responsible for yourselves." He gave her a look and shook his head. "Let's go over the route." In spite of his disclaimer, he made everybody note on the map exactly where they'd cross the field, where the summit was, where they'd have to take off their skis and walk, where they'd stop and make a fire. The whole nine yards, just in case anything happened to him or if somebody got lost. Unlikely, but you never knew.

They went outside and strapped on their skis. Will asked Naomi and Eddie to take a couple of laps around the yard just so he could see how they managed. Eddie went first, making long, smooth strides over the darkening snow. He was graceful and well taught. Naomi went behind, copying him step for step.

"They're okay," Will said. "Physically, anyway." He raised his arms to get everybody's attention. "Listen up. We've been over the route. Everybody knows the drill. Just one more thing before we leave. I want everybody to be aware of the person behind them tonight. That's behind. Not in front, but behind. If you turn around and you don't see your person, you wait until you do. Got that? That way the line stops from the back to the front." With that, he took off at a run, herringboned up the rise in the driveway, crossed the culvert, and headed off across the stretch of pasture to the woods. The night was crisp, and once they got going, after all the remarks about the beauty and the cold, after they'd established their places in the line and gotten into a rhythm, they fell silent. All that could be heard was the sound of breathing, the snap of twigs, and the soft thunk of poles and skis. The surface was a silky powder threaded with every whiff of wind.

Carole concentrated on what she was doing, on each brief thrust of ski, on her balance. She listened to herself breathe—anything to be there, in the moment, in all that rugged dark beauty surrounding her, and not with her fury. Behind, she could hear Eddie and Naomi laughing, their voices ringing out over the night.

As they began the climb up through the forest, the spaces between them grew long and irregular. The full moon on the snow made the night strangely bright, turning shadows blue. At the point where the terrain shot up steeply, they stopped to remove their skis and hoist them onto their shoulders. Will shone his flashlight up through the trees to show how the trail cut diagonally to the right and then switched back to the left about halfway up. Then they set off again, ducking the branches to keep their skis from snagging. It was slow, hard going, and they stopped to take off jackets and sweaters and tie them around their waists or stuff them into backpacks. Twice there was a little shriek from behind, and when she turned, she saw three figures huddling. Naomi must have fallen each time and asked for help. Carole needed to stay away from them. Once when she looked back, she saw the quick bright light of a match and knew Naomi had stopped for a cigarette.

At the point where the trail began to level out again, before they traversed the ridge to the summit, they stopped to put on their skis. Will opened the flap of Rachel's backpack and pulled the layers of wool from Dylan's little face. In the sudden light, the baby blinked and yawned.

Morgan caught up to them. "We'll check, man. Don't worry," he said. But how could he be checking? He'd been way behind.

They set out again, faster now, following a trail that was packed solid and firm. Will got into the lead followed by Pepper and then Naomi. Rachel was next and then Carole. The person behind Carole was Eddie, and all she wanted was distance in spite of Will's rule. Every so often she'd stop and listen. As soon as she heard laughter or the loud punch line to a joke, she'd take off again. She didn't want to have to see him. Didn't want Will to see her waiting for him either, even though it was his rule.

When they reached the summit, Rachel was waiting for her. "Take a look at the baby, okay?" Carole maneuvered her skis so she stood side by side with Rachel on the narrow trail, a little behind so she could lift the cover and turn her flashlight on the child, aslant to keep the light out of his eyes. He squinted and would have turned his head, but he was so bundled in and covered over that only his eyes peeked out from between the hat and the scarf. Carole pulled lightly at the scarf. A small white dot had blossomed on the child's nostril.

"Uh-oh," Carole said.

"What?" Rachel asked. "What is it?"

"He's got a spot on his nose."

"Get him out," Rachel said. "Let me see."

Carole undid the straps and lifted the baby, who was heavy and solid, from the backpack. She had to stand a moment to rebalance herself. Rachel backed up a few steps on her skis until they were side by side. She took the baby from Carole.

"Where?"

The frostbite was whiter than snow, arcing around the edge of the tiny nostril. The baby flinched at the light but smiled when he saw his mother's face.

"He'll be okay," Rachel said. "We just need to warm it up."

"Will," Carole called. He was the authority. He'd know what to do.

"Morgan!" Rachel called for her husband. They both listened in the silence for the sound of Will from in front or Morgan from behind, but there was nothing. Rachel bent over the baby and tried to warm the small nose with her breath.

"The flesh can die," Carole said.

"That's a myth," Rachel said.

Carole shone her light at Rachel to see if she was serious. What else did she think frostbite *was*? Rachel was shaking her head and blowing softly on the baby's nose, smiling slightly. "Maybe if he walks around a little," Carole said. "To help his circulation."

"Look," Rachel said. "The spot's gone."

"It could come back," Carole said. "We should check his fingers."

"Morgan," Rachel called out again, but again there was only silence. "We should have stayed closer," she said. "I thought he was right behind you."

"I kept checking," Carole said. "I heard them. Where's Pepper?"

"Up with Will," Rachel said.

"They'll come back," Carole said, realizing as she spoke that Naomi was the next person ahead and would have forgotten the instruction. She was also drunk. Carole should have told Will that. She also should have been checking for Eddie behind her. She felt ill with shame at what she'd done. She had risked everybody's safety over something personal.

"Morgan!" Rachel yelled out again. They listened but could hear nothing over the child's cries. Carole fumbled to unlatch her skis and got to her feet. She picked up the baby and gave Rachel a hand. "We've got to get moving," she said. "Turn around." Rachel turned, and Carole was able, with some difficulty, to get Dylan back into the carrier and cover him as well as she could against the cold.

Carole fell into line behind Rachel. After the summit, the trail dipped down and it was more difficult to maneuver. They had to side-step carefully, staying in the tracks of the three ahead. At the base of the hill there were flashlights shining in their direction. Will was coming quickly up the path toward them. "We've been waiting. What happened?" His voice was brisk and clipped. He was concerned, allowing himself the luxury of anger now that he'd found them. "What about the other two?"

"They're in back," Carole said. "We had to hurry. Dylan got frostbite on his nose."

"Damn," Will said.

"I once knew a guy who said he got frostbite on his dick," Naomi said. She shined her light at Carole, blinding her for a moment. Carole waved it away, would have knocked it from Naomi's hand if she'd been close enough.

"You two go ahead," Will barked at them. "It's not far. Half a mile. Take Pepper with you. I'll wait for Morgan and that other guy."

Carole didn't hesitate. She pushed past Naomi to Pepper. "Come on, toots." She paused only long enough to organize them. "Rachel behind me, then Naomi, then Pepper, you sweep." And she was off.

Will had been right. They skied for only fifteen minutes before they saw the cabin. Carole stopped and waited for the flashlights of the others to burst one by one over the top of the hill behind her, three in all. Then she turned and skied the rest of the way down. The snow was so deep they could ski across the deck railing and down to the door.

They didn't bother to take off their mittens but went to work right away. Carole lifted Dylan from his pack and handed him to Rachel, who fell heavily onto the couch. She shouted at Naomi to light the paper in the woodstove and told Pepper to make sure the kettles were full—if not, to use the pitchers near the door—then light the kerosene lamps and turn off the battery-powered lamp that Will and Morgan had left burning earlier that day. Then she lit the fireplace in the corner of the main room. The newspaper caught immediately with a whoosh. Carole watched while the kindling took and then reached the logs on top. Then she sat beside Rachel to help her check the baby. Rachel had opened her parka and sweater and was warming the child's face with her breast. Carole removed his mittens and boots to examine his feet and hands. They were pink and cold but not frostbitten. "He's okay," she said.

From the kitchen came the sounds of Naomi giggling.

"Is that stove lit?" Carole called out.

"She doesn't know how to light the stove. I'm doing it now," Pepper replied.

"What about the water and the lights?"

"Water's on," Pepper said. "I'll get the lights in a sec."

Naomi came to the door. "I'm just hopeless in a kitchen."

Carole turned away to give the fire a hard stab with the poker. She couldn't stop thinking about what she'd done. Maybe Naomi had put herself at risk by drinking. Maybe Naomi was pushing her patience to the limits, but Carole had upped the stakes dangerously and she knew it. Pepper and the baby were safely here, but she couldn't take credit for that. If it hadn't been for her, Will would have forbidden Eddie to come, and probably the baby too. She'd lost control back there at the house. Eddie had threatened her, and she'd spread the risk to protect herself.

She went to the kitchen to help Pepper with the cookstove, brushing by Naomi as she went. The stove was a massive cast-iron job with nickel trim. Once it was going, it would throw out more heat than the fireplace, so much that the kitchen would overheat, while the rest of the cabin, the big room with the musty old couches and chairs, would be just right. Pepper was on his knees, watching the flames inside. He shut the grate. "Okay," he said. Just then sounds outside made her stop. The door was flung open and there they were. She counted. Three. All safe, all accounted for. She took a deep breath in relief as they entered one by one. She hadn't lost them.

The chill was off the air enough for people to shed their parkas and mittens and hats. They stripped off their long wool socks and hung gear everywhere, draping it over the fireplace screen, along the hearth, and on the pipe from the woodstove, where it sizzled and filled the air with the smell of wet wool. Rachel had the seat before the fire, at the center of a brown sofa. Dylan, his small patch of frost-bite gone now, had begun to nurse hungrily.

Will scootched the furniture forward, pushing the couch with Rachel and Dylan on it, and moving the two ratty green armchairs and a couple of smaller wooden chairs into a tight semicircle in front of the fireplace. Morgan swept up the mouse droppings and chunks of mortar that were always coming loose from the walls. The room warmed quickly and was fragrant with fire and must. Eddie watched the women take off their parkas and sweaters. Sly but apparent to Carole was the way he settled down on the couch beside Rachel and peered in to watch Dylan at Rachel's breast.

Rachel pulled away, covering the nursing baby with her clothing. She shot Carole a warning glance. I know who he is now, her look said. She shook her head, frowning.

Just then, Morgan and Will brought in food. They laid platters of bread and cheese and bowls of soup on the rickety table behind the circle of chairs and sofas, but Carole was still looking at Rachel, who was looking back at her with a take-no-prisoners expression. Eddie got up to help himself, to be first in line. Carole had lost her appetite. Rachel took the plate of food Morgan brought to her, then looked again at Carole.

"I can explain," Carole said in just a whisper. "There's more to it than it looks."

But Rachel was not about to wait this one out. "Pepper," she said, "does Eddie remind you of somebody?"

Pepper shook his head.

"Say, Eddie," she said. "Take a good look at my son."

"We're not going on," Will broke in. By now everyone was squeezed into the circle, their plates on their laps. "It's too risky with the baby. With Dylan. And we were getting sloppy out there. People aren't keeping an eye on the ones behind. Me included, I guess."

"I got cold waiting all the time," Naomi said in a thin little whine. She was the only one on the floor, wedged in between Eddie's knees. She finished off her glass of wine, and Eddie leaned forward, picked up the bottle, and filled her glass again.

"Something you ought to know about alcohol," Will said. "It makes blood come to the surface of the body, so you cool off faster. You don't want to mess with it if you're going to be in wilderness."

"But we're all cozy inside," Naomi said, as though Will was nuts.

Will shrugged in annoyance at her. "We'll try to get some sleep after we eat," he said.

"I was *speaking*!" Rachel practically shouted out the words, and the others stopped eating and looked at her.

"Rach," Carole said, extending a hand as if to stave off a blow. "Maybe we can talk about this later, just the two of us."

Rachel ignored her. "I believe I asked Eddie to take a good look at Pepper. At his forehead, in particular."

"Rachel!" Pepper covered the scar with his hand. "Cut it out."

"What's going on?" Naomi said. "What are we talking about?"

"Your boyfriend here gave Pepper that scar," Rachel said. "In San Francisco. He was four years old, and the love of your life threw him against a countertop and split open his forehead, and then he took off like the coward he is. I'm right, aren't I? Carole? Tell everybody. I'm right about this."

Naomi craned her neck to see Eddie. "You never told me you saw Carole in San Francisco."

Eddie leaned his head against the back of the couch, his eyes shut.

"I can explain it, Rachel," Carole said. "Please."

But Rachel was having none of it. "I asked you back there before we started and you didn't have the decency to tell me. You might as well have lied to my face. You did lie. You've been lying for weeks just by keeping quiet." She looked at Will. "Did you know about this? Who he is? Did she tell *you*?"

Will had settled on the wide arm of Carole's chair. He looked down at her and then at Rachel and shook his head. "No," he said. "She didn't."

"I recognized the voice when we were skiing," Rachel said, looking right at Eddie, who opened his eyes and stared at her. "There was something familiar about you, but then it was dark in the kitchen in San Francisco and you look different now. Fatter, for one thing. But your voice, you bastard. It was you."

Eddie's face filled with loathing. "Christ," he said, slow as syrup. "You're that bitch that spat on me."

"And I'll spit again," Rachel said, getting up. "In a heartbeat." Morgan held her back.

"You never told me you went to see Carole," Naomi said.

"I was passing through," Eddie said. "After 'Nam. I dropped in to say hello."

"And you." Rachel directed her fury at Carole. "You knew it was him all this time. You let him come in here." She motioned around to the others, to the cabin. "When you *knew* what he *did*."

"I'm sorry," Carole said.

"Sorry?" Rachel bellowed as if she couldn't believe her ears. "*Sorry* is all you can say? What the hell does that even mean? If I hadn't figured it out, you weren't going to say anything. Am I right?"

Carole nodded. She owed Rachel that much. She looked at everyone in turn; they were all watching her. "I wanted them to leave," she said to Rachel. "I tried to talk Naomi out of coming in the first place. You know I did. I didn't want them on this trip. I went about it all wrong. I should have told you who he was, I know."

"But we were a *family* here, Carole. At least I thought we were. The six of us. You and me and Will and Morgan and the kids. Family. But I was wrong about that, because you let this monster in the fold and not just once but twice."

"Wait just a second," Naomi said.

"Oh, shut up," Rachel said.

Carole glanced at Will, but his expression was unreadable. She was too ashamed to look at anybody else. There was nothing to say. No explanation.

"I guess that's it for us," Rachel said. "Fool me once, shame on you. Fool me twice, shame on me. Look at me, Carole." Carole looked up. "Shame on you," Rachel told her.

She lay wide-eyed, watching the fire die down. Pepper had the couch. Morgan, Dylan, and Rachel were the heap below him on the floor. Everybody had gone to their corners without any more discussion, slinking away, afraid to say more. Naomi and Eddie were by the window. Will was at Carole's side, lying on his back. She waited until she was sure everyone was asleep before getting up. She couldn't sleep. She might never sleep again.

She slipped on her boots, wrapped a blanket around herself, and tiptoed to the door to the deck. Someone had shoveled a path to the railing, and beyond that the hill was smooth, broken only by ski tracks. It was breathtaking and bitter cold. The moon was just behind some thin clouds. She'd done the unforgivable, keeping Eddie's identity from Rachel. *Shame on you.* There would be no restoring the friendship. Rachel was dead right about what she'd done.

She didn't hear the door open behind her, and she jumped when a thick hand covered her mouth. "Just shut up," he said.

She pulled at his hand, but he wouldn't yield.

"Now look what the fuck you've gone and done," he said.

The feel of him, the smell of him so close, made her sick. He let go but pressed her against the railing. "You and I have to get a couple of things straight." She looked back at the cabin, afraid the door would open and Will would find her with Eddie. It looked like an embrace. "That stunt your friend pulled tonight. You talk to her. You straighten it out."

"What do you think I can do? Tell Rachel she's wrong? She's not stupid. She remembered you." She felt exhausted.

"She's a walking freak show, that one. Tell her something. Make it right. Settle the thing. And talk to Naomi. That's the main thing. She thinks I went out there to see you."

"You did."

"You tell her what really happened. That it was you bird-dogging me and not the other way around. You who asked me. You gave me the address, *capisce*?"

"Me bird-dogging you? Oh, please."

"Keep your voice down."

"I just lost my best friend. God knows what Will's going to do, and you want me to care about *Naomi*? That's a joke. Did you take a good look at that scar? Did you see what you did to him? We had to take him up to the hospital for stitches. He was just a little kid."

"She *spat* at me," he said, as if it justified not just that but a whole lot of worse things. He was crazy. She'd always known it. He was missing something. A conscience. That was it. He wasn't all there. "So just do what I say, Carole. Like you always do." He twisted the flesh at the back of her neck, and she yelped, her cry cutting the night air. Both of them were silent to see if anyone came to the door to see what was going on. "Holy shit," Eddie said, laughing softly and letting her go. "You were scared just then, weren't you? Scared that somebody would hear you and come out and find the two of us together. Hell. You're not going to yell, are you? And you're going to do what I tell you."

She looked away to the hill of smooth, unbroken snow.

"You'll do it, Carole, because you always do what Eddie says." His breath was foul, soaked in sleep. "You talk a good game. You strut around like you've got the world by the balls, but I know better." His voice lowered an octave. "All you really know how to do is roll over and spread your legs. Since you were sixteen years old. Since you were taught by old Eddie. Right?"

The moon was sliding behind the trees on a spear of cloud.

"You ever tell Sambo about what happened?" His fingers tapped her neck lightly, traveled up to her chin and down again. "I asked you a question."

"No."

"But you told that freak show, right? Girlfriend to girlfriend."

"No."

He tightened his grasp on her. "Fix it," he said. "Make up a story she believes, then invite Naomi over, you know? Confide in her. Like you used to do when you were in school. You dig?" He turned to go back inside, but then stopped and faced her. "I mean it. No more surprises." Then he went inside. The deck, brittle with cold, groaned noisily under his footsteps. She stood in the chill, watching the door close behind him. She felt weak, her heart thundering. She waited until she was sure Eddie was gone before she made her way back across the deck to the door and tiptoed to where Will lay. As quietly as she could she lay down beside him, but when she reached for the blanket, she saw that his eyes were wide open and he was staring at her.

Chapter Seventeen

One by one, they dragged themselves out of the warmth of their dusty old blankets and took up the chairs that were still around the fire, nobody speaking. Carole escaped to the kitchen to put a bucket of snow on the stove to boil and to heat some of the food from the night before that would serve as breakfast. She hadn't slept at all, and she was dreading the morning.

She was afraid of having to face Rachel. *Shame on you* kept ringing in her ears. Or Will. She took a deep breath and pulled her attention toward the task at hand, the food. Something she knew how to do. She spread an oilcloth over the table, smoothing it carefully so there were no ripples in it. When the water on the stove came to a boil, she poured some of it into a tub and rewashed the dishes from the night before, which still had bits of food and grease on them. Naomi's work. She set the food to warm in a makeshift double boiler on the stove. Everybody was leaving her alone in here. Nobody came in to help or even to talk.

When everything was ready, she took the food out and laid it on the table in the main room, not looking at the others. "Breakfast" was all she said. They got up like a bunch of zombies. It looked as though no one had slept. They were in line, helping themselves in silence, when Pepper dropped the bomb.

"They got married," he said. "Eddie and Naomi got married."

"We were going to announce it ourselves, thank you very much," Naomi said.

"Maybe you can still get it annulled," Rachel said to Naomi, her voice dull.

Naomi let it go. "Last week. Justice of the peace. Eddie didn't want anything big and flashy. Just the two of us, and Zoë to stand up for me." She looked around, her eyes glassy. "Eddie has such great plans for the house," she said. "A study he can use. Maybe even a studio out in back."

"And a place in the islands," Eddie said, getting up and heading into the kitchen. "So we can get away in the winter, right, babe?" He came back with a half-full bottle of red wine. "Calls for a toast."

"None of that," Will said. "We still have the trip to finish, and I don't want anybody drinking."

"Just a little sip," Eddie said.

"I said no," Will said. "And I'm in charge here."

Eddie poured a glass for Naomi and handed it to her.

"You drink that, you're not on the trip," Will said to her. "You can get back to the road on your own, the both of you."

Naomi put the glass down. "Isn't anybody going to even congratulate us?" she said. "Carole?"

"Yeah, Carole," Eddie said. "Aren't you going to congratulate us?"

Naomi came to life then, as if she'd just woken up. She threw her arms around Carole's neck and let herself hang there for a moment as dead weight until Carole pulled herself free. "Aren't you happy for me?" Naomi said. "Please be happy for me. I hope you're not jealous." She turned to Morgan and Will, who were standing together. "You boys going to kiss the bride?" She reached up to Will the way she had to Carole and kissed him full on the lips before he pulled away, and she went on to Morgan and then to Pepper, who at ten was more her own height, and kissed him in a way that must have been brand new to him. Eddie stood apart watching as his bride went from one man to the next, and he was pleased as hell. Carole could tell how pleased he was, as though he'd bagged a big one. Pudgy face trying to contain the size of his smile. That was her impression, and that's what she said to Will later, after they'd skied down the rest of the way and arrived at the cars. "He's done it this time," she seethed, watching them pull away. "That son of a bitch."

Will said nothing. He stopped for the mail at the bottom of their driveway and handed it to her. She sat with it in her lap as the car labored up the hill to the house, slipping and sliding. She remembered Will's open eyes in the dark. "Look, I went to the deck because I couldn't sleep," she said. "He followed me."

"You were out there a long time."

"He wants me to be nicer to Naomi," she said.

"I asked you once how Pepper got that scar," he said. "You told me it was a fight, that Pepper got in the way. Didn't you think it mattered that that son of a bitch was the one who did it? And let's see. 'I met him briefly.' I think that's how you put it. But now it turns out he came looking for you in San Francisco. Or you went looking for him, depending on who you believe. That doesn't sound like briefly to me."

All during the unpacking and putting away of their gear, Will didn't say another word. She put the food into the refrigerator and emptied her pack, hanging the ski clothes in the closet by the front door. When she'd finished, she sat down at the dining room table to go through the mail, anything to stay busy right now. It was standard stuff. Some catalogs and a few bills. But there was also a long white envelope. She stared at it for several moments.

It was addressed to her in an old spidery handwriting. In the upper-left corner was the name Conrad Mason and an address in Albany. She took a knife from the drawer, slit it open, and took out a single sheet of thin blue paper. The letter was typed, but there were cross-outs and words written in the margins. She knew the handwriting instantly.

My dear Carole,

First, I don't mean to alarm you with this letter. Do not think that I write from my deathbed. To the contrary, I am in good health.

I know that Naomi has been in touch with you. She telephoned me last year to ask your whereabouts, and I gave them to her on condition that she be in touch once she had spoken to you. She has written several times since. I'm pleased that you two have reestablished the friendship you once had and pleased that I played some small part in your reunion. This renewed connection to Naomi is what gives me the wherewithal to write.

I shall tell you something of my life now. I remarried after your mother died. Gloria and I lived in New York, in the Sixty-second Street apartment, until I left my practice and we moved here to Albany to be close to family.

Gloria has two sons and now six grandchildren, all of whom live nearby. They are lovely children, a joy to us both. We travel a good deal. Gloria shares my interest in geology and we have spent many wonderful days in the world's faraway places examining rocks and caves, even the edges of sleeping volcanoes!

Often in our travels, the conversation among people our age turns to our children. I have been surprised at how many of these strangers' children left as you did. They ran away from home or disappeared into cities and communes in the 1960s. Gloria's sons too disappeared into Europe and broke contact for a time. I tell you this only because it's so much on my mind. The heartbreak, however, is that those young people came home again, and you did not.

Over the years, I have known your whereabouts. I hired someone to find you, to report to me where you were living and with whom. You did little to erase yourself. Over the years, I've received his reports, consoling myself that you were alive and surrounded by others. I know we both disappointed each other.

Your abrupt departure from your mother's memorial service and subsequent flight came as an additional blow. I had thought we were on the way to mending the rift between us. I was mistaken.

I don't expect fondness or affection from you. I'm beyond that, but I wonder if you will consent to see me. I would like to talk to you. No one else remains from that time. Not even your aunt Emily, who died last September in a convalescent home.

Gloria thinks the time to respect privacy is long over. Perhaps she's correct that it is my right, my duty, to see you regardless. And there is the money as well. I suspect that money holds no interest for you, judging from the life you lead, but you should know that you are of course entitled to a share of your mother's and my estate. If I should die, you would be contacted by Gloria. So, you see, one way or another there will be contact. I prefer it to be now, while I am alive.

Love,
Dad

P.S. Your mother wanted you to have the ancestor prints that once hung in the foyer of our apartment. I'm sure you remember them. They were very special to her.

Carole sat, dazed. A detective. She pictured her elegant father slitting open the detective's envelopes with his silver letter opener. All this time he had known where she was and not stepped up. Not that she would have wanted it, but he hadn't. That was the part she didn't understand. The worst part. She remembered that evening, after her mother's service, heading out of New York City on the bus, positive that everything was behind her, that nobody would ever find her, how she'd felt real hope for the first time since the night in Stowe. Only she'd been so wrong. All this time, somebody had been watching. She felt weak at the thought. A spy. His eyes on her all the time. Sitting in a parked car watching through binoculars, coming into Chacha's. Everything.

"What's that?" Will's voice startled her and she jumped.

Out of habit, she curled a hand around the paper and crushed it.

"Why don't you stuff it in your mouth and swallow it?" he said. "One more secret from me."

"I'm sorry." She smoothed it out and handed it to him.

Will pulled out a chair and sat down opposite. He put on his reading glasses and read slowly, casting his eyes back up the page from time to time, turning the letter to read the notes in the margins, rereading before going on. "Carole," he said in a whisper, shaking his head as though this time she'd gone too far. "You told me he was dead."

"He is to me."

"Oh, no, you don't," Will said, smacking the table with his hand. "No way. I don't want to hear it. Dead to you. You're not going to keep lying to me like this. The man's alive. He lives in Albany." He scanned the letter. "With Gloria and a mess of kids. That ain't dead, baby."

"I'm sorry," she said. "I had no idea he knew where I was."

"That's not the point."

"I said I was sorry."

"Sorry doesn't cut it. Jesus Christ, what else don't I know? Eddie gave Pepper his scar. Your father's alive. Christ, Carole. What else? Rachel and Morgan. They're probably in on it too. I feel like a fool to tell you the truth. Am I the only one in the dark around here?"

"Rachel and Morgan don't know everything."

"What exactly do they not know?"

"It's ancient history, Will."

"No, it's not," he said. "It's right now. I'm talking about right now. You and me. We are not ancient history. That's the point I'm trying to make." He banged the table again, then leaned toward her. "We're right now."

"I knew them in high school. Naomi was a friend. The three of us went up to Stowe one year to go skiing." She looked away.

"And?" he said.

"I got drunk one night," she said. "I might have . . . I slept with him. He slept with both of us. It was the sixties."

"And now?"

"Now nothing."

He covered his eyes with his hand and rubbed hard, as though he had a headache. He smoothed out the letter on the table. "Write him back."

"I don't know," she said.

"You'd better. He's your only family now, Carole." Will stood up from the table and went upstairs. It was over. She knew it. She sat staring at the letter from her father. Gloria. She reread the letter several times and then got out a note card to write him back.

I got your letter. I think we should all get used to the idea for a while before we talk about seeing each other. I work six days a week at Chacha's on Main Street, so there isn't a lot of time. Carole.

Chapter Eighteen

Gloria. Carole's life was disintegrating, and that was the word she couldn't get out of her head. It was an annoying name, a blowsy name. As she shaved carrots for lunch, throwing herself into work with everything she had, running behind today, she pictured a woman with fake blond hair and lots of jewelry, thick in the middle with thin legs, the kind of woman her mother would say had had too much gin in her life. Carole had never known a Gloria. Only film stars had names like that. And the song, of course. The Doors had done it, and Van Morrison. Gloria.

Her father had another family. He wrote about them with the familiarity that came only from permanence. She was the outsider now, the one he told stories about, his long-lost daughter. Just like she was the outsider to Will and to Rachel. She hadn't seen Rachel in four days, not since the night ski. Rachel hadn't been in Chacha's once. And Will was moving about the house in silence. He was waiting for her to say something, but she hadn't been able to. Every day she expected him to announce that he was moving out.

She'd assumed her father would have remarried. Men like him did. But the new wife had always been a cipher, without a face, without a name. Nobody important. She pictured a new Gloria, impatiently nagging Conrad about his earlier life. *The time for privacy is over.* Gloria the tough. Gloria the shot caller. Carole would bet she had a charm bracelet with the silhouettes of all those grandchildren dangling from it. She imagined her fancy old hands, the hands of rich New York women. Brown and spotted, with thickly lacquered nails.

A pounding sound started out on the floor, and Carole went to see what was happening through the glass in the door. The customers were banging the tables with their fists, led by an old farmer with pure white hair in a ponytail. "We want Hector. We want Hector."

"Where is he?" Carole asked Rudy, tying on an apron. "Don't tell me he's not here yet. I don't know how to run this. I don't know the frigging answers."

"Over here." Hector was at the back of the kitchen in his usual white suit, grinning from ear to ear. "They want me," he said. "But I like to make them wait. It heightens the moment." He sauntered through the kitchen and out the swinging doors, and the noise subsided.

Sandy swung back in through the door with a tray. "Everybody wants club sandwiches today. Every other Thursday it's been the dinner specials, and today they want clubs. Must be the phase of the moon or something."

Carole rolled up her sleeves and took a station to help. "One of these days we'll get it right," she said.

They put together sixteen plates with turkey clubs, and Sandy took them out. People were ordering all sorts of things they normally didn't. The pickled herring salad, the vegetarian lasagna. Carole picked up a menu to make sure they had everything in stock and looked at the games. A winter acrostic. A word jumble. A little crossword puzzle and a photograph of a circle of men staring at the ground. "You know this one?" she asked Sandy.

Sandy shrugged. "I never know any of them," she said.

They pushed out dozens of lunches and were just taking a breather before the dessert orders came through when Hector came into the kitchen, out of breath. "Victor Champine from Aubuchon's downstairs thinks he knows. He just ran like a bat out of hell for the library."

"Full house today?" Carole asked.

"*Everybody's* here, dearie. Including that fabulous friend of yours and her husband. The ones from New York. She was telling me all about your wicked girlhood. Your exploits at Lamston's. And here I always thought you were so sweet."

"Where are they?"

"Over with that Weaver woman. Lear. You know what I mean. A very odd-looking threesome, if you ask me, but they do seem to be getting on."

Together? Impossible. Carole went out on the floor to see. From over near the windows, Naomi lifted her glass and gave Carole a big glittery smile. She'd invited her to drop by the restaurant. Her concession to Eddie after the night ski. What difference did it make now, anyway? Rachel looked at Carole and then away, without a sign of recognition. She was sitting on one side of Naomi, and Eddie was on the other, his back to her.

The crowd had settled down, and people were talking to one another. Once in a while somebody would raise a hand and suggest an answer, but Hector would tell them with glee that they were off by a mile. Rachel and Naomi were huddled together now, talking about something. It gave Carole a terrible ominous feeling. They must be talking abut her. About what happened in the cabin after the night ski. But where had Eddie gone?

When dessert was being served, Victor Champine returned, dragging a chunky, giggling young woman along by the hand and waving some sheets of paper in the air. He went over to the bar and started to show Hector what he had, but Hector made him stand beside him. He quieted the people. "Attention, everyone," he called. All over the place people looked up and dropped forks and spoons onto their plates. "Go ahead," he said to Victor.

Victor read from some notes. "June 14 or 15, 1965," he said. Hector's eyebrows jumped a mile. Victor seemed nervous all of a sudden. His hands started to shake, and he had to go behind the bar and lay the menu down with his notes beside it so that nobody would notice. "This photo from the menu was taken on June 14, 1965, but it ran in the *Times Argus* on June 15, so you can take your pick of the date." He held up a Xerox that had the photo as well as a newspaper cutline beneath it. "Left to right," he said, reading from the cutline. He gave people a couple of seconds to fish glasses out of their pockets and purses and put them on. "Brad Wendel on the left is the guy who found her. He was up there surveying. Next to him is Russ Reed, the sheriff, then George Brown, the deputy sheriff, and then Alden Coburn, the medical examiner. On the far right, that's Pete Cambio, who owned the motel next door. And that thing they're looking at? That was a woman, five-five, brown hair, a hundred fifty pounds."

"What was her name?" Hector asked Victor.

"They never found out," Victor said. "It was an unsolved mystery."

"Not really," the woman with him said but didn't press it.

"So do I win or what?" Victor said.

"Where?" Hector said. "You need location. Without that, you don't win."

"Stowe," Victor said immediately. "Mountain Road. Woods back of the old Snowtown Motel."

"And the event?" Hector seemed very put out that someone had gotten the answer so quickly.

"They didn't know. They thought she was strangled," Victor said, flicking the article with a snap of his fingers to show the source of his facts. He made a choking sound in his throat and let his head fall to the side, then grinned. "According to this, anyway, and this is the only article about it. I checked the index. End of story."

Carole lowered herself onto a barstool. Her legs were suddenly loose and weak under her. The voices around her became a low roar in her ears, distorted by the sound of her own breathing, the pounding of her heart. She furtively sought out Rachel and Naomi in case they'd seen, but they were still so deep in conversation. She watched the article in Victor's hand as he flicked it again, the snap of his finger against the paper sudden and painful. He put it down on the bar, raised his hands, as if in victory, and turned toward the crowd, who erupted in applause. Carole reached over and slid the paper toward herself. In the picture, the men were standing in a small clearing of thick brush and long grass. You couldn't make out what they were looking at at all. She followed through the account without being able to read the words. She felt the panic slide up her throat.

"Carole?" Hector said. "Are you okay?"

If she tried to stand, she might fall over. "Where did you get this?" she asked Hector, pointing to the photograph on the menu.

"Archives," Hector said. "I showed it to you last month. Remember?"

"No. I mean, yes, maybe. But I didn't—"

Naomi and Rachel had stopped talking, their attention drawn to something at the adjacent table. Eddie had come back and was sitting beside Naomi again.

"So?" Victor said. "We get two free lunches. Fair and square."

"After the last one," Hector said to Carole. "Don't you remember? Over at the bar." He pouted. "I went through them all. You said to pick one."

Carole pointed to an empty table for Victor and the woman.

"Is she going to wait on us?" the woman with Victor asked.

Carole got to her feet but felt so nauseated that she had to run from the room. In the ladies' room she bent over the toilet and vomited. Someone came in while she was there and then left right away. Carole walked out of the stall and splashed cold water on her face. She was afraid to look in the mirror, to see what other people could see.

Just outside the door she hesitated to see if Eddie and Naomi had picked up on what was happening, but they weren't paying attention. Eddie had a hand over Naomi's mouth, kidding around. Rachel was standing, looking around for something. *For her.* As soon as she spotted Carole, she signaled for her to come to the table.

Carole held up a finger to say *in a minute.* No way was she going over there. She had to go along with things, do what Victor wanted, but she could barely move. When she was back out on the floor, she asked Victor and the woman, whose name was Mindy, what they wanted. Maybe she could save herself the way she always did, with work. They wanted a lot, and Carole tried to keep it in her memory but brought over a 7-Up instead of a Coke and onion rings instead of French fries and had to go back and change the orders. Then she cleared off the silverware before they had dessert and they had to ask her for more. They ordered a couple of pieces of pie, a lemon square, and some ice cream. Hector ordered raspberry sherbet. Carole brought it all over on a big tray without making a mistake. Then she sat down between Mindy and Hector.

"What did you mean when you said 'not really'?"

Mindy's eyes brightened as she looked over the desserts.

Carole had to press her. "Mindy? When Hector said they never found out the name, that it wasn't solved, you said 'not really.'"

Mindy looked up at her, frowning. "Oh," she said. "Yeah." She had the kind of voice that attracted attention. "My uncle is from up there, from Morris Center. People up there knew who the woman was." She said it partly to Carole but more to the people around her now that she was the center of attention. She took a large bite of pie. "Her name was Rita. She was a nurse or maybe going to school to be a nurse. Whoever did it just dumped her. They didn't even bury her or anything."

Oh, but they did, Carole thought.

"They left her in the woods to rot," Mindy continued, looking pleased with herself. "But she must have stayed frozen a long time. I heard she wasn't in that bad shape when they found her except for her face. Ugh."

From the corner of her eye, Carole could see Eddie struggling with Naomi, as if he were trying to hold her back. Hector nudged her. "I've got the rest," he said. "If you're interested."

"The rest of what?"

"Come on, I'll show you."

He led her behind the bar and knelt down. She got down on her knees beside him. "The others," he whispered. "The one on the menu was part of a series." He was so proud of himself. "I did a little free-lance police work I never told you about." He laid the photographs on the floor, side by side in front of Carole. She leaned over to look. Her stomach heaved at the sight of Rita's calf and ankle, the small ankle bracelet still intact over flesh that appeared mottled and waxy. She sought out the only benign photo on the floor, the one that showed the larger scene. In it, Rita's body was barely visible in deep grass, surrounded by shrubs and trees newly in leaf. In all the times she'd pictured this scene, she'd never imagined it would be so serene and lush.

"There you are, Hector." The voice made her jump. She looked up and saw two grinning faces staring down at them. A man and a woman, both strangers to Carole. She gathered up the pictures so they could not be seen. Hector rose and spoke to the two people. There was laughter. He tapped her on the shoulder and said he would be right back. She used the moment to slip the photos into a wrinkled manila envelope from the box and stood to see what Eddie and Naomi were doing. They were still at their table, arguing now. Naomi was drunk and becoming belligerent. Eddie seemed to be grabbing for her, trying to keep her from getting up. Rachel was no longer at the table. The *Times Argus* article still sat where Victor had left it on the bar. Carole swept it up and headed for the door.

Chapter Nineteen

But they did. Had she said it aloud? Had Victor and Mindy heard her say it? Please, no. She tried to remember if there'd been any indication on Mindy's face that she'd heard the words. And then the vomiting. That was Mindy in the ladies' room, Mindy who stood there listening and then bolted, probably blabbing to Victor, how the proprietor was ralphing in the head.

As she drove, Carole rolled down the window and got just a whiff of the thaw. It was still snowing a bit, big, soft spring snowflakes, lifting and hovering, exploding wetly on the windshield. The flakes plopped and dribbled down until the whole glass was awash in rivulets.

Oh, they did. They had buried her, or at least tried. They hadn't just gone off and left her like Mindy said. Halfway up East Hill, after the Doyle farm, where there were no more houses, she pulled to the side of the road. The manila envelope lay on the seat beside her. She reached into it and drew out the article. Victor had only read from the cutline and paraphrased the content. Her hands trembled as she read.

STOWE—The remains of an unidentified woman were found in a wooded area off Mountain Road in this wealthy tourist community on Wednesday.

Lamoille County Sheriff Russell Reed made the grim announcement about 6 P.M. "The investigation into the manner and cause of death indicates that the woman was approximately thirty years of age and died of strangulation," he said. "Efforts are being made to establish her identity and the date of death."

The remains were found by Brad Wendel, a surveyor for Hiram Corporation in Stowe, owners of the land on which the remains were found. He was alerted to the remains by his dog.

Reed said it is likely the woman died at the scene. It is too soon to know if the body was buried, although he said there was no indication of a grave.

Persons with information regarding the woman's identity or circumstances of her death are asked to contact the Lamoille County Sheriff's Office.

June 14. That spring. All these years, thinking Rita had never been found, and now this. She'd been found three months later. Carole read it again, and then once more. The errors! The newspaper said Rita was about thirty when she was twenty-eight, that she'd died of strangulation when it had been a broken neck. That she'd died on the spot and not somewhere else. Even the date she'd died was in question.

Victor had said that this was the only account. He said he'd checked it out in the archives, which meant there never was a public announcement of who she was or any of the rest of it. But how could that be? Mindy had said people knew. And that man in the drugstore. Howie. Howie had known. And those people she called. All these loose ends and nobody tying them together. It was as though people had just given up, as though they weren't interested enough or Rita wasn't important enough for them to make the effort. The sheriff and everybody else had let it drop.

Carole returned the article to the envelope and started the truck again. Nobody had gone looking for Rita. And that knowledge mingled unpleasantly with Carole's own relief that she had been protected by exactly that. Rita's anonymity and the lack of urgency into solving her death had allowed Carole to live freely all these years.

She stopped the truck in front of the house, but she didn't have the will to get out at first. It was the woodpile that finally got her attention. How could they have let it get that way? A ragged mess. They'd taken logs from it all winter willy-nilly, pulling out the good big ones and leaving all the ugly odd-shaped bits with branch stumps sticking out and slabs of wet bark falling off. It looked like a war zone, a good half cord of junk wood strewn over the dooryard. Why hadn't she noticed it before?

She didn't go into the house at all but put on gloves and started to work. Midway through, she stopped and looked. She'd made progress. The new pile was large and tidy. There was little left to move. She swept the bits of wood and bark off the tarmac and rinsed it down with buckets of water from the house. The water turned instantly to ice, and the black tarmac glistened in the bright midday light. The tarmac was so shiny, she could see her reflection. She stared down at her rippling upside-down self. She would tell Will everything. For sure. It had to be today. She didn't know how or when, just that she would tell him what had happened and who she was. It was time.

She removed the manila envelope from the truck, took it inside, and laid it on the dining room table. The telephone rang, and she let the machine take the message. Then she made herself a cup of tea in the kitchen and sat down, the envelope before her. One by one, she laid the photographs facedown on the table. When she was ready, she turned the first one over. It was the close-up that Hector had shown her earlier, of Rita's calf with its tiny ankle chain. The next one made her gag. In crisp detail, it showed Rita's face and neck, the flesh partly gone and the teeth set in a ghastly grin.

The front door banged with a solid shuddering that made her jump. "Where are you?" Will, home early. His steps came loudly across the living room floor toward her. "I called work, and they said you went home early, that you left without telling anybody," he said, approaching. His voice sounded wary, as if to say, Now what is it? He paused in the doorway and looked at the table and then at her. "What's all that?"

She stayed in place, staring at the photos spread out before her.

"Carole?" he said.

She turned the photos over. They'd come later. She indicated the chair opposite for him and waited until he sat down, until he was quiet, waiting. "I did something a long time ago. I need to tell you about it." She could feel the color drain from her face. "I don't know how to do this." She shut her eyes and let the stillness of the room settle her thoughts. Will said nothing.

"When I was sixteen." She stopped. I *killed someone,* she thought. In all her imagined conversations with Will, it was how she began. What she hadn't expected was the panic. She hadn't expected to be back suddenly in that cabin. Images from that night presented themselves one after the other. Rita's body on the bed. Her body in the snow. The girl in the shower at the Double Hearth, saying, "You've been through the mill." It all came at once, the way they said your life flashed before your eyes when you died. The images appeared and disappeared like the images rising from the dark water in an eight ball. She saw the beds pushed together and splitting so there wasn't enough room for the three of them. She'd been the odd man out. The weird blue light of the lamp under a towel. That bucking bronco. And Eddie's hair slick with sweat, slapping against her. Rita's voice. *It's okay, honey.* She dared to look at Will. She had to look away.

"When you were sixteen . . ." Will prompted her.

The night of Rachel's CR group, when Jo had confessed to her infidelity, she'd given only fragments of facts and feelings, and yet the story had emerged as a whole. It had stayed with Carole, as though one day she would need to use it. How else could she tell Will what had happened? How could she begin with the worst thing?

"I'll start with the day I ran away," she said.

"Anywhere. Just do it."

"Right after my mother's memorial service in New York City. I'd dropped out of Vassar by then. I'd been working in a restaurant, but my dad found me and told me my mother was dead. I couldn't believe it at first. Sometimes I still can't. Eddie showed up at the service, and I was so scared, I bolted. He wanted money again. I ran from the University Club and got out of there." Will raised his eyebrows at Eddie's name, but she kept on. She was feeling stronger. "I took the bus from the Port Authority to Newark, and I was this boiling pot inside, just sitting there on the bus sobbing because of the enormity of everything. Just the sheer size of everything. My mother was dead.

"This woman at the service had held my dad's ears. She reached up and took them in her hands and pulled his head down and kissed him, and in that gesture, I knew he would be okay. Women would take care of him. Women like her. A single older guy like him? The women were already jockeying around him at the memorial service. Maybe she was Gloria.

"And then I got to San Francisco. I knew Rachel was out there and I found her. She was already married to Morgan by then. Pepper is from another man. I don't know if you knew that or not. We lived in a house. Sort of a commune, but not really. There was always stuff going on. Noise, people coming and going. Drugs. I could go for days without thinking about why I was there."

She paused, took a deep breath. "Eddie found out about my mom's service, getting back to that. He had ways. That's what made him so scary. *Makes* him so scary. He said he'd been her lover. My mother." She looked down at her hands, which looked like a couple of white spiders. "I might have delivered my mother to him. That's what's so awful. I'm to blame for that. They ran into each other on the street because of me. My mother was *forty*. Eddie was a lot younger. After I disappeared, they got together again. Or maybe they still were together. Maybe it started before. I don't know. My mother was desperate not knowing where I was. My father would have been no help. All the time what Eddie wanted from my mother was to be there if she ever found out where I was. He always wanted to know where I was."

Here it came. "But where it really began was when Naomi and I went to Stowe, senior year." She was able to look at him now, saying all this. "We stayed in this place, a dorm called the Double Hearth, and there was a motel down the road called the Snowtown. Eddie had a room there. The point was to lose our virginity before graduation, and he was the guy. I told you that part, but the real story is that we went up there on purpose. It wasn't that I got drunk and he took advantage. I did it on purpose, eyes wide open. I lied to my parents about going there and why. I said it was only me and Naomi, and that we were going to learn to ski."

She took another breath, still looking at him square on. "I was asleep in his motel room, and really late, about one or two I think, a woman came to the room and he let her in. I thought it was the owner. But she was this *woman*. Here I'd just lost my virginity to this guy, and already this other woman was there." She felt the words ripping out of her faster than she could think them. "Rita was her name, and she kept worrying if it was okay with me. We started doing things. Together. The three of us."

There was no way of telling what was going on behind Will's calm face, but it was too late now. The words wouldn't stop. "If she'd been bitchy, maybe I wouldn't have gone along with what we did. Not that I'm blaming her. It's just one of those things you think. If this, if that. You can't imagine the times I've wondered how my life would have been different if I had just left. But I didn't leave. I didn't want to be the one to leave. I wanted her to go because I was the one who deserved him, and who was she to come barging in? But they were really going at it, so I drank some more scotch.

"Her name was Rita." She slowed down her speech. She had to. "The beds kept sliding apart, so we had to stay on just one of them, and it was way too small for all three of us. Eddie said to get out of his way. He said to go sit on the other bed and watch, and I didn't want to, although maybe I would have, but Rita said I should get up at the

303

head of the bed near the wall, which is what I did. I was drunk. I climbed over all these ropes he had. He'd tied her wrists. I was so drunk. The only time in my life. I can't remember anything in sequence. That's what is always so hard. I try, Will. I've tried for years, but it won't come. All I know is, I was hitting the wall. I was looking down on them. It was really dark in there. It went on forever." Will's eyes narrowed slightly. Here it came. "I killed her." A shudder bolted through her, and she looked up. His eyes were wide, his mouth open, but he didn't speak. "I killed her," she said again.

"I don't understand," he said.

She looked away, breathing fast as though she'd just run a race. "I must have leaned on her too hard. I was a big girl then."

"Wait a minute," he said, shaking his head. "I still don't get it."

"I lied to you because I was so ashamed. Am so ashamed."

He was staring at her with his mouth open. He shook his head as if to clear it. "Go back a minute. I don't understand how you killed her."

"What is there to understand?" she wailed. "You asked me, Will. You asked what happened, and I told you. Why do you need to make me repeat it?"

"But how? How did she die?"

"Broken neck," she whispered.

"How do you know that?"

"He said! He felt along her neck, and it was broken."

"Eddie?"

"Of course, Eddie."

"Calm down," he said. "Calm down. I want to understand this, Carole. I just want to get it straight. You're all doing your thing there in the motel, and her neck just breaks?"

She nodded.

"Because—" he said, drawing out the word. "Because you what, twisted her head?"

"That's the problem. I don't *remember* the part where it happened. I must have blocked it out." In the news, there were always stories about people who remembered traumatic events years after they happened, and she'd assumed that one day that would happen. One day when she didn't expect it, it would come back, complete with the sound of bone and the lewd, crazed behavior that must have overtaken her.

She tidied the photos into a stack and pushed them across the table, along with the newspaper story. "It's her. It's Rita. You'll see."

He turned over the stack and sat staring at the one on top. From where she sat, she could see that it was one of those she hadn't seen yet. She made out the way Rita's hand was caught under her body, exactly as it had been that night. She had to look away. She could hear him going through the rest, one at a time, and then the slight fluttering of paper as he read the newspaper account. She looked up at him. "I was bigger then. A lot bigger. So strong. I didn't know my own strength."

He tapped the photos. "Where did you get all this stuff? Have you been keeping it or something?"

"Oh, God, no," she said. "They're Hector's. That's another story. He used one of them on the menu. That one." She pointed to the photo of the men standing around the remains of Rita Boudreau, shielded in the long grass. "Victor Champine guessed it. He got the article at lunch. Oh, my God." She was near tears now.

He waited for what seemed like forever. Finally he leaned across the table and took her wrist in his hand. "Okay," he said. "What did you do? I mean after. What happened then?"

"We took the body way up in back in the woods. It was woods then. There's a parking lot there now."

"You *buried* her?" Will put his hands to his temples, shocked, concentrating.

"Eddie and Naomi and me." Her voice trailed off, and she felt afraid again. "I shouldn't be telling. I swore I never would."

"You didn't get help?"

"I wanted to. I remember that. It was so obvious that we had to. I wanted to call the police or the hospital or something, but he wouldn't let me. He said if it got out what I did—"

Will looked down at the photographs again and spread them out facing him. "You say you broke her neck?"

She nodded.

"Look here." He pushed one of the photographs across the table toward her, tapping the place he wanted her to see with his index finger. "Her neck isn't broken. It's intact."

It was a photo she hadn't yet seen, a close-up showing the jaw and jointed bones of the neck. She shut her eyes.

"Come on, Carole, look at it." He sifted through the pile for other photos and examined each one. "Hector took a lot of pictures of the neck. Looks as though insects got to the exposed parts. The neck would have been important. It doesn't look broken."

"But how—?" Her hope rose. Was this possible? Was he just trying to make her feel better?

"Let me explain something to you," he said. "The newspaper is accurate. A broken neck is fairly obvious. They knew early on that it wasn't broken, that she was strangled. What was Eddie doing? You told me what you were doing, but what about him?"

"He was, you know. He was fucking her, I guess." *Why was Will doing this to her?*

"Show me, babe. Say that's the bed." He pointed to the floor. "Where were you?"

She hesitated, then dropped to the floor, knees apart, sobbing now. "Here," she said.

"And them?"

She motioned with her hands to the spot between her knees. "I could see his back mostly. I really couldn't see her too much."

"What about his hands?"

"I don't know. It was dark. I don't remember."

"What did you hear?"

"The bed hitting the wall. Them breathing. A lot of groaning."

Will breathed in hard and fast, the way he did when they made love. "Like that?"

"I guess," she said.

He made another sound so labored and obstructed it made her stomach pitch, and she had to cover her ears to keep from hearing it.

He pulled her hands away. "What about that? Answer me." He made the hateful sound again, and she felt the fear spread hotly through her, as though it was happening all over again, the nausea, the shame, the pitching, rocking bed in that fetid disgusting room.

She nodded. "Yes, like that. She called him the wrong name. Garrett, that was it." And now she recalled something else. She put her hand up to Will's throat. "Like that," she said. "He put his hand on her neck like that."

Will whistled.

"What is it?"

"I think the paper was right. She was strangled."

"But—"

"Not you. Eddie." He looked at her for a moment, his lips pursed. "She was probably saying 'garrote,' not 'Garrett.' It's something people do to enhance sexual pleasure, and it's dangerous as hell. They cut off the oxygen supply to the brain. Nobody knows why it happens, it just does. Usually it's men, but women get orgasm with it. There's plenty written about it."

Sitting in that car outside her dorm at Vassar that time, Eddie had asked if she'd ever heard of it, and she'd said no. She'd thought he was making it up, grossing her out, but he'd been testing her. He wanted to know what she knew.

"They press on the windpipe," Will said.

"She would have had a spasm, though, right? Wouldn't she have gagged? Like any choking victim, sexual or not. I read it in one of your Red Cross books."

"Not necessarily," Will said. "Maybe she passed out and then she never got enough air because he kept the pressure on a couple more minutes, and then it was done."

"But we would have *noticed*," she said, desperate to believe him but not daring to. "We would have seen. She was right there. She would have shuddered. Something."

Will shook his head. "Not if she passed out."

Carole shut her eyes. She was back in that darkened room again now, reeking of sweat, a glimpse of Rita's upturned face and a detail she'd forgotten. It was the moment when Rita went quiet. She'd thought Eddie would stop. She'd thought Rita wasn't going anymore, and he didn't seem to care. He'd kept on going. It must have been the moment Rita passed out.

"I didn't kill her?" she whispered.

"You didn't break her neck," Will said.

She opened her eyes and stared at him.

"Because her neck's not broken," he said. "You didn't do it. And all this time you thought—"

"Are you sure?"

Will looked through the pictures again. "I'm sure," he said.

She sat there, her anger gathering, unaware of Will or even her surroundings. It was as though the monster had finally broken through the gluey murk with its sickening, familiar fragmented images, and now, in all its brilliant and steely clarity, was what she'd really done.

Oh, yes, she had touched the dead woman's naked body. She had felt it grow cool and seen close up the expressionless face. She had carried it up the slope, hefting it over and over as it slipped from her grip. She had helped to bury it wetly in the snow. She had pushed in the snow every bit as much as Naomi and Eddie. She had let Eddie talk her out of getting help when she knew it was wrong. She had kept everything quiet all these years. Yes. But she had not killed Rita Boudreau, and all these years she'd thought their knowledge, Eddie's and Naomi's, was her problem, when the truth was, she was theirs.

She pulled the stack of photos toward herself and spread them out. Rita's remains lay in the twisted pose she remembered. Now she had the courage to see these shots taken from every angle. The abundant dark hair, the ravaged lower face, the body that was left mostly intact.

"She would have died quickly," Will said. "She slipped away."

It didn't matter. She had given Eddie her mother's little silver cigarette box. She had given him her mother. *If the three of us keep our mouths shut, nobody will be the wiser.* He hadn't ever been protecting her. She'd been protecting him. That was why he kept asking. *Did you tell? Does anybody know? Does Sambo know?*

She knew what it meant when people said they saw red. The sudden fury was like nothing she'd ever felt. "I'm going over there." She was barely aware of Will any longer. She looked forward to it. She was hungry for this. "I need to know," she said out loud, although it was to herself, not to Will. "I need to know if Naomi knew. If she was in on it all this time." She stood up, knocking her chair over and leaving it there. "That son of a bitch. They were laughing at me."

"Think this through, Carole. Don't go tearing out of here."

"I'm finished thinking," she said.

"Don't go alone, then. I'll come with you."

"No." She could hear the fury in her voice. She wasn't going to hide behind anybody else this time. "This is my mess. I'm going to clean it up."

309

Chapter Twenty

The rage built as she drove. It made her sharp and quick at the wheel, speeding over the snow-covered roads and once accelerating out of a skid. She was alert to the overcast sky, the jade color of frosted evergreens. And so many hateful images, all of them newly lit by this information. She saw Rita in that pointed rabbit fur hat, shaking out her hair when she took it off. And then Eddie's hand at Rita's throat, like he was trying to feel for words he couldn't hear.

She swerved along the shoulder of the road, half on, half off, recalling again what she'd thought that night. *So there. She doesn't want to play anymore, and neither do I.* She veered back onto the pavement and gunned the motor, thinking of Eddie that morning in the cabin, spread out across the couch, talking about all the things he and Naomi would be buying now that they were married. A welter of images followed. Eddie in that god-awful yellow cashmere sweater that belonged to the owner of the brownstone on Sixty-sixth Street. *Like mother, like daughter,* he had said. And Naomi, so recklessly in his thrall. As Carole drove, she was convinced Naomi had to have known. How easy it had been to pull the wool over her eyes. What a loser, to believe it all this time.

At West Hill, she hooked a left and flew over the snow-packed dirt roads, wheels slipping here and there as the road slush turned to ice in shadow. She went right on Molly Supple, and finally up Naomi's long, messy driveway. When she was almost at the house, the green Jaguar blocked her way, the passenger-side door wide open. Carole stopped the truck and leaned on the horn.

She waited. As soon as either one of them showed his or her face, she was going to let it rip. She wasn't scared anymore. She wasn't responsible for Rita Boudreau's death. Eddie was. She let the horn blare again. But there was only silence. She got out of the truck, slammed closed the door on the Jag, and walked toward the house. The back storm door was ajar. She rapped and waited, then opened the inside door and called in; her voice was met by silence. The kitchen was piled with filthy plates and open containers of food. Naomi's big patent-leather purse was on the floor, as if thrown, the contents spread out across the shiny wood. A lipstick, her car keys, junk.

They could be in bed. They could have come home from Chacha's lusting for each other and gone upstairs to the bedroom. It would explain the car in the driveway, the open doors. They could be lying there, waiting for her to leave. She wouldn't put it past them. "I'm coming up," she yelled at the base of the stairs. The outside door swung shut on a breeze and slammed, causing her to jump.

She took the stairs two at a time to the wide-open bedroom, but it was empty. The huge king bed was unmade, littered with boxes from Tripler's, the men's store in Manhattan. Tissue from the boxes was strewn around, and so were sweaters and slacks and socks, all still with the tags on. There were two suits, one brown and one blue, in a heap on the couch. And several pairs of shoes. Eddie had been on a shopping spree. She flung open the closet door, but it was empty. Then she raced back downstairs and did the same, opening and slamming doors all through the house, even into the cellar with its dank walls. And she would have left, would have assumed they'd gone out again, except for one thing. She checked the garage and there was the Land Cruiser.

So they had come home, and something had made Naomi throw down her purse, and now the only place they could be was outside.

She went to check, and sure enough there were footprints, freshly made in the snow, heading downhill in back. Eddie's big boots and Naomi's little high-heeled ones. It infuriated her all over again, the irresponsibility of everything they did, running into the woods too late in the day, letting the battery run down on the car, letting the heat out of the house. She'd just add that to the list when she found them.

In the back of the truck she kept, among other emergency items, snowshoes and a small pack. Will had drummed preparation into her. She wasn't supposed to take any trail, summer or winter, without that little pack with its plastic bags of gorp, water bottle, dry socks, and a little first-aid kit whose contents were probably reduced to dust by now. She went into the house to fill the bottle of water. She tied the snowshoes to a loop on the pack, then entered the woods, following their footprints. They were mostly Eddie's, only occasionally the little pointed triangular ones. In one place, the snow was freshly roiled. In another there were long troughs where something had been dragged. It all continued clearly enough, and Carole followed them. What were they doing? Where were they going? They couldn't have gone too far, certainly not with Naomi in those stupid boots.

The snow had softened in the midday sun, then firmed to ice. In minutes, the hem of her skirt was waterlogged from dragging in the snow, and salty sweat stung in her eyes. The trail flattened out for a good distance and then turned down again through the forest. She scanned the thickly wooded terrain, called Naomi's name, waited, then continued. She must be on a snowmobile trail because the footing was so solid. In the distance was the sound of running water. She decided to keep going a bit more. If she couldn't see them soon, then to hell with it, she'd go back and wait for them at the house.

She went carefully down the incline, calling out as she went, stopping at a junction where another snowmobile trail came in from the left. They could have gone either way, she thought, and she was about to turn back when a little fleck of black in the distance caught her eye. It moved, stopped, moved again. She stopped to watch, lost it, found it again. A person, she was sure.

The sun was falling behind the mountains now, casting everything in shadow. As she headed down, holding on to trees for support, crouching to keep herself from falling, she could feel moisture seep through her skirt and her gloves. Will had taught her to turn and look behind her periodically, making a mental note of landmarks so she would know what to look for when she doubled back. But the light in the woods was already too dim to get a good fix on any rocks or trees, so she concentrated on the sound of the water, which was ahead now and much closer.

She kept going, testing her weight with each step. Then Eddie came full into view perhaps twenty yards away, a thick, dark shadow standing with his back to her. Beyond him, Naomi swayed on hands and knees, her head lolling as though it was too heavy to raise. Carole watched as Eddie took Naomi under the arms and lifted her like some limp little doll, then toppled her on purpose and left her sitting in the snow, her head drooping. He lit a cigarette. The smell hit Carole and she stood up.

Naomi saw her at once and made a sound that caused Eddie to spin around and look. He was massive in all his winter gear. Carole didn't have time to move before he spotted her. "Oh, Christ," he said.

"What's going on? What's wrong with Naomi?"

"She's drunk," Eddie said with a laugh. "As usual."

Carole approached Naomi. Up close she could see that Eddie had on a new down parka, a new ski hat. Naomi had only her thin jacket. Even from several yards away, Carole could tell that she was dripping wet. Naomi tried to stand again but fell and broke into a giggle.

"Give me a hand," Eddie said.

Carole approached warily. Something was way off. "How did she get so wet? That's really dangerous. We have to—" she said, forgetting her anger.

"She fell in," Eddie said. "Get over here, okay?"

Carole held back, afraid of what Eddie might do if she got too close to him. She stalled for time, removing her pack, dumping it at her feet. "I might have dry clothes in here. Something." She rummaged around but caught a glimpse of Eddie at the same time holding up Naomi's hair. He seemed to be trying to tell how wet it was.

"Help me." Naomi was looking at Carole, her eyes wide and frightened. "Please."

"Relax, will you?" Eddie said to her. "Bring that pack of yours over here," he said to Carole. He was beckoning, snapping his fingers with impatience, a gesture she remembered from that night in the motel when he'd been so agitated. She edged closer. Maybe Naomi *was* drunk, and maybe Eddie *was* trying to help. But when she drew close, Naomi said, "Look out," and Carole stopped.

He looked from Carole to Naomi and back, then laughed. "My wife pulled some very stupid shit," he said. "Back there at your place, she wanted to go for the free lunch. Fill in the blanks down there at your place. She thought it would be fun for people to hear who *actually* did it. She's waving her hand around for your friend to come over so she could give him a blow-by-blow, and I had to manhandle her a little to get her out of there. It was extremely stupid what you did with that picture. Extremely."

"You lied to me," Carole said. "I never killed her. You did. She died of asphyxiation, not a broken neck."

He stared at her, took a long drag on his cigarette.

"What's the difference?" he said. "It was an accident."

"But it was your accident, Eddie, not mine."

"We got away with it, okay? You should have left it alone."

She moved in closer to him, all her fury back. "You said it was my fault, you son of a bitch. You said you were covering up for me when all the time I was covering up for you."

He was standing before her, legs slightly apart, arms taut. All black except for his pale, round face. "And you believed it," he said. "A smart girl like you. I wondered when you'd figure it out."

"I was sixteen."

"You were a kid. I knew that. There was no telling what you'd do. You were in a shitload of trouble no matter whose fault it was. You should have thanked me a million times over. Instead you make a federal case of it. She"—he pointed to Naomi—"she was ready to tell the world today. Shit. She thought it was *funny*."

"Tell them what? That I did it or that you did it, Eddie? That's what she wanted to shout out today, isn't it? That it was you and not me?"

A long moan came from Naomi.

"We've got to get her warm, Eddie. This is serious."

Eddie took a step toward Carole. "When we got back from town, she jumped out of the car and ran for the woods, drunk as a skunk. I came after her, and when she stopped, she was in this creek. All I was trying to do was settle her down so I could get her home and get her dry. I didn't know what else to do."

He was lying, and Carole knew it. Naomi's purse had been on the floor, which meant she had gone into the house first. She hadn't bolted from the car to the woods like he said. Naomi rolled herself around and sat on the snow, her legs straight out in front of her like a doll. She began tugging at the zipper on her jacket and finally got it down, then she pulled open her shirt, exposing her neck. "Hot in here," she said.

In that instant it all made sense. Eddie had brought Naomi out here. He might even have carried her, dragged her. It explained the troughs she'd seen in the snow. In a sudden fury, Carole ran at Eddie, ramming him with her body, and felt him give, massive and soft. She felt him fall beneath her and grappled for his face. Will had taught her how once, made her show him the claw her hand could make, the index and middle fingers crooked to plunge into the eyes. But Eddie was powerful. He rolled away, loomed over her, and pinned her to the snow. They lay panting and gasping.

"You stupid bitch." He pulled himself up and planted a knee hard on Carole's shoulder. He took a few more breaths, rolled her over, and pushed her arms painfully up. She tried to pull away, but he had her tight. "You're not as strong as you think you are." He dragged her a few feet to the stream. She struggled and tried to kick, but he had her too firmly, and she was facedown, her arms pinned. He plunged her down into the icy water. It was everywhere at once. In her mouth and her nose and ears. It rushed under her clothing at the neck of her parka, her wrists and ankles and waist, searing her skin all over. He pushed her down farther, so far under the water now that the cold attacked her back and her legs, it soaked her hair, burned her scalp. She couldn't breathe. She had to fight against taking in a great sucking breath from the shock of the cold, but if she did, she would drown. She shook her head, clamped her lips shut against it, writhed like an eel until he let go, and burst through the surface of the water, dragging the cold night air into her lungs like fire. He flung her back onto the snow and planted his knee in the small of her back.

"You girls are a couple of losers. Always were." Still holding her down, he rummaged through her pack, came up with the flashlight, and shone it into her face. The light was so weak she could see its filaments, the shape of the bulb. It would never last. "I can use this." He took out the socks and a windbreaker, then threw the pack down.

"I'm hot." Naomi was sitting cross-legged a few feet from where Eddie had Carole pinned.

"You're gone." Eddie raised himself up, putting more weight on his knee, digging it deeply into Carole's shoulder. He took a handful of snow and shoved it into Naomi's face, down her neck. "Better?" he said.

Carole tried to pull away but couldn't. "Let me lay it down for you," he said. "Now that I have your attention." He laughed. "I've been reading your boyfriend's column in the newspaper," he said. "What's his name?"

Keep him calm, keep him talking, Carole thought, but her body was starting to convulse with shivers. Don't let him get a rise out of you. He laughed again. "Will," she said.

"That's right. Will. It occurred to me that all I needed to do is wet her down and leave her here like she slipped and fell in the brook and was trying to crawl out. Hypothermia. I didn't believe it at first, but I asked around, and it's true. You girls are just going to cool down to nothing."

"What did she ever do to you?"

"It's not what she did *to* me. It's what she might do with that mouth of hers. And it's what she can do *for* me. I'll be the grieving widower. Need I say more?"

"She would give it to you," Carole said. "She was giving away money all the time."

"Exactly," Eddie said. "She's very careless."

"You're despicable," Carole said.

Eddie sighed. "And fast too," he said. "The hypothermia, I mean. That's the interesting thing. It happens fast. Well, not death itself, but the disorientation, and he said once a person is disoriented they're dead, because they do all the wrong things. They can't help themselves. It's irreversible at some point. Oh, skinny and wet speed things up even more." He paused. "I'll be leaving once you girls are ready. I'll go back to the house, my house now, for a bowl of hot soup or something. In a few hours I'll call the police about my missing wife." He paused and then laughed. "When they find you, they'll just think it's a couple of dumb broads, which it is." He laughed. "That's got possibilities." His knee dug deeper into her back, pressing her abdomen harder into the snow. "I wish you could thank Will for me," he said.

By now Naomi was whimpering rhythmically. Eddie straddled Carole's back, keeping her down. She didn't know how long they stayed like that, and in spite of trying not to, she slipped in and out of sleep. She began to shiver violently, picturing her wet clothing welding to the icy ground beneath her. She shut her eyes and must have dozed because when she opened them again, the woods had darkened. Eddie switched on the light. Its thin yellow beam flickered. "Come on," he said. "Time to get up and go home to a nice warm bed, okay?"

She tried to pull herself up but felt a tug and realized her clothing had begun to freeze to the ground. She lay back down again and felt his bare hand under her clothes. His face came close to hers, and she could feel his breath. He raised her eyelid with his finger and she stared into his face, training her eye on the bridge of his nose so it wouldn't flicker. "That boyfriend gives you a couple of hours, maybe," he said to her. "A lot less for my wife here."

He let go of her, rolled over, and got to his feet.

Naomi lay back in the snow.

Eddie laughed. "Just like Will said." Carole shivered again, a racking spasm that made her teeth rattle. "'The body shivers to create heat and by that very act depletes itself more quickly.' I remember that line. A genius, that boy of yours. I'll be going now before I start to get hypothermia myself. I've been here much too long." He jiggled her foot. "I got wet, too. My cuffs." He got to his feet, and she saw him shine the light into her pack, take out the food, start to walk away, and then stop again. "One more for good measure," he said, and she felt more liquid sluicing over her hair and the back of her neck. He must have found the water bottle in her pack.

She listened as his footsteps retreated and stopped. "Think I'll take these snowshoes too," he said. "If neither of you ladies mind." He sat down to put them on, cursing and muttering about the straps. They were beavertail snowshoes, old bentwood ones, three feet long including the tail. They had makeshift rawhide laces you had to wrap around your ankles several times to secure them. She wished he'd hurry up. She didn't have too long now before she started to lose it for real, before she was so disoriented she'd do something suicidal. She watched Eddie stand and lose his balance. He righted himself, then headed out slowly, knowing enough to keep his feet wide apart as he walked.

As soon as he was gone, Carole rose to her knees and brushed off the bits of ice clinging to her. The moon was rising, casting just enough light to see Naomi lying with her arms outstretched.

Carole got to her feet. The air was very cold now and her skin stung everywhere. "Nay?"

Silence.

She could see Eddie lumbering up the snowmobile trail. It took only seconds to decide to follow him out. She didn't dare stay. Her judgment would start to go. Maybe it already had. That was the trouble. You didn't know. Eddie had been right about that much. She opened her pack as wide as it would go and spread it over Naomi. It was all she had. "I'll come back," she whispered.

He was struggling upward, and she followed at a distance. He would fight up a ways, stop, turn, and look back, as though to check his progress. She would stop and wait for him to turn again and to keep going. She was shivering violently. She crept behind, adjusting to his speed. When they reached the house, she would wait until he went inside, then run for her truck and get help.

They kept going, Eddie ahead and Carole far enough behind that he wouldn't see her. It seemed so much longer than it had taken to come in. After a time she realized they were still struggling up the slope, when it should have leveled out by now. The flat part had been the longest. The slope had been short. She looked for landmarks, but it was too dark to see. The water. She remembered now. She'd used the water as the trail marker. She listened for it, and yes, there it was, but wait. It was close by, and the sound was coming from the right. She had to stop and think, to orient herself, knowing her mind was going fuzzy. If the water had been ahead coming in, it should be behind her coming out. So how could it be to the right? Then she remembered the trail junction. Oh, God, they'd taken the wrong fork. They were deeper in the woods. They were moving farther from the house.

She picked out Eddie's thick, dark form from the sound of his footsteps. He stopped, waited for several beats, catching his breath, then continued on. She tried to think what she needed to do but couldn't. Her indecision was so confusing. If only she could decide, then she would know. In that state, she kept walking, but the cold air had hardened the path to slippery ice beneath her. The sound of her own boots seemed to echo everywhere, and she was afraid he'd hear her. She stepped to the edge of the path where the snow was soft and quiet and continued along that way.

When she looked up again, Eddie was startlingly clear in a wide snowfield broken only by small clumps of evergreens. Where were they? He wasn't on the trail anymore. He'd headed off into the deep snow where his snowshoes had purchase. He was going away from her, across the snow, unsteadily, sinking to his knees and losing his balance.

The way the snow lay on the land was trying to tell her something. It was all wrong, lumpy and uneven in a way that suggested forms underneath. Here and there, dense clumps of new evergreens peeked through, like a Christmas tree farm. Then she remembered. Those small trees weren't new growth at all but the tips of mature spruce trees. The actual trees were fifteen or twenty feet tall, and these were their tops. Over time, the drifting snow had accumulated on the branches. Under the branches, all the way down, were dozens of air pockets.

Instinctively, she stepped back onto the hard-packed snowmobile trail, where the footing was safe, while up ahead, Eddie stopped. He turned this way and that, his body language that of somebody lost, somebody about to panic.

"Eddie," she called to him. She was feeling very calm. She knew what she was about to do.

The faltering little beam of flashlight jiggled crazily, trying to find the source of the sound. "Who's out there?" he yelled.

"Carole." The sound of her name rang out in the quiet evening.

The beam of his light clicked off. She felt a flutter of sympathy for the pathetic gesture. He thought she wouldn't know where he was if he turned off the flashlight. He was scared.

"Come and get me," she said.

He began to move toward her. She could hear the *thumpf thumpf,* a sound made more distinctive by the hollows beneath him. She pictured what it looked like under the snow, fragile as a spiderweb, airy as a honeycomb. A person's weight could never be supported by that. It was like ocean foam.

He must have felt the snow give way, felt the way his weight sank oddly down because he made a sudden, clumsy motion to recover, his arms spiraling. The effect was to drop him farther. Even in that dim light, she could see the thrust of his arms reaching out. She heard the quick suck of breath, the snap of branches deep underneath as his weight broke them and he fell. A dark shadow widened at the spot he'd gone down. *It's like quicksand,* Will had said of a spruce trap. *Like being buried alive. The more you struggle, the worse you become ensnared.*

She stood listening to his muffled screams, and she made no move to help him. He would be twisting among the branches. He would be grabbing for them, trying to climb back out, but the more he tried, the more snow would cascade down on him. The horror of it. Snow would be filling his mouth and his nose. It would be finding every opening in his clothing.

"Help me," he shouted. The whole dark gash began to quiver. He would understand now that to survive, he had to remove his snowshoes. He would try to undo them, but they would be tangled up with the branches. He would reach down first one way and then another, trying to snake his hands through the branches to his feet. With every effort, and she could almost see it happen, he would panic more, realizing that he could never reach his feet. The panic would sink him farther, cause him to sweat, soak his clothing from the inside out.

She remembered Rita right then, dead on a cold night like this, her naked body deep under snow. She remembered looking down, how she had tried to keep Naomi and Eddie from pushing the snow in on top of her. How she had tried to say something to the dead woman that night. "Rita Boudreau," Carole called out. "Her name was Rita Boudreau."

The shaking stopped. "Carole," he screamed at her, his voice rising from the pit, bouncing off the mountains. The awareness would be dawning in full. Of the cold and of the fact that he could not get out. He could not remove the snowshoes, could not rid himself of those big paddles anchoring him to the trap, and she would not come to his aid. He called out again. "Please."

She looked around. It was so much darker. She'd stayed too long. The movement, the rustling where Eddie had gone down, stopped. Suddenly it was quiet. "Marie," she shouted. "Her name was Rita *Marie* Boudreau."

Who's the most important person in a rescue? Will's mantra, that one. *The rescuer* was the answer. The person with the strength and the wherewithal. Not the victim. Never the victim. *If somebody has to die, it's got to be the victim, not you. Because if you die, the victim is going to die. Two instead of one. Simple arithmetic.*

Those were the words circulating through Carole's mind as she felt her way back along the trail, testing each step to make sure she was still on hard pack and not on the edges. She had to fight to keep remembering, fight to focus on what she knew she had to do. She was thinking victim and rescuer, that she had to find the house now and get help. She had to stay on that path. Back to the house. Test, step. Test, step. It was all she thought about. Have to stay out of the deep snow. Have to stay on solid snow. Not until she stumbled, hearing the stream right there before her, did she realize her mistake. She'd forgotten about the trail back to the house. Again. The other path, the same one Eddie had missed. She was losing it. *Focus,* she told herself.

Naomi lay with her hands crossed over her breasts and her wet hair hanging like tree vines, soaking wet. She'd sloughed off the pack and taken off her shirt. Her silver rings were loose on her fingers and her nails black, no gloves on. Carole touched her hair, which had begun to form ice crystals.

"I need to get you out of here," Carole said. But Naomi made no effort to stand, and Carole had to help her. She pulled gently at first and then with more force until she felt the give as Naomi let herself be lifted. Carole stood slowly, Naomi's slight body resting against her own, the incredibly fragile bones. When Carole let go, Naomi fell like stone to the ground. Carole wasn't sure Naomi even knew if she was there. *Do not let the victim of hypothermia go to sleep.* She shook Naomi. Her mind groped the whole disaster lexicon. *Advanced confusion, feeling hot, stripping off clothing.* Will had been so expansive. She pulled Naomi's clothing back up to cover her, but Naomi clawed it off.

She felt along the ground, hands raking under the snow for dead leaves, but the leaves were wet. She worked her way up the hill on her hands and knees, feeling the snow deepen quickly, unable to feel anything. Her skin was numb everywhere. She dug with her hands. Under the crust, the snow was mercifully soft and yielding, and she was able to move armfuls of it aside, to get into the hole and press it down, enlarging it. She took Naomi under the arms and inched up the rise to the hole.

The torso. The heart. Will's words again. Those were the important parts now. Arms and legs didn't matter.

She fingered her own frozen clothing, feeling for something dry, but there was nothing. Everything was soaked through. She felt Naomi's icy wet sweater. Fumbling, shivering. All she wanted was to lie beside Naomi, to warm her and to sleep.

Worst thing you can do, Will had said. They'd been in the car, and he'd talked about it. *The transfer works against you. Your heat going into the victim. The victim's cold coming into you. Irreversible. You slip from sleep into death. Just like that.* He'd snapped his fingers to show how fast. *Need to get out of here.* But she didn't want to. She felt so tired.

Who's the most important person in a rescue? She wanted to stay there, to close her eyes and sleep, but Will's words kept intruding. *If you die, the victim will surely die.* She was feeling so drowsy, far off and strange, but at least she wasn't feeling the cold anymore. Against her chest, Naomi's heart pounded like a jackhammer.

"Don't go to sleep." She slapped Naomi's arm, then her face lightly. "Say something."

But there was only silence. Carole watched the light of the moon on the stream. Cries sounded in the distance. Eddie. *One degree of body temperature is lost for every five minutes on uninsulated frozen ground. If you're wet, the cooling process is twenty-five times faster. At 90 degrees of body heat, the direction is irreversible.*

As if someone had wound her up, she rose to her knees and began to crawl back up the path. She felt nothing. She had to get there, back to the house, to a telephone. *The most important person in any rescue.* But she was so sleepy. So intoxicatingly sleepy. Take the left path, she told herself. Look for the left path.

Chapter Twenty-one

In the hospital, she breathed warm air from a funnel, aware in her sleepy haze of the nurses coming and going, of Rachel and her tinkling bells, and of Will reading to her from something that had a soothing cadence, although she couldn't much follow the words. Was it a dream? The cold and Eddie's dark form disappearing into a gash in the snow and Naomi's dangling broken foot. Lying there, she would shiver so hard, the nurse would have to heap heated blankets over her and wait with her until it stopped.

When she opened her eyes for the first time, Will was beside her bed. The light was so bright it hurt. "Hey," she said.

"Hey." He pulled the curtains closed and came back to sit on her bed. He took her hand.

"Where is Naomi?" she asked him.

He shook his head. "She didn't make it."

Carole closed her eyes in defeat. "And him? Eddie?"

"Dead."

Could it be true? She exhaled, as though Eddie's hold on her was finally released and she could breathe again.

"They want to talk to you," Will said. "I asked them to wait a little bit longer."

She dozed off again. She didn't know exactly when they came, maybe later that same day or the next, when she felt stronger and she'd started to eat. Sheriff Art Weed pulled one of the side chairs over to the bed. Two other men stood behind him. She listened, blinking up at them and trying hard to follow the thread.

They were pretty sure they knew what had happened, they said. Just wanted some corroboration. Tragedy, it was. City people like that, like herself even, out there in those woods in those temperatures. "Foolers," they call those days when it's hot at noon and the temperature skids down to zero by evening time. "And that Mrs. Lindbaeck out in almost nothing at all. Well . . ." Weed blushed crimson, and Carole, remembering that Naomi had stripped off her shirt, shut her eyes against the image of Naomi's bare frozen torso. "You know what I mean. Light little jacket like that. Mr. Burbank tells us you went off to the Lindbaecks' house around four. From the looks of things, you parked behind their car. Did you all go out into the woods together? Is that what happened?"

Carole had to stop and think. She was so tired. "No." She shook her head as if to loosen the memory. "They were already gone. I went looking for them."

"Oh."

"She was—" She couldn't remember the word, a word she should know. "Naomi wasn't making any sense," she said. Then she remembered Eddie saying, *It's called hypothermia,* and she shivered. "Hypothermic," she said to Weed. "She was already hypothermic."

"And Mr. Lindbaeck must have gone off to get help?"

She just stared into Weed's round pleasant face. He was smiling at her with concern, urging her on. She smiled back and nodded.

"You're a lucky woman," he said. He held up his thumb and forefinger an inch apart. "You came this close." After they left, she fell into a deep, long sleep.

In the days that followed, she watched the story spin out on the little TV that hung over her bed. Sometimes Rachel would be there with her, sitting on the bed. Rachel had told her, breathlessly, agog, what had happened that day in Chacha's, how she'd tracked Naomi down, determined to get the whole story and how Naomi had given her the years at Spence, the night in Stowe, the shocker about Rita, and the other shocker that all these years Carole had thought it was her fault when it wasn't. It was Eddie's, something Eddie had told Naomi only the day before, had bragged about it even, and oh, God, Rachel said, if only you'd told us.

On TV, Eddie was described as a thirty-six-year-old man who had come to Montpelier from New York City and recently married Naomi Irving Lindbaeck, one of two women found earlier by state police and volunteers. Mrs. Lindbaeck had died at Central Vermont Hospital in Berlin. The couple's friend, Carole Mason of Montpelier, was in stable condition. Implications of tragedy hung everywhere. The newly marrieds had died before their lives together had had a chance to begin. "Authorities tell us that Lindbaeck was going for help for the two women when he became lost in the darkness, fell through the snow, and was unable to extricate himself," the reporter said. There was no suggestion that Carole was concealing anything. Reporters kept the story alive, but only as an excuse to educate people about spruce traps and hypothermia and to warn them against going into the woods without food. Water. Dry clothes. Flashlight and batteries. Above all, pay attention to weather forecasts. In the accounts of her ordeal, it was clear that Carole had broken every one of the winter safety rules.

But she'd come through it, she thought, lying in her hospital bed and drifting in and out of sleep. It was over. Naomi was dead. Eddie was dead. The threat was gone. There would be no more dread, that constant companion, that spirit guide, that force whispering always to hold back, to keep a part of herself in reserve, because there was no telling when she'd need it, when she'd have to pull up stakes again and move on. The truth was a stubborn animal snuffling and nudging at the edges, looking for a way in. You might plug the holes, but there it was, never sleeping, never going away, the awful, exhausting truth. In spite of all her vigilance, in spite of her efforts to keep everybody separate from one another—Eddie from Naomi from Will and Rachel and Morgan and Pepper—to keep them mute and looking the other way, in spite of all that, they'd swum together, sought one another out, until in that small cabin deep in the woods and in the dark of night, with everyone accounted for, the truth had begun to come and then wouldn't stop, kept on coming and coming.

And now? She rose and went to the mirror in the bathroom, let the cotton gown fall to the floor, and looked hard at her long white body. Naked but for the bandages on her fingers, she looked at her jutting hip- and collarbones, the pale swath of pubic hair, her small breasts, her dark nipples, and then at her own face. Her eyes were a deep-sea blue against skim-milk skin. She thrust out her chin and stood up straight.

"Now what?" She said the words aloud and touched her fingers to the glass, joining hands with herself. She'd held that secret for so long, it had become her life—the strongest facet of her personality, with everything else in service to it. It often caused her to fall mute during conversations or to leave the room when the fun began. It held her back, fueled that aloofness, so that she was never able to share the abandon she saw in Rachel and Will and Morgan, the way they could throw themselves fully into laughter and conversation without a second thought—giddy and reckless. But never Carole. Never, because there was always the chance that she would slip, that if she ever dared to speak from the heart, she would reveal herself, and people would know.

Rachel and Will had filled her hospital room with snapshots. They were taped to the walls and propped up on the dresser, the night table, and the vacant second bed. She supposed it was a type of therapy for when she came out of her sleep, to remind her of who she was, to pull her back into the world again. She went through the room, looking at each one. Carole and Rachel as hippie chicks in

Golden Gate Park, Carole holding Dylan as a brand-new baby, the six of them—Will, Carole, and all the Weaver-Lears—crammed onto the sofa at Chacha's. She took several to the window and studied them in the light. In each one, she was the one with the half smile, the reluctant one, like in that children's song, *Which one of these is not like the others?* It was staggering to see this, to see in these pictures how different she was from everybody else, and it made her wonder if there was any undoing what she'd done, any chance that she would ever be free of what she'd done, and worse, what she'd done to them, how she'd betrayed her friends, one after the other, for years. She went back to look at the pictures spread out in the room, looking for what else, but of course it wasn't there. Her life had begun with Rita's death, so there was nothing from before, not here, not at home, not anywhere. She had betrayed not only the people in these pictures, but everyone. Her mother, her father, her aunt. Everyone.

She looked at a picture of Will and herself on Mount Hunger, a picture they'd had in the house for years. Why hadn't she ever noticed before the way he held on to her with such gusto, for dear life, his arm tightly around her and not letting go, his smile huge and happy, while she, smaller and slighter beside him, looked stiff and tentative, seemed even to be pulling away, her head tilted just slightly away from him as if she wasn't sure? Oh, how she wished she could just go back and hug him to her, open her mouth the way he did in that wide, carefree smile.

She could hear him out in the corridor, talking to one of the nurses or to her doctor as he did each time he visited her. He was the one in charge, the one they talked to. He would put her well-being ahead of everything else. He would never do anything to interfere with her recovery from the trauma of that night. The door swung open, and he came in. He kissed her lightly on the cheek, put a hand to her forehead to check her temperature the way he always did, then held up her hand to check the bandages on her fingers. "How are you?" he asked her.

"Good," she said.

"How good?" His face was empty of expression, as though he was about to give her bad news.

"Good enough," she said. She knew it was coming, and it made her heart pound.

"I can't keep waiting on it, Carole," he said. "But I don't want to do this too soon."

"Do it now," she said, feeling tears building in her eyes. She'd opened the dialogue on the day she told him about Eddie. She knew he would have his say.

He walked to the window and looked out, then turned. "That day?" he said. "I need to tell you what happened that day. I want you to know." He came back toward her, but instead of sitting on the bed as he usually did, he drew up a chair and sat facing her, eye to eye, the same chair Weed had sat in, and began. "When I came home that day and found you with those pictures and you told me about Eddie and what happened." He shook his head. "It was like I didn't even know you. And then you went flying out of our house like it was all between you and him, and I was left sitting with the pictures all spread out and the sight of your truck going like hell down East Hill Road. And I thought to myself, shit. What just happened? I watched your truck lay rubber, and you know what kept coming into my head?" His eyes wouldn't let hers go. "Fuck you, Carole Mason," he said, and the shock of it, like this, face to face, was like a blow. "I thought we knew each other pretty well. I know two people can't know everything. But the major stuff. And all that time you had that guy, Eddie, on the brain. You thought you killed somebody and you didn't tell me. Me. Will." His hand rose and thudded against his heart. "I was in your corner, baby. Flat out. That's the way it was, and I always thought you knew that. But then, see, I began to wonder if maybe I'd just been the jerk all along. Maybe I was just part of the disguise. Like who's going to come looking for you here? With me? With that ol' nigga boy Will Burbank."

"Oh, Will."

"Shut up." He glared at her. "You didn't trust me, Carole. I saw you ride off, and I knew what a son of a bitch Eddie was, and I didn't care. They all deserve each other, I thought. You lied through your teeth to me." He shook his head without taking his eyes from hers. "It's still hard to believe. I put on my coat and I left. I walked almost to Shady Rill, and when it got dark, I turned around. I was gone maybe three hours. When I came back, you were still gone. I kicked around here for a while. I ate dinner by myself at the table. And then just to drive the spike further into my heart, I turned over all those pictures again and I read that article. If I hadn't done that, I'd have stayed there feeling pissed off, and you'd be dead. But those pictures. What kind of a guy would do that with a kid? That's a sick guy who would show you that. And you still hadn't come back. By then it must have been four hours. Four hours. I called over there and got no answer. I called Chacha's just in case you went there—"

She reached out to touch him, but he folded his arms over his chest and leaned back. "I knew what to do." He smiled but without warmth. "At least I'm good for that much. When something goes wrong, I know what to do, and I do it. I went over there. I called emergency from Naomi's phone." He looked at the backs of his hands briefly and then back at her. "You almost didn't make it, Carole. You'd done all the wrong things. You know it. I don't have to tell you."

All the wrong things, and for a long time too, not just that night. "I—" she began.

"I'm not done. Where they found you, you weren't even very far in the woods. I knew Naomi was dead when I saw her, and so did Weed, but he did everything by the book. Nobody's ever dead until they're warm and dead. They got you both into hypothermia wraps. It took a while to get you out. They found Eddie the next day with dogs. He was pretty twisted up. What happened out there?"

"He pushed us both into the brook and then left us to die of hypothermia," she said. "I followed him out, and he took the wrong path. I was there when he went into that spruce trap. I knew exactly

330

what it was and I called to him so he would fall in." She looked into his dark eyes. "I wanted to be the one who did it."

"Oh, man," he said.

"He tried to kill us both. He used the information in your column, Will. He knew all about it."

"You should have told me about him." His eyes were wet. "None of that needed to happen if you'd just said something."

It might all have been taken care of some other way. The thought was staggering. It was true. Naomi would be alive. Eddie. She wouldn't have nearly died herself. Will would never have had to find her. *If she'd just said something.* She remembered all the times she'd almost told him, all the times she'd imagined taking charge, telling Will to sit down and listen and not say a word until she was through telling him and to hell with the consequences. She'd imagined that dozens of times, yearned for it. And she knew the reason she'd never done it. Because of what might happen if she did, what he would be faced with. She'd never had the courage to find out before, and while it wasn't exactly courage now, the time had come and there was no getting around it. She was surprised at how calm she felt, how sure of the truth.

"You said I never told you because I didn't trust you, Will." He nodded. "But that's not true. The reality is, Will, that I did trust you, and I do trust you now. I trusted you to understand the choice you would have had to make once you knew. To stay with me knowing what you knew, or to leave me because of it. I didn't know which you would do, and I was too afraid to find out." She was looking directly into his eyes. "I still am," she said. She waited for what seemed like forever. He sat back, not taking his eyes from hers. He blinked once, but he never looked away. She could hear the PA system in the hall, the little chimes, and then "Will Dr. Adams please pick up on seven. Paging Dr. Adams."

He was studying her face the way he had that first night at Chacha's, the night they met. Her eyes, her nose, her lips. "I'm not going to leave," he said.

*   *   *

The day Carole returned to work was sunny and warm. All the hill-
sides were that pale chartreuse that comes only for a few days in May.
The bandages were off her hands and feet, and there was only a little
permanent damage. The tips of the index and middle fingers of her
right hand were gone. Otherwise, she was fine. She caressed the two
smooth mounds with her thumb. In the month she'd spent at home
after her release from the hospital, she'd gained six pounds and had
to buy some clothes. Will had gone along to help her. He had picked
out the dress she had on today. Lighter than air, and pretty. White
with blue flowers. She had on white sandals, and her hair was loose
around her shoulders, a strand of white beads warm at her throat.

She was resting at a table at the front when she heard unbroken
honking in the street below. She stepped to the window to see that
an old man was standing in the middle of Main Street, stopping traffic with one hand while the woman with him crossed the street. The
woman had on a red cape and was younger, with jet-black hair
drawn so tightly back that even from where Carole stood, the sharp
line of the woman's part was clear. It was pretty obvious they weren't
from here, and pretty obvious the man was showing off for her. A
couple of people yelled out at him, and then the two of them disappeared on Carole's side of the street under the window, where she
couldn't see them anymore.

A few minutes later, she was in the kitchen, and Sandy came
through the swinging doors. "People out there want to speak to the
owner," she said.

Carole came out to the floor, drying her hands on a towel. First
she recognized the red cape of the woman from the street, and a moment later, once she could see his face, she knew the man.

Her father was standing tight at the woman's side, glancing about
the room. Carole stopped and took a breath at the same moment her
father saw her and raised an arm like a salute. She was stunned to see
how old he'd become. His hair was white and coarse, and he walked
toward her tilted slightly, as if making an effort to conceal a real
limp. In all these years, whenever she'd thought of him, she'd re-

called the man he was at her mother's memorial service, gliding around the place fully in charge. And handsome. The women that day had been all over him.

They stood facing each other for several seconds. She wasn't sure what to do. Then he wrapped his arms around her, and she was filled with the familiar smell of him—at once bitter and clean. He held her for several seconds and then backed off, staring at her. He shook his head. "My God," he said. "Look at you. More like your mother than ever."

The woman stepped forward and gave her a strong, hard handshake. Her wrist was harnessed in silver and bone jewelry. "I'm Gloria," she said. "At last we meet."

"May we sit down?" her father asked.

She led the way to a free table close to the front. Her father attended to Gloria, pulling out her chair a bit, standing behind her as she pulled the chair in. Then he sat opposite Carole and looked around, surveying the restaurant.

"I've had it for four years. It keeps me busy." She knew how great it looked, full and bustling, and it smelled great too. Her father had to see that. He had to be impressed.

But he made a slight grimace and held his hand to his eyes. "I wonder if we could take the table over there?" He pointed a few tables away. "We'll be looking directly into the sun in a few minutes." Gloria was already gathering up her big slouchy bag for the move. She was obviously used to this.

When they were settled again, her father looked around. "Hard to find you here," he said. "We had to ask a number of times where Chacha's was. You should hang a sign out there. Advertise."

Gloria gave Carole's hand a reassuring pat as if to say, Don't take your father too seriously, dear. He means well. Her mother used to run interference for him that way, but it irritated her coming from Gloria.

"I don't want a sign," Carole said to her father. "I've never needed one. People know—"

He looked around. "But more people would know if—"

"Daddy," she said. "Please. I said I didn't need one."

"Your father and I went back and forth, didn't we, Conrad?" Gloria said, changing the subject for them. "Should we just arrive and surprise you, or call ahead? Well, we just took a chance and came. We've been in Montreal, and we have to go on this afternoon. I hope it isn't too big a shock, dear. We didn't mean for that, of course."

Carole felt all at sixes and sevens with him. Familiar, strange, with everything to talk about and nothing at all. He was out of context, like someone she barely knew. She'd bolted from that memorial service and left him stranded, and she'd often thought how he must have looked for her, how bitter he would have been and disappointed. But then he'd had detectives. "You've always known where I was," she said. "And yet you never came."

He sucked in his lips in the way she remembered. "I hit you that time," he said. "I was never able to forgive myself."

"It was never because you hit me," she said. "You had every right."

He put a finger to his lips. "No."

"Not for that, for something else."

Now the tears were coming, one trail then two, streaming down his old cheeks. "Let's not," he said.

She wiped her own tears away with the back of her hand and smiled at him and then at Gloria. "I used to go back and look at our building on Sixty-second," she said. "I'd stand out there and look up."

"Oh, my," he said. And she was aware of Gloria moving closer to him protectively.

"Are you hungry?" Carole said.

"I think just a tuna sandwich for me," her father said. Gloria ordered a salad. It wasn't exactly the kind of food that would show off her restaurant, but she called Sandy over and placed the orders. Her father took out a handkerchief and blew his nose, then sat up straight, his eyes dry. He nudged Gloria and pointed to her purse.

"Oh, yes!" Gloria said. She removed a stack of photographs and handed them to him. He spread them on the table. "The family," he said. He pointed to the smiling faces. Carole looked eagerly for pictures of herself, her mother. Instead they were photographs of strangers. Schoolchildren with missing teeth. Smiling families. Her father became animated, naming these new stepbrothers and sisters-in-law. Her new nieces and nephews. Gloria told little stories about some of them. All the faces blurred.

"You'll come to visit us," her father said. "You're welcome anytime, and of course the kids will all be so happy to meet you." Her father had that old way of owning a conversation, as though after all these years and then coming into her world, he was still the person in charge, still the daddy.

At that moment, Sandy arrived and slid the platters onto the table.

"Marvelous," Gloria said. Carole looked at the two of them, inspecting their plates the way people did, and she knew then. *Let's not,* her father had said. He didn't want to know why she left.

He made a fuss of repositioning his plate as though it had been done all wrong. He paused and looked at Carole. "You're very changed." He glanced at Gloria. "Right? Isn't she very different from the pictures I showed you?"

Gloria studied her before speaking. Then she smiled and didn't look so hard. "She's very lovely, Conrad," she said.

"We've lost so much time," he said, his eyes on Carole. "Ten years. All those years. And now this." He gestured to the restaurant and shook his head. "Hardly what we—" he began.

"But quite wonderful," Gloria said.

"Hardly what your mother and I had in mind for you."

"What you had in mind?" she said, feeling momentarily blindsided the way she used to, as a girl, by how easy it was to disappoint him. How, once, she would have needed to find out what they had in mind and then try to make it happen, but that no longer mattered. Well, this is what I'm doing, she thought to herself. She looked over to where Rachel and Morgan and the kids were sitting, their usual place by the window. "Some people you should meet," she said to them. "Come on over. Sandy will bring your sandwiches."

When they were settled on the couches at the window, Carole introduced them all to one another. "Get out!" Rachel said. "You're Carole's dad?" She drew closer, her bells jingling. Morgan sprawled beside her, an arm slung over her shoulders.

Her father was immediately taken with Pepper. Pepper now ironed all his own clothes, and it showed in the crisp seams running down the fronts of his secondhand pants. He went to the barber on his own every five weeks and looked like a kid who'd stepped right out of the 1950s. Her father quizzed the boy about school, about what he liked to do, and Pepper explained that he had been home-schooled at times in the past, but this fall he was entering seventh grade at Union 32, the regional school. He was interested in math. Somehow Pepper knew to call him "sir" at the end of every answer.

Carole enjoyed seeing them hit it off so well, enjoyed seeing her father smile and nod with interest at the things Pepper said. She enjoyed seeing Pepper sit with his erect posture, understanding that he was making a good impression, playing to his audience. And it gave her pleasure to think about the time all those years ago when she'd gone to her father's office and asked for legal advice about Rachel's pregnancy. He'd refused to give it to her because he'd had contempt for the girls at the home. She'd known her own mind better than she knew at the time, and she'd chosen well. Rachel was the person to whom she had remained loyal. Now here was her father, enchanted by that same baby. She wanted to tell him, but to do so would be to embarrass Rachel and Pepper both, so she kept quiet.

Her father started going through the pictures again for Pepper, sliding them around on the table like a shell game. When he finished showing the photographs, Gloria put them back into the envelope and slid it into her purse. There was a long silence.

"What's Naomi up to?" her father asked at last. "I haven't heard from her in a while."

"You don't know?"

"Know what?"

She spotted Will behind the bar, talking to a customer, and waved him over. She wanted him there while she told the story, because she was still shaky telling it.

"This is Will," she said to her father and Gloria. "Will, my dad and Gloria." She touched Will's arm. She'd learned to do this, to get it over with, so people wouldn't spend time guessing: Were they or weren't they? At the gesture, her father gave Will a hard, appraising look. Years ago that look would have undone her. Now she saw how little his judgment mattered.

"They don't know about Naomi," she said to Will, and then she began. She described finding them at the stream that evening, Naomi's hypothermia, her broken ankle, and Eddie's departure using Carole's snowshoes. She spoke of trying to make Naomi stand up, then going for help and collapsing on the path, that if it hadn't been for Will getting worried about her and coming to look, she'd have died too.

"What about the husband?" her father asked.

"They found him a day later way off the trail," Will said. "He died of exposure too. He must have gotten lost on the way out."

"Poor guy tried," her father said. Whenever she told the story of that night, the effect was always the same. People went away with the belief that Eddie had struggled off to get help for her and Naomi and then died cruelly from the effort. They always reacted as her father had. *Poor guy.* In the weeks right after it had happened, this had galled her. Now, however, the impression of Eddie as heroic was always and easily erased by the true one that belonged to her alone. Her memory of the dark gash in the snow into which Eddie had sunk. That and knowing that the last words he had ever heard were *Rita Marie Boudreau.*

Her father cleared his throat and settled back in the chair. He took a breath and held forth, the paterfamilias reminiscing for this little circle of his daughter's friends, as if she was still his little girl, as if he was the adult, the person of wisdom. He cast Naomi's legacy for them as if only he had ever known her, as if they all needed his great wisdom to give shape to the tragedy of Naomi. He said she was a striking girl, intelligent but troubled, given over to urges. It was a shame, a blow for Carole to lose a longtime friend. He said, after a moment's thought, that Carole's mother had actually been quite fond of Naomi, but she would have liked the friendship better if Naomi hadn't wielded so much influence. "Our Carole was an impressionable girl."

Hearing about Naomi, seeing her again cast as the troubled but irrepressible girl she remembered, before alcohol, before Eddie, before everything, Carole wished with a sudden and overwhelming urgency that Naomi could hear all this. Whoever thought her parents had ever liked anything about Naomi? It was as though Naomi's death were suddenly brand new, as if it had just happened, and Carole missed her sharply. She wanted Naomi to walk in with her red nails and her high heels and stolen jewelry. She wished she could tell Naomi about that night, about how she'd tried to save her life and how she had tracked Eddie down and heard him die.

That day in Chacha's, Naomi had been trying to say out loud to everyone there that she knew who had killed Rita Boudreau, who had *really* done it. Not Carole, but Eddie. Eddie Lindbaeck, her own husband. Naomi had learned the truth and must have been ready to reveal Eddie to everybody. Naomi had married him, but in their ancient triangle, she had finally opted for Carole after all, the way Carole, in the end, had tried to save Naomi's life.

Her father always picked out one person to direct his remarks to. In fact, he'd told her about that once when she had to give a report at Spence during assembly. *Find a friendly face,* he'd said. *And speak to it.* And now he found Pepper to speak to. "My Carole skipped the fourth grade. She was a precocious girl, always one's best friend, interested in everything back then." He glanced at her and then said to Pepper, "A bit like you, I suspect."

Carole was awash in the warm familiarity of his voice when he checked his watch, a signal to Gloria. She waited a few moments and then started to collect things, making it clear that they would have to be leaving. Headed back home, she explained. Something about a birthday party for one of the grandchildren. Otherwise, of course, they would have stayed longer, but they hadn't known for sure if Carole would be here. They'd taken a chance to find her here, and wonderful to meet her after all this time, and the next time, of course, they wouldn't rush off. "And wonderful to meet your friends," her father was saying, winding down. "How much this means to me. To us."

She rose and walked with them to the top of the stairs, Will and the Weaver-Lears following. Her father gave her the same stiff hug he'd given her when he came in. They'd be in touch, he said. She'd have to come visit them. Gloria leaned in and kissed her once on each cheek. Carole watched her father and Gloria go downstairs and pause before opening the door to the street, where her father turned and raised a hand. "Sweetie," he said, and smiled up at her. It was the name he'd had for her all those years ago, when it used to annoy her, when she'd taken her parents' affection for granted.

Will put a hand on her shoulder, and they walked back to the sofas by the window, where she stood for a moment, looking at them all, at Rachel and Morgan and Pepper. Coming back here with them, back to Vermont, had been no accident, she now understood. She recalled her shock in that dark candlelit room on the night they'd had the conference, when Morgan suggested they move to Vermont. She could have refused. She could have easily split off from them and gone anywhere in the country, in the world for that matter. Anywhere but here. Anywhere but Vermont. Instead she recalled the slight frisson at the very idea of it. She remembered taking the map to the bathroom, greedy to see how close the place they were going to would be to Stowe. At the time she'd said to herself that it was to make sure there was *enough* distance, but that hadn't been it. No. She'd been hungry to come back here. And for the whole long drive back across the country, her heart had often beat faster at the thought of where she was going. From fear, oh, yes, fear. But anticipation too, because a part of her had always needed to face what she had done.

For a very long time, she had marked the start of her life from one single terrible night in a motel room in Stowe. What went before had been lost, or lied about, or muddied, and what came after had become her life. What she did that terrible night had driven her from her family and her past, across the country and back again. In the new life she had made for herself she'd kept her distance. She'd kept her silence. Now her mother was dead. Naomi was dead. Eddie too.

Carole sat on the sofa before the tall windows of Chacha's, safely among her friends. These people, this place, they were now her life. She shuddered to think that she'd almost lost them. At sixteen, with her whole life ahead of her, she'd had no way to see Eddie for what he was, to understand his cruelty. Neither had she understood the power of the secret she was keeping. She'd had no idea that a secret could grow with such speed and intensity, coloring all her decisions, governing her life.

And what did she know now? Something simple and powerful. There can be no love when people are divided by a secret. To be loved is to be known fully. To be known and still to be loved.

Acknowledgments

For their many readings and consistently helpful critiques, I offer grateful acknowledgment to Bruce Cohen, Leslie Johnson, Terese Karmel, Wally Lamb, and Ellen Zahl; also to Jane Christensen and Gene Young. Thanks also to my agent, Jennifer Rudolph Walsh, for the speed and enthusiasm with which she responded to this book, and to my editor, Rob Weisbach, who knew just how to help me make the book better, and then better again. Most of all, to Robert Haskins Funk, whose knowledge of survival in the outdoors informs this book and whose patience, love, and support helped me to complete it.

About the Author

Pam Lewis's fiction has appeared in *The New Yorker* and other literary publications. She lives in Storrs, Connecticut. This is her first novel.